For
PHILIPPA and SUE
Anglo-Oc Caterers
Fiendishly Good Food!

Contents

Introduction

Acknowledgements

Introduction

The scene is a small dinner party. Three couples are sitting round a table, and the sound of chinking cutlery and the gentle buzz of conversation create an atmosphere of enjoyment and general well-being. One of the guests, the rather effusive man on the left of the hostess, takes another mouthful of food, swallows it, and then, suddenly, clutching his throat, makes a horrible choking sound. Before any of the other five diners has a chance to move, the man slumps forward onto the table . . . dead.

It is not only in crime fiction that stories such as this are to be found. History, too, can provide similar instances in which poison has brought a dramatic end to some unsuspecting diner's meal.

The ways in which mealtime killers, whether real or fictional, have dispatched their victims are many and varied, and the place of death may have been a restaurant, café, club or inn as often as a private home. But truth is always stranger than fiction, and I doubt if any author could possibly have matched the fiendish ingenuity of Cardinal Ferdinando de' Medici, one of the hugely wealthy Florentine dynasty, some four hundred years ago.

It appears that the Cardinal was anxious to rid himself of his elder brother and had hit upon the idea of poisoning him with a peach which he would share. Using a golden knife, he sliced the fruit precisely down the middle, then passed one half to his brother, proceeding to munch the rest contentedly himself. A moment later, the elder man sank dying to the floor.

How had the Cardinal survived the poisoned peach? The blade of the knife had been carefully smeared with poison on only *one* side – and the half *it* had cut de' Medici handed to his unsuspecting brother.

Of course, poisoning men and women through their palates was much easier in the past when food was often over-salted, over-spiced or rancid; and even in the earlier part of this century, when there seemed to be something of a vogue for killing people with toxic doses, forensic science was still in its infancy and there were plenty of substances extremely difficult to trace in a corpse.

Where a dose of poison has always had the advantage over other forms of murder is that the victim has no time to duck as he or she may do when confronted by a gun, or to ward off the lunge of a knife thrust. And getting the person to take the bait is simplicity itself if it is served up in a favourite dish.

Looking through the crime novels of the genre's 'Golden Age', between the two World Wars, it is interesting to draw up a list of the poisons that were used. Naturally enough, arsenic, cyanide, hemlock, nitrobenzene and strychnine were essential ingredients in many killers' pharmacopoeias. Weed killer was a very popular choice in country house murders, while botulism in tinned foods was ideal for use in the city. Some of the cleverer criminals even managed to come up with arcane poisons from far-off places like South America.

Equally interesting are the dishes in which the poison was served. Porridge and eggs (unless they were hard-boiled) were breakfast favourites; Dover sole, either baked or poached, was the ideal lunchtime killer; while for the evening meal, a meat dish or any cream sauce seemed to avoid suspicion until it was too late. Spirits, too, were easy to doctor, as were boxes of chocolates. And the glass of warm milk (or cocoa) taken before going to bed probably killed off more victims in these novels than all the rest put together!

Of course, not all mealtime murders have been committed with the aid of poison. The good old-fashioned blunt instrument has cropped up on a number of occasions, as have the gun and the knife, all striking down diners when they least expected it. Nor does the list end there, as the reader will find in this book.

For the gourmet of crime stories, the composition of the fateful meal often holds as much interest as trying to solve the cause of death. The more exotic the dishes, and the more succulently they are described, the greater the sensation of pleasure experienced by the reader. Even the finest *cordon bleu* cookbook cannot offer quite the same *frisson* as some of these mixtures of crime and culinary delights.

In this anthology the reader will find a wide variety of short stories mixing food and murder – not to mention some mystery and horror – and because they fall neatly into categories I have divided them into three main 'courses'. Firstly, some outstanding stories by famous writers like Paul Gallico, Ruth Rendell and L. P. Hartley, set mainly in fine restaurants, clubs, and cafés; then a selection of historical culinary tales ranging from the activities of the infamous Borgias to a modern variation on the Last Supper; and, finally, a group of detective cases featuring such famous gourmet sleuths as Hercule Poirot, Nero Wolfe and Inspector Maigret. All the stories are written with the same skill that one would expect from a master chef, and it is no surprise to learn that most of the authors were gourmets and proud of it. Some of them were excellent cooks, too.

One of my favourite stories about food and death was told some years ago by Lord Dunsany, that larger-than-life Irish nobleman who was known around the clubs and restaurants of London and Dublin as 'the worst dressed man in Ireland'. One of Dunsany's pet hates was the adulteration of food, and he recounted a parable concerning Death and what happened when he became ill and his followers set about curing him with modern nutriments.

'One day,' Dunsany said, 'they carried Death into the dining-room of a great hotel and brought him bread such as the modern bakers make, whitened with alum, and the tinned meats of Chicago, with a pinch of our modern substitute for salt. They brought him a bottle of wine that they called champagne and gave him their cheap Indian tea. They also bought a newspaper and looked up the patient medicines and gave him the foods that it recommended for invalids. And after a while, Death arose ravening and strong and strode once again through the cities.'

Having survived thanks to those adulterated foods, Death will be found stalking the following pages where the dishes are rather richer and certainly more exotic. The menu is ready for the reader's selection. Dine well!

Peter Haining
Boxford, Suffolk
February 1991.

I

SPÉCIALITÉS DE LA MAISON

Stories by Some Famous Authors

The Speciality of the House

STANLEY ELLIN

Every major city in the world has a little restaurant that looks like Sbirro's in this opening story by Stanley Ellin (1916–1986): inconspicuous, but highly regarded by its gourmet clientele. Appearances, however, can be deceptive, especially in the hands of a writer whom *The Times* described as 'a master of the thriller, a man in the tradition of great storytellers'. Some readers may well have seen the films from his works, including *Nothing but the Best* (1964, starring Alan Bates) and *House of Cards* (1968, with Orson Welles). 'The Speciality of the House' was Stanley Ellin's first published story, written in 1948, and it has been widely praised. Alfred Hitchcock presented a brilliant television adaptation some years ago, claiming that he had had to overcome strong resistance from the TV network. After reading the denouement the reader will undoubtedly understand why!

'And this,' said Laffler, 'is Sbirro's.' Costain saw a square brownstone façade identical with the others that extended from either side into the clammy darkness of the deserted street. From the barred windows of the basement at his feet a glimmer of light showed behind heavy curtains.

'Lord,' he observed, 'it's a dismal hole, isn't it?'

'I beg you to understand,' said Laffler stiffly,

'that Sbirro's is the restaurant without pretensions. Besieged by these ghastly, neurotic times, it has refused to compromise. It is perhaps the last important establishment in this city lit by gas jets. Here you will find the same honest furnishing, the same magnificent Sheffield service, and possibly, in a far corner, the very same spider webs that were remarked by the patrons of a half-century ago!'

'A doubtful recommendation,' said Costain, 'and hardly sanitary.'

'When you enter,' Laffler continued, 'you leave the insanity of this year, this day, and this hour, and you find yourself for a brief span restored in spirit, not by opulence, but by dignity, which is the lost quality of our time.'

Costain laughed uncomfortably. 'You make it sound more like a cathedral than a restaurant,' he said.

In the pale reflection of the street lamp overhead, Laffler peered at his companion's face. 'I wonder,' he said abruptly, 'whether I have not made a mistake in extending this invitation to you.'

Costain was hurt. Despite an impressive title and large salary, he was no more than clerk to this pompous little man, but he was impelled to make some display of his feelings. 'If you wish,' he said coldly, 'I can make other plans for my evening with no trouble.'

With his large, cowlike eyes turned up to Costain, the mist drifting into the ruddy, full moon of his face, Laffler seemed strangely ill at ease. Then 'No, no,' he said at last, 'absolutely not. It's important that you dine at Sbirro's with me.' He grasped Costain's arm firmly and led the way to the wrought-iron gate of the basement. 'You see, you're the sole person in my office who seems to know anything at all about good food. And on my part, knowing about Sbirro's but not having some appreciative friend to share it, is like having a unique piece of art locked in a room where no one else can enjoy it.'

Costain was considerably mollified by this. 'I understand there are a great many people who relish that situation.'

'I'm one of that kind!' Laffler said sharply. 'And having the secret of Sbirro's locked in myself for years has finally become unendurable.' He fumbled at the side of the gate and from within could be heard the small, discordant jangle of an ancient pull-bell. An interior door opened with a groan, and Costain found himself peering into a dark face whose only discernible feature was a row of gleaming teeth.

'Sair?' said the face.

'Mr Laffler and a guest.'

'Sair,' the face said again, this time in what was clearly an invitation. It moved aside and Costain stumbled down a single step behind his host. The door and gate creaked behind him, and he stood blinking in a small foyer. It took him a moment to realise that the figure he now stared at was his own reflection in a gigantic pier glass that extended from floor to ceiling. 'Atmosphere,' he said under his breath and chuckled as he followed his guide to a seat.

He faced Laffler across a small table for two and

peered curiously around the dining-room. It was no
size at all, but the half-dozen guttering gas jets which
provided the only illumination threw such a deceptive
light that the walls flickered and faded into uncertain
distance.

There were no more than eight or ten tables about,
arranged to ensure the maximum privacy. All were
occupied, and the few waiters serving them moved
with quiet efficiency. In the air was a soft clash and
scrape of cutlery and a soothing murmur of talk.
Costain nodded appreciatively.

Laffler breathed an audible sigh of gratification. 'I
knew you would share my enthusiasm,' he said.
'Have you noticed, by the way, that there are no
women present?'

Costain raised inquiring eyebrows.

'Sbirro,' said Laffler, 'does not encourage members
of the fair sex to enter the premises. And, I can tell you,
his method is decidedly effective. I had the experience
of seeing a woman get a taste of it not long ago. She sat
at a table for not less than an hour waiting for service
which was never forthcoming.'

'Didn't she make a scene?'

'She did.' Laffler smiled at the recollection. 'She
succeeded in annoying the customers, embarrassing
her partner, and nothing more.'

'And what about Mr Sbirro?'

'He did not make an appearance. Whether he
directed affairs from behind the scenes, or was
not even present during the episode, I don't know.
Whichever it was, he won a complete victory. The

woman never reappeared nor, for that matter, did the witless gentleman who by bringing her was really the cause of the entire contretemps.'

'A fair warning to all present,' laughed Costain.

A waiter now appeared at the table. The chocolate-dark skin, the thin, beautifully moulded nose and lips, the large liquid eyes, heavily lashed, and the silver white hair so heavy and silken that it lay on the skull like a cap, all marked him definitely as an East Indian. The man arranged the stiff table linen, filled two tumblers from a huge, cut glass pitcher, and set them in their proper places.

'Tell me,' Laffler said eagerly, 'is the special being served this evening?'

The waiter smiled regretfully and showed teeth as spectacular as those of the majordomo. 'I am so sorry, sair. There is no special this evening.'

Laffler's face fell into lines of heavy disappointment. 'After waiting so long. It's been a month already, and I hoped to show my friend here . . .'

'You understand the difficulties, sair.'

'Of course, of course.' Laffler looked at Costain sadly and shrugged. 'You see, I had in mind to introduce you to the greatest treat that Sbirro's offers, but unfortunately it isn't on the menu this evening.'

The waiter said: 'Do you wish to be served now, sair?' and Laffler nodded. To Costain's surprise the waiter made his way off without waiting for any instructions.

'Have you ordered in advance?' he asked.

'Ah,' said Laffler, 'I really should have explained.

Sbirro's offers no choice whatsoever. You will eat the same meal as everyone else in this room. Tomorrow evening you would eat an entirely different meal, but again without designating a single preference.'

'Very unusual,' said Costain, 'and certainly unsatisfactory at times. What if one doesn't have a taste for the particular dish set before him?'

'On that score,' said Laffler solemnly, 'you need have no fears. I give you my word that, no matter how exacting your tastes, you will relish every mouthful you eat in Sbirro's.'

Costain looked doubtful, and Laffler smiled. 'And consider the subtle advantages of the system,' he said. 'When you pick up the menu of a popular restaurant, you find yourself confronted with innumerable choices. You are forced to weigh, to evaluate, to make uneasy decisions which you may instantly regret. The effect of all this is a tension which, however slight, must make for discomfort.

'And consider the mechanics of the process. Instead of a hurly-burly of sweating cooks rushing about a kitchen in a frenzy to prepare a hundred varying items, we have a chef who stands serenely alone, bringing all his talents to bear on one task, with all the assurance of a complete triumph!'

'Then you have seen the kitchen?'

'Unfortunately, no,' said Laffler sadly. 'The picture I offer is hypothetical, made of conversational fragments I have pieced together over the years. I must admit, though, that my desire to see the functioning

of the kitchen here comes very close to being my sole
obsession nowadays.'

'But have you mentioned this to Sbirro?'

'A dozen times. He shrugs the suggestion away.'

'Isn't that a rather curious foible on his part?'

'No, no,' Laffler said hastily, 'a master artist is never
under the compulsion of petty courtesies. Still,' he
sighed, 'I have never given up hope.'

The waiter now reappeared bearing two soup bowls
which he set in place with mathematical exactitude,
and a small tureen from which he slowly ladled a
measure of clear, thin broth. Costain dipped his
spoon into the broth and tasted it with some curiosity. It was delicately flavoured, bland to the verge
of tastelessness. Costain frowned, tentatively reached
for the salt and pepper cellars, and discovered there
were none on the table. He looked up, saw Laffler's
eyes on him, and although unwilling to compromise
with his own tastes, he hesitated to act as a damper
on Laffler's enthusiasm. Therefore he smiled and
indicated the broth.

'Excellent,' he said.

Laffler returned his smile. 'You do not find it excellent at all,' he said coolly. 'You find it flat and badly
in need of condiments. I know this,' he continued
as Costain's eyebrows shot upward, 'because it was
my own reaction many years ago, and because like
yourself I found myself reaching for salt and pepper
after the first mouthful. I also learned with surprise
that condiments are not available in Sbirro's.'

Costain was shocked. 'Not even salt!' he exclaimed.

'Not even salt. The very fact that you require it for your soup stands as evidence that your taste is unduly jaded. I am confident that you will now make the same discovery that I did: by the time you have nearly finished your soup your desire for salt will be nonexistent.'

Laffler was right; before Costain had reached the bottom of his plate he was relishing the nuances of the broth with steadily increasing delight. Laffler thrust aside his own empty bowl and rested his elbows on the table. 'Do you agree with me now?'

'To my surprise,' said Costain, 'I do.'

As the waiter busied himself clearing the table, Laffler lowered his voice significantly. 'You will find,' he said, 'that the absence of condiments is but one of several noteworthy characteristics which mark Sbirro's. I may as well prepare you for these. For example, no alcoholic beverages of any sort are served here, nor for that matter any beverage except clear, cold water, the first and only drink necessary for a human being.'

'Outside of mother's milk,' suggested Costain dryly.

'I can answer that in like vein by pointing out that the average patron of Sbirro's has passed that primal stage of his development.'

Costain laughed. 'Granted,' he said.

'Very well. There is also a ban of the use of tobacco in any form.'

'But, good heavens,' said Costain, 'doesn't that make Sbirro's more a teetotaller's retreat than a gourmet's sanctuary?'

'I fear,' said Laffler solemnly, 'that you confuse the words, *gourmet* and *gourmand*. The gourmand, through glutting himself, requires a wider and wider latitude of experience to stir his surfeited senses, but the very nature of the gourmet is simplicity. The ancient Greek in his coarse chiton savouring the ripe olive; the Japanese in his bare room contemplating the curve of a single flower stem – these are the true gourmets.'

'But an occasional drop of brandy, or pipeful of tobacco,' said Costain dubiously, 'are hardly over-indulgences.'

'By alternating stimulant and narcotic,' said Laffler, 'you seesaw the delicate balance of your taste so violently that it loses its most precious quality: the appreciation of fine food. During my years as a patron of Sbirro's I have proved this to my satisfaction.'

'May I ask,' said Costain, 'why you regard the ban on these things as having such deep aesthetic motives? What about such mundane reasons as the high cost of a liquor licence, or the possibility that patrons would object to the smell of tobacco in such confined quarters?'

Laffler shook his head violently. 'If and when you meet Sbirro,' he said, 'you will understand at once that he is not the man to make decisions on a mundane basis. As a matter of fact, it was Sbirro himself who first made me cognisant of what you call "aesthetic" motives.'

'An amazing man,' said Costain, as the waiter prepared to serve the entrée.

Laffler's next words were not spoken until he had savoured and swallowed a large portion of meat. 'I hesitate to use superlatives,' he said, 'but to my way of thinking Sbirro represents man at the apex of his civilisation!'

Costain cocked an eyebrow and applied himself to his roast which rested in a pool of stiff gravy ungarnished by green or vegetable. The thin steam rising from it carried to his nostrils a subtle, tantalising odour which made his mouth water. He chewed a piece as slowly and thoughtfully as if he were analysing the intricacies of a Mozart symphony. The range of taste he discovered was really extraordinary, from the pungent nip of the crisp outer edge to the peculiarly flat yet soul-satisfying ooze of blood which the pressure of his jaws forced from the half-raw interior.

Upon swallowing, he found himself ferociously hungry for another piece, and then another, and it was only with an effort that he prevented himself from wolfing down all his share of the meat and gravy without waiting to get the full voluptuous satisfaction from each mouthful. When he had scraped his platter clean, he realised that both he and Laffler had completed the entire course without exchanging a single word. He commented on this, and Laffler said: 'Can you see any need for words in the presence of such food?'

Costain looked round at the shabby, dimly lit room, the quiet diners, with a new perception. 'No,' he said humbly, 'I cannot. For any doubts I had I apologise unreservedly. In all your praise of Sbirro's there was not a single word of exaggeration.'

'Ah,' said Laffler delightedly. 'And that is only part of the story. You heard me mention the special which unfortunately was not on the menu tonight. What you have just eaten is as nothing when compared to the absolute delights of that special!'

'Good Lord!' cried Costain; 'What is it? Nightingales' tongues? Fillet of unicorn?'

'Neither,' said Laffler. 'It is lamb.'

'Lamb?'

Laffler remained lost in thought for a minute. 'If,' he said at last, 'I were to give you in my own unstinted words my opinion of this dish you would judge me completely insane. That is how deeply the mere thought of it affects me. It is neither the fatty chop, nor the too solid leg; it is, instead, a select portion of the rarest sheep in existence and is named after the species – lamb Amirstan.'

Costain knit his brows. 'Amirstan?'

'A fragment of desolation almost lost on the border which separates Afghanistan and Russia. From chance remarks dropped by Sbirro, I gather it is no more than a plateau which grazes the pitiful remnants of a flock of superb sheep. Sbirro, through some means or other, obtained rights to the traffic in this flock and is, therefore, the sole restaurateur ever to have lamb Amirstan on his bill of fare. I can tell you that the appearance of this dish is a rare occurrence indeed, and luck is the only guide in determining for the clientele the exact date when it will be served.'

'But surely,' said Costain, 'Sbirro could provide some advance knowledge of this event.'

'The objection to that is simply stated,' said Laffler. 'There exists in this city a huge number of professional gluttons. Should advance information slip out, it is quite likely that they will, out of curiosity, become familiar with the dish and thenceforth supplant the regular patrons at these tables.'

'But you don't mean to say,' objected Costain, 'that these few people present are the only ones in the entire city, or for that matter, in the whole wide world, who know of the existence of Sbirro's!'

'Very nearly. There may be one or two regular patrons who, for some reason, are not present at the moment.'

'That's incredible.'

'It is done,' said Laffler, the slightest shade of menace in his voice, 'by every patron making it his solemn obligation to keep the secret. By accepting my invitation this evening, you automatically assume that obligation. I hope you can be trusted with it.'

Costain flushed. 'My position in your employ should vouch for me. I only question the wisdom of a policy which keeps such magnificent food away from so many who would enjoy it.'

'Do you know the inevitable result of the policy *you* favour?' asked Laffler bitterly. 'An influx of idiots who would nightly complain that they are never served roast duck with chocolate sauce. Is that picture tolerable to you?'

'No,' admitted Costain, 'I am forced to agree with you.'

Laffler leaned back in his chair wearily and passed his hand over his eyes in an uncertain gesture. 'I am a solitary man,' he said quietly, 'and not by choice alone. It may sound strange to you, it may border on eccentricity, but I feel to my depths that this restaurant, this warm haven in a coldly insane world, is both family and friend to me.'

And Costain, who to this moment had never viewed his companion as other than tyrannical employer or officious host, now felt an overwhelming pity twist inside his comfortably expanded stomach.

By the end of two weeks the invitations to join Laffler at Sbirro's had become something of a ritual. Every day, at a few minutes after five, Costain would step out into the office corridor and lock his cubicle behind him; he would drape his overcoat neatly over his left arm, and peer into the glass of the door to make sure his Homburg was set at the proper angle. At one time he would have followed this by lighting a cigarette, but under Laffler's prodding he had decided to give abstinence a fair trial. Then he would start down the corridor, and Laffler would fall in step at his elbow, clearing his throat. 'Ah, Costain. No plans for this evening, I hope.'

'No,' Costain would say, 'I'm foot-loose and fancy-free,' or 'At your service,' or something equally inane. He wondered at times whether it would not be more tactful to vary the ritual with an occasional refusal, but the glow with which Laffler received his answer, and the rough friendliness of Laffler's grip on his arm, forestalled him.

Among the treacherous crags of the business world, reflected Costain, what better way to secure your footing than friendship with one's employer. Already, a secretary close to the workings of the inner office had commented publicly on Laffler's highly favourable opinion of Costain. That was all to the good.

And the food! The incomparable food at Sbirro's! For the first time in his life, Costain, ordinarily a lean and bony man, noted with gratification that he was certainly gaining weight; within two weeks his bones had disappeared under a layer of sleek firm flesh, and here and there were even signs of incipient plumpness. It struck Costain one night, while surveying himself in his bath, that the rotund Laffler himself might have been a spare and bony man before discovering Sbirro's.

So there was obviously everything to be gained and nothing to be lost by accepting Laffler's invitations. Perhaps after testing the heralded wonders of lamb Amirstan and meeting Sbirro, who thus far had not made an appearance, a refusal or two might be in order. But certainly not until then.

That evening, two weeks to a day after his first visit to Sbirro's, Costain had both desires fulfilled: he dined on lamb Amirstan, and he met Sbirro. Both exceeded all his expectations.

When the waiter leaned over their table immediately after seating them and gravely announced:

'Tonight is special, sair,' Costain was shocked to find his heart pounding with expectation. On the table before him he saw Laffler's hands trembling violently. 'But it isn't natural,' he thought suddenly: 'Two full-grown men, presumably intelligent and in the full possession of their senses, as jumpy as a pair of cats waiting to have their meat flung to them!'

'This is it!' Laffler's voice startled him so that he almost leaped from his seat. 'The culinary triumph of all times! And faced by it you are embarrassed by the very emotions it distils.'

'How did you know that?' Costain asked faintly.

'How? Because a decade ago I underwent your embarrassment. Add to that your air of revulsion and it's easy to see how affronted you are by the knowledge that man has not yet forgotten how to slaver over his meat.'

'And these others,' whispered Costain, 'do they all feel the same thing?'

'Judge for yourself.'

Costain looked furtively around at the nearby tables. 'You are right,' he finally said. 'At any rate, there's comfort in numbers.'

Laffler inclined his head slightly to the side. 'One of the numbers,' he remarked, 'appears to be in for a disappointment.'

Costain followed the gesture. At the table indicated a grey-haired man sat conspicuously alone, and Costain frowned at the empty chair opposite him.

'Why, yes,' he recalled, 'that very stout, bald man,

isn't it? I believe it's the first dinner he's missed here in two weeks.'

'The entire decade more likely,' said Laffler sympathetically. 'Rain or shine, crisis or calamity, I don't think he's missed an evening at Sbirro's since the first time I dined here. Imagine his expression when he's told that on his very first defection lamb Amirstan was the *plat du jour*.'

Costain looked at the empty chair again with a dim discomfort. 'His very first?' he murmured.

'Mr Laffler! And friend! I am so pleased. So very, very pleased. No, do not stand; I will have a place made.' Miraculously a seat appeared under the figure standing there at the table. 'The lamb Amirstan will be an unqualified success, hurr? I myself have been stewing in the miserable kitchen all the day, prodding the foolish chef to do everything just so. The just so is the important part, hurr? But I see your friend does not know me. An introduction, perhaps?'

The words ran in a smooth, fluid eddy. They rippled, they purred, they hypnotised Costain so that he could do no more than stare. The mouth that uncoiled this sinuous monologue was alarmingly wide, with thin mobile lips that curled and twisted with every syllable. There was a flat nose with a straggling line of hair under it; wide-set eyes, almost oriental in appearance, that glittered in the unsteady flare of gaslight; and long, sleek hair that swept back from high on the unwrinkled forehead – hair so pale that it might have been bleached of all colour. An amazing face surely, and the sight of it tortured

Costain with the conviction that it was somehow familiar. His brain twitched and prodded but could not stir up solid recollection.

Laffler's voice jerked Costain out of his study. 'Mr Sbirro. Mr Costain, a good friend and associate.' Costain rose and shook the proffered hand. It was warm and dry, flint-hard against his palm.

'I am so very pleased, Mr Costain. So very, very pleased,' purred the voice. 'You like my little establishment, hurr? You have a great treat in store, I assure you.'

Laffler chuckled. 'Oh, Costain's been dining here regularly for two weeks,' he said. 'He's by way of becoming a great admirer of yours, Sbirro.'

The eyes were turned on Costain. 'A very great compliment. You compliment me with your presence and I return same with my food, hurr? But the lamb Amirstan is far superior to anything of your past experience, I assure you. All the trouble of obtaining it, all the difficulty of preparation, is truly merited.'

Costain strove to put aside the exasperating problem of that face. 'I have wondered,' he said, 'why with all these difficulties you mention, you even bother to present lamb Amirstan to the public. Surely your dishes are excellent enough to uphold your reputation.'

Sbirro smiled so broadly that his face became perfectly round. 'Perhaps it is a matter of the psychology, hurr? Someone discovers a wonder and must share it with others. He must fill his cup to the brim, perhaps, by observing the so evident pleasure of those who explore it with him. Or,' he shrugged, 'perhaps it is just a matter of good business.'

'Then in the light of all this,' Costain persisted, 'and considering all the conventions you have imposed on your customers, why do you open the restaurant to the public instead of operating it as a private club?'

The eyes abruptly glinted into Costain's, then turned away. 'So perspicacious, hurr? Then I will tell you. Because there is more privacy in a public eating place than in the most exclusive club in existence! Here no one inquires of your affairs; no one desires to know the intimacies of your life. Here the business is eating. We are not curious about names and address or the reasons for the coming and going of our guests. We welcome you when you are here; we have no regrets when you are here no longer. That is the answer, hurr?'

Costain was startled by this vehemence. 'I had no intention of prying,' he stammered.

Sbirro ran the tip of his tongue over his thin lips. 'No, no,' he reassured, 'you are not prying. Do not let me give you that impression. On the contrary, I invite your questions.'

'Oh, come, Costain,' said Laffler. 'Don't let Sbirro intimidate you. I've known him for years and I guarantee that his bark is worse than his bite. Before you know it, he'll be showing you all the privileges of the house – outside of inviting you to visit his precious kitchen, of course.'

'Ah,' smiled Sbirro, 'for that, Mr Costain may have

to wait a little while. For everything else I am at his beck and call.'

Laffler slapped his hand jovially on the table. 'What did I tell you!' he said. 'Now let's have the truth, Sbirro. Has anyone, outside of your staff, ever stepped into the sanctum sanctorum?'

Sbirro looked up. 'You see on the wall above you,' he said earnestly, 'the portrait of one to whom I did the honour. A very dear friend and a patron of most long standing, he is evidence that my kitchen is not inviolate.'

Costain studied the picture and started with recognition. 'Why,' he said excitedly, 'that's the famous writer – you know the one, Laffler – he used to do such wonderful short stories and cynical bits and then suddenly took himself off and disappeared in Mexico!'

'Of course!' cried Laffler, 'and to think I've been sitting under his portrait for years without even realising it!' He turned to Sbirro. 'A dear friend, you say? His disappearance must have been a blow to you.'

Sbirro's face lengthened. 'It was, it was, I assure you. But think of it this way, gentlemen: he was probably greater in his death than in his life, hurr? A most tragic man, he often told me that his only happy hours were spent here at this very table. Pathetic, is it not? And to think the only favour I could ever show him was to let him witness the mysteries of my kitchen, which is, when all is said and done, no more than a plain, ordinary kitchen.'

'You seem very certain of his death,' commented

Costain. 'After all, no evidence has ever turned up
to substantiate it.'

Sbirro contemplated the picture. 'None at all,' he
said softly. 'Remarkable, hurr?'

With the arrival of the entrée Sbirro leaped to his
feet and set about serving them himself. With his eyes
alight he lifted the casserole from the tray and sniffed
at the fragrance from within with sensual relish. Then,
taking great care not to lose a single drop of gravy,
he filled two platters with chunks of dripping meat.
As if exhausted by this task, he sat back in his chair,
breathing heavily. 'Gentlemen,' he said, 'to your good
appetite.'

Costain chewed his first mouthful with great deliberation and swallowed it. Then he looked at the empty
tines of his fork with glazed eyes.

'Good God!' he breathed.

'It is good, hurr? Better than you imagined?'

Costain shook his head dazedly. 'It is as impossible,'
he said slowly, 'for the uninitiated to conceive the
delights of lamb Amirstan as for mortal man to look
into his own soul.'

'Perhaps,' Sbirro thrust his head so close that
Costain could feel the warm, fetid breath tickle his
nostrils, 'perhaps you have just had a glimpse into
your soul, hurr?'

Costain tried to draw back slightly without giving
offence. 'Perhaps,' he laughed, 'and a gratifying picture it made: all fang and claw. But without intending
any disrespect, I should hardly like to build my church
on *lamb en casserole*.'

Sbirro rose and laid a hand gently on his shoulder. 'So perspicacious,' he said. 'Sometimes when you have nothing to do, nothing, perhaps, but sit for a very little while in a dark room and think of this world – what it is and what it is going to be – then you must turn your thoughts a little to the significance of the Lamb in religion. It will be so interesting. And now,' he bowed deeply to both men, 'I have held you long enough from your dinner. I was most happy' – he nodded to Costain – 'and I am sure we will meet again.' The teeth gleamed, the eyes glittered, and Sbirro was gone down the aisle of tables.

Costain twisted around to stare after the retreating figure. 'Have I offended him in some way?' he asked.

Laffler looked up from his plate. 'Offended him? He loves that kind of talk. Lamb Amirstan is a ritual with him; get him started and he'll be back at you a dozen times worse than a priest making a conversion.'

Costain turned to his meal with the face still hovering before him. 'Interesting man,' he reflected. 'Very.'

It took him a month to discover the tantalising familiarity of that face, and when he did, he laughed aloud in his bed. Why, of course! Sbirro might have sat as the model for the Cheshire cat in *Alice*!

He passed this thought on to Laffler the very next evening as they pushed their way down the street to the restaurant against a chill, blustering wind. Laffler only looked blank.

'You may be right,' he said, 'but I'm not a fit judge. It's a far cry back to the days when I read the book. A far cry, indeed.'

As if taking up his words, a piercing howl came ringing down the street and stopped both men short in their tracks. 'Someone's in trouble there,' said Laffler. 'Look!'

Not far from the entrance to Sbirro's two figures could be seen struggling in the near darkness. They swayed back and forth and suddenly tumbled into a writhing heap on the sidewalk. The piteous howl went up again, and Laffler, despite his girth, ran toward it at a fair speed with Costain tagging cautiously behind.

Stretched out full length on the pavement was a slender figure with the dusky complexion and white hair of one of Sbirro's servitors. His fingers were futilely plucking at the huge hands which encircled his throat, and his knees pushed weakly up at the gigantic bulk of a man who brutally bore down with his full weight.

Laffler came up panting. 'Stop this!' he shouted. 'What's going on here?'

The pleading eyes almost bulging from their sockets turned towards Laffler. 'Help, sair. This man – drunk – '

'Drunk am I, ya dirty – ' Costain saw now that the man was a sailor in a badly soiled uniform. The air around him reeked with the stench of liquor. 'Pick me pocket and then call me drunk, will ya!' He dug his fingers in harder, and his victim groaned.

Laffler seized the sailor's shoulder. 'Let go of him,

do you hear! Let go of him at once!' he cried, and the next instant was sent careening into Costain, who staggered back under the force of the blow.

The attack on his own person sent Laffler into immediate and berserk action. Without a sound he leaped at the sailor, striking and kicking furiously at the unprotected face and flanks. Stunned at first, the man came to his feet with a rush and turned on Laffler. For a moment they stood locked together, and then as Costain joined the attack, all three went sprawling to the ground. Slowly Laffler and Costain got to their feet and looked down at the body before them.

'He's either out cold from liquor,' said Costain, 'or he struck his head going down. In any case, it's a job for the police.'

'No, no, sair!' The waiter crawled weakly to his feet, and stood swaying. 'No police, sair. Mr Sbirro do not want such. You understand, sair.' He caught hold of Costain with a pleading hand, and Costain looked at Laffler.

'Of course not,' said Laffler. 'We won't have to bother with the police. They'll pick him up soon enough, the murderous sot. But what in the world started all this?'

'That man, sir. He make most erratic way while walking, and with no meaning I push against him. Then he attack me, accusing me to rob him.'

'As I thought.' Laffler pushed the waiter gently along. 'Now go on in and get yourself attended to.'

The man seemed ready to burst into tears. 'To you, sair, I owe my life. If there is anything I can do – '

Laffler turned into the areaway that led to Sbirro's door. 'No, no, it was nothing. You go along, and if Sbirro has any questions send him to me. I'll straighten it out.'

'My life, sair,' were the last words they heard as the inner door closed behind them.

'There you are, Costain,' said Laffler, as a few minutes later he drew his chair under the table: 'civilised man in all his glory. Reeking with alcohol, strangling to death some miserable innocent who came too close.'

Costain made an effort to gloss over the nerve-shattering memory of the episode. 'It's the neurotic cat that takes to alcohol,' he said. 'Surely there's a reason for that sailor's condition.'

'Reason? Of course there is. Plain atavistic savagery!' Laffler swept his arm in an all-embracing gesture. 'Why do we all sit here at our meat? Not only to appease physical demands, but because our atavistic selves cry for release. Think back, Costain. Do you remember that I once described Sbirro as the epitome of civilisation? Can you now see why? A brilliant man, he fully understands the nature of human beings. But unlike lesser men he bends all his efforts to the satisfaction of our innate natures without resultant harm to some innocent bystander.'

'When I think back on the wonders of lamb Amirstan,' said Costain, 'I quite understand what you're driving at. And, by the way, isn't it nearly due to appear on the bill of fare? It must have been over a month ago that it was last served.'

The waiter, filling the tumblers, hesitated. 'I am so sorry, sair. No special this evening.'

'There's your answer,' Laffler grunted, 'and probably just my luck to miss out on it altogether the next time.'

Costain stared at him. 'Oh, come, that's impossible.'

'No, blast it.' Laffler drank off half his water at a gulp and the waiter immediately refilled the glass. 'I'm off to South America for a surprise tour of inspection. One month, two months, Lord knows how long.'

'Are things that bad down there?'

'They could be better.' Laffler suddenly grinned. 'Mustn't forget it takes very mundane dollars and cents to pay the tariff at Sbirro's.'

'I haven't heard a word of this around the office.'

'Wouldn't be a surprise tour if you had. Nobody knows about this except myself – and now you. I want to walk in on them completely unsuspected. Find out what flimflammery they're up to down there. As far as the office is concerned, I'm off on a jaunt somewhere. Maybe recuperating in some sanatorium from my hard work. Anyhow, the business will be in good hands. Yours, among them.'

'Mine?' said Costain, surprised.

'When you go in tomorrow you'll find yourself in receipt of a promotion, even if I'm not there to hand it to you personally. Mind you, it has nothing to do with our friendship either; you've done fine work, and I'm immensely grateful for it.'

Costain reddened under the praise. 'You don't expect to be in tomorrow. Then you're leaving tonight?'

Laffler nodded. 'I've been trying to wangle some reservations. If they come through, well, this will be in the nature of a farewell celebration.'

'You know,' said Costain slowly, 'I devoutly hope that your reservations don't come through. I believe our dinners here have come to mean more to me than I ever dared imagine.'

The waiter's voice broke in. 'Do you wish to be served now, sair?' and they both started.

'Of course, of course,' said Laffler sharply, 'I didn't realise you were waiting.'

'What bothers me,' he told Costain as the waiter turned away, 'is the thought of the lamb Amirstan I'm bound to miss. To tell you the truth, I've already put off my departure a week, hoping to hit a lucky night, and now I simply can't delay any more. I do hope that when you're sitting over your share of lamb Amirstan, you'll think of me with suitable regrets.'

Costain laughed. 'I will indeed,' he said as he turned to his dinner.

Hardly had he cleared the plate when a waiter silently reached for it. It was not their usual waiter, he observed; it was none other than the victim of the assault.

'Well,' Costain said, 'how do you feel now? Still under the weather?'

The waiter paid no attention to him. Instead, with the air of a man under great strain, he turned to

Laffler. 'Sair,' he whispered. 'My life. I owe it to you. I can repay you!'

Laffler looked up in amazement, then shook his head firmly. 'No,' he said; 'I want nothing from you, understand? You have repaid me sufficiently with your thanks. Now get on with your work and let's hear no more about it.'

The waiter did not stir an inch, but his voice rose slightly. 'By the body and blood of your God, sair, I will help you even if you do not want! *Do not go into the kitchen, sair.* I trade you my life for yours, sair, when I speak this. Tonight or any night of your life, do not go into the kitchen at Sbirro's!'

Laffler sat back, completely dumbfounded. 'Not go into the kitchen? Why shouldn't I go into the kitchen if Mr. Sbirro ever took it into his head to invite me there. What's all this about?'

A hard hand was laid on Costain's back, and another gripped the waiter's arm. The waiter remained frozen to the spot, his lips compressed, his eyes downcast.

'What is all *what* about, gentlemen?' purred the voice. 'So opportune an arrival. In time as ever, I see, to answer all the questions, hurr?'

Laffler breathed a sigh of relief. 'Ah, Sbirro, thank heaven you're here. This man is saying something about my not going into your kitchen. Do you know what he means?'

The teeth showed in a broad grin. 'But of course. This good man was giving you advice in all amiability. It so happens that my too emotional chef heard some rumour that I might have a guest into his precious kitchen, and he flew into a fearful rage. Such a rage, gentlemen! He even threatened to give notice on the spot, and you can understand what that should mean to Sbirro's, hurr? Fortunately, I succeeded in showing him what a signal honour it is to have an esteemed patron and true connoisseur observe him at his work first hand, and now he is quite amenable. Quite, hurr?'

He released the waiter's arm. 'You are at the wrong table,' he said softly. 'See that it does not happen again.'

The waiter slipped off without daring to raise his eyes and Sbirro drew a chair to the table. He seated himself and brushed his hand lightly over his hair. 'Now I am afraid that the cat is out of the bag, hurr? This invitation to you, Mr Laffler, was to be a surprise; but the surprise is gone, and all that is left is the invitation.'

Laffler mopped beads of perspiration from his forehead. 'Are you serious?' he said huskily. 'Do you mean that we are really to witness the preparation of your food tonight?'

Sbirro drew a sharp fingernail along the tablecloth, leaving a thin, straight line printed in the linen. 'Ah,' he said, 'I am faced with a dilemma of great proportions.' He studied the line soberly. 'You, Mr Laffler, have been my guest for ten long years. But our friend here – '

Costain raised his hand in protest. 'I understand perfectly. This invitation is solely to Mr Laffler, and naturally my presence is embarrassing. As it happens,

I have an early engagement for this evening and must be on my way anyhow. So you see there's no dilemma at all, really.'

'No,' said Laffler, 'absolutely not. That wouldn't be fair at all. We've been sharing this until now, Costain, and I won't enjoy this experience half as much if you're not along. Surely Sbirro can make his conditions flexible, this one occasion.'

They both looked at Sbirro, who shrugged his shoulders regretfully.

Costain rose abruptly. 'I'm not going to sit here, Laffler, and spoil your great adventure. And then too,' he bantered, 'think of that ferocious chef waiting to get his cleaver on you. I prefer not to be at the scene. I'll just say good-bye,' he went on, to cover Laffler's guilty silence, 'and leave you to Sbirro. I'm sure he'll take pains to give you a good show.' He held out his hand and Laffler squeezed it painfully hard.

'You're being very decent, Costain,' he said. 'I hope you'll continue to dine here until we meet again. It shouldn't be too long.'

Sbirro made way for Costain to pass. 'I will expect you,' he said. '*Au 'voir.*'

Costain stopped briefly in the dim foyer to adjust his scarf and fix his Homburg at the proper angle. When he turned away from the mirror, satisfied at last, he saw with a final glance that Laffler and Sbirro were already at the kitchen door; Sbirro holding the door invitingly wide with one hand, while the other rested, almost tenderly, on Laffler's meaty shoulders.

Bribery and Corruption

RUTH RENDELL

The setting for this next story is very different from Sbirro's.
It is a grand and imposing place – one of the most expensive
in London – and certainly does not hide the same kind of
dark secrets in its kitchen. There is, however, a surprise
awaiting Nicholas Hawthorne when he takes a friend to
dine there and finds himself thrust into a situation fraught
with danger – the kind of danger and intrigue for which the
author, Ruth Rendell (1930–), has become internationally
famous. Described as 'a natural storyteller' and the winner
of innumerable literary prizes on both sides of the Atlantic,
she always provides a chilling finale to her short stories.
This is precisely what awaits Nicholas after his night out
at Potters . . .

Everyone who makes a habit of dining out in London
knows that Potters in Marylebone High Street is one
of the most expensive of eating places. Nicholas
Hawthorne, who usually dined in his rented room
or in a steak house, was deceived by the humble-
sounding name. When Annabel said, 'Let's go to
Potters,' he agreed quite happily.

It was the first time he had taken her out. She was
a small pretty girl with very little to say for herself.
In her little face her eyes looked huge and appealing

– a flying fox face, Nicholas thought. She suggested they take a taxi to Potters 'because it's difficult to find'. Seeing that it was a large building and right in the middle of Marylebone High Street, Nicholas didn't think it would have been more difficult to find on foot than in a taxi but he said nothing.

He was already wondering what this meal was going to cost. Potters was a grand and imposing restaurant. The windows were of that very clear but slightly warped glass that bespeaks age, and the doors of a dark red wood that looked as if it had been polished every day for fifty years. Because the curtains were drawn and the interior not visible, it appeared as if they were approaching some private residence, perhaps a rich man's town house.

Immediately inside the doors was a bar where three couples sat about in black leather chairs. A waiter took Annabel's coat and they were conducted to a table in the restaurant. Nicholas, though young, was perceptive. He had expected Annabel to be made as shy and awkward by this place as he was himself but she seemed to have shed her diffidence with her coat. And when waiters approached with menus and the wine list she said boldly that she would start with a Pernod.

What was it all going to cost? Nicholas looked unhappily at the prices and was thankful he had his newly acquired credit card with him. Live now, pay later – but, oh God, he would still have to pay.

Annabel chose asparagus for her first course and roast grouse for her second. The grouse was the

most expensive item on the menu. Nicholas selected
vegetable soup and a pork chop. He asked her if she
would like red or white wine and she said one bottle
wouldn't be enough, would it, so why not have one
of each?

She didn't speak at all while they ate. He remembered reading in some poem or other how the poet
marvelled of a schoolmaster that one small head could
carry all he knew. Nicholas wondered how one small
body could carry all Annabel ate. She devoured roast
potatoes with her grouse and red cabbage and runner
beans, and when she heard the waiter recommending
braised artichokes to the people at the next table she
said she would have some of those too. He prayed
she wouldn't want another course. But that fawning
insinuating waiter had to come up with the sweet
trolley.

'We have fresh strawberries, madam.'

'In November?' said Annabel, breaking her silence.
'How lovely.'

Naturally she would have them. Drinking the dregs
of his wine, Nicholas watched her eat the strawberries
and cream and then call for a slice of chocolate
roulade. He ordered coffee. Did sir and madam wish
for a liqueur? Nicholas shook his head vehemently.
Annabel said she would have a green chartreuse.
Nicholas knew that this was of all liqueurs the pearl
– and necessarily the most expensive.

By now he was so frightened about the bill and so
repelled by her concentrated guzzling that he needed
briefly to get away from her. It was plain she had

come out with him only to stuff and drink herself into a stupor. He excused himself and went off in the direction of the men's room.

In order to reach it he had to pass across one end of the bar. The place was still half-empty but during the past hour – it was now nine o'clock – another couple had come in and were sitting at a table in the centre of the floor. The man was middle-aged with thick silver hair and a lightly tanned taut-skinned face. His right arm was round the shoulder of his companion, a very young, very pretty blonde girl, and he was whispering something in her ear. Nicholas recognised him at once as the chairman of the company for which his own father has been sales manager until two years before when he had been made redundant on some specious pretext. The company was called Sorensen-McGill and the silver-haired man was Julius Sorensen.

With all the fervour of a young man loyal to a beloved parent, Nicholas hated him. But Nicholas was a very young man and it was beyond his strength to cut Sorensen. He muttered a stiff good evening and plunged for the men's room where he turned out his pockets, counted the notes in his wallet and tried to calculate what he already owed to the credit card company. If necessary he would have to borrow from his father, though he would hate to do that, knowing as he did that his father had been living on a reduced income ever since that beast Sorensen fired him. Borrow from his father, try and put off paying the rent for a month if he could, cut down on his smoking, maybe give up altogether . . .

When he came out, feeling almost sick, Sorensen and the girl had moved farther apart from each other. They didn't look at him and Nicholas too looked the other way. Annabel was on her second green chartreuse and gobbling up *petit fours*. He had thought her face was like that of a flying fox and now he remembered that flying fox is only a pretty name for a fruit bat. Eating a marzipan orange, she looked just like a rapacious little fruit bat. And she was very drunk.

'I feel ever so sleepy and strange,' she said. 'Maybe I've got one of those viruses. Could you pay the bill?'

It took Nicholas a long time to catch the waiter's eye. When he did the man merely homed in on them with the coffee pot. Nicholas surprised himself with his own firmness.

'I'd like the bill,' he said in the tone of one who declares to higher authority that he who is about to die salutes thee.

In half a minute the waiter was back. Would Nicholas be so good as to come with him and speak to the maître d'hôtel? Nicholas nodded, dumbfounded. What had happened? What had he done wrong? Annabel was slouching back in her chair, her big eyes half-closed, a trickle of something orange dribbling out of the corner of her mouth. They were going to tell him to remove her, that she had disgraced the place, not to come here again. He followed the waiter, his hands clenched.

A huge man spoke to him, a man with the beak

and plumage of a king penguin. 'Your bill has been paid, sir.'

Nicholas stared. 'I don't know what you mean.'

'Your father paid it, sir. Those were my instructions, to tell you your father had settled your bill.'

The relief was tremendous. He seemed to grow tall again and light and free. It was as if someone had made him a present of – well, what would it have been? Sixty pounds? Seventy? And he understood at once. Sorensen had paid his bill and said he was his father. It was a little bit of compensation for what Sorensen had done in dismissing his father. He had paid out sixty pounds to show he meant well, to show that he wanted, in a small way, to make up for injustice.

Tall and free and masterful, Nicholas said, 'Call me a cab, please,' and then he went and shook Annabel awake in quite a lordly way.

His euphoria lasted for nearly an hour, long after he had pushed the somnolent Annabel through her own front door, then climbed the stairs up to the furnished room he rented and settled down to the crossword in the evening paper. Things would have turned out very differently if he hadn't started that crossword. 'Twelve across: Bone in mixed byre goes with corruption. (7 letters)' The I and the Y were already in. He got the answer after a few seconds – 'Bribery'. 'Rib' in an anagram of 'byre'. 'Bribery'.

He laid down the paper and looked at the opposite wall. That which goes with corruption. How could he ever have been such a fool, such a naive innocent fool, as to suppose a man like Sorensen cared about injustice or ever gave a thought to wrongful dismissal or even believed for a moment he *could* have been wrong? Of course Sorensen hadn't been trying to make restitution, of course he hadn't paid that bill out of kindness and remorse. He had paid it as a bribe.

He had paid the bribe to shut Nicholas's mouth because he didn't want anyone to know he had been out drinking with a girl, embracing a girl, who wasn't his wife. It was bribery, the bribery that went with corruption.

Once, about three years before, Nicholas had been with his parents to a party Sorensen had given for his staff and Mrs Sorensen had been the hostess. A brown-haired mousey little woman, he remembered her, and all of forty-five which seemed like old age to Nicholas. Sorensen had paid that bill because he didn't want his wife to find out he had a girlfriend young enough to be his daughter.

He had bought him, Nicholas thought, bribed and corrupted him – or tried to. Because he wasn't going to succeed. He needn't think he could kick the Hawthorne family around any more. Once was enough.

It had been nice thinking that he hadn't after all wasted more than half a week's wages on that horrible girl but honour was more important. Honour, surely, meant sacrificing material things for a principle. Nicholas had a bad night because he kept waking up and thinking of all the material things he would have to go short of during the next few weeks on account of his honour. Nevertheless, by the morning his resolve was fixed. Making sure he had his cheque book with him, he went off to work.

Several hours passed before he could get the courage together to phone Sorensen-McGill. What was he going to do if Sorensen refused to see him? If only he had a nice fat bank account with five hundred pounds in it he could make the grand gesture and send Sorensen a blank cheque accompanied by a curt and contemptuous letter.

The telephonist who used to answer in the days when he sometimes phoned his father at work answered now.

'Sorensen-McGill. Can I help you?'

His voice rather hoarse, Nicholas asked if he could have an appointment with Mr Sorensen that day on a matter of urgency. He was put through to Sorensen's secretary. There was a delay. Bells rang and switches clicked. The girl came back to the phone and Nicholas was sure she was going to say no.

'Mr Sorensen asks if one o'clock will suit you?'

In his lunch hour? Of course it would. But what on earth could have induced Sorensen to have sacrificed one of those fat expense account lunches just to see him? Nicholas set off for Berkeley Square, wondering what had made the man so forthcoming. A weak hopeful little voice inside him began once again putting up those arguments which on the previous evening the voice of a common sense had so decisively refuted.

Perhaps Sorensen really meant well and when

Nicholas got there would tell him the paying of the bill had been no bribery but a way of making a present to the son of a once-valued employee. The pretty girl could have been Sorensen's daughter. Nicholas had no idea if the man had children. It was possible he had a daughter. No corruption then, no betrayal of his honour, no need to give up cigarettes or abase himself before his landlord.

They knew him at Sorensen-McGill. He had been there with his father and, besides, he looked like his father. The pretty blonde girl hadn't looked in the least like Sorensen. A secretary showed him into the chairman's office. Sorensen was sitting in a yellow leather chair behind a rosewood desk with an inlaid yellow leather top. There were Modigliani-like murals on the wall behind him and on the desk a dark green jade ashtray, stacked with stubs, which the secretary replaced with a clean one of pale green jade.

'Hallo, Nicholas,' said Sorensen. He didn't smile. 'Sit down.'

The only other chair in the room was one of those hi-tech low-slung affairs made of leather hung on a metal frame. Beside it was a black glass coffee table with a black leather padded rim and on the glass lay a magazine open at the centrefold of a nude girl. There are some people who know how to put others at their ease and there are those who know how to put others in difficulties. Nicholas sat down, right down – about three inches from the floor.

Sorensen lit a cigarette. He didn't offer the box. He

looked at Nicholas and moved his head slowly from side to side. At last he said:

'I suppose I should have expected this.'

Nicholas opened his mouth to speak but Sorensen held up his hand. 'No, you can have your say in a minute.' His tone became hard and brisk. 'The girl you saw me with last night was someone – not to put too fine a point on it – I picked up in a bar. I have never seen her before, I shall never see her again. She is not, in any sense of the words, a girlfriend or mistress. Wait,' he said as Nicholas again tried to interrupt. 'Let me finish. My wife is not a well woman. Were she to find out where I was last night and whom I was with she would doubtless be very distressed. She would very likely become ill again. I refer, of course, to mental illness, to an emotional sickness, but . . .'

He drew deeply on his cigarette. 'But all this being so and whatever the consequences, I shall not on any account allow myself to be blackmailed. Is that understood? I paid for your dinner last night and that is enough. I do not want my wife told what you saw, but you may tell her and publish it to the world before I pay you another penny.'

At the word blackmail Nicholas's heart had begun to pound. The blood rushed into his face. He had come to vindicate his honour and his motive had been foully misunderstood. In a choked voice he stuttered:

'You've no business – it wasn't – why do you say things like that to me?'

'It's not a nice word, is it? But to call it anything else

would merely be semantics. You came, didn't you, to ask for more?'

Nicholas jumped up. 'I came to give you your money back!'

'Aah!' It was a strange sound Sorensen made, old and urbane, cynical yet wondering. He crushed out his cigarette. 'I see. Youth is moralistic. Inexperience is puritanical. You'll tell her anyway because you can't be bought, is that it?'

'No, I can't be bought.' Nicholas was trembling. He put his hands down flat on Sorensen's desk but still they shook. 'I shall never tell anyone what I saw, I promise you that. But I can't let you pay for my dinner – and pretend to be my father!' Tears were pricking the backs of his eyes.

'Oh, sit down, sit down. If you aren't trying to blackmail me and your lips are sealed, what the hell did you come here for? A social call? A man-to-man chat about the ladies you and I took out last night? Your family aren't exactly my favourite companions, you know.'

Nicholas retreated a little. He felt the man's power. It was the power of money and the power that is achieved by always having had money. There was something he hadn't ever before noticed about Sorensen but which he noticed now. Sorensen looked as if he were made of metal, his skin of copper, his hair of silver, his suit of pewter.

And then the mist in Nicholas's eyes stopped him seeing anything but a blur. 'How much was my bill?' he managed to say.

'Oh, for God's sake.'

'How much?'

'Sixty-seven pounds,' said Sorensen, 'give or take a little.' He sounded amused.

To Nicholas it was a small fortune. He got out his cheque book and wrote the cheque to J. Sorensen and passed it across the desk and said, 'There's your money. But you needn't worry. I won't say I saw you. I promise I won't.'

Uttering those words made him feel noble, heroic. The threatening tears receded. Sorensen looked at the cheque and tore it in two.

'You're a very tiresome boy. I don't want you on my premises. Get out.'

Nicholas got out. He walked out of the building with his head in the air. He was still considering sending Sorensen another cheque when, two mornings later, reading his paper in the train, his eye caught the hated name. At first he didn't think the story referred to 'his' Sorensen – and then he knew it did. The headline read: 'Woman Found Dead in Forest. Murder of Tycoon's Wife.'

'The body of a woman,' ran the story beneath,

was found last night in an abandoned car in Hatfield Forest in Hertfordshire. She had been strangled. The woman was today identified as Mrs Winifred Sorensen, 45, of Eaton Place, Belgravia. She was the wife of Julius Sorensen, chairman of Sorensen-McGill, manufacturers of office equipment.

Mrs Sorensen had been staying with her mother, Mrs Mary Clifford, at Mrs Clifford's home in Much Hadham.

Mrs Clifford said, 'My daughter had intended to stay with
me for a further two days. I was surprised when she said
she would drive home to London on Tuesday evening.'

'I was not expecting my wife home on Tuesday,' said Mr
Sorensen. 'I had no idea she had left her mother's house
until I phoned there yesterday. When I realised she was
missing I immediately informed the police.'

Police are treating the case as murder.

That poor woman, thought Nicholas. While she had
been driving home to her husband, longing for him
probably, needing his company and his comfort, he
had been philandering with a girl he had picked up,
a girl whose surname he didn't even know. He must
now be overcome with remorse. Nicholas hoped it
was biting agonised remorse. The contrast was what
was so shocking, Sorensen cheek to cheek with that
girl, drinking with her, no doubt later sleeping with
her; his wife alone, struggling with an attacker in a
lonely place in the dark.

Nicholas, of course, wouldn't have been surprised
if Sorensen had done it himself. Nothing Sorensen
could do would have surprised him. The man was
capable of any iniquity. Only this he couldn't have
done, which none knew better than Nicholas. So it
was a bit of a shock to be accosted by two policemen
when he arrived home that evening. They were
waiting in a car outside his gate and they got out
as he approached.

'Nothing to worry about, Mr Hawthorne,' said the
older of them who introduced himself as a Detective
Inspector. 'Just a matter of routine. Perhaps you read

about the death of Mrs Winifred Sorensen in your
paper today?'

'Yes.'

'May we come in?'

They followed him upstairs. What could they want
of him? Nicholas sometimes read detective stories
and it occurred to him that, knowing perhaps of
his tenuous connection with Sorensen-McGill, they
would want to ask him questions about Sorensen's
character and domestic life. In that case they had come
to the right witness.

He could tell them all right. He could tell them
why poor Mrs Sorensen, jealous and suspicious as
she must have been, had taken it into her head
to leave her mother's house two days early and
drive home. Because she had intended to catch her
husband in the act. And she would have caught
him, found him absent or maybe entertaining that
girl in their home, only she had never got home.
Some maniac had hitched a lift from her first. Oh
yes, he'd tell them!

In his room they sat down. They had to sit on the
bed for there was only one chair.

'It has been established,' said the Inspector, 'that
Mrs Sorensen was killed between eight and ten p.m.
on Tuesday.'

Nicholas nodded. He could hardly contain his
excitement. What a shock it was going to be for
them when he told them about this supposedly
respectable businessman's private life! A split second
later Nicholas was left deflated and staring.

'At nine that evening Mr Julius Sorensen, her husband, was in a restaurant called Potters in Marylebone High Street accompanied by a young lady. He has made a statement to us to that effect.'

Sorensen had told them. He had confessed. The disappointment was acute.

'I believe you were also in the restaurant at that time?' In a small voice Nicholas said, 'Oh yes. Yes, I was.'

'On the following day, Mr Hawthorne, you went to the offices of Sorensen-McGill where a conversation took place between you and Mr Sorensen. Will you tell me what that conversation was about, please?'

'It was about my seeing him in Potters the night before. He wanted me to . . .' Nicholas stopped. He blushed.

'Just a moment, sir. I think I can guess why you're so obviously uneasy about this. If I may say so without giving offence you're a very young man as yet and young people are often a bit confused when it comes to questions of loyalty. Am I right?'

Mystified now, Nicholas nodded.

'Your duty is plain. It's to tell the truth. Will you do that?'

'Yes, of course.'

'Good. Did Mr Sorensen try to bribe you?'

'Yes.' Nicholas took a deep breath. 'I made him a promise.'

'Which must carry no weight, Mr Hawthorne. Let me repeat. Mrs Sorensen was killed between eight and ten. Mr Sorensen has told us he was in Potters at nine, in the bar. The bar staff can't remember him. The surname of the lady he says he was with is unknown to him. According to him you were there and you saw him.' The Inspector glanced at his companion, then back to Nicholas. 'Well, Mr Hawthorne? This is a matter of the utmost seriousness.'

Nicholas understood. Excitement welled in him once more but he didn't show it. They would realise why he hesitated. At last he said:

'I was in Potters from eight till about nine-thirty.' Carefully he kept to the exact truth. 'Mr Sorensen and I discussed my being there and seeing him when I kept my appointment with him in his office on Wednesday and he – he paid the bill for my dinner.'

'I see.' How sharp were the Inspector's eyes! How much he thought he knew of youth and age, wisdom and naivety, innocence and corruption! 'Now then – did you in fact see Mr Sorensen in Potters on Tuesday evening?'

'I can't forget my promise,' said Nicholas.

Of course he couldn't. He had only to keep his promise and the police would charge Sorensen with murder. He looked down. He spoke in a guilty troubled voice.

'I didn't see him. Of course I didn't.'

Chef d'Oeuvre

PAUL GALLICO

Many readers will be familiar with those superior French country restaurants to be found along the River Loire, havens of gourmet excellence and with a far-flung reputation. But times have suddenly become hard for Monsieur Armand Bonneval, the proprietor of the auberge in the following story, and he is in desperate need of money to avoid financial ruin – when a most unexpected customer calls in. Paul Gallico (1897–1976), novelist, journalist and bon vivant, whose classic novels like *The Snow Goose* (1941), *The Small Miracle* (1951) and the series featuring the irrepressible Mrs Harris have been read all over the world, reveals in 'Chef d'Oeuvre' both his knowledge of French cuisine and his skill at weaving a murder story full of suspense and surprises . . .

You who recall the tale of the secret ingredient added to the recipe for Chicken Royal Surprise by means of which Monsieur Armand Bonneval, proprietor of the Auberge Château Loiret on the Loire, won his two-star rating in the famous Guide Michelin, bible of the touring gastronome, will be astonished to learn that this was not an unmixed blessing.

In ordinary circumstances this designation would have guaranteed Monsieur Bonneval, retired Chef of the Cordon Bleu, and Madame, his faithful partner through life's vicissitudes, an old age of ease if not of affluence. But considering what, weatherwise, the previous season had been like abroad, the circumstances were not ordinary at all.

In fact, so miserable had it been – wet, cold, and stormy – that it drove all the visitors away from France, southwards to Italy and Spain in search of sun, bringing Bonneval to the brink of bankruptcy, the loss of the Auberge Château Loiret, and of his life-savings which it represented.

The five crossed spoons and forks and two stars that Monsieur Bonneval had won for his great dish meant that his was a superior restaurant with an excellent cuisine, 'worthy of a detour,' and a 'must' stop for lunch or dinner en route past the châteaux.

But it also required the proprietor always to have on hand an adequate supply of the delicious but expensive Loire salmon, prohibitively-priced lobsters and langoustes, sweet water crayfish, legs of lamb, poulets de Bresse, duck from Nantes, truffles from Perigord, goose-livers from Strasbourg . . .

When the customers came, the profit was adequate if not handsome. But when they did not, as happened during that disastrous season, the spoilage was catastrophic. Now Monsieur Bonneval found himself unable to meet the interest payment on the mortgage due on the auberge, and likewise lacking money to discharge his obligations to the provisioners.

Thus, on one of those wretched end-of-October days, with the rain pouring down in torrents after a severe all-night gale, Monsieur Bonneval sat with Madame in the little office where she kept the cash accounts and sought for some means of evading the ruin that stared them both in the face.

'If we could only win the lottery,' sighed Madame Bonneval. She was a stout, red-cheeked woman with fine eyes, who believed in God and her husband.

'Or receive a small unexpected legacy,' brooded Bonneval.

Short, rotund, clad in classic light-blue trousers, white coat, napkin about his neck, and high stiffly-starched chef's toque on his head, he looked exactly like what he was, a kind man and one of the great cooks of France.

But alas, the letters which Madame Bonneval was engaged in opening consisted of accounts pressing for payment, circulars, and a police handbill warning of a dangerous criminal at large.

There had been an unhappy spate of such notices recently, with the usual ugly rogues'-gallery photograph of some desperate character wanted for murder, kidnapping, or bank robbery, and more often than not the warning: *Dangerous! May be armed! Notify the police at once if you encounter this man*.

Such notices were sent regularly to Monsieur Bonneval in his capacity as innkeeper, and he was supposed to display them prominently, which however he did not do, considering such a spectacle depressing to the appetites of his clientele.

'Oh, là là,' murmured Madame Bonneval, 'but here is a wicked one indeed!' as she drew forth the police handbill with a photograph of a lean man with a fierce, beaked nose. But Bonneval had eyes only for the black type topping the sheet:

500,000 FRANCS REWARD!
HAVE YOU SEEN THIS MAN?
IF SO, NOTIFY THE POLICE IMMEDIATELY!

'Five hundred thousand francs!' he cried. 'Exactly the sum we are lacking to save us. Ah ah, it is unkind of Fate to remind us so violently of our insoluble dilemma.'

'He must have done something fearful for them to offer so much,' his wife remarked. 'I read of a frightful murder in Paris a week ago. A fellow cut the throat of his mistress, and placed the corpse in a cistern. This one looks quite capable of it.'

Together they read the description: *Goes under the name of Henri Blanchard; six feet four inches tall; extremely powerful physique; age between fifty and fifty-five; slight cast in left eye; old scar running from right eyebrow to jawbone . . .*

Madame Bonneval shuddered. 'The poor girl! The paper said that she was nearly decapitated.'

'I don't doubt it,' Bonneval commented. 'Hah! If it were only our good fortune to have him appear here, our troubles would soon be over.'

'You mean he would quickly murder us both,' shrieked Madame Bonneval. 'Heuh! Do not ask for such a thing.'

But Monsieur Bonneval, it seems, *had* asked and Fate was already organising the reply. For at that very moment, no more than a kilometre away, up the road leading from Blois there trudged a tall man with a beaked nose under a battered hat, his worn clothes and knapsack soaked by the driving downpour.

It was the custom of Monsieur Bonneval, when a client or party arrived at his inn, to make a brief appearance at the service door of the dining-room to appraise them. For when he went to work on a dish he liked to have a mental image of the person who was going to enjoy it, to know whether he was lean and hungry or fat and well-fed, whether he looked like a bon viveur or gourmet, a bourgeois, a tourist, or a gentleman. He felt that this knowledge aided him in his creations.

Thus, on this rainy autumn day when Monsieur Bonneval heard the scrape of a chair in the dining-room and saw Odette, the waitress, give her hair a pat before going in, he stepped as usual into the doorway for reconnaissance.

What he saw caused him to turn as white as his coat. For he recognised immediately, seated, menu in hand, at a side table in the empty room, Henri Blanchard, murderer.

Certainly he answered every descriptive detail of the man Madame Bonneval decided had brutally slain a young girl in a Left Bank Paris attic. There was the great size, the powerful frame, the beaked nose, greying hair, the cast in one eye, and the sinister disfiguring scar from temple to jaw. There could be no mistaking him.

A frisson of terror ran through Monsieur Bonneval's

portly frame as he contemplated the formidable customer, but along with the shudder a wave of joy, also. For seated likewise at the table, in the person of Henri Blanchard, were 500,000 sorely-needed francs.

A man of rapid decisions, Bonneval quickly signalled the waitress back, whispered in the ear of Brazon, the man-of-all-work – so as not to alarm Céleste, the kitchenmaid – setting him to watch the front door, and then nipped round through the passage that ran behind the dining-room to the front of the house and joined Madame Bonneval in her office.

There he slid back a small panel in the wall, permitting a glimpse into the dining-room. 'Maman,' he cried, 'look there. Tell me what you see.'

Madame Bonneval applied her eye, gave a shriek, and seizing the black-japanned cashbox, proceeded to conceal it beneath her many black petticoats. 'Armand! It is he, the murderer!' She appeared about to faint as, remembering the handbill, she quaked, 'He may be armed. We shall all be slaughtered.'

'Pssst, woman! Keep quiet!' the chef hissed. 'Do you not realise it is the opportunity of a lifetime? I will telephone the police. They will come to arrest him. We shall collect the reward and pay the interest as well as our bills.'

Strangely, Madame Bonneval did not react to this as Bonneval expected. 'Oh, Armand,' she said, 'do you think that is right? He is a human being after all. Blood money is never lucky.'

'Are you out of your senses?' Bonneval whispered. 'This is the answer to our prayers. Keep your eye on him. Brazon is watching at the other door.'

He seized the telephone to connect with the gendarmerie at Blois, thirty kilometres distant, and the nearest police post capable of coping with so dangerous and valuable a customer. The sorely-needed 500,000 francs was practically in the till.

Yet, not quite. For no sooner had Bonneval picked up the receiver to listen for the buzzes, clicks, wails, hums, and cracklings which would indicate that the machine was activating itself than he realised that on this of all days, the telephone – never a fully developed invention in France at any time – was silent. As a matter of fact, the great windstorm during the night had taken down the lines between Loiret and Chaumont, and the instrument contained not so much as a whisper.

The only alternative then was for him to leap swiftly into his ancient shooting brake, and drive to Blois to alert the authorities. Yet, even as he rushed into the courtyard where the vehicle stood, he was aware of a serious dilemma. If he went himself, he exposed Madame Bonneval to a dangerous killer. And if he sent Brazon to break the news, he risked losing the reward or a substantial share of it.

The car solved this impasse for him as Monsieur Bonneval trod on the starter. Water from the torrential rain had managed to intrude itself into a sensitive chamber in the engine reserved to petrol. The resulting dilution caused the ignition to respond with a splutter and a sigh, after which it went as dead as the telephone. With 500,000 francs and a dangerous man at large in the dining-room, Monsieur Bonneval found himself with neither means of communication nor transport.

It was enough to try the stoutest heart. Yet stout-hearted was an exact description of Monsieur Bonneval when the survival of Madame Bonneval and himself was threatened. The telephone, it developed, when Brazon nipped over to the tiny exchange nearby, might be a matter of two or three hours, one could not say exactly.

The garage men fetched in haste estimated the same time to mobilise the vehicle. But by that time, Henri Blanchard would be many kilometres away, and the reward for his apprehension lost to them for ever.

Unless . . . Unless . . . A plan formed itself.

Shaking, inwardly, Monsieur Bonneval entered the dining-room, presented himself at the table occupied by the fugitive, and said, 'Bonjour, monsieur. I am sorry you have been kept waiting. What may I serve you?'

The stranger replied amiably enough, 'Waiting does not matter. It is good to be out of the rain. A plate of soup, a little bread, a glass of wine.'

Monsieur Bonneval thought, Ha, playing the innocent, eh? You do not realise that I know all. The cast in Blanchard's left eye made him look shifty, the nose gave him an aspect of ferocity, the scar an appearance of evil.

'Eh, now,' said the host in his most seductive voice, 'soup, a crust, and a glass of wine? Impossible at the

Auberge Loiret. You must permit me to create a meal for you.'

Had Blanchard not appeared so sinister, his smile might have seemed wistful. 'You are good,' he said, 'but forgive me, I am poor and a stranger here. I cannot afford more.'

Monsieur Bonneval thought, Ho ho, you smooth villain. And your wallet probably bulging with stolen notes.

Aloud he said, 'No, no! I will not hear of it. I was about to prepare something special for Madame and myself, to keep my hand in. With this wretched weather we have not had a customer for days. You will see, it will cost you no more than you can afford.'

'If you are so kind then,' the huge man replied, his eyes lighting up, his voice slightly hoarse.

'To begin with,' temporised Monsieur Bonneval, racking his brains for dishes that would be not only succulent but a long time in preparation, since it was his bold and ingenious plan to keep Blanchard there by the art of his cookery until either the wretched telephone or the miserable vehicle should be restored to him. 'But, of course. Mousseline de Saumon de Loire Dijonnaise, a recipe of my old friend, host of a famous restaurant in Dijon.'

The formula for preparing this superb creation was unreeling through his head. Pound in a mortar a half-kilo of magnificent fresh salmon. Force the pounded flesh through a strainer, and work it again lovingly in the mortar, incorporating little by little three to four cups of pure sweet butter, two fresh eggs, two egg yolks, a delicate head of lettuce parboiled and forced through a sieve, a tablespoon chopped chervil, two tablespoons chopped parsley, one and a half teaspoons salt, freshly-ground pepper, and a pinch of nutmeg.

Work for thirty minutes with a wooden spatula in a bowl placed in ice. Stir in two cups whipped cream.

An attractive three-quarters of an hour would be occupied by this step.

And this, the chef recalled with immense satisfaction, was but the beginning.

Turn this delectable mixture, the recipe continued, into a buttered ring mould, and poach it over hot water for forty minutes.

In an hour and a half, that wretched shooting brake might have composed itself.

Unmould the Mousseline on a round platter and place in the centre the twenty-five finest cooked crayfish tails or shrimps, and thirty small mushroom caps sauté'd in butter.

Then occupy yourself with the following sauce: to two cups warm stock made of the bones, head, and trimmings of the salmon, add one cup cream combined with four beaten egg yolks. Heat gradually, stirring. Do not let the sauce boil. Add five tablespoons butter, a little at a time, and the crayfish or shrimp shells in butter, adding a little hot water and reducing. Serve over and with the Mousseline.

By this time life could have returned to that salaud telephone.

'If you think . . .' said Henri Blanchard.

'But of course. First, however, an appetiser. Ha! Oeufs Meurette will be just the thing. After the Mousseline, I suggest a dish from the Auvergnat made famous by my old colleague Monsieur Laronde – Escalope de Veau à la Brune et à la Blonde. Then, to finish, an Omelette Norvégienne.'

'A meal fit for a king!' said Henri Blanchard.

Or the last dinner of a condemned murderer, thought Monsieur Bonneval, but aloud said, 'Of course, it will take a little time. Everything is freshly cooked.'

The wanted man smiled. 'I have nothing but time,' he said.

Time! Ha ha, Bonneval thought to himself, that is what you think, my villainous-looking friend. But it is the guillotine that awaits just round the corner.

He returned to the kitchen through the pantry, but then quickly scuttled via the passage to the front office where he cautioned Madame Bonneval. 'Signal to me immediately the telephone functions again. I will deal with him in the meantime.'

'Oh, Armand! I am terrified for your life.'

'Never fear. I will tame him with my cooking. For, once he has tasted my first dish, he will never leave.'

And this indeed proved to be the case.

When the Oeufs Meurette appeared, afloat in a sauce compounded of bacon, garlic, onion, and red wine, Blanchard sniffed, passed a hand over his brow as though he was in a dream, fell to, and in a short time put away the entire quantity of the recipe of eight eggs intended for four persons, causing Monsieur Bonneval to gape, for the chef had a true admiration for big eaters, holding with regret that they were a vanishing species. But the Mousseline, when at last Monsieur Bonneval brought it in triumphantly and set it before his unsuspecting victim, had an even more outstanding effect.

Henri Blanchard regarded the composition for an instant, the delicate pink mould, the tantalising parade of crayfish tails, the exquisite sauce, and a tear ran down his cheek and fell on to the plate. Then he tasted the first mouthful, and turned upon Monsieur Bonneval a smile which, to the host's horror, transfigured his face most astonishingly. 'Oh, mon cher chef!' he murmured, deeply moved.

The horror was that, for an instant, the smile seemed to wipe all the evil from his countenance, leaving Monsieur Bonneval badly shaken as he watched the man again devour the portion for four with undiminished appetite. For, Monsieur Bonneval found himself suddenly asking in his mind, what really was an evil face. A flaw in a retina, a misfortune of birth, a beak nose, a family inheritance, a scar caused by an accident? The smile had nullified them all.

Was it not easy to find a wicked gleam in the eye of almost anyone, a smirk, a baring of the teeth, a disarrangement of the hair, an irregularity in the walk, a twitching of the fingers, leading one to imagine one is to be butchered on the spot? But then Bonneval's mind returned to the police notice which left no room for doubt. He went into the kitchen to complete the weaving of the culinary net about the man he intended to betray.

But, truth to tell, his conscience was far from easy as he set about pounding six thin escalopes of veal quite flat, and cooked them slowly in butter a fine golden brown on both sides. For the words of his wife were weighing upon him: 'He is a human being after all. Blood money is never lucky.'

True, the 500,000 francs was desperately needed. Yet the sum was to be obtained at the price of the life of a man who had shed a tear over his Mousseline and called him, 'My dear chef.'

Thoughtfully Monsieur Bonneval removed the meat, adding a half cup of white wine to the pan, stirring, then adding another half cup of strong veal stock flavoured with a tablespoon of meat glaze. He reduced and thickened the brown sauce slightly with a teaspoonful of potato starch.

A drastic idea came to him. Madame Bonneval suffered from migraine and frequently took a sleeping powder. Two of these added to the sauce would guarantee the presence of Henri Blanchard until the police came, as well as spare Bonneval the reproachful look at the betrayal. When Blanchard woke up he would be in goal.

Bonneval the archconspirator actually held the powder in his fingers. But Bonneval the master chef found himself unable to add them to the mixture, for who could tell what undesirable alteration in flavour might result?

Disposing of it in the waste bucket, he stuffed a

pound of cooked white mushroom caps with chopped ham and pâté-de-foie-gras; then with the mushroom stock, heavy cream, and egg yolks he confected one and three-quarter cupfuls of cream sauce. A sudden vision of Blanchard's head laid upon the block of the guillotine assailed him, inducing in Monsieur Bonneval a shudder that almost caused a fatality to the sauce.

Now, with care, he heated in butter six slices of Normandy ham on both sides just long enough, and then arranged the escalopes of veal and ham slices alternately on the serving platter. Glancing at the clock he noted that it was four in the afternoon, three hours since his dangerous guest had arrived. It did not make him happy.

Filling in the centre of the veal and ham ring with the stuffed mushrooms, he carefully spooned the aromatic brunette gravy over the meat and the magnificent blonde sauce over the fungi. Then he carried it in to Henri Blanchard.

The reaction was spontaneous and startling.

A look, a sniff, a taste! Then the man rose to his feet and folded Monsieur Bonneval to his breast with his enormous and powerful arms. A good thing that Madame Bonneval was engaged on the telephone at that moment, and not applying her eye to the panel in the wall, for she would have thought certainly that Bonneval's last moment had come.

'Maître!' exclaimed Blanchard, and then he cried, 'Magus!' or magician.

To his surprise, Monsieur Bonneval found himself

with his eyes quite moist, returning the pressure. 'Friend,' he said, 'Grand gourmet! Connoisseur! Bon appétit! Enjoy yourself. I go to prepare the Omelette Norvégienne for you.'

It was only when he was delicately folding the ten stiffly-beaten eggwhites into the soufflé mixture of four yolks, mixed with a cup of sugar, almonds, and a glass of 1901 Armagnac, that it came to him he had been wrapped in the embrace of a murderer.

The next instant, a lightning bolt smote him as he clapped his hand to his sweating brow; he was riven by the thought that Henri Blanchard must be innocent. For no man who loved good food and cooking, and so appreciatively filled his belly with it, could be a murderer. In all the history of crime there was no record of a hungry or even starving gourmet having slain anyone. The two were incompatible.

Have you ever, Monsieur Bonneval would have asked you, after a satisfying repast, when you sat half drowsy, hands folded over paunch, the fragrance of the good cigar still lingering, rememorising the tastes, flavours, aromas, the blends and clashes of spices, colour and texture of meat, fish, or fowl, the subtleties of the sauces, the airiness of the soufflé, contemplated murder?

But when the mind is not on food . . . you might suggest.

The mind of a great gourmet, Monsieur Bonneval would assure you, is always on food.

At this moment, the startled chef became aware that Madame was signalling frantically to him from the passage. When he went to her she whispered, 'The telephone is restored. I have been through to the police at Blois a short while ago. They will arrive in less than ten minutes now.'

'Woman,' Bonneval cried, 'what have you done? You yourself declared that it was wrong to accept blood money – '

'But, Armand! It was only because I feared for your life!'

There was not a moment to be lost. Frantically, Bonneval burst into the dining-room where sat Henri Blanchard, the last vestige of Escalope Brune et Blonde scraped from the platter, an expression of ineffable bliss upon a face that now appeared not only handsome but even somewhat noble.

'You must fly!' Bonneval shouted. 'All is known. The police will be here at any moment!'

The violence of Bonneval's entrance brought Henri Blanchard to his feet, and for an instant he looked stupefied.

'Fly?' he said. 'Where to? Why?'

'You are accused of murder. There is a reward of 500,000 francs offered for your apprehension; but only I, Armand Bonneval, know that you are innocent. Go now, while there is still time. You must leave the country at once.'

'But I have no money with which to leave the country. And I have never murdered anything but a little white paper.'

'Ah ah, but once the police have captured you they will see that you go to the block. Wait here an instant.'

Bonneval rushed into the little office and, opening the cashbox, extracted eighty thousand francs. It was their last reserve, but his conscience was very bad for he knew that he had come close to selling the life of a fellow man.

Returning to the dining-room he thrust the notes into the hands of Henri Blanchard.

'Here,' he said, 'take this. It is all I have. It will get you across the border.'

But it was already too late.

From without came the wailing of sirens, the squealing of brakes, the slamming of car doors, the running of feet. Monsieur Bonneval had time only to leap to the sideboard and seize a carving-knife and fork with which he ranged himself fiercely before Henri Blanchard as the gendarmes, led by a lieutenant, burst into the room.

'You shall not take him. He is innocent. Advance at your peril!' Bonneval challenged.

But the gendarmes made no attempt to advance, and only ranged themselves opposite the tall man and his stout little protector, while the lieutenant consulted a copy of the handbill he had brought with him.

Finally the police officer spoke. 'Monsieur le Duc,' he said.

'Oh,' said the tall man softly. 'So that is how it is.'

'Forgive this means of tracing you,' the lieutenant continued, 'but the word from Paris is that the lawyers are frantic. They know you never see newspapers or listen to the radio when you are abroad. I have to inform you that His Grace, your uncle, died some months ago. The message is that if you do not immediately assume the title and its responsibilities his entire fortune will be devoted to the propagation of the giant grasshoppers that were the subject of his lifelong research.'

Blanchard said, 'I am happier to remain poor, and a poet, roaming the highways and byways of France as I have done in the past.'

There was a moment of silence broken uncomfortably by Monsieur Bonneval, who suddenly felt slightly ridiculous brandishing his massive knife and fork. 'But the handbill: the charge of murder of that unfortunate girl!' he said.

The lieutenant turned to him with some amusement. 'What are you talking about, little puff-pigeon? There is nothing here about murder, only that we wished to be put in touch with Henri Blanchard, here pictured.'

Seizing the handbill, Monsieur Bonneval examined it closely as Madame Bonneval, Odette, and the others crowded into the room. It was true. The overheated imaginations of his wife and himself had supplied all the rest.

'Oh,' he cried in such anguish that Madame at once rushed to his side and slipped her arm through his, 'I am the greatest fool alive!'

Henri Blanchard said gravely, 'Not the greatest fool but, surely, the greatest chef.' He asked the officer, 'How much time is there left to decide?'

'Only eight hours, under the terms of the will, Your Grace. We must drive you to Paris at once.'

Henri Blanchard went to the window and gazed down the rain-swept road for a moment. Then he said to Bonneval, 'If it had not been for you and your magnificent cookery, I should long have been down that road and free for ever, for tomorrow it would have been too late. So you took me for a murderer, and kept me here that you might gain the reward?'

Bonneval turned a brilliant scarlet.

'But when you became convinced of my innocence you thrust upon me your last sou to help me to escape. You have taught me that people may yet be generous, noble, and kind, Monsieur Bonneval.'

He came over and placed his hands on the shoulder of the chef, saying, 'But you have also taught me something else by the artistry of your creations; namely, that there is another kind of good life besides that of a wandering vagabond. The beauties of art of every kind await me. A rich man can support and perpetuate these beauties. I believe I shall essay this kind of life for a time.

'Besides – ' he smiled suddenly – 'I do not very much care for those giant grasshoppers . . .'

Henri Blanchard fingered the banknotes Bonneval had thrust upon him and, smiling, patted the little chef on the shoulder. 'I shall need these when I arrive in Paris. But they will be returned to you manifold, along with the reward for my – ah – apprehension. Come, lieutenant, we had better hasten.'

He strode from the room, followed by the gendarmes, leaving Monsieur Bonneval feeling a little ashamed, yet also deeply touched and extraordinarily happy.

La Spécialité de M. Duclos

OLIVER LA FARGE

Pierre Duclos is also a *maître de cuisine*, although he has
chosen to practise his art across the Atlantic, in America.
He, too, has his own restaurant and sets a standard of
excellence that seems to please all his customers – all, that is,
except one. The result is murder, and the subsequent trial is
reported hereunder in 'La Spécialité de M. Duclos' by Oliver
La Farge (1901–1963). La Farge, who was best-known as an
anthropologist and led archaeological expeditions in Mexico
and Guatemala, as well as being a Pulitzer Prize winner for
his novel *Laughing Boy* (1929), here created a most ingenious
tale of a courtroom drama where the question being debated
is whether homicide might be justifiable on the grounds of
culinary interference!

The jurists of Paris were surprised when Maître
Béchamil, the famous advocate, undertook the defence
of Pierre Duclos. The United States had asked for
Duclos's extradition to the province of Connecticut to
be tried for a homicide that he himself admitted he had
committed. His extradition seemed certain. Moreover,
Duclos was an Auvergnat, and Maître Béchamil, a
Norman, had often and openly expressed his dislike
for the people of Auvergne. He detested their accent.
He distrusted their smallness, their darkness, their

ferocity. He said that they were emotional primitives in a country founded upon civilisation and pure reason, more Spanish than French, more Latin than Gallic, and that they used too much garlic.

Maître Béchamil was an effective trial lawyer, a brilliant legal thinker, a gourmet, and a man of sound common sense. His taking of the case attracted attention that was further heightened when he exercised great ingenuity to have the case put over from the winter to the spring sessions. He did nothing without cause. The delay was essential, for the whole matter hung upon a proper understanding of the *haute cuisine française*. The later sessions would insure that the presiding judge would be no less a person than the president of the Société Gastronomique des Légistes, that famous organisation of jurist-connoisseurs, with two other members of the society as his associates. The winter sessions, Béchamil confided to his client, would be presided over by a man who had been seen – here he lowered his voice – sprinkling vinegar upon *rognons sautés madère*. They shuddered together.

Maître Béchamil had equally good reasons for taking the case to begin with. In the privacy of the advocate's bachelor apartment Duclos had amply proven that he was a *maître chef*. Above all, his amazing variation upon ordinary *sauce blanche*, which was the very heart of the case, was one of those great innovations that enshrine an artist's name in history. The advocate saw a good chance of success. He also thought he saw the means of at last winning membership in the Société Gastronomique, which was not only a constellation of gourmets but the controlling inner circle of his profession.

Duclos planned, if he was set free, to proceed immediately to Auvergne, where he would visit his relatives and marry his fiancée. With her and her dowry he would return to Paris and open a restaurant. Maître Béchamil found this plan commendable. He asked how long the master chef would stay in Auvergne. Duclos said about a month. The advocate nodded. Inwardly, he smiled. A month would do nicely, he thought.

The case was heard by the panel of three judges for which Béchamil had hoped. The courtroom was well filled, and the presence of an American attaché testified to the importance of the matter. The prosecution put its case bluntly. The evidence was inescapable. The accused had run a restaurant in Connecticut. One evening he invited a group of his patrons to a dinner. In the course of the meal, for no apparent reason, the accused stabbed one of them, a M. Hathaway, through the heart with a carving knife. (The pronunciation of the names 'Hathaway' and 'Connecticut' caused the prosecutor no slight difficulty.) It was not for the present court to find the named Duclos innocent or guilty, but merely to determine, as it could not help but determine, that there existed a sufficient shadow of guilt to require him to return to the suburb or province of Connecticut where he would receive a fair trial under American law.

When Maître Béchamil rose, the audience felt that

his case was already lost. The great advocate surveyed the bench. He shook back the sleeves of his robe and adjusted his cravat. He would not, he said, deny the facts set forth by his learned colleague. His client had indeed stabbed one of his guests and patrons through the heart as he sat at the table. He would, however, show the court that this act had been honourable and completely justified. He would further show that it would be a travesty upon justice to deliver a man who was in effect a hero to the jurisdiction of a people incapable of grasping the principles involved.

'I must give you,' he said, 'some little idea of the populace of that province of Connecticut, adjoining the metropolis of New York. I must describe them from the point of view of a *maître de cuisine*, a gastronome, and an artist, such as my client.'

He described how these people daily wolfed a hurried breakfast, sped to New York by train or automobile, and, after a day of the intensely sustained work characteristic of American energy, hastened home, to arrive exhausted, in time only to numb themselves against their fatigue with an excess of cocktails before approaching the pleasures of the table. From this point, by an interesting transition, he reached the subject of clam chowder.

Maître Béchamil described that bivalve, paler than a mussel, tougher than a scallop, less succulent than an oyster, mere leather when cooked. He described the process of the chowder from the crude salt pork smoking in the pan to the completed dish with spots of grease floating in the milk. The bench was impressed, but it was apparent that the judges were wondering what this description of monstrosities had to do with the case.

'Among these people,' he went on, 'there is a certain affectation of epicureanism. There is also an affectation of the *cuisine*, with a creditable desire to emulate *la cuisine française*. But the mastery of great art requires generations. Just as that great nation leads all others in questions of the machine, so has it a long way to go before its members have absorbed a true sense of gastronomy. Many among them have formed some palate – enough so that they patronised my client's little restaurant. They have not, however, learned to cook. They may produce their chowders, and they are fairly good with a simple beef-steak, but when they step beyond that point, they err.

'It is impossible to persuade them that very little of anything is enough. If one pinch of sweet basil is good, they think, then two are better. In their cooking they seek to taste not the influence of the ingredients but the ingredients themselves. One of those gentlemen concocting a dish in his kitchen and finding that the recipe calls for a teaspoonful of dry Sauternes will unhesitatingly substitute for it a tablespoon of one of their wines of California.'

Maître Béchamil paused dramatically. The judges looked profoundly shocked. Everyone glanced toward the representative of the American Embassy, who was staring at his clasped hands and blushing. Nothing had yet been brought out to prevent Duclos's extradition, but the atmosphere in the court was now strongly in his favour.

'Among my client's patrons was that M. Hathaway,' the advocate resumed, 'a man blindly pleased with his own cookery. A man who prided himself upon his omelettes, and yet insisted publicly that oleo-margarine was just as good as butter.' His eyes flickered toward the judge on the right, who was internationally famous for his omelettes.

'Now, Messieurs, I have set the stage. We approach the day and hour of the act, an act far more deserving of reward than of punishment. My client, ever improving his art, discovered an amazing variation upon one of the simplest of all elements of cookery – white sauce – that elevated it to a celestial plane. I shall not elaborate, as the court will have the opportunity to judge for itself the deliciousness of this compound, a product of the purest essentials of French cookery, of simplicity, perfect timing, and restraint.

'This sauce, my client realised, would become his chiefest *spécialité de la maison*. It would become famous as *sauce blanche Duclos*. It assured at last his successful return to his native land. Launched in Connecticut, then transferred to France, where it belonged, it would be a magnet to Americans, a source of dollar exchange, an aid to his country in her restoration of herself under the Marshall Plan. To introduce this sauce, he invited a select group of patrons to dinner. Among them was the individual Hathaway, included not for his personal character or for his palate but because of his wealth and position, which dictated even that he be seated upon my client's left.

'The sauce was served with the *entrée* exactly as it will shortly be served to the court. Everyone exclaimed over it. The guests toasted their host and *sauce blanche Duclos*. They asked for the recipe, but my client only smiled. They tasted, they guessed, but the new elements – the secret – were beyond them.

'Supremely happy, my client went into the kitchen to supervise the final moments of the *pièce de résistance*. This man named Hathaway, pretending good-fellowship, followed him. Before my client knew what was happening, the man had stepped quickly to the small stove at which my client prepared his personal creations. There was the saucepan with remnants of *sauce blanche Duclos* in it, and there, on the shelf, were all the ingredients. Hathaway scanned the shelf, chuckled, and returned to the table. Shaken, but ever courtly, my client saw the main course made ready and returned to his seat.

'The individual Hathaway sat at his left. He had prepared himself for the feast in the usual manner, with an excess of cocktails. Now he leaned over and in my client's ear he said these terrible words: 'Come to dinner next Wednesday, old boy'. And then he named three names, the secret of *sauce blanche Duclos*, and again he chuckled.'

Maître Béchamil was silent long enough to let the full horror of the situation sink in. 'My client's years in the Resistance had taught him speed of thought and action. Instantly, as fast as ever in a crisis confronting the Gestapo, he grasped the situation. With heavy hand, this individual would prepare a travesty that from then on he would serve under the name of *sauce blanche Duclos*. Before ever the creation was launched, a counterfeit would be in circulation, its reputation would be destroyed, and not only its creator but the French Republic would have been robbed.

'What could be done? How can knowledge be removed from a mind? There was only one thing to do, and my client did it, knowing full well that thus once more he offered the sacrifice of his life if the Good God so willed. The essence of what followed you already know. He miraculously made good his escape. I shall not waste the court's time with details of his voyage to Mexico or of his embarkation from there. Suffice in that, having set foot once more upon the soil of his beloved France, this patriot openly assumed his own name, conscious of the correctness of his position, desiring only his vindication.'

Maître Béchamil fell silent. The President of the Court said that it was indeed essential that the court examine this *spécialité de M. Duclos*. A table was wheeled in, bearing cooking equipment and ingredients. M. Duclos stepped forward, bowed to the court, and went to work without speaking.

While he made his preparations, the advocate explained that the *entrée* consisted simply of slices of breast of chicken, broiled, and seethed in white Burgundy. That the court might be sure what was the contribution of the sauce to the whole, a plate with slices of the meat was passed to them. The judges entertained themselves determining the wine and vintage used.

At a certain point the little chef took three phials from an envelope and emptied them into his saucepan. He then dropped the phials into the trash receptacle. The sauce was poured over the warmed meat. The combination was allowed to simmer briefly. Then it was placed on dishes and served, with thin slices of good bread and a well-chosen Graves. As the judges tasted, it could be seen that the effect upon them was electric. It began to seem that Maître Béchamil was winning.

The judges withdrew to consider. Maître Béchamil waited calmly. He was sure he had made and sustained all his points. He was confident, too, that no member of the Société Gastronomique could permit the secret of such a sauce to be eliminated from the world. He was inwardly pleased, in addition, because he had obtained possession of the three phials as the table had been wheeled out, and already had identified the contents of one of them.

The judges returned. The President of the Court spoke well of the Marshall Plan, and with deep feeling of the liberation of France. He pointed out that these matters, however, were not on trial in his court. It was the specific act of the defendant, which must be considered in its context. There was a man's inherent right to protect his livelihood. There was the sacredness of art. There were questions of national interest. There was the matter of delivering a man for trial under circumstances such that, with all admiration for American jurisprudence, it must be assumed that true justice would not be done, because of a fundamental conflict of mores and of cultures. One must doubt that any court in a land of chowder and oleo-margarine could understand the values involved.

'Finally,' he said, 'the theft of a recipe of this order, aggravated by the incompetence of the thief, is an especially despicable form of larceny. The killing of the thief in the very act is legally identical with, but far more noble than, the shooting of a common burglar as he enters one's window. Extradition is denied.'

The courtroom cheered. The American attaché departed furtively. M. Duclos embraced Maître Béchamil. The victory was tremendous.

At 11 o'clock the following morning the advocate told his staff that he would be absent for several hours on personal business. He then repaired to his apartment, proceeding directly to the kitchen. With precise, delicate motions he laid out the publicly known ingredients of *sauce blanche Duclos*. From a locked drawer he took out the three secret elements, identified by him the night before. The crucial question now was: How much of each?

He did not expect truly to duplicate the sauce. Connoisseur that he was, he knew he was a mediocre cook. Duclos would be a month in Auvergne. Time enough to come so close to the real thing that even the fine palate of the president of the society, after the lapse of a few weeks, would believe that he had indeed duplicated *sauce blanche Duclos* simply from having tasted it once before the trial. Election to the Société Gastronomique would then be certain.

He removed his frock coat, put on a large apron, and went to work. A very little of this, he suspected, rather more of that, and of the third – barely a drop? Or was that merely his timidity? Perhaps, in his greatness, M. Duclos had dared use as much as half a teaspoonful. One must experiment, that was all. This time, one-quarter of a teaspoonful.

The result was not right. It missed being very good – probably by some indefinable yet disagreeable imbalance of the elements. Béchamil sighed and started again. As he stirred and meditated, lost to the world, he was startled into dropping the spoon with a clatter by the sound of a step behind him and a familiar Auvergnat voice saying, 'Good day, Maître Béchamil.'

He whirled about. Duclos, who should have been in Auvergne by now, walked toward him. He wore a black suit, a white shirt with stiff collar, and a sober tie. Maître Béchamil noticed that his shoes squeaked slightly. He laid his bowler hat on a chair, and took from under his arm a case about half a metre long, covered with purplish plush.

'I am on my way to the station,' he said. 'I just stopped by to show you the bargain I picked up. Look.' He opened the case. In it lay a carving knife of fine steel, moderately worn and very sharp. M. Duclos placed the case on the table and took out the knife. 'Believe you, Monsieur, this is almost the exact duplicate of the fine knife I sacrificed when I eliminated the individual Hathaway.'

Maître Béchamil said something vague.

The little man glanced at the articles on the table. 'You experiment, Monsieur l'Avocat? You encounter trouble?' The Auvergnat accent was stronger than ever. 'Incompetence, I fear. No good cook would think that I ever put that' – he pointed at one ingredient – 'in a sauce. I had a phial of it along as a blind. Incompetent.'

He smiled. He was dark, small, ferocious, the light in his eyes was primitive, he was more Spanish than French, more Latin than Gallic. He caressed the blade of the knife with the fingers of his left hand. Softly, in that detestable accent, he quoted, ' "The killing of the thief in the very act is legally identical with, but far more noble than . . ." '

Three, or Four, for Dinner

L. P. HARTLEY

The Italians, like the French, enjoy a cuisine unmistakably
their own, and there are restaurants and hotels to be found
all over Italy which can provide the setting for meals that
please the eye as well as the appetite. Few cities, however,
can match the places to choose from in Venice, the location
of this unnerving story by L. P. Hartley (1895–1972), author
of those two remarkable novels *The Go-Between* (1953) and
The Hireling (1957). Hartley was a sedate man of letters
with a devotion to Italy which took him to the country on
numerous occasions. The Hotel San Giorgio in Venice, in
which he sets his grim story of an unexpected dinner guest,
was, apparently, among his favourite places to eat . . .

It was late July in Venice, suffocatingly hot. The
windows of the bar in the Hotel San Giorgio stood
open to the Canal. But no air came through. At
six o'clock a little breeze had sprung up, a feebler
repetition of the mid-day sirocco, but in an hour it
had blown itself out.

One of the men got off his high stool and walked
somewhat unsteadily to the window.

'It's going to be calm all right,' he said. 'I think
we'll go in the gondola. I see it's there, tied up at
the usual post.'

'As you please, Dickie,' said his friend from the other stool.

Their voices proclaimed them Englishmen; proclaimed also the fact that they were good clients of the barman.

'Giuseppe!' called the man at the window, turning his eyes from the Salute with its broad steps, its mighty portal and its soaring dome back to the counter with the multi-coloured bottles behind it. 'How long does it take to row to the Lido?'

'Sir?'

'Didn't you say you'd lived in England, Giuseppe?'

'Yes, sir, eight years at the Hôtel Métropole.'

'Then why?'

His friend intervened, pacifically, in Italian.

'He wants to know how long it takes to row to the Lido.'

Relief in his voice, the barman answered, 'That depends if you've got one oar or two.'

'Two.'

'If you ask me,' said Dickie, returning to his stool, 'I don't think Angelino, or whatever his damned name is, counts for much. It's the chap in front who does the work.'

'Yes, sir,' said the barman, solicitously. 'But the man at the back he guide the boat, he give the direction.'

'Well,' said Dickie, 'as long as he manages to hit the Lido. . . . We want to be at the Splendide by eight. Can we do it?'

'Easily, sir, you have got an hour.'

'Barring accidents.'

'We never have accidents in Venice,' said the barman, with true Italian optimism.

'Time for another, Phil?'

'Three's my limit, Dickie.'

'Oh, come on, be a man.'

They drank.

'You seem to know a lot,' said Dickie more amiably
to the barman. 'Can you tell us anything about this
chap who's dining with us – Joe O'Kelly, or whatever
his name is?'

The barman pondered. He did not want to be called
over the coals a second time. 'That would be an English
name, sir?'

'English! Good Lord!' exploded Dickie. 'Does it
sound like English?'

'Well, now, as you say it, it does,' remonstrated his
companion. 'Or rather Irish. But wait – here's his card.
Does that convey anything to you, Giuseppe?'

The barman turned the card over in his fingers. 'Oh,
now I see, sir – Giacomelli – il Conte Giacomelli.'

'Well, do you know him?'

'Oh yes, sir. I know him very well.'

'What's he like?'

'He's a nice gentleman, sir, very rich . . .'

'Then he must be different from the rest of your
aristocracy,' said Dickie, rather rudely. 'I hear they
haven't two penny pieces to rub together.'

'Perhaps he's not so rich now,' the barman admitted, mournfully. 'None of us are. Business is bad.
He is *grand azionista* – how do you say?' he stopped,
distressed.

'Shareholder?' suggested Philip.

'Good Lord!' exclaimed Dickie, 'I didn't know you were so well up in this infernal language. You're a regular Wop!'

The barman did not notice the interruption.

'Yes, shareholder, that's it,' he was saying delightedly. 'He is a great shareholder in a *fabbrica di zucchero –* '

'Sugar-factory,' explained Philip, not without complacence.

The barman lowered his voice. 'But I hear they are . . .' He made a curious rocking movement with his hand.

'Not very flourishing?' said Philip.

The barman shrugged his shoulders. 'That's what they say.'

'So we mustn't mention sugar,' said Dickie, with a yawn. 'Come on, Phil, you're always so damned abstemious. Have another.'

'No, no, really not.'

'Then I will.'

Philip and even the barman watched him drink with awe on their faces.

'But,' said Philip as Dickie set down his glass, 'Count Giacomelli lives in Venice, doesn't he?'

'Oh yes, sir. Usually he comes in here every night. But it's four – five days now I do not see him.'

'Pity,' said Philip, 'we might have given him a lift. But perhaps he has a launch?'

'I don't think he's using his launch now, sir.'

'Oh well, he'll find some way of getting there, you

may be sure,' said Dickie. 'How shall we know him, Giuseppe?'

'I expect you'll see him double, my poor Dickie,' remarked his friend.

The barman, with his usual courtesy, began replying to Dickie's question.

'Oh, he's a common-looking gentleman like yourself, sir. . . .'

'I, common?'

'No,' said the barman, confused. 'I mean *grande come lei* – as tall as you.'

'That's nothing to go by. Has he a beard and whiskers and a moustache?'

'No, he's clean-shaven.'

'Come on, come on,' said Philip. 'We shall be late, and perhaps he won't wait for us.'

But his friend was in combative mood. 'Damn it! how are we to dine with the chap if we don't recognise him? Now, Giuseppe, hurry up; think of the Duce and set your great Italian mind working. Isn't there anything odd about him? Is he cross-eyed?'

'No, sir.'

'Does he wear spectacles?'

'Oh no, sir.'

'Is he minus an arm?'

'*Nossignore*,' cried the barman, more and more agitated.

'Can't you tell us anything about him, except that he's common-looking, like me?'

The barman glanced helplessly round the room.

Suddenly his face brightened. 'Ah, *ecco*! He limps a little.'

'That's better,' said Dickie. 'Come on, Philip, you lazy hound, you always keep me waiting.' He got down from the stool. 'See you later,' he said over his shoulder to the barman. 'Mind you have the whisky pronto. I shall need it after this trip.'

The barman, gradually recovering his composure, gazed after Dickie's receding, slightly lurching figure with intense respect.

The gondola glided smoothly over the water towards the island of San Giorgio Maggiore, the slender campanile of which was orange with the light of the setting sun. On the left lay the Piazzetta, the two columns, the rich intricate stonework of St Mark's, the immense façade of the Ducal Palace, still perfectly distinct for all the pearly pallor in the air about them. But, as San Giorgio began to slide past them on the right, it was the view at the back of the gondola which engrossed Philip's attention. There, in the entrance of the Grand Canal, the atmosphere was deepening into violet while the sky around the dome of the Salute was of that clear deep blue which, one knows instinctively, may at any moment be pierced by the first star. Philip, who was sitting on his companion's left, kept twisting round to see the view, and the gondolier, whose figure blocked it to some extent, smiled each time he did so, saying *'Bello, non è vero?'* almost as though from habit. Dickie, however, was less tolerant of his friend's aesthetic preoccupations.

'I wish to goodness you wouldn't keep wriggling about,' he muttered, sprawling laxly in the depths of the more comfortable seat. 'You make me feel seasick.'

'All right, old chap,' said Philip, soothingly. 'You go to sleep.'

Dickie hauled himself up by the silk rope which was supported by the brass silhouette of a horse at one end and by a small but solid brass lion at the other.

He said combatively: 'I don't want to go to sleep. I want to know what we're to say to this sugar-refining friend of yours. Supposing he doesn't talk English? Shall we sit silent through the meal?'

'Oh, I think all foreigners do.' Philip spoke lightly; his reply was directed to the first of Dickie's questions; it would have been obviously untrue as an answer to the second. 'Jackson didn't tell me; he only gave me that letter and said he was a nice fellow and could get us into palaces and so on that ordinary people don't see.'

'There are too many that ordinary people do see, as it is, if you ask me,' groaned Dickie. 'For God's sake don't let him show us any more sights.'

'He seems to be a well-known character,' said Philip. 'He'll count as a sight himself.'

'If you call a limping dago a sight, I'm inclined to agree with you,' Dickie took him up crossly.

But Philip was unruffled.

'I'm sorry, Dickie, but I had to do it – couldn't ignore the letter, you know. We shall get through the evening somehow. Now, sit up and look at the lovely scenery. *Cosa è questa isola?*' he asked the gondolier, indicating an island to the right that looked as if it might be a monastery.

'*Il manicomio*,' said the gondolier, with a grin. Then, as Philip looked uncomprehending, he tapped his forehead and smiled still more broadly.

'Oh,' said Philip, 'it's the lunatic asylum.'

'I do wish,' said Dickie, plaintively, 'if you must show me things, you'd direct my attention to something more cheerful.'

'Well, then,' said Philip, 'look at these jolly old boats. They're more in your line.'

A couple of tramp-steamers, moored stern to stern, and, even in the fading twilight, visibly out of repair – great gangrenous patches of rust extending over their flanks – hove up on the left. Under the shadow of their steep sides the water looked oily and almost black.

Dickie suddenly became animated. 'This reminds me of Hull,' he exclaimed. 'Good old Hull! Civilisation at last! Nothing picturesque and old-world. Two ugly useful old ships, nice oily water and lots of foreign bodies floating about in it. At least,' he said, rising unsteadily to his feet, 'I take that to be a foreign body.'

'*Signore, signore!*' cried the first gondolier, warningly.

A slight swell, caused perhaps by some distant motor-boat, made the gondola rock alarmingly. Dickie subsided – fortunately, into his seat; but his hand was still stretched out, pointing, and as the water was suddenly scooped into a hollow, they all saw what he meant: a dark object showed up for an instant in the trough of the wave.

'Looks like an old boot,' said Philip, straining his eyes. '*Cosa è, Angelino?*'

The gondolier shrugged his shoulders.

'*Io non so. Forsè qualche gatto,*' he said, with the light-heartedness with which Italians are wont to treat the death of animals.

'Good God, does the fellow think I don't know a cat when I see one?' cried Dickie, who had tumbled to the gondolier's meaning. 'Unless it's a cat that has been in the water a damned long time. No, it's – it's . . .'

The gondoliers exchanged glances and, as though by mutual consent, straightened themselves to row. '*E meglio andare, signori,*' said Angelino firmly.

'What does he say?'

'He says we'd better be going.'

'I'm not going till I've found out what that is,' said Dickie obstinately. 'Tell him to row up to it, Phil.'

Philip gave the order, but Angelino seemed not to understand.

'*Non è niente interessante, niente interessante,*' he kept repeating stubbornly.

'But it is interesting to me,' said Dickie, who like many people could understand a foreign language directly his own wishes were involved. 'Go to it! There!' he commanded.

Reluctantly the men set themselves to row. As the boat drew up alongside, the black patch slid under the water and there appeared in its place a gleam of whiteness, then features – a forehead, a nose, a mouth. . . . They constituted a face, but not a recognisable one.

'Ah, *povero annegato*,' murmured Angelino, and crossed himself.

The two friends looked at each other blankly.

'Well, this has torn it,' said Dickie, at last. 'What are we going to do now?'

The gondoliers had already decided. They were moving on.

'Stop! Stop!' cried Philip. 'We can't leave him like this.' He appealed to the men. '*Non si può lasciarlo così.*'

Angelino spread his hands in protest. The drowned man would be found by those whose business it was to patrol the waters. Who knew what he had died of? Perhaps some dreadful disease which the signori would catch. There would be difficulties with the police; official visits. Finally, as the Englishmen still seemed unconvinced, he added, '*Anche fa sporca la gondola. Questo tappeto, signori, m'ha costato più che mille duecento lire.*'

Somewhat grimly Philip explained to Dickie this last, unanswerable reason for not taking the drowned man on board. 'He will dirty the gondola and spoil the carpet, which cost twelve hundred lire.'

'Carpet be damned!' exclaimed Dickie. 'I always told you dagoes were no good. Here, catch hold of him.'

Together they pulled the dead man into the boat, though not before Angelino had rolled back his precious carpet. And when the dead man was lying in the bottom of the boat, decently covered with a piece of brown water-proof sheeting, he went round with sponge and wash-leather and carefully wiped away every drop of water from the gunwale and its brass fittings.

Ten minutes sufficed to take them to the Lido. The little *passeggiata* that had started so pleasantly had become a funeral cortège. The friends hardly spoke. Then, when they were nearing the landing-stage and the ugly white hotel, an eyesore all the way across the lagoon, impended over them with its blazing lights and its distressing symmetry, Dickie said:

'By Jove, we shall be late for that fellow.'

'He'll understand,' said Philip. 'It'll be something to talk to him about.'

He regretted the words the moment they were out of his mouth: they sounded so heartless.

The landing-stage was almost deserted when the gondola drew up at the steps; but the aged, tottering and dirty *rampino* who hooked it in and held out his skinny hand for *soldi*, soon spread the news. While Philip was conferring with the gondoliers upon the proper course to be taken, a small crowd collected and gazed, expressionlessly but persistently, at the shapeless mound in the gondola. The *rampino* professed himself capable of keeping watch; the gondoliers declared they could not find a *vigile* unless they went together; they hinted that it might take some time. At last Dickie and Philip were free. They walked along the avenue under acacia trees stridently lighted by arc-lamps, towards the sea and the Hotel Splendide. As they looked back they saw that the little knot of spectators was already dispersing.

No, they were told: Count Giacomelli had not yet arrived. But that is nothing, smiled the *maître d'hôtel*; the Signor Conte is often late. Would the gentlemen take a cocktail while they waited?

Dickie agreed with enthusiasm. 'I think we've earned it,' he said. 'Think of it, but for us that poor chap would be floated about the lagoons till Doomsday and none of his dusky offspring know what had happened to him.'

'Do you think they will now?' asked Philip.

'You mean . . .? Oh, I think anyone who really knew him could tell.'

They were sitting at a table under the trees. The air was fresh and pleasant; the absence of mosquitoes almost miraculous. Dickie's spirits began to rise.

'I say,' he said. 'It's damned dull waiting. He's twenty minutes late. Where's that boy?'

When a second round had been served, Dickie motioned the page to stay. Philip looked at him in surprise.

'Listen,' said Dickie, in a thick, excited undertone. 'Wouldn't it be a lark if we sent this lad down to the gondola and told him to ask the chap that's resting inside to come and dine with us?'

'A charming idea, Dickie, but I doubt whether they understand practical jokes in this country.'

'Nonsense, Phil, that's a joke that anyone could understand. Now, put on your thinking-cap and find the appropriate words. I'm no good; you must do it.'

Philip smiled.

'We don't want to be four at dinner, do we? I'm sure

the Count wouldn't like having to sit down with a – a drowned rat.'

'That's absurd; he may be a man of excellent family; it's generally the rich who commit suicide.'

'We don't know that he did.'

'No, but all that's beside the point. Now just tell this boy to run down to the jetty, or whatever it is called, give our message and bring us back the answer. It won't take him ten minutes. I'll give him five lire to soothe his shattered nerves.'

Philip appeared to be considering it. 'Dick, I really don't think – a foreign country and all, you know. . . .'

The boy looked interrogatively from one to the other.

'It's a good idea,' repeated Philip, 'and I don't want to be a spoilsport. But really, Dickie, I should give it up. The boy would be very scared, perhaps tell his parents, and then we might be mobbed and thrown into the Canal. It's the kind of thing that gives us a bad name abroad,' he concluded, somewhat pompously.

Dickie rose unsteadily to his feet.

'Bad name be hanged!' he said. 'What does it matter what we do in this tuppenny ha'penny hole? If you won't tell the boy I'll arrange it with the concierge. He understands English.'

'All right,' agreed Philip, for Dickie was already lurching away, the light of battle in his eye. 'I don't expect it'd do any harm, really. *Senta, piccolo!*' He began to explain the errand.

'Don't forget,' admonished Dickie, 'we expect the

gentleman *subito*. He needn't bother to dress or wash or brush up or anything.'

Philip smiled in spite of himself.

'*Dica al signore*,' he said, '*di non vestirsi nero.*'

'Not "smoking"?' said the boy, pertly, delighted to display his English.

'No, not "smoking".'

The boy was off like a streak.

It must be boring waiting for a bomb to go off; it is almost equally tedious waiting for a practical joke to take effect. Dickie and Philip found the minutes drag interminably and they could think of nothing to say.

'He must be there now,' said Dickie, at last, taking out his watch.

'What's the time?'

'Half-past eight. He's been gone seven minutes.'

'How dark it is,' said Philip. 'Partly the trees, I suppose. But it wouldn't be dark in England now.'

'I've told you, much better stick to the Old Country. More daylight, fewer corpses, guests turn up to dinner at the proper time. . . .'

'Giacomelli's certainly very late. Over half an hour.'

'I wonder if he ever got your message.'

'Oh yes, he answered it.'

'You never told me. How long ago was that?'

'Last Wednesday. I wanted to give him plenty of time.'

'Did he write?'

'No, he telephoned. I couldn't understand very well. The servant said the Count was away but he would be delighted to dine with us. He was sorry he couldn't write, but he had been called away on business.' .

'The sugar factory, perhaps?'

'Very likely.'

'It's bloody quiet, as the navvy said,' remarked Dickie.

'Yes, they are all dining in that glass place. You can see it through the leaves.'

'I suppose they'll know to bring him here.'

'Oh, yes.'

Silence fell, broken a moment later by Philip's exclamation, 'Ah, here's the boy!'

With no little excitement they watched his small figure approaching over the wilderness of small grey pebbles which serve the Venetians in lieu of gravel. They noticed at once that his bearing was erect and important; if he had had a shock he bore no traces of it. He stopped by them, smiling and breathing hard.

'Ho fatto un corso,' he said, swelling with pride.

'What's that?'

'He says he ran.'

'I expect he did.'

The friends exchanged amused glances.

'I must say he's got a good pluck,' remarked Dickie, ruefully admiring. Their joke had fallen flat. 'But I expect these Italian kids see corpses every day. Anyhow, ask him what the gentleman said.'

'Che cosa ha detto il signore?' asked Philip.

Still panting, the boy replied:

'Accetta con molto piacere. Fra pochi minuti sarà qui.'

Philip stared at the page in amazement.

'*Si, si, signore,*' repeated the boy. '*Cosi ha detto, "vengo con molto piacere"*.'

'What does he say?' asked Dickie irritably.

'He says that the gentleman accepts our invitation with great pleasure and will be here in a few minutes.'

'Of course,' said Dickie, when the boy had gone off with his *mancia*, 'he's having us on. But he's a tough youngster. Can't be more than twelve years old.'

Philip was looking all around him, clenching and unclenching his fingers.

'I don't believe he invented that.'

'But if he didn't?'

Philip did not answer.

'How like a cemetery the place looks,' he said, suddenly, 'with all the cypresses and this horrible monumental mason's road-repairing stuff all round.'

'The scene would look better for a few fairy-lights,' rejoined Dickie. 'But your morbid fancies don't help us to solve the problem of our friend in the boat. Are we being made fools of by this whippersnapper, or are we not?'

'Time will show,' said Philip. 'He said a few minutes.'

They both sat listening.

'This waiting gives me the jim-jams,' said Dickie at last. 'Let's call the little rascal back and make him tell us what really did happen.'

'No, no, Dickie, that would be too mortifying. Let's try to think it out; let's proceed from the known to

the unknown, as they do in detective stories. The boy
goes off. He arrives at the landing stage. He finds some
ghoulish loafers hanging about . . .'

'He might not,' said Dickie. 'There were only two or
three corpse-gazers when we left.'

'Anyhow, he finds the *rampino* who swore to mount
guard.'

'He might have slipped in for a drink,' said Dickie.
'You gave him the wherewithal, and he has to live like
others.'

'Well, in that case, the boy would see – what?'

'Just that bit of tarpaulin stuff, humped up in the
middle.'

'What would he do, then? Put yourself in his place,
Dickie.'

Dickie grimaced slightly.

'I suppose he'd think the man was resting under
the water-proof and he'd say, "Hullo, there!" in that
ear-splitting voice Italians have, fit to wake. . . .'

'Yes, yes. And then?'

'Then perhaps, as he seems an enterprising child,
he'd descend into the hold and give the tarpaulin
a tweak and well, I suppose he'd stop shouting,'
concluded Dickie lamely. 'He'd see it was no good.
You must own,' he added, 'it's simpler to assume that
half way down the street he met a pal who told him he
was being ragged: then he hung about and smoked a
cigarette and returned puffing with this cock-and-bull
story – simply to get his own back on us.'

'That is the most rational explanation,' said Philip.
'But just for fun, let's suppose that when he called, the

tarpaulin began to move and rear itself up and a hand
came round the edge, and – '

There was a sound of feet scrunching on the stones,
and the friends heard a respectful voice saying, '*Per
qui, signor Conte.*'

At first they could only see the robust, white-
waistcoated figure of the concierge advancing with
a large air and steam-roller tread; behind him they
presently descried another figure, a tall man dressed
in dark clothes, who walked with a limp. After the
concierge's glorious effulgence, he seemed almost
invisible.

'Il Conte Giacomelli,' announced the concierge,
impressively.

The two Englishmen advanced with outstretched
hands, but their guest fell back half a pace and raised
his arm in the Roman salute.

'How do you do?' he said. His English accent was
excellent. 'I'm afraid I am a little late, no?'

'Just a minute or two, perhaps,' said Philip. 'Nothing to speak of.' Furtively, he stared at the Count. A
branch of the overhanging ilex tree nearly touched
his hat; he stood so straight and still in the darkness that one could fancy he was suspended from
the tree.

'To tell you the truth,' said Dickie bluntly, 'we had
almost given you up.'

'Given me up?' The Count seemed mystified. 'How
do you mean, given me up?'

'Don't be alarmed,' Philip laughingly reassured
him. 'He didn't mean give you up to the police. To

give up, you know, can mean so many things. That's the worst of our language.'

'You can give up hope, isn't it?' inquired the Count.

'Yes,' replied Philip cheerfully. 'You can certainly give up hope. That's what my friend meant: we'd almost given up hope of seeing you. We couldn't give you up – that's only an idiom – because, you see, we hadn't got you.'

'I see,' said the Count. 'You hadn't got me.' He pondered.

The silence was broken by Dickie.

'You may be a good grammarian, Phil,' he said, 'but you're a damned bad host. The Count must be famished. Let's have some cocktails here and then go in to dinner.'

'All right, you order them. I hope you don't mind,' he went on when Dickie had gone, 'but we may be four at dinner.'

'Four?' echoed the Count.

'I mean,' said Philip, finding it absurdly difficult to explain, 'we asked someone else as well. I – I think he's coming.'

'But that will be delightful,' the Count said, raising his eyebrows slightly. 'Why should I mind? Perhaps he is a friend of mine, too – your – your other guest?'

'I don't think he would be,' said Philip, feeling more than ever at a loss. 'He – he . . .'

'He is not *de notre monde*, perhaps?' the Count suggested, indulgently.

Philip knew that foreigners refer to distinctions of

class more openly than we do, but all the same, he found it very difficult to reply.

'I don't know whether he belongs to our world or not,' he began, and realising the ludicrous appropriateness of the words, stopped suddenly. 'Look here,' he said, 'I can't imagine why my friend is staying so long. Shall we sit down? Take care!' he cried as the Count was moving towards a chair. 'It's got a game leg – it won't hold you.'

He spoke too late; the Count had already seated himself. Smiling, he said: 'You see, she carries me all right.'

Philip marvelled.

'You must be a magician.'

The Count shook his head. 'No, not a magician, a – a . . .' he searched for the word. 'I cannot explain myself in English. Your friend who is coming – does he speak Italian?'

Inwardly Philip groaned.

'I – I really don't know.'

The Count tilted his chair back.

'I don't want to be curious, but is he an Englishman, your friend?'

Oh God, thought Philip. Why on earth did I start this subject? Aloud he said: 'To tell you the truth I don't know much about him. That's what I wanted to explain to you. We only saw him once and we invited him through a third person.'

'As you did me?' said the Count, smiling.

'Yes, yes, but the circumstances were different. We came on him by accident and gave him a lift.'

'A lift?' queried the Count. 'You were in a hotel, perhaps?'

'No,' said Philip, laughing awkwardly. 'We gave him a lift – a ride – in the gondola. How did you come?' he added, thankful at last to have changed the subject.

'I was given a lift, too,' said the Count.

'In a gondola?'

'Yes, in a gondola.'

'What an odd coincidence,' said Philip.

'So, you see,' said the Count, 'your friend and I will have a good deal in common.'

There was a pause. Philip felt a growing uneasiness which he couldn't define or account for. He wished Dickie would come back: he would be able to divert the conversation into pleasanter channels. He heard the Count's voice saying:

'I'm glad you told me about your friend. I always like to know something about a person before I make his acquaintance.'

Philip felt he must make an end of all this. 'Oh, but I don't think you will make his acquaintance,' he cried. 'You see, I don't think he exists. It's all a silly joke.'

'A joke?' asked the Count.

'Yes, a practical joke. Don't you in Italy have a game on the first of April making people believe or do silly things? April Fools, we call them.'

'Yes, we have that custom,' said the Count, gravely, 'only we call them *pesci d'Aprile* – April Fish.'

'Ah,' said Philip, 'that's because you are a nation of fishermen. An April fish is a kind of fish you don't expect – something you pull out of the water and – '

'What's that?' said the Count. 'I heard a voice.'

Philip listened.

'Perhaps it's your other guest.'

'It can't be him. It can't be!'

The sound was repeated: it was only just audible, but it was Philip's name. But why did Dickie call so softly?

'Will you excuse me?' said Philip. 'I think I'm wanted.'

The Count inclined his head.

'But it's the most amazing thing,' Dickie was saying, 'I think I must have got it all wrong. But here they are and perhaps you will be able to convince them. I think they're mad myself – I told them so.'

He led Philip into the hall of the hotel. The concierge was there and two *vigili*. They were talking in whispers.

'*Ma è scritto sul fazzoletto*,' one of them was saying.

'What's that?' asked Dickie.

'He says it's written on his handkerchief,' said Philip.

'Besides, we both know him,' chimed in the other policeman.

'What *is* this all about?' cried Philip. 'Know whom?'

'Il Conte Giacomelli,' chanted the *vigili* in chorus.

'Well, do you want him?' asked Philip.

'We *did* want him three days ago,' said one of the men. 'But now it's too late.'

'Too late? But he's . . .' Philip stopped suddenly and looked across at Dickie.

'I tell them so,' shouted the concierge, who seemed

in no way disposed to save Count Giacomelli from the hands of justice. 'Many times, many times, I say: "The Count is in the garden with the English gentlemen." But they do not believe me.'

'But it's true!' cried Philip. 'I've only just left him. What do the *vigili* say?'

'They say that he is dead,' said the concierge. 'They say he is dead and his body is in your boat.'

There was a moment of silence. The *vigili*, like men exhausted by argument, stood apart, moody and indifferent. At last one of them spoke.

'It is true, *signori*. *Si è suicidato*. His affairs went badly. He was a great swindler – and knew he would be arrested and condemned. *Così si è salvato*.'

'He may be a swindler,' said Philip, 'but I'm certain he's alive. Come into the garden and see.'

Shaking their heads and shrugging their shoulders, the *vigili* followed him out of the hotel. In a small group they trooped across the stony waste towards the tree. There was no one there.

'You see, *signori*,' said one of the *vigili*, with an air of subdued triumph, 'it's as we said.'

'Well, he must have gone away,' said Philip, obstinately. 'He was sitting on this chair – so . . .' But his effort to give point to his contention failed. The chair gave way under him and he sprawled rather ludicrously and painfully on the stony floor. When he had picked himself up one of the policemen took the chair, ran his hand over it, and remarked:

'It's damp.'

'Is it?' said Philip expressionlessly.

'I don't think anyone could have sat on this chair,' pursued the policeman.

He is telling me I am a liar, thought Philip, and blushed. But the other *vigile*, anxious to spare his feelings, said:

'Perhaps it was an impostor whom you saw – a confidence man. There are many such, even in Italy. He hoped to get money out of the *signori*.' He looked round for confirmation; the concierge nodded.

'Yes,' said Philip, wearily. 'No doubt that explains it. Will you want us again?' he asked the *vigili*. 'Have you a card, Dickie?'

The *vigili*, having collected the information they required, saluted and walked off.

Dickie turned to the concierge.

'Where's that young whippersnapper who took a message for us?'

'Whippersnapper?' repeated the concierge.

'Well, page-boy?'

'Oh, the *piccolo*? He's gone off duty, sir, for the night.'

'Good thing for him,' said Dickie. 'Hullo, who's this? My poor nerves won't stand any more of this Maskelyne and Devant business.'

It was the *maître d'hôtel*, bowing obsequiously.

'Will there be three gentlemen, or four, for dinner?' he asked.

Philip and Dickie exchanged glances and Dickie lit a cigarette.

'Only two gentlemen,' he said.

II

ENTRÉES HISTORIQUES

Tales from the Culinary Past

Guests from Gibbet Island

WASHINGTON IRVING

Unexpected dinner guests are the theme of this next story by Washington Irving (1783–1859), the first American writer to gain an international literary reputation. Irving, who was the son of an Englishman, was very interested in the early history of the United States, and wrote a number of tales about the pre-Revolutionary Dutch culture along the Eastern seaboard. Pre-eminent among these was the classic 'Rip Van Winkle' and the equally evocative 'Guests From Gibbet Island'. It is a chilling story of an old pirate who, wanting to see his old shipmates again, decides to invite a group of them to a meal . . .

Whoever has visited the ancient and renowned village of Communipaw may have noticed an old stone building, of most ruinous and sinister appearance. The doors and window-shutters are ready to drop from their hinges; old clothes are stuffed in the broken panes of glass, while legions of half-starved dogs prowl about the premises, and rush out and bark at every passer-by; for your beggarly house in a village is most apt to swarm with profligate and ill-conditioned dogs. What adds to the sinister appearance of this mansion is a tall frame in front, not a little resembling a gallows, and which looks as if waiting to accommodate some of the inhabitants with a well-merited airing. It is not a gallows, however, but an ancient sign-post; for this dwelling, in the golden days of Communipaw, was one of the most orderly and peaceful of village taverns, where public affairs were talked and smoked over. In fact, it was in this very building that Oloffe the Dreamer, and his companions, concerted that great voyage of discovery and colonisation, in which they explored Buttermilk Channel, were nearly ship-wrecked in the strait of Hell-gate, and finally landed on the island of Manhattan, and founded the great city of New Amsterdam.

Even after the province had been cruelly wrested from the sway of their High Mightinesses by the combined forces of the British and the Yankees, this tavern continued its ancient loyalty. It is true, the head of the Prince of Orange disappeared from the sign, a strange bird being painted over it, with the explanatory legend of 'DIE WILDE GANS,' or, The Wild Goose; but this all the world knew to be a sly riddle of the landlord's, the worthy Teunis Van Gieson, a knowing man, in a small way, who laid his finger beside his nose and winked when any one studied the signification of his sign, and observed that his goose was hatching, but would join the flock whenever they flew over the water – an enigma which was the perpetual recreation and delight of the loyal but fat-headed burghers of Communipaw.

Under the sway of this patriotic, though discreet

and quiet publican, the tavern continued to flourish in primeval tranquillity, and was the resort of true-hearted Nederlanders, from all parts of Pavonia, who met here quietly and secretly, to smoke and drink the downfall of Briton and Yankee, and success to Admiral Van Tromp.

The only drawback on the comfort of the establishment was a nephew of mine host, a sister's son, Yan Yost Vanderscamp by name, and a real scamp by nature. This unlucky whipster showed an early propensity to mischief, which he gratified in a small way by playing tricks upon the frequenters of the Wild Goose: putting gunpowder in their pipes, or squibs in their pockets, and astonishing them with an explosion, while they sat nodding round the fireplace in the bar-room; and if perchance a worthy burgher from some distant part of Pavonia lingered until dark over his potation, it was odds but young Vanderscamp would slip a brier under his horse's tail as he mounted, and send him clattering along the road, in neck-or-nothing style, to the infinite astonishment and discomfiture of the rider.

It may be wondered at, that mine host of the Wild Goose did not turn such a graceless varlet out of doors; but Teunis Van Gieson was an easy-tempered man, and, having no child of his own, looked upon his nephew with almost parental indulgence. His patience and good nature were doomed to be tried by another inmate of his mansion. This was a crossgrained curmudgeon of a negro, named Pluto, who was a kind of enigma in Communipaw. Where he came from, nobody knew. He was found one morning after a storm, cast like a sea-monster on the strand, in front of the Wild Goose, and lay there, more dead than alive. The neighbours gathered round, and speculated on this production of the deep; whether it were fish or flesh, or a compound of both, commonly yclept a merman. The kind-hearted Teunis Van Gieson, seeing that he wore the human form, took him into his house, and warmed him into life. By degrees, he showed signs of intelligence, and even uttered sounds very much like language, but which no one in Communipaw could understand. Some thought him a negro just from Guinea, who had either fallen overboard, or escaped from a slave-ship. Nothing, however, could ever draw from him any account of his origin. When questioned on the subject, he merely pointed to Gibbet Island, a small rocky islet, which lies in the open bay, just opposite Communipaw, as if that were his native place, though everybody knew it had never been inhabited.

In the process of time, he acquired something of the Dutch language – that is to say, he learnt all its vocabulary of oaths and maledictions, with just words sufficient to string them together. '*Donder en blicksem!*' – thunder and lightning – was the gentlest of his ejaculations. For years he kept about the Wild Goose, more like one of those familiar spirits, or household goblins, we read of, than like a human being. He acknowledged allegiance to no one, but performed various domestic offices, when it suited his humour: waiting occasionally on the guests; grooming the horses, cutting wood, drawing water; and all this without being ordered. Lay any command on him, and the stubborn sea-urchin was sure to rebel. He was never so much at home, however, as when on the water, plying about in skiff or canoe, entirely alone, fishing, crabbing, or grabbing for oysters, and would bring home quantities for the larder of the Wild Goose, which he would throw down at the kitchen door, with a growl. No wind nor weather deterred him from launching forth on his favourite element: indeed, the wilder the weather, the more he seemed to enjoy it. If a storm was brewing, he was sure to put off from shore; and would be seen far out in the bay, his light skiff dancing like a feather on the waves, when sea and sky were in a turmoil, and the stoutest ships were fain to lower their sails. Sometimes, on such occasions, he would be absent for days together. How he weathered the tempest, and how and where he subsisted no one could divine, nor did any one venture to ask, for all had an almost superstitious awe of him. Some of the Communipaw oystermen declared they had more than once seen him suddenly disappear, canoe and all, as if plunged beneath the waves, and after a while come up again, in quite a different part of the bay; whence they concluded that he could live under water like that notable species of wild duck commonly called the hell-diver. All began to consider him in the light of a foul-weather bird, like the Mother Carey's Chicken or stormy petrel; and whenever they saw him putting far out in his skiff, in cloudy weather, made up their minds for a storm.

The only being for whom he seemed to have any liking was Yan Yost Vanderscamp, and him he liked for his very wickedness. He in a manner took the boy under his tutelage, prompted him to all kinds of mischief, aided him in every wild harum-scarum freak, until the lad became the complete scapegrace of the village; a pest to his uncle, and to every one else. Nor were his pranks confined to the land: he soon learned to accompany old Pluto on the water. Together these worthies would cruise about the broad bay, and all the neighbouring straits and rivers; poking around in skiffs and canoes; robbing the set nets of the fishermen; landing on remote coasts, and laying waste orchards and water-melon patches; in short, carrying on a complete system of piracy, on a small scale. Piloted by Pluto, the youthful Vanderscamp soon became acquainted with all the bays, rivers, creeks, and inlets of the watery world around him; could navigate from the Hook to Spitting-devil on the darkest night, and learned to set even the terrors of Hell-gate at defiance.

At length, negro and boy suddenly disappeared, and days and weeks elapsed, but without tidings of them. Some said they must have run away and gone to sea; others jocosely hinted that old Pluto, being no other than his namesake in disguise, had spirited away the boy to the nether regions. All, however, agreed in one thing – that the village was well rid of them.

In the process of time, the good Teunis Van Gieson slept with his fathers, and the tavern remained shut up, waiting for a claimant, for the next heir was Yan Yost Vanderscamp, and he had not been heard of for years. At length, one day, a boat was seen pulling for shore, from a long, black, rakish-looking schooner, that lay at anchor in the bay. The boat's crew seemed worthy of the craft from which they debarked. Never had such a set of noisy, roistering, swaggering varlets landed in peaceful Communipaw. They were outlandish in garb and demeanour, and were headed by a rough, burly, bully ruffian, with fiery whiskers, a copper nose, a scar across his face, and a great Flaunderish beaver slouched on one side of his head, in whom, to their dismay, the quiet inhabitants were made to recognise their early pest, Yan Yost Vanderscamp. The rear of this hopeful gang was brought up by old Pluto, who had lost an eye, grown grizzly-headed, and looked more like a devil than ever. Vanderscamp renewed his acquaintance with the old burghers, much against their will, and in a manner not at all to their taste. He slapped them familiarly on the back, gave them an iron grip of the hand, and was hail fellow well met. According to his own account, he had been all the world over; had made money by bagsful; had ships in every sea, and now meant to turn the Wild Goose into a country-seat, where he and his comrades, all rich merchants from foreign parts, might enjoy themselves in the interval of their voyages.

Sure enough, in a little while there was a complete metamorphose of the Wild Goose. From being a quiet, peaceful Dutch public-house, it became a most riotous, uproarious private dwelling; a complete rendezvous for boisterous men of the seas, who came here to have what they called a 'blow out' on dry land, and might be seen at all hours, lounging about the door, or lolling out of the windows; swearing among themselves, and cracking rough jokes on every passer-by. The house was fitted up, too, in so strange a manner: hammocks slung to the walls, instead of bedsteads; odd kinds of furniture, of foreign fashion; bamboo couches, Spanish chairs; pistols, cutlasses and blunderbusses, suspended on every peg; silver crucifixes on the mantelpieces, silver candlesticks and porringers on the tables, contrasting oddly with the pewter and Delf ware of the original establishment. And then the strange amusements of these sea-monsters! Pitching Spanish dollars, instead of quoits; firing blunderbusses out of the window; shooting at a mark, or at any unhappy dog, or cat, or pig, or barn-door fowl, that might happen to come within reach.

The only being who seemed to relish their rough waggery was old Pluto; and yet he led but a dog's life of it; for they practised all kinds of manual jokes upon him; kicked him about like a football; shook him by his grizzly mop of wool, and never spoke to him without coupling a curse by way of adjective to his name, and consigning him to the infernal regions. The old fellow, however, seemed to like them the better the more they cursed him, though his utmost expression of pleasure never amounted to more than the growl of a petted bear, when his ears are rubbed.

Old Pluto was the ministering spirit at the orgies of the Wild Goose; and such orgies as took place there! Such drinking, singing, whooping, swearing; with an occasional interlude of quarrelling and fighting. The noisier grew the revel, the more old Pluto plied the potations, until the guests would become frantic in their merriment, smashing everything to pieces, and throwing the house out of the windows. Sometimes, after a drinking bout, they sallied forth and scoured the village, to the dismay of the worthy burghers, who gathered their women within doors, and would have shut up the house. Vanderscamp, however, was not to be rebuffed. He insisted on renewing acquaintance with his old neighbours, and on introducing his friends, the merchants, to their families; swore he was on the look-out for a wife, and meant, before he stopped, to find husbands for all their daughters. So, will-ye, nill-ye, sociable he was; swaggered about their best parlours, with his hat on one side of his head; sat on the good wife's nicely waxed mahogany table, kicking his heels against the carved and polished legs; kissed and tousled the young *vrouws*; and, if they frowned and pouted, gave them a gold rosary, or a sparkling cross, to put them in good humour again.

Sometimes nothing would satisfy him, but he must have some of his old neighbours to dinner at the Wild Goose. There was no refusing him, for he had the complete upper hand of the community, and the peaceful burghers all stood in awe of him. But what a time would the quiet, worthy men have, among these rake-hells, who would delight to astound them with the most extravagant gunpowder tales, embroidered with all kinds of foreign oaths; clink the can with them; pledge them in deep potations; bawl drinking-songs in their ears; and occasionally fire pistols over their heads, or under the table, and then laugh in their faces, and ask them how they liked the smell of gunpowder.

Thus was the little village of Communipaw for a time like the unfortunate wight possessed with devils; until Vanderscamp and his brother merchants would sail on another trading voyage, when the Wild Goose would be shut up, and everything relapse into quiet, only to be disturbed by his next visitation.

The mystery of all these proceedings gradually dawned upon the tardy intellects of Communipaw. These were the times of the notorious Captain Kidd, when the American harbours were the resorts of piratical adventurers of all kinds, who, under pretext of mercantile voyages, scoured the West Indies, made plundering descents upon the Spanish Main, visited even the remote Indian Seas, and then came to dispose of their booty, have their revels, and fit out new expeditions, in the English colonies.

Vanderscamp had served in this hopeful school, and, having risen to importance among the buccaneers, had pitched upon his native village and early home as a quiet, out-of-the-way, unsuspected place, where he and his comrades, while anchored at New York, might have their feasts, and concert their plans, without molestation.

At length the attention of the British Government

was called to these piratical enterprises, that were becoming so frequent and outrageous. Vigorous measures were taken to check and punish them. Several of the most noted freebooters were caught and executed, and three of Vanderscamp's chosen comrades, the most riotous swashbucklers of the Wild Goose, were hanged in chains on Gibbet Island, in full sight of their favourite resort. As to Vanderscamp himself, he and his man Pluto again disappeared and it was hoped by the people of Communipaw that he had fallen in some foreign brawl, or been swung on some foreign gallows.

For a time, therefore, the tranquillity of the village was restored; the worthy Dutchmen once more smoked their pipes in peace, eyeing, with peculiar complacency, their old pests and terrors, the pirates, dangling and drying in the sun, on Gibbet Island.

This perfect calm was doomed at length to be ruffled. The fiery persecution of the pirates gradually subsided. Justice was satisfied with the examples that had been made, and there was no more talk of Kidd, and the other heroes of like kidney. On a calm summer evening, a boat, somewhat heavily laden, was seen pulling into Communipaw. What was the surprise and disquiet of the inhabitants, to see Yan Yost Vanderscamp seated at the helm, and his man Pluto tugging at the oar! Vanderscamp, however, was apparently an altered man. He brought home with him a wife, who seemed to be a shrew, and to have the upper hand of him. He no longer was the swaggering, bully ruffian, but affected the regular

merchant, and talked of retiring from business, and
settling down quietly, to pass the rest of his days in
his native place.

The Wild Goose mansion was again opened, but
with diminished splendour, and no riot. It is true,
Vanderscamp had frequent nautical visitors, and the
sound of revelry was occasionally overheard in his
house; but everything seemed to be done under the
rose; and old Pluto was the only servant that officiated
at these orgies. The visitors, indeed, were by no means
of the turbulent stamp of their predecessors; but quiet,
mysterious traders, full of nods, and winks, and
hieroglyphic signs, with whom, to use their cant
phrase, 'everything was smug'. Their ships came to
anchor at night, in the lower bay; and, on a private
signal, Vanderscamp would launch his boat, and,
accompanied solely by his man Pluto, would make
them mysterious visits. Sometimes boats pulled in at
night, in front of the Wild Goose, and various articles
of merchandise were landed in the dark, and spirited
away, nobody knew whither. One of the more curious
of the inhabitants kept watch, and caught a glimpse of
the features of some of these night visitors, by the cas-
ual glance of a lantern, and declared that he recognised
more than one of the freebooting frequenters of the
Wild Goose, in former times; whence he concluded
that Vanderscamp was at his old game, and that this
mysterious merchandise was nothing more nor less
than piratical plunder. The more charitable opinion,
however, was, that Vanderscamp and his comrades,
having been driven from their old line of business,

by the 'oppressions of Government', had resorted to
smuggling to make both ends meet.

Be that as it may: I come now to the extraordinary
fact, which is the butt-end of this story. It happened
late one night that Yan Yost Vanderscamp was returning across the broad bay, in his light skiff, rowed by
his man Pluto. He had been carousing on board of a
vessel, newly arrived, and was somewhat obfuscated
in intellect by the liquor he had imbibed. It was a still,
sultry night; a heavy mass of lurid clouds was rising in
the west, with the low muttering of distant thunder.
Vanderscamp called on Pluto to pull lustily, that they
might get home before the gathering storm. The old
negro made no reply, but shaped his course so as to
skirt the rocky shores of Gibbet Island. A faint creaking
overhead caused Vanderscamp to cast up his eyes,
when, to his horror, he beheld the bodies of his three
pot companions and brothers in iniquity dangling in
the moonlight, their rags fluttering, and their chains
creaking, as they were slowly swung backward and
forward by the rising breeze.

'What do you mean, you blockhead!' cried Vanderscamp, 'by pulling so close to the island?'

'I thought you'd be glad to see your old friends once
more,' growled the negro. 'You were never afraid of a
living man; what do you fear from the dead?'

'Who's afraid?' hiccupped Vanderscamp, partly
heated by liquor, partly nettled by the jeer of the
negro; 'who's afraid? Hang me, but I would be glad
to see them once more, alive or dead, at the Wild
Goose. Come, my lads in the wind!' continued he,

taking a draught, and flourishing the bottle above his head, 'here's fair weather to you in the other world; and if you should be walking the rounds tonight, odd's fish! but I'll be happy if you will drop in to supper.'

A dismal creaking was the only reply. The wind blew loud and shrill, and, as it whistled round the gallows and among the bones, sounded as if they were laughing and gibbering in the air. Old Pluto chuckled to himself, and now pulled for home. The storm burst over the voyagers, while they were yet far from shore. The rain fell in torrents, the thunder crashed and pealed, and the lightning kept up an incessant blaze. It was stark midnight before they landed at Communipaw.

Dripping and shivering, Vanderscamp crawled homeward. He was completely sobered by the storm; the water soaked from without having diluted and cooled the liquor within. Arrived at the Wild Goose, he knocked timidly and dubiously at the door, for he dreaded the reception he was to experience from his wife. He had reason to do so. She met him at the threshold, in a precious ill-humour.

'Is this a time,' said she, 'to keep people out of their beds, and to bring home company, to turn the house upside down?'

'Company?' said Vanderscamp meekly; 'I have brought no company with me, wife.'

'No indeed! they have got here before you, but by your invitation; and blessed-looking company they are, truly!'

Vanderscamp's knees smote together. 'For the love of Heaven, where are they, wife?'

'Where? – why, in the blue room upstairs, making themselves as much at home as if the house were their own.'

Vanderscamp made a desperate effort, scrambled up to the room, and threw open the door. Sure enough, there at a table, on which burned a light as blue as brimstone, sat the three guests from Gibbet Island, with halters round their necks, and bobbing their cups together, as if they were hob-or-nobbing, and trolling the old Dutch freebooter's glee, since translated into English:

> 'For three merry lads be we,
> and three merry lads be we;
> I on the land, and thou on the sand,
> And Jack on the gallows-tree.'

Vanderscamp saw and heard no more. Starting back with horror, he missed his footing on the landing-place, and fell from the top of the stairs to the bottom. He was taken up speechless, and, either from the fall or the fright, was buried in the yard of the little Dutch church at Bergen, on the following Sunday.

From that day forward, the fate of the Wild Goose was sealed. It was pronounced a *haunted house*, and avoided accordingly. No one inhabited it but Vanderscamp's shrew of a widow, and old Pluto, and they were considered but little better than its hobgoblin visitors. Pluto grew more and more haggard and morose, and looked more like an imp of darkness than a human being. He spoke to no one, but went about muttering to himself; or, as some hinted, talking with the devil, who, though unseen, was ever at his elbow. Now and then he was seen pulling about the bay alone, in his skiff, in dark weather, or at the approach of nightfall; nobody could tell why, unless on an errand to invite more guests from the gallows. Indeed, it was affirmed that the Wild Goose still continued to be a house of entertainment for such guests, and that, on stormy nights, the blue chamber was occasionally illuminated, and sounds of diabolical merriment were overheard, mingling with the howling of the tempest. Some treated these as idle stories, until on one such night – it was about the time of the equinox – there was a horrible uproar in the Wild Goose, that could not be mistaken. It was not so much the sound of revelry, however, as strife, with two or three piercing shrieks, that pervaded every part of the village. Nevertheless, no one thought of hastening to the spot. On the contrary, the honest burghers of Communipaw drew their nightcaps over their ears, and buried their heads under the bed-clothes, at the thoughts of Vanderscamp and his gallows companions.

The next morning, some of the bolder and more curious undertook to reconnoitre. All was quiet and lifeless at the Wild Goose. The door yawned wide open, and had evidently been open all night, for the storm had beaten into the house. Gathering more courage from the silence and apparent desertion, they gradually ventured over the threshold. The house had indeed the air of having been possessed by devils. Everything was topsy-turvy; trunks had been broken open, and chests of drawers and corner cupboards turned inside out, as in a time of general sack and pillage; but the most woeful sight was the widow of Yan Yost Vanderscamp, extended a corpse on the floor of the blue chamber, with the marks of a deadly gripe on the windpipe.

All now was conjecture and dismay at Communipaw; and the disappearance of old Pluto, who was nowhere to be found, gave rise to all kinds of wild surmises. Some suggested that the negro had betrayed the house to some of Vanderscamp's buccaneering associates, and that they had decamped together with the booty; others surmised that the negro was nothing more nor less than a devil incarnate, who had now accomplished his ends, and made off with his dues.

Events, however, vindicated the negro from this last imputation. His skiff was picked up, drifting about the bay, bottom upward, as if wrecked in a tempest; and his body was found, shortly afterward, by some Communipaw fishermen, stranded among the rocks of Gibbet Island, near the foot of the pirates' gallows. The fishermen shook their heads, and observed that old Pluto had ventured once too often to invite Guests from Gibbet Island.

The Compleat Housewife

RICHARD DEHAN

American regional cookery owes a great deal to the influence of the recipes brought to the continent by the first settlers from Britain and Europe. This is the theme taken up by Richard Dehan (1863–1932) in 'The Compleat Housewife', which was originally published with the sub-heading 'The story of a Battaglio Pie'. Dehan, a playwright and novelist whose real name was Clotilde I. M. Graves, actually owned a copy of the rare eighteenth-century recipe book, *The Compleat Housewife*, which plays such a sinister role in the story, and later donated it to the British Museum where it can be seen to this day!

So many male members of the British aristocracy find their feminine complements in American social circles, that I guess I won't astonish any one that reads this when I announce myself, *née* Lydia Randolph, of Savannah – described in Glatt's *Guide to the United States* as 'the chief city and commercial metropolis of Georgia' – as a slip of Southern wild orange grafted by marriage upon one of the three-hundred-year-old citron trees that are the pride of the greenhouses at Hindsway Abbey, Deershire.

Bryan – my husband is Sir Bryan Corbryan,

sixteenth baronet of that name – was travelling in
the Southern States when we met at the Jasper House
at Thunderbolt, a fashionable early summer resort on
the Warsow River. I had seen clean-made, springy,
red-and-white, handsome Englishmen before, but
there was something particularly distinguished about
this one, or it seemed so. We were neighbours at
the *table d'hôte*, and Sir Bryan had no idea how to
eat green corn until I gave him an object lesson,
and was wonderfully ignorant about simple things
like fried egg-plant. Chicken gumbo reminded him
of Indian curries, and he thought our green oysters
as good as those of Ostend, but he drew the line at
raw canvas-back and roast ices. We became so friendly
over the *carte de jour* that Mamie – my second sister –
parodied the old rhyme about love –

'Oh, 'tis food, 'tis food, 'tis food
That makes the world go round!'

she sang, as we moved towards the ladies' drawing-room.

'*Grow* round, you mean,' said I scornfully, as the
elevator carried us upwards, and the coloured boy
grinned.

'After all,' said Mamie thoughtfully – she is considered a very brainy girl by her school professors – 'without food there would be no love. People would just
pine and dwindle and die. Wouldn't they, Belvidere?'

'Iss, missus,' said the lift-boy, catching and biting
the quarter Mamie tossed him.

Well, next day we met Sir Bryan again. After that
it was usually me. We all greatly enjoyed that June
holiday in our differing ways. Marma simply drank
in the restfulness of a hotel with three or four hundred
guests in it, after the harassing worries of a household
consisting of a husband, three daughters, and seven
servants, and rocked and fanned from morning until
night. For us young folks there were drives, fishing
parties, walking excursions, and bathing sociables.
My! the time flew, but the world stood still quite
suddenly, or seemed to, when Sir Bryan asked me
to be his wife. He said I was the loveliest girl
on the Salts or the face of Creation, and he just
burned with longing to carry me home as his bride
to Deershire, and walk with me under the Tudor oaks
he had told me about. Tudor oaks! And a girl whose
father was making a corner in cotton on Bay Street at
that very moment! But Sir Bryan appeared to see no
discrepancy, and that corner in cotton made me quite
an heiress, as it afterwards turned out.

Well, our wedding – Bryan's and mine – was sol-
emnised at the Savannah Episcopal Church, fronting
Madison Square. It was a jessamine and tuberose
wedding, cart-loads of those blooms being employed.
I had privately begged Bryan to send home for the first
baronet's gold inlaid suit of tilting armour to be married
in; but he begged to be excused, as wrought steel is such
heavy summerwear. Otherwise, he thought, considering the almost Presidential amount of handshaking a
bridegroom usually has to go through, gauntlets would
be rather an advantage than otherwise.

We spent a week of our honeymoon trip at Newport and one on the ocean, and two in that Eden of the modern Adam and Eve, Paris, and then we went home to Deershire and Hindway Abbey, driving the whole way from the station under festoons of parti-coloured flags, while the bells rang peals of welcome, and school-children and tenants cheered, and the guard of honour supplied by the Deershire Mounted Volunteers kept up a deafening clatter behind that made the spirited horses more spirited still: and then we turned in between old stone entrance gate-pillars crested with heraldic monsters like those on Bryan's coat-of-arms, and drove along the wide avenue under those Tudor oaks Bryan had talked about, and the Abbey, a glorious old building of ancient red brick faced with white stone, rose up before us, girt with its ancient terraced walks and clipped hedges of yew and holly, and smothered in roses and wistaria to its mossy tiled roofs and the very tips of its twisted chimneys.

'Oh,' I cried to Bryan, 'never tell *me* that gentlemen in trunks and ladies in farthingales, or *beaux* in powdered periwigs and laced brocade coats, and *belles* in hoops and furbelows don't promenade here in the witching hours of night under the glimpses of the waning moon, because I simply shan't believe you!'

'So you like it?' said my husband, looking pleased and proud.

'Like it!' was all I could say; but it seemed enough for Bryan. He took my hand and led me into our home, and the red light of the great wood fire upon the gleaming hearth-dogs of the old wainscoted hall shone upon two very happy people.

Then – I just hate to think of it! – hard upon all the cheering and curtseying welcome came the blue-enveloped cablegram from Marma, with its brief, sharp, clearly worded message of misfortune. Parpa had had a spell of hemiplegia in consequence of a slump in lumber, which he had tided through, poor dear, at the expense of his health. I cried and begged to go back to the States at any risk, but Bryan was firm. I could see that if I had owned three fathers, all lying in imminent peril, it would have been just the same. *He* would go, he declared, in my place. Parpa had two daughters on the spot, and a son ought to be an appreciated change.

I loathed to let him go, but I loved him for wanting to. I put my head right down on his dear tweed shoulder and told him so. He lifted up my face and kissed it.

'You'll be brave, little woman' – I am five feet eight – 'and, Phee, I know you will take care of your mistress?' he said, looking hard at my coloured maid.

'Bless Grashus, Marsa, co'se I will!' said Phee, with a wide, brilliant smile.

And within two hours my husband had driven from the door of his ancestral dwelling, and I was a grass widow. I made this observation to Phee.

'Lor', honey,' said she, 'ain' dat heaps better dan bein' de real kin'?'

I had not regarded the situation previously from this point of view, and I could not deny that Phee was in the right. But I cried myself to sleep all the same, and woke feeling pretty cheerful, and when I had bathed and dressed, and breakfasted in the morning-room that looked upon the quaintest of old-world gardens bounded with rose-hedges and centred with a splendid four-faced dial, lifted aloft upon a twisted and carven pillar, adorned with the motto, *Nunc sol nunc umbra*, I received a respectful message from Mrs Pounds, the housekeeper, asking for an audience.

She was a handsome old lady in a lace cap and rustling black silk gown, and when she had handed me a bunch of keys similar to the bunch that dangled at her waist, she launched into many revelations concerning household affairs, to which I fear I listened absently, being mentally absorbed upon the question of the arrival or non-arrival of Bryan's letter. Joy! a guardedly expressed but distinctly affectionate telegram was handed to me before Mrs Pounds had got through. Bryan had engaged a deck cabin on the biggest of the Atlantic ferries, and would steam out of Southampton Docks precisely at two p.m. A letter was following. Dear telegram! Dear letter! Dearest Bryan! My eyes swam with tears. Oh, how I meant to try to be an ideal wife! How I –

'It being a rainy morning, and unpleasant for walking or driving,' I heard Mrs Pounds say, 'and the Abbey being one of the most interesting Tudor residences in the county, perhaps her ladyship would wish to go over the house.'

The notion was invigorating.

'Why, certainly!' I exclaimed. 'I should just adore to!'

'If her ladyship permits,' said Mrs Pounds, with refrigerating stateliness, 'I will act as her ladyship's guide!'

I thanked her and rang for Phee.

'Did her ladyship wish the young black person to attend her?' Mrs Pounds inquired, with a perfectly glacial stiffness.

'I guess so,' I said; 'since she is to live in this house, she may as well learn her way about it – the sooner, the better.'

'As her ladyship pleases,' said Mrs Pounds, and unhooked her bunch of keys with a shiver of virtuous resignation. Then she said that if her ladyship permitted, she would lead the way, and glided out of the morning-room.

What a refined and subtle pleasure there lies in going over every nook and corner of a noble, ancient house, in traversing the echoing galleries, looking from the mullioned windows upon garden, terrace, alley, pleasaunce, and park, in gazing at ancient pictures painted by inspired hands long since dust, in fingering antique china and glorious old tapestries, tapping ringing corselets and engraven helms, touching gleaming or rusty weapons, looking respectfully on chairs that have upheld historical personages, and carven, canopied beds in which they have slept! That pleasure was to me intensified a thousandfold because the house was Bryan's and mine.

Phee was as enthusiastic in her way as I was, though

my way was less ebullient. Her vociferations of 'Lordy! Lawd sakes! Bless grashus!' with other kindred ejaculations, seemed to pain Mrs Pounds a good deal. But presently that rustling embodiment of respectability threw open a door on the first floor landing of what she termed the west wing, saying –

'This is called Lady Deborah's room, which, although carefully kept free from dust, as her ladyship sees, has never been occupied since the death of Lady Deborah, which occurred of quinsy in the reign of King George the Second, and the lifetime of the tenth baronet, her son. The portrait in oils by Jongmans, set in panel over the chimney-piece, is considered to be a speaking likeness. Her ladyship is wearing the very cap and gown in which she is said to haunt this house, and that book that lies upon the escritoire in the window is the identical volume she is said to carry in her hand.'

'Fo' de Lawd!' I heard Phee say gutturally behind me. As for myself, I felt no chill of awe. The triumph of being the mistress of an undeniably ancient, undoubtedly ghost-haunted abbey fired my blood and thrilled my whole being. I advanced to the escritoire, an ancient, brass-handled piece of furniture with flowers in Dutch marquetry, and opened the book – a dilapidated volume in brown leather binding – at the title-page. 'The Compleat Housewife,' I read, 'or Accomplished Gentlewoman's Companion. A Collection of Prov'd Recipys in Cookery and Confectionary, With Instructions for the Making of Wines and Cordyals, Also Above 200 Family Specificks, viz. Drinks, Syrups, Salves, Oyntments and Cures For

Varyous Distempers. By Eliz. Smith; The Second
Edycion. London; Printed for J. Pynkerton agaynst
S'Dunstan's Church in Fleet street in the Reign of His
Ma'sty King George II.'

Phee had backed nervously into the corridor. With
the book in my hand, I glanced a friendly adieu
towards the portrait of Lady Deborah, whose mob-cap
and black silk calash encircled a wrinkled yet pleasant
and placid countenance, embellished with the fine
streakings of rosy red one sees on a good eating apple,
and ornamented by huge round spectacles rimmed
with silver.

'Thank you,' I said to the housekeeper, 'but I think
I have seen enough for one while. So many stairs are
fatiguing to a person accustomed to elevators.'

'Her ladyship means lifts?' said Mrs Pounds,
making allowances for the foreigner.

'Not at all,' I said. 'But I guess you mean elevators.'
The stout brown leather volume under my arm
inspired me to ask a question: 'With regard to Lady
Deborah, Mrs Pounds, you will not think it a very odd
question if I ask you, have you ever seen her?'

'I will not deceive her ladyship,' said the housekeeper. 'There have been alarms among the maids
and reports circulated by guests long, long before
my time, and *in* my time, but never having viewed
the apparition myself, I never gave such credit
for an instant. Ghostly hauntings argue unquiet
consciences, I have always understood; and what
should a virtuous, housekeeping lady, such as Lady
Deborah was, by all accounts – and the alms-houses

she built and endowed are the pride of the village to this day! – have upon her conscience? Her still-room is in the wing, though now turned into a store-room; and my jams, not to say jellies, are made after recipes in ancient writing which I believe to have been hers.'

'And this must have been the cookery-book out of which she copied them,' said I, glancing into the well-thumbed volume, 'which I am going to carry away and look over.'

'Oh, my – my lady!' exclaimed Mrs Pounds, paling slightly and forgetting the third person in her perturbation. 'I beg your ladyship's pardon, but your ladyship had best not. They do say – '

'Ah! what do they say?' I asked.

'They say,' said Mrs Pounds, nervously smoothing her muslin apron, 'that whenever or however that book is removed from this room, it is always found in its place upon Lady Deborah's escritoire next morning. Which would argue, my lady, that she fetches it back herself!'

My Southern blood ran less warmly through my veins, but I held my head up bravely.

'Has any one put that tradition to the test, to your knowledge?' I asked.

Mrs Pounds pursed her lips and shook her head.

'Very well!' I said in my stateliest manner, and I swept down the corridor, whose ancient oaken planking creaked under my high-heeled French shoes.

It still rained. Two huge fires of apple-wood burned in my great panelled drawing-room, where tall, carved cabinets of Indian ebony, Dutch marquetry, and

Chinese lacquer, crowned with lovely vases and bowls
of Oriental pottery, stood sentinel on the edges of the
worn but beautiful Turkey carpet. I sank into a low,
deep chair near the lower hearth-place and stared up
at the carvings over the bossed mantelshelf, represent-
ing Dante and Beatrice, and other personages from
the *Divina Commedia*, all wearing Elizabethan ruffs,
trunk hose and farthingales. The rain splashed from
the leaden mouths of the lion-headed water-pipes
upon the flags of the terrace. It sounded like the
tap-tapping of high-heeled brodequins. There was a
high-backed, narrow, black oak chair on the opposite
edge of the rug, an armless, stiff, uncomfortable chair,
and upholstered in gilded leather – or leather that
had once been gilded, fastened on with gilt nails,
or nails that were once gilt, driven through little
round pieces of faded green and red felt. There are
articles of furniture that irresistibly evoke in the mind
fancy portraits of the people who must have owned
them. As I looked at that chair, its outlines became
obscure . . . Gradually enormously hooped petticoats
of strong, flowered brocade, green with a shrimp-pink
pattern of roses, came into view, from the border of
which peeped the ends of narrow, square-toed shoes
adorned with silver buckles. Languidly and without
surprise my eyes travelled from these upwards to the
cobweb-lace border of a very fine Swiss – I should say
muslin – apron. In the centre of the apron were a
pair of withered hands adorned with antique jewelled
rings, and covered to the bony knuckles with black silk
mittens. I followed the mittens to the lace ruffles of the

sleeves, which matched the cinnamon satin peaked
bodice – so tightly laced that one could hardly credit
a human body being inside – trimmed with heavy
silver lace and having puffed *paniers* on either side.
The neck of the bodice was cut square and filled in
with soft folds of muslin, and about a withered throat
I caught the gleam of a gold and amber necklace.
The body I have described ended in the face I had
expected. The peaked chin, the pursed-up lips, the
withered rose-apple cheeks, slightly pinched nose,
and huge silver-rimmed spectacles – all belonged
to Lady Deborah's portrait. Almost with gladness I
recognised the rolled-up, powdered hair, crowned
with the enormous, lappeted mob-cap. It affected
me strangely that the old lady did not wear the
black silk calash or bonnet, but carried it slung
over her thin arm by its wide strings, and that a
tortoiseshell-headed cane not represented upon the
canvas – a kit-kat – leaned against a little Indian cabinet
of striped calamander wood which stood near.

Bryan's family ghost – mine, by virtue of my rights
as Bryan's wife! The cold chills and crisping sensations
of fear were banished by the pleasant glow of pride
which stole over my being as I gazed upon the dear
old lady. I had so much regretted Bryan's not having
any mother or pleasant elderly women relatives living
for me to be cosy and confidential with – and here was
one! Not living, but still visible; not to be felt, perhaps,
but possibly to be heard. All this while Lady Deborah
stared piercingly in my direction. She was not looking
at me, but at the open book upon my knee, which had

nearly slipped off it, and just as I had made up my mind to venture on a very delicate cough, she spoke, in a dry, rasping old voice –

'Child, if you thought to persuade me you was asleep, you may spare' yourself the trouble, for I have seen your eyelids blink these dozen times.'

'Oh, Lady Deborah – ' I began, but the old lady caught up her cane and rapped me over the knuckles – hard, with the end of it!

'Is that the way you give greeting to your elders, Mistress Impertinence?' she cried shrilly. 'Truly, I don't know where the young women are coming to! Dry your eyes, chit!' – they were watering from the smart of my rapped knuckles – 'and let me see you make a proper reverence!'

Her cane was hovering. I hastily got out of my chair and made the lowest cotillon-curtsey I had ever achieved.

'Pish!' ejaculated the Lady Deborah Corbryan, with perfectly withering contempt. She waved me aside and rose to her feet. 'Fold the arms, thus, cross the legs at the knees, bend them outwards, sink – and recover.' She sank as though the floor had opened under her, she recovered – apparently upon the point of vanishing. 'Madam,' she said, with an agreeable smile which revealed a set of boxwood teeth strung on gold wire, 'I vow I am vastly happy to see your ladyship, and venture to hope that your ladyship enjoys good health?'

'Perfectly, thank you. And – dear Lady Deborah, you can't begin to know how real glad I am to see you.

I was just expiring to have you drop in!' I stopped, for
the old lady's eyes were beginning to snap behind her
spectacles.

'Drop in,' she said severely, 'is not a seemly expression for a young woman. But be seated, child, and tell
me your name. . . . Lydia Randolph, of Georgia, d'ye
say? My young descendant was travelling in the East,
I presume, when he encountered you? I hoped, for
the honour of the Corbryans, you was a relative of the
Grand Turk, or of the Sophy, at least, for our family is
very ancient and honourable, let me tell you!'

After an effort or two I gave up the task of trying to
persuade Lady Deborah that the State of Georgia was
located in America, which she persisted in calling 'the
Virginias'. She was aware that a person named Smith
had devoted his life to the exploration and colonisation
of New England, and that the English, in 1664, had
held possession of New York. She approved of those
commodities which came from my country. American
rum, cane sugar, coffee, and tobacco, and helped
herself to snuff from an amethyst-topped box as she
approved.

'My young descendant will take you up to London
in the family coach when he returns (I had explained
why I figured as a lonely bride) and initiate you into the
pleasures of the gay world of fashion,' she said. 'You
must see Mr Garrick in *Hamlet*, the dear, ingenious
man! and Mrs Siddons as Belvidera – Lud! how she
frightened me in her frenzy. And Mr Johnson – you
must see that great, if uncouth, personage – and Mr
Reynolds, the painter – he must be prevailed upon

to paint you, for you are not ill-looking, chit, and would be positively handsome was you dressed. Dear me, what junketings I had in my time! . . . Ranelagh, Hampstead, Vauxhall, Marybone Gardens and Totnam Farm . . . where we went for syllabubs new from the cow – and the *beaux* quarrelled among them which should have the glass I had drank out of. For I was a toast and a beauty, and a sad coquette, too, my dear!' said the old lady, complacently nodding her great cap. 'Sir George Cockerell, of Bangwood – a mon'sous rake – tried to carry me off from Bath Wells in a coach with four, in broad day, for which Sir Bryan ran him through, my dear, under the second rib on the left side – and – "You've nicked it, Corbryan," says Sir George, "and – and I lose! – but I don't apologise," and swooned away. And D'Arcy D'Urfée writ a poem upon a pair of fringed gloves I wore at an assembly, and my Lord Chesterfield himself hath paid me compliments. But beauty is a passing flower, child, and so I found it when I took the smallpox and rose from my bed – hung with scarlet cloth, by orders of His Majesty's own physician – to find my face all pitted and my beautiful eyebrows and lashes gone – to a hair!'

'Oh, how dreadful!' I cried. 'And – and Sir Bryan?'

'Sir Bryan took to the claret bottle in his sorrow, and to the punch-bowl,' said Lady Deborah.

'Drank!' I cried. 'Oh, how dreadful!'

'Tush, child!' snapped the old lady. 'Don't all our men drink? And our women, too, for that matter! Liquor was made for man, we have the authority of the Ancients upon it! But Sir Bryan took to other things as well – gaming at the Grecian and White's, and other follies – and I was a very unhappy woman for a time. Then I found comfort, chit – in a book with which you are acquainted!'

'The Scriptures, madam?' I said, my lips trembling with sympathy and admiration of the simple piety of the poor, deserted wife.

'My dear mother's Cookery Book. You have it in your lap, child, and by constant study of it I became the most notable housewife in my county . . . Let me trust you have read and pondered its pages,' said Lady Deborah, nodding solemnly. ''Tis as unseemly for a young lady to enter the world without a knowledge of the art of carving, for instance, as to appear at a ball without her sacque and paniers and hooped petticoat. Thou canst unjoint a bittern, I trust? Souse a capon, unlace a crane, dismember a heron, lift a swan and rear a bustard with elegance and discretion?'

'I – I am afraid not,' I stammered, keeping the tears back with difficulty as I realised my ignorance of English social customs. 'You see, Parpa wished me to be educated in the State where I was raised, and this is my first visit to England. Possibly I could souse a capon, but swans are such vicious things, I should never dare to lift one. And as to rearing a bustard, I've never seen one yet.'

'Lydia, I vow you horrify me! No more, child, or I shall have a fit of the spleen!' Lady Deborah fanned herself with the cunningest tortoiseshell fan, and sniffed at the silver apple pricked full of holes that

hung from her *châtelaine*. 'I shall have to take a dram
of gentian wine or carduus-seed bruised in old sack,'
she added. 'Either is sovereign, both for spleen and
the vapours. Remember that, should you happen to
be attacked by these distempers.'

'I'm sure I hope I shan't be!' said I fervently.

'Rue-water is also excellent in fits,' said the old
lady loftily. 'My rue-water was justly celebrated. I
distributed it on Thursdays to all the poor who chose
to bring bottles to contain it. The juice of the plant
distilled, and mingled in the strongest brown ale,
a gallon and a half to a pint. 'Twas extraordinary
much sought by the labourers on Sir Bryan's estate.
Even more eagerly begged for and carried away was
my Palsy and Surfeit Water composed of the juice of
poppies, mint, cloves, and coriander seeds, mingled
with crushed loaf-sugar and the best French brandy.'

'I guess so!' I said.

'Did you suffer from dropsy, child, or gout,' said
Lady Deborah, 'you would find in that volume the
absolute specific.'

I said I was afraid I had never had gout, or dropsy
either.

'Consumption, then, or sore throat?' said Bryan's
ancestress anxiously.

I had had sore throat, and allowed as much.

'For sore throat, an excellent water is made of a
peck of snails laid in hyssop, bruised and distilled in
new milk,' said Lady Deborah, 'and drunk fasting.
By discreet use of this cordial any sore throat can be
cured.'

'Why, of course,' said I. 'The mere thought of the snails would effect the cure. One would get well directly – at least, I should!'

'Then in the treatment of jaundice I have worked absolute wonders, child, with conserve of prepared earthworms, turmeric, and rhubarb, mixed. The complaint flies before it positively,' continued Lady Deborah.

'Or the patient does,' I said to myself, but inwardly, remembering the cane.

'You never was bit by a mad dog, was you, chit?' was the astonishing question that came next.

'Good gracious, no!' I exclaimed energetically.

'Because sage, garlic, treacle, and tin filings boiled in a quart of strong mead or clary will serve in this disorder,' said Lady Deborah. 'You pour it into the party bitten by a quarter of a pint at a time.'

'I should never pour it,' I said decidedly. 'I should be too scared the party would bite *me*, and then there'd be two of us, foaming and acting awful!'

'But supposing you was pitted after a bout of smallpox, and desired to efface the scars,' continued Lady Deborah, just as though I had not spoken, 'you would find on the hundredth page the worthy Dr Burgess's recipe for a salve, of oil of tartar, pounded docks and green goose fat, considered infallible.' She sighed meditatively.

'Did you –?' I hinted, as delicately as I could.

'The ingredients must be mingled at the time of the new moon, when Venus is in the ascendant, and Jupiter is an evening star. I fear, chit,' she sighed, 'that my knowledge of astronomics was faulty. So little result I obtained that for a while I was plunged in despair.'

'I'm real sorry, dear Lady Deborah!' I said gently.

'But I despaired not long,' resumed Bryan's ancestress. 'I shut myself in my still-room and kitchen – not to weep and lament, but to work. I had ceased to be the queen of my husband's heart, but I learned to be the goddess of his table. Men are stomach first, child, and heart afterwards. What man would not lose a lover to gain so accomplished a cook as I became?' Her lean, narrow figure dilated, her expanding hoops seemed to fill the room, her keen grey eyes flamed like burning knots of lightwood behind her glasses. 'My fame was sounded throughout the county. "Lady Deb's battaglio pie," the bloods toasted now, instead of Lady Deb's skin of cream and roses, and Lady Deb's salmigondin, her patty royal, her cock salmon with buttered lobster, and her tansy fritters, they raved upon, instead of her bright eyes, red lips, pearly teeth, and clustered hair. And I bore it, chit! and curtsied and thanked 'em kindly, though I wished the dishes might surfeit 'em, with all my heart!'

'Oh, poor Lady Deborah!' I said, my heart in my voice.

'I blame them not now!' She lifted her lean hand. 'There are no men that love not good eating and drinking – even the saints that denied themselves; and for the women – I'm one of 'em myself, chit, or was – and know whether they sip nectar from blossoms, as they would have the silly men believe,

or have at the cold chine and apple-tart in the buttery
on the sly, an hour before the dinner-bell.'

She fanned herself, and producing from a deep,
swinging pocket a thin, black bone rod with a little
hand carved at the end, put it to its definite purpose
with an energy that made me shiver. William Blake
drew the ghost of a flea, I remembered, as Lady
Deborah pocketed the little black rod again.

'Please go on, madam . . . You interested me *so*
much about Sir Bryan. Did he reform and become a
real devoted husband again?' I asked timidly.

'I tell thee, Lyddy – they call you Lyddy for short,
don't they?' resumed Lady Deborah – 'he was mine
from his shoe-buckle to his wig-tie. He worshipped
the tiles of my kitchen – blue-and-white Dutch, and of
a pretty fancy. He took glory to himself in the envy of
other men; fox-hunting lords and squires, fat-jowled
justices of the peace, doctors of divinity, and doctors of
law. He never wearied to his dying day of the triumphs
of my cookery, especially roasted sucking-pig stuffed
with farced chestnuts, and battaglio pie.'

'I guess that's good, anyhow!' I said. 'It sounds so.'

''Tis made of young chickens, squab pigeons,
quails, partridges and larks,' said the ghost of Lady
Deborah, drying a shadowy tear. 'You truss them, put
'em in your dish lined with rich paste, add sweetbreads, cockscombs, a quart of oysters, sliced sheep's
tongues, the marrow of a dozen bones, cloves, mace,
nutmegs, the yolks of hard eggs, and forced-meat
balls . . . Cover with butter, pour in a pint of cream,
and draw the paste over the pie. When done – '

'It's soon done, I guess,' said I, for the recital made me feel quite hungry. 'My! it must have been rich!'

'That is why I was left a widow, my dear,' said the poor old ghost of Lady Deborah, applying the ghost of a lace pocket-handkerchief – darned – to her eyes.

'Through – through a battaglio pie?' I gasped, appalled by the savour of tragedy that rose from the dish.

'Through a battaglio pie. Mr Pope made use of the incident in his *Moral Essays*,' said Lady Deborah, 'where 'tis a jowl of salmon and not a pie. Alas, yes! Odious as it sounds, I was the cause of my Bryan's too early end. Year by year he had, thanks to the perfection of my cookery, become more and more addicted to the pleasures of the table. Racing, gaming, hunting, had become in his eyes the mere means to gain the appetite for fresh enjoyment. His fine complexion had become a dusky red, his chiselled features swelled, his eyes retired behind cushions of fat, his waist vanished, and three chins depended upon his laced cravat.'

'Oh!' I cried in horror.

'He drank hugely, but his drinking was moderate in proportion to his eating,' said Sir Bryan's widow. 'Too well I remember the odious event . . . 'Twas his name-day; he had five boon companions join him at the table, I put forth all my powers fitly to celebrate the anniversary. There could not be a prettier supper than that my husband sat to – not if I was to die this minute – I crave pardon, dear Lydia, for forgetting that I am dead! The first course was roasted pike and smelts – being June, pike was in season. Westphalia ham and young fowls, marrow puddings, haunch of venison roasted, ragout of lamb, sweetbreads, *fricassée* of young rabbits, umbles, a dish of mullets, roasted ducks, and custards.'

'And six men sat down to a supper like that?' I said, feeling my eyes opening to their widest extent.

'Nay, child, that was only the first course,' said Lady Deborah, sniffing at her silver pomander. 'The second course was a dish of young pheasants, a dish of soles and eels, a potato-salad, a jowl of sturgeon, a dish of tarts and cheese-cakes, a rock of snow with syllabubs, *and* that fatal, that ever-to-be-regretted battaglio pie!' She wiped her eyes and fanned herself. ' 'Twas the crown of the banquet . . . Sir Bryan and his guests called for a fresh magnum of claret when it appeared . . . "Gentlemen and boon companions," said he, with the drops of perspiration standing on his purple forehead, and his wig pushed back – I can see it now, for I was peeping through the old buttery dish-slide the servants scarce ever used – "Gentlemen, here's another bumper to the health of Lady Deborah Corbryan, the best wife and the best cook in the Four Kingdoms!" And the gentlemen tossed down the wine, child, but they were full to the throats. Justice Sir Barnwell Plumptree and Sir George Cockerell (for he and Bryan became great friends in later years), Nainby Friswell and Mr Selwyn, and Colonel Sir Harry Firebrace of the King's Dragoons. They could only look and water at the chops as my dear Sir Bryan cut into the battaglio pie. He cleared a platter full and wiped up the gravy with crust. "Do ye check?'' says he in scorn of the others. "Do ye balk at the best dish in Christendom? I've supped already, but I wager ye a guinea to a tester all round that I finish the dish!'' They took the bet, child, and Sir Bryan put ladle to dish. The ladle dropped with a clatter . . . a surge of blackish purple rose from his chins to his crown . . . "Death and fire!" says he, "you've won your money!'' and fell, and never uttered word again until he had been blooded by three chirurgeons one after the other, and had had the actual cautery applied. Oh, my dear! Then he came to himself, and "Is that thou, Deb?" says he. "I always loved thee, lass! Tell me the truth now, do I live or die?" And the doctor shook his head. "No hope?" says Sir Bryan. "Why, then, I'll e'en die as I have lived. Bring me the dish here – I'll e'en finish the rest o' the battaglio pie and turn the tables on Plumptree and the others." And he did, child – he did. And I lived to wear out my weeds and con over my cookery book but a dozen years after him, and now I'm dead' – the poor lady sobbed – 'I do it still, chit – I do it still! My hapless spirit is bound up in the yellow pages of that cookery book. I know not when my bondage shall cease, and rest be mine at last!'

'Poor lady – unhappy ghost!' I cried. 'Will nothing bring you peace?'

You would have known you had been interviewing a ghost by the fading outlines of Lady Deborah's form and features, and the way in which the black oak chair upholstered with old gilt leather showed through the hooped skirts of green and pink brocade. Her vanishing lips framed but two other words . . .

'Battaglio pie,' she said, and was gone in an instant; and with a crash the cookery book fell to the floor, and I sat up, wondering whether I had been dreaming? On the whole, I guessed I had not. When I picked up the prostrate cookery book, I knew I had not, for one of the many-time dogs'-eared pages was doubled over in a perfectly fresh place, *and the page bore the famous recipe for battaglio pie*.

The post that followed brought my promised letter. The next day brought a marconigram from Bryan. Marconi is hardly the language of love, but it did at a pinch. Parpa was no worse, it said, and I was not to be anxious. Indeed, by the time the liner picked up her pilot off Sandy Hook, the bulletins were so favourable that Bryan decided to return right away, Parpa being quite out of danger. He did return – one of our great Atlantic ferryboats being on the point of starting – and I marconied a message which hit the ship 1,065 miles west of the Lizard, to say I was well and happy, and learning to cook!

That was so. I had respectfully replaced Lady Deborah's cookery book upon her escritoire, after copying the fatal and famous recipe for battaglio pie . . . I had made friends with the ruler of the Abbey kitchen, and under her tuition was rapidly mastering the secret of flaky pastry.

June was scarcely over our heads; all the ingredients were procurable, though the heavy groan that burst from the head gamekeeper's bosom, when I demanded three young partridges, I never shall

forget. He brought them, though, and I had but to
amass the quail, the squab pigeon, the cockscombs,
sweetbreads, oysters, sheep's tongues, and so forth,
from other sources. Thus on the afternoon previous
to Bryan's return, I lined a stately dish with rich
pie-paste, I piled in all the good things, added
the eggs, forcemeat, spices, cream and butter, and
drew the cover over all, ornamenting it with devices
cut with antique pewter moulds that Lady Deborah
herself may have used. I glazed the outside with
egg-white. And then I saw the pie slide into a
gentle oven, and knew my task would soon be
done. An hour later, as I lay resting in my favourite
corner of the spindle-legged, tapestry-covered sofa
in the long drawing-room, I had a second visit from
Lady Deborah. She wore her black silk calash this
time, and behind her great silver-rimmed spectacles
her eyes snapped and sparkled with a joy that
was – was it malign? She spread out her rustling
brocade skirts as I rose up, and responded to my
hesitating curtsey with the grandest cheese I had
ever seen.

'I am vastly obleeged, Lydia,' she said, smiling
her old cheeks into creases. 'You have behaved
monstrous genteelly, child, and I feel that I shall
owe my freedom to your generosity. I have taken
measures that the reputation of the Abbey shall not
suffer, as there is a lamentable lack of *ton* about a
family residence without a ghost. Sir Umphrey, who
got grant of the demesne from King Henry VIII,
and, as you may have heard, murdered the abbot

who took exception to the grant, has arranged to haunt the inhabited wings as well as the shut-up portion. You have also a third share in a banshee brought into the family by one of the Desmonds, who intermarried with us in 1606, and there is a hugely impressive death-watch in the wainscoting of your room. Therefore, I need have no scruples in taking the change of air so necessary for vapours.'

She took her great calash and spreading brocades away. I forgot her – forgot the pie – forgot everything an hour later, in the joy of Bryan's arrival. With the aid of the housekeeper and by the advice of the cook, I had had prepared a real traveller's dinner, and at last my battaglio pie was placed upon the table before the master of the house.

Such a pie! a mountain of golden flaky crust, exhaling delicious, tempting, savoury odours. I looked across it at Bryan, and laughed in sheer delight at his astonishment.

'So this is the joke you have been keeping to yourself all the evening. Lydia, you little witch!' said Bryan, laughing too. 'A pie – a monster pie – and a savoury pie, too, made by your own hands, what?' He sniffed the delicious steam with expanded nostrils and filled his glass with port. 'Here's to the health of Lady Lydia Corbryan,' he cried gaily, 'the best wife and the best cook in the Four Kingdoms – not to mention the Realms beyond the Seas!'

Where had I heard those words – most of them
– before? I grew dizzy as Bryan seized the silver
pastry-knife and spoon and plunged into the depths
of the battaglio pie . . . A change seemed to have come
over him, the outlines of his face and figure seemed to
waver and alter as I gazed speechlessly, waiting for
something to come . . .

'I've dined already,' my husband cried in a thick
voice that frightened me, 'but I'll bet you a sovereign
to a sixpence that I finish the dish!'

'Bryan!' I screamed. 'Bryan!' and barely recognised
him to whom I appealed. That crimson face, with
the moist shine of perspiration glossing it, the powdered wig pushed back from the swollen forehead,
the piggish, twinkling eyes, gross, flabby mouth,
and three chins dropping over the flowing lace
cravat . . . Strange to me . . . all strange, yet so
horribly, horribly, familiar! I must have risen from
my chair and rushed to him, for I found myself
clinging to a man's arm and crying, 'Don't touch
it! If you love me, Bryan, don't touch it!' over and
over again.

'Of course not, if you don't wish it, little woman!'
said the dear familiar voice. Bryan was holding
me, and the face I loved was pressed comfortingly
to mine. 'Look here, Pet, I didn't mean to vex
you. I'll throw it out of the window if you want
me to.'

'Y-yes!' I sobbed, with chattering teeth. 'Th-throw
it out . . . do, please!' and Bryan heaved up the huge
pie-dish in his muscular hands.

'Open the window, please,' he said, and I hurried to obey. The casement swung wide upon a square of star-jewelled darkness . . . Did I hear a shrill, thin, eerie scream? Did I hear another casement crash open, somewhere in the west wing, as the battaglio pie was hurled into the night?

I asked Phee next morning to accompany me to Lady Deborah's room. The intrepid girl followed, only delaying to wind a thread of red marking-cotton nine times round her left thumb, and tuck her Aunt Dinah's hymn-book into what she termed 'de bosom' of her gown. As I climbed the stairs, threaded recollected passages, and with just a little qualm of nervousness opened the not-to-be-forgotten door, a blast of cold air saluted me. The casement swung open, fragments of its shattered panes still jagging in the leads, and a yellowish snow of torn papers littered the floor. They were fragments of the cookery book, torn to atoms by a force unknown . . . What force? The portrait of Lady Deborah gazed stonily from over the fireplace and made no answer.

What would have happened had Bryan indulged the hereditary instinct that led him to hunger, even after a full meal, for battaglio pie? Would he have ended existence like the unlucky glutton, his ancestor, in stertorous coma, unrelieved by depletion? Should I have died of grief, and haunted the Abbey in Lady Deborah's stead, a disconsolate, widowed shade, continually brooding over a battered edition of the *Compleat Housewife*? Who can say?

But it smelt wonderfully good. There have been hungry moments when I have half regretted not tasting it, the sole achievement in the cookery line I am destined ever to accomplish.

I have never seen Lady Deborah since!

(The recipes quoted by the ghost of Lady Deborah have been taken from a copy of THE COMPLEAT HOUSEWIFE *in the author's possession, dated 1733.)*

The Case of Mr Lucraft

WALTER BESANT AND JAMES RICE

The supernatural element is also to be found in this next
story, 'The Case of Mr Lucraft', which has been described by
several critics as a mixture of Charles Dickens and F. Anstey
at their respective bests! The story of a penniless young man
who sells his one outstanding asset – an enormous appetite
– and then has to suffer the excesses of the purchaser, was
first published anonymously in the magazine *Once A Week*
in 1875, but such was its reception by readers that the
authors, Sir Walter Besant (1836–1901) and James Rice
(1843–1882), owned up and were acclaimed both in the
national press and by that most renowned of all writers
on cookery, Mrs Beeton.

I have more than once told the story of the only
remarkable thing which ever happened to me in the
course of a longish life, but as no one ever believed me,
I left off telling it. I wish, therefore, to leave behind
me a truthful record, in which everything shall be
set down, as near as I can remember it, just as it
happened. I am sure I need not add a single fact. The
more I consider the story, the more I realise to myself
my wonderful escape and the frightful consequences
which a providential accident averted from my head,
the more reason I feel to be grateful and humble.

I have read of nothing similar to my own case. I have consulted books on apparitions, witchcraft, and the power of the devil as manifested in authentic history, but I have found absolutely nothing that can in any way compare with my own case. If there be any successor to my Mr Ebenezer Grumbelow, possessed of his unholy powers, endowed with his fiendish resolve and his diabolical iniquity of selfishness, this plain and simple narrative may serve as a warning to young men situated as I was in the year 1823. Except as a moral example, indeed, I see no use in telling the story at all.

I have never been a rich man, but I was once very poor, and it is of this period that I have to write.

As for my parentage, it was quite obscure. My mother died when I was still a boy; and my father, who was not a man to be proud of as a father, had long before run away from her and disappeared. He was a sailor by profession, and I have heard it rumoured that sailors of his time possessed a wife in every port, besides a few who lived, like my mother, inland; so that they could vary the surroundings when they wished. The wives were all properly married in church too, and honest women, every one of them. What became of my father I never knew, nor did I ever inquire.

I went through a pretty fair number of adventures before I settled down to my first serious profession. I was travelling companion and drudge to an itinerant tinker, who treated me as kindly as could be expected when he was sober. When he was drunk he used to throw the pots and pans at my head. Then I became a cabin-boy, but only for a single voyage, on board a collier. The ship belonged to a philanthropist, who was too much occupied with the wrongs of the West Indian niggers to think about the rights of his own sailors; so his ships, insured far above their real value, were sent to sea to sink or swim as it might please Providence. I suppose no cabin-boy ever had so many kicks and cuffs in a single voyage as I had. However, my ship carried me safely from South Shields to the port of London. There I ran away, and I heard afterwards that on her return voyage the *Spanking Sally* foundered with all hands. In the minds of those who knew the captain and his crew personally, there were doubtless, as in mine, grave fears as to their ultimate destination. After that I became steward in an Atlantic sailing packet for a couple of years; then clerk to a bogus auctioneer in New York; cashier to a store; all sorts of things, but nothing long. Then I came back to England, and not knowing what to do with myself, joined a strolling company of actors in the general utility line. It was not exactly promotion, but I liked the life; I liked the work; I liked the applause; I liked wandering about from town to town; I even liked, being young and a fool, the precarious nature of the salary. Heaven knows mine was small enough; but we were a cheery company, and one or two members subsequently rose to distinction. If we had known any history, which we did not, we might have remembered that Molière himself was once a stroller through France.

Some people think it philosophical to reflect, when they are hard up, how many great men have been hard up too. It would have brought no comfort to me. Practically I felt little inconvenience from poverty, save in the matter of boots. We went share and share alike, most of us, and there was always plenty to eat even for my naturally gigantic appetite. Juliet always used to reckon me as equal to four.

Juliet was the manager's daughter – Julie Kerrans, acting as Miss Juliet Alvanley. She was eighteen and I was twenty-three, an inflammable and romantic time of life. We were thrown a good deal together too, not only off the stage but on it. I was put into parts to play up to her. I was Romeo when she played her namesake, a part sustained by her mother till even she herself was bound to own that she was too fat to play it any longer; she was Lady Teazle and I was Charles Surface; she was Rosalind and I Orlando; she was Miranda and I Ferdinand; she was Angelina and I Sir Harry Wildair. We were a pair, and looked well in love scenes. Looking back dispassionately on our performances, I suppose they must have been as bad as stage-acting could well be. At least, we had no training, and nothing but a few fixed rules to guide us; these, of course, quite stagey and conventional. Juliet had been on the stage all her life, and did not want in assurance; I, however, was nervous and uncertain. Then we were badly mounted and badly dressed; we were ambitious, we ranted, and we tore a passion to rags. But we had one or two good points – we were young and lively. Juliet had the most charming of faces and the most delicious of figures – mind you, in the year 1823, girls had a chance of showing their figures without putting on a page's costume. Then she had a soft, sweet voice, and pretty little coquettish ways, which came natural to her, and broke through the clumsy stage artificialities. She drew full houses; wherever we performed, all the men, especially all the young officers, used to come after her. They wrote her notes, they lay in wait for her, they sent her flowers; but what with old Kerrans and myself, to say nothing of the other members of the company, they might as well have tried to get at a Peri in Paradise. I drew pretty well too. I was – a man of seventy and more may say so without being accused of vanity – I was a good-looking young fellow; you would hardly believe what quantities of letters and *billets-doux* came to me. I had dozens, but Juliet found and tore them up. There they were; the note on rose-coloured note-paper with violet ink, beginning with 'Handsomest and noblest of men', and ending with 'Your fair unknown, Araminta'. There was the letter from the middle-aged widow with a taste for the drama and an income; and there was the vilely spelled note from the foolish little milliner who had fallen in love with the Romeo of a barn. Perhaps ladies are more sensible now. At all events, their letters were thrown away upon me, because I was in love already, head over ears, and with Juliet.

Juliet handed over her notes to her father, who found out their writers, and made them take boxes and bespeak plays. So that all Juliet's lovers got was the privilege of paying more than other people, for the girl was as good as she was pretty – a rarer combination of qualities on the stage fifty years ago than now. She was tall and, in those days, slender. Later on she took after her mother; but who would have thought that so graceful a girl would ever arrive at fourteen stone? Her eyes and hair were black – eyes that never lost their lustre; and hair which, though it turned grey in later years, was then like a silken net, when it was let down, to catch the hearts of lovers. Of course she knew that she was pretty; what pretty woman does not? And of course, too, she did not know and would not understand the power of her own beauty; what pretty woman does? And because it was the very worst thing she could do for herself, she fell in love with me.

Her father knew it and meant to stop it from the beginning: but he was not a man to do things in a hurry, and so we went on in a fool's paradise, enjoying the stolen kisses, and talking of the sweet time to come when we should be married. One night – I was Romeo – I was so carried away with passion that I acted for once naturally and unconventionally. There was a full house; the performance was so much out of the common that the people were astonished and forgot to applaud. Juliet caught the infection of my passion, and for once we acted well, because we acted from the heart. Never but that once, I believe, has *Romeo and Juliet* been performed by a pair who felt every word they said. It was only in a long, low room, a sort of corn exchange or town hall, in a little country town, but the memory of that night is sacred to me.

You know the words –

> See, how she leans her cheek upon her hand!
> O, that I were a glove upon that hand,
> That I might touch that cheek!

And these –

> 'O, for a falconer's voice,
> To lure this tassel-gentle back again!
> Bondage is hoarse and may not speak aloud,
> Else would I tear the cave where Echo lies,
> And make her airy tongue more hoarse than
> mine
> With repetition of my Romeo!'

Splendidly we gave them.

Why, even now, old as I am, the recollection of these lines and the thought of that night warm my heart still and fire my feeble pulses. I have taught them to my grandchild. She takes after my poor Juliet, and would succeed on the stage, if only her father would let her. But he is strait-laced. Ah! he should have seen the temptations which beset a girl on the stage in my time. We are Puritans now, almost –

And a good thing, too. It is time for me to own it.

Well – old Kerrans was in the front, looking after the money, as usual, and always with one eye on the stage, to see how his daughter was getting on. He was puzzled, I think, to make out the meaning of the unaccustomed fire, but he came to the conclusion that if Juliet was going to remain Miss Juliet, instead of becoming Mrs Mortimer Vavasseur (my stage name), he had better interfere at once.

So after the play, and over the domestic supper-table, he had it out with his daughter.

Juliet swore that nothing should induce her to marry another man.

'Bless the girl!' said her father; 'I don't want you to marry anybody at all.'

Juliet declared that she never, never would forget me.

'I don't want you to forget him,' Mr Kerrans replied. 'Remember him as much as you like.'

Juliet announced her intention of retiring from the stage and going into a convent. There were no convents in England in 1823, so that the threat was not so serious as it would be now.

Her father promised her that when the company passed by any respectable convent on the road, he would certainly knock at the door and inquire about the accommodation and the terms.

'Lor!' he said, caressing his weeping daughter, 'do you think I want to be cruel to you, my pretty? Not a bit. Let young Lucraft go and prove himself a man, and he shall have you. But, you see, it wouldn't do to add to the expenses of the company just now, with business so bad and all, would it, my dear? Why, you might be confined in a twelvemonth, and laid by for half the year ever after, with a troop of young children. Where should we be then?'

The next day was Saturday. As usual, I went into the treasury to draw my money, and found the old fellow with rather a red face, and a hesitation in his manner.

He told me the whole story, just as I have told it to you. And then he gave me my dismissal.

'Look here,' he said, handing me the money, 'you are a capital young fellow, Lucraft, and a likely actor. There's merit in you. But I can't have you spoiling my Juliet for the stage. So I'm going to put her up without you. After a bit I daresay I shall find another Romeo. You get away to London and find another engagement – there's a week's pay in advance – and when Juliet is married, or when you get rich, or when anything happens to make things different, why, you see, we shall all be glad to see you back. Go and make your farewells to Juliet, and don't be more sentimental than you can help. Good-bye, my boy, and good luck to you.'

Good luck! Had he known the kind of luck which awaited me!

I sought my girl, and found her crying. I remember that we forgot all the fine verses of Shakespeare, and just put our faces close to each other and cried together.

It did seem hard upon both of us. We were really and truly in love, and that in a good, honest, determined way. To me there was no other girl in the world except Juliet. To her there was no other man besides Luke Lucraft. We had come to an understanding for three months, and had been quietly dropping deeper and deeper in love during all that time.

And now we were to part.

'Don't forget me, dear Luke,' she sobbed. 'There are lots of prettier and finer girls in the world than I am, who will try to take away your love from me. I wish I could kill the creatures!' she added, stamping her foot.

Juliet always had a high and generous spirit. I like women to have a high spirit.

'And will you have no admirers, Juliet?' I replied. 'Why, half the town' – we were in Lancaster then – 'half the town is at your feet already. I intercepted two love-letters yesterday, and I kicked the grocer's apprentice the day before for trying to get Mrs Mould to give you a *billet-doux* from himself. Come, dear, we will trust one another. I will try and prove myself a man – get an engagement, make a name on the London stage, and come back with money and an offer to act Romeo to your Juliet at Drury Lane. Think of that, my dearest, and dry your eyes. Your father does not object to me, you know; he only wants me to make an income. Come, Juliet, let us say good-bye. It is only for a short time, and I shall come back with all sorts of reasons in my pocket for persuading your father's consent.'

So we parted, with many more promises of trust and fidelity, and after breaking a sixpenny-bit between us. Juliet's piece is buried with her; mine is hanging at my heart, and will be, before long, buried with me beside her.

Oh! the weary journey to London in those days, especially outside the coach, and for a poor man not encumbered with too many wraps. However, I arrived at length, and found myself in the streets that are supposed to be paved with gold, with a couple of sovereigns in my pocket.

But I was brimful of hope. London was a kindly step-mother, who received adopted sons by the thousand, and led them to fame and wealth. I thought of Garrick, of Dick Whittington, and all the rest who came up to town poorer, far poorer than myself, and took comfort. I secured a lodging at a modest rent, and made my way to Drury Lane – the stage door.

I found no opening at Drury Lane; not even a vacancy for a supernumerary. There were not many London theatres in 1823, and I found the same thing everywhere – more applications than places to give.

I tried the Greenwich and the Richmond theatres with the same ill-success.

Then I endeavoured to get a country engagement, but I even failed there. I had no friends to recommend me, and my single experience with Kerrans's strolling troupe did not tell so much in my favour as I had hoped.

My ambition naturally took a town flight. I had intended to make my appearance on the metropolitan stage as Romeo, my favourite part, and at once to take the town by storm. I was prepared to give them an intelligent and novel interpretation of Hamlet. And I was not unwilling to undertake Macbeth, Othello, or even Prince Hal.

When these hopes became evidently grounded on nothing but the baseless fabrication of a dream, I resolved on beginning with second parts. Horatio, Mercutio, Paris, were, after all, characters worthy the work of a rising artist.

Again there seemed no chance.

The stage always wants young men of general utility. I would go anywhere and take anything. I offered to do so, but although hopes were held out to me by the theatrical agent, somehow he had nothing at the moment in his gift. Nothing: not even a vacancy for a tragedian at Richardson's Show; not even a chance for Bartholomew Fair.

It took me a fortnight to run down the scale from Hamlet, say, to Francis the warder. While I passed through this descending gamut of ambition, my two sovereigns were melting away with a rapidity quite astonishing.

The rent took five shillings: that was paid in advance. Then I was extravagant in the matter of eating, and took three meals a day, finding that not enough to satisfy my vigorous appetite. Once or twice, too, I paid for admission to the pit, and saw, with a sinking heart, what real acting means. My heart failed, because I perceived that I had to begin all over again, and from the very bottom of the ladder.

Then I had to buy a new pair of boots. It was always a trouble to me, the rapid wearing out of leather.

And then there was something else; and then one

morning I found myself without a sixpence in my pocket. And then I began for the first time to become seriously alarmed about the future.

I had one or two things which I could pawn – a watch, a waistcoat, a few odds and ends in the way of wardrobe, and a few books – on the proceeds of them I lived for a whole week; but at last, after spending two-pence in the purchase of a penny loaf and a saveloy for breakfast, I found myself not only penniless, but also without the means of procuring another penny at all, because I had nothing left to pawn.

Many a young fellow has found himself in a similar predicament, but I doubt whether anyone ever became so desperately hungry as I did on that day. I recollect that, having rashly eaten up my sausage before eight o'clock, I felt a sinking towards twelve; it was aggravated by the savoury smell of roast meat which steamed from the cookshops and dining-rooms as I walked along the streets. About one o'clock I gazed with malignant envy on the happy clerks who could go in and order platefuls of the roast and boiled which smoked in the windows, and threw a perfume more delicious than the sweetest strains of music into the streets where I lingered and looked. And at two I observed the diners come out again, walking more slowly, but with an upright and satisfied air, while I – the sinking had been succeeded by a dull gnawing pain – was slowly doubling up. At half-past two I felt as if I could bear it no longer. I had been walking about, trying different offices for a clerkship. I might as well have asked for a partnership. But I could walk no more. I leaned against a post – it was in Bucklersbury – opposite a dining-room, where hares, fowls, and turkeys were piled in the window among a boundless prodigality and wealth of carrots, turnips, and cauliflowers, till my senses swam at the contemplation. I longed for a cauldron in which to put the whole contents of the shop front, and eat them at one Gargantuan repast. My appetite, already alluded to, was hereditary; one of the few things I can remember of my mother was a constant complaint that my father used to eat her out of house and home. To be sure, from other scraps of information handed down by tradition, I have reason to believe that the word eating was used as a figure of speech – the part for the whole – and included drinking. I was good at both, and as a trencherman I had been unsurpassed, as I said above, in the company, the dear old company among whom I have so often eaten beefsteak and fried onions with Juliet. The door of the place opened now and then to let a hungry man enter or a full man go out, and I caught a glimpse of the interior. Dining-rooms were not called restaurants in those days. They had no gilding, no bright paint, no pretty barmaids, and no silver-plated forks and spoons. Nor were they brilliant with gas. All London – that is, all working London – dined before four o'clock; the clerks from twelve to two, and the principals, except a few of the big wigs, from two to four. The cheaper rooms were like one or two places still to be found in Fleet Street. There were sanded floors; there were hard benches; you had your beer out of pewter, not plated tankards;

there was no cheap claret, and the popular ideal of wine was a strong and fiery port. Also, candles stood upon the tables – not wax candles, but tallow, with long wicks which required snuffing. They dropped a good deal of mutton fat about the table, and it was not uncommon to find yourself eating a little tallow with your bread, which was not nice even to men of a strong stomach. Finally, you had steel forks, which are just as good, to my thinking, as plated silver, and more easily cleaned.

I stood by the post and watched with hungry eyes. From within I heard voices, stifled voices, as those sent up a pipe, calling for roast beef with plenty of brown – good heavens! plenty of brown; roast mutton, underdone – I loved my mutton underdone; boiled beef with suet-pudding and fat – I always took a great deal of pudding and fat with my boiled beef; roast veal and bacon with stuffing – a dish for the gods; calves' head for two – I could have eaten calves' head for a dozen; with orders pointing to things beyond my hungry imagination – hunger limits the boundaries of fancy – puddings, fish, soup, cheese, and such delicacies. Alas! I wanted the solids. I felt myself growing feebler; I became more and more doubled up; I had thoughts of entering this paradise of the hungry, and, after eating till I could eat no longer, calmly laying down my knife and fork and informing the waiter that I had no money. There was a farce in which I had once played where the comic actor sent for the landlord, after a hearty meal, and asked him what he would do in case a stranger, after ordering and eating his dinner, should declare his inability to pay. 'Do, sir?' cried the host; 'I should kick him across the street.' 'Landlord,' said the low comedian, and it always told – 'Landlord,' he used to rise up slowly as he spoke, and solemnly draw aside his coat-tails, turning his face in the direction of the street-door – 'landlord, I'll trouble you.' I used to play the landlord.

It struck half-past three; the dead gnawing of hunger was followed by a sharp pain, irritating and much more unpleasant. The crowd of those who entered had been followed by the crowd of those who came out and the heaven of hungry men was nearly empty again. I gazed still upon the turkeys and the hares, but with a lack-lustre eye, for I was nearly fainting.

Presently there came down the street an elderly gentleman, bearing before him, like a Lord Mayor in a French tale, his enormous abdomen: he had white hair, white eyebrows, white whiskers, and a purple face. He walked very slowly, as if the exertion might prove apoplectic, and leaned upon a thick stick. As he passed the shop he looked in at the window and wagged his head. At that moment I groaned involuntarily. He turned round and surveyed me. I suppose I presented a strange appearance, leaning against the post, with stooping figure and tightly-buttoned coat. He had big projecting eyes flushed with red veins, which gave him a wolfish expression.

'Young man,' he said, not benignantly at all, but severely, 'you look ill. Have you been drinking?'

I shook my head.

'I am only hungry,' I said, telling the truth because

I was too far gone to hide it, 'I am only hungry; that is the matter with me.'

He planted his stick on the ground, supporting both his hands upon the gold head, and wagged his head again from side to side with a grunting sound in his throat like the sawing of bones.

Grunt! 'Here's a pretty fellow for you!' Grunt! 'Hungry, and he looks miserable.' Grunt! 'Hungry, and he groans.' Grunt! 'Hungry – the most enviable position a man can be in – and he dares to repine at his lot.' Grunt! 'What are the lower classes coming to next, I wonder? Aren't you ashamed of yourself? Aren't you a model of everything that is ungrateful and' – grunt! – 'and flying in the face of Providence? He lives in a land of victuals. London is a gigantic caravan, full of the most splendid things, the most glorious things to eat and drink; it only wants an appetite; and he's got that, and he laments!'

'What is the use of an appetite if you have no money to satisfy it with?'

Grunt! 'Is it a small appetite, as a rule, or is it a large appetite?'

'Large,' I replied. 'It is an awkward thing for a poor beggar like me to have such a devil of a twist. I was born with it. Very awkward just now.'

'Come with me, young man,' he grunted. 'Go before me. Don't talk, because that may interfere with the further growth of your appetite. Walk slowly, and keep your mouth shut close.'

He came behind me, walking with his chuckle and grunt.

'So. What a fine young fellow it is!' Grunt! 'What room for the development of the Alderman's Arch! What a backbone for the support of a stomach! What shoulders for a dinner-table, and what legs to put under it! Heavens! what a diner might be made of this boy if he only had money.' Grunt! 'Youth and appetite – health and hunger – and all thrown away upon a pauper! What a thing, what a thing! This way, young man.'

Turning down a court leading out of Bucklersbury, he guided me to a door, a little black portal, at which he stopped; then stooping to a keyhole of smaller size than was generally used in those days, he seemed to me to blow into it with his mouth; this was absurd, of course, but it seemed so to me. The door opened. He led the way into a passage, which, when the door shut behind us, as it did of its own accord, was pitch dark. We went up some stairs, and on the first landing the old gentleman, who was wheezing and puffing tremendously, opened another door, and led me into a room. It was a large room, resplendent with the light of at least forty wax candles. The centre was occupied by a large dining-table laid for a single person. Outside it was broad daylight, for it was not yet four o'clock.

'Sit down, young man, sit down,' puffed my host. 'Oh dear! oh dear! Sit down, do. I wish I was as hungry as you.'

I sat down in the nearest chair, and looked round the room. The first thing I remarked was that I could not see the door by which we had been admitted. The room was octagonal, and on every side stood some

heavy piece of furniture; a table with glass, a case
of bookshelves, a sofa, but no door. My heart began
to go round as I continued my observations. There
was no window either, nor was there any fireplace.
Then I felt a sudden giddiness, and I suppose I fell
backwards on my chair. It was partly the faintness of
hunger, but partly it was the strange room, and that
old man glaring at me with his great wolfish eyes.

When I recovered I was lying on a sofa, and soft
cold fingers were bathing my head, and pressing a
perfumed handkerchief to my lips. I opened my eyes
suddenly and sat up completely recovered. At the foot
of the sofa stood my entertainer.

'Easy with him, Boule-de-neige; make him rest for
a moment. Perhaps his hunger has been too much
for him.'

I turned to see who Boule-de-neige was. He was a
negro of the blackest type, ancient and withered as
some old ourang of tropical woods; his cheeks hung in
folds, and his skin seemed too much for his attenuated
body; his wool was white, and his gums were almost
toothless; and his nose so flattened with age as to be
almost invisible, looking at him as I was looking, in
profile. His hands were as soft as any woman's, but
icy cold; and his eyes were red and fiery.

'Boule-de-neige, what do you think of him?'

'Him berry fine young man, massa: him beautiful
young man; got lubly abbatite develoffed, I tink; him
last long time, much longer time dan last oder young
man. Cluck! Him poor trash, dat young man; dam
poor trash; use up and go to debbel in a month.

Cluck! Dis young man got lubly stumjack, strong as bull. Cluck-cluck! How much you tink him eat tonight?'

'We shall see, Boule-de-neige. We will try him with a simple dinner, and then pronounce on his performances. Young men do not always come up to their professions. But he looks well, and perhaps, Boule-de-neige – perhaps – ah!' He nodded with a deep sigh.

'What time massa dine himself?'

'I don't know,' the old gentleman answered, with another heavy sigh. 'Perhaps not till nine o'clock; perhaps not then. It all depends on this youth. Vanish, Boule-de-neige, and serve.'

There was evidently something in my host's mind by the way he sighed. Why did it depend upon me? And did Boule-de-neige go through the floor? Did the table sink when he disappeared, and come up loaded with dishes? It seemed so.

I sprang from the couch. The sight and smell of the food brought back my raging hunger.

'Let me eat!' I cried.

'You shall. One moment first – only a single moment. Young man, tell me again and explicitly the nature and extent of your appetite. Be truthful, oh, be truthful! Our little tongues should never lie for mutton-chop or apple-pie. You know the hymn. I hope you have been religiously brought up, and know that hymn.'

'I've got a devil of an appetite. What is there to lie about?'

'My dear young friend, there are many kinds of appetites. Yours may be fierce at first and promise great things, and then end in a miserably small performance. I have known such, and mourned to see them. Is it a lasting appetite, now? Is it steady through a long dinner? Is it regular in its recurrence?'

'You shall see something of my performance,' I laughed, insensate wretch. 'You shall see. I never had a long dinner in my life, because I always made short work of mine. It is steady through a good many pounds of steak, and as regular as a clock.'

'That is always something. Steak is as healthy a test as I know. Is it, secondly, an appetite that recovers itself quickly? That is very important. Is it a day-by-day or an hour-by-hour appetite? Is it good at all times of the day?'

'Alas, I wish it were not!'

'Hush, young man; do not blaspheme! Tell me, if you eat your fill now – it is half-past four – when do you think you might be ready again?' His eyes glistened like a couple of great rubies in the candlelight, and his hands trembled.

'I should say about eight. But I might do something light at seven, I daresay. Just now I feel as if I could eat a mountain.'

'He feels as if he could eat a mountain! Wonderful are the gifts of Providence! My dear young friend, I am very thankful – deeply thankful – that I met you. Sit down, and let me take the covers off for you; I long to see you eat. This is a blessed day – a truly blessed day! I will wait upon you myself. No one else. Boule-de-neige, vanish!'

As he was about to take off the covers he stopped short.

'Stay. You are without occupation?'

'I can get none.'

'You are of any trade?'

'I am an actor.'

'A bad trade – an un-Christian trade. Actors are vagabonds by Act of Parliament. Actors can never be in a state of grace. I shall be happy in being a humble instrument in removing you from a calling fatal to the Christian warrior. Why did you leave your last situation? No dishonesty? No embezzlement? No tampering with accounts?'

'Sir, I have always been an honest man. And, besides, I have never been tempted by the handling of other people's money.'

'Ha! You have got no wife?'

'No, sir; I am unmarried.'

'You have got no – I trust I am taking to my bosom no deceiver of women. You are not the father of an illegitimate offspring, I hope and pray.'

'No, sir; I am not.'

'Young man, you are about to enter upon a most serious act, perhaps the most serious act of your life, and these questions may appear to you trivial and tedious. As a Christian, and a member of the congregation of Mr – But never mind; you are hungry now, and wish to eat. We will talk after dinner.'

He took off the covers. The table was spread with a

dozen different dishes, all served up together. Others
I noticed, standing with bottles and decanters, on a
large sideboard. As my generous benefactor removed
the silver covers, his face, which had assumed during
his questioning an austere gravity, suddenly lit up,
and he laughed as the perfume of the hot food
mounted to his nostrils. He seemed all at once a
different man.

'Gently, gently, my dear young friend. Here is a
dinner fit for a king; fit for *me*, if I could eat it. Oh!
my dainty Boule-de-neige! Ha! is it right to waste
such a dinner upon a youth whose only dreams are
of a sufficiency of steak? Young man, in after years –
ahem! – in after days you will remember this dinner.
You will recall every item in this delicious bill of fare
which Boule-de-neige has set before you. Let me teach
you to eat it properly. Weigh your morsels.'

Heaven! how I cursed his delay. He kept one great
hand between me and the dishes, for fear, I suppose,
that I should pounce upon them and clear them off
all at once.

'Patience, patience. Consider each mouthful. Try
to be thankful that cooks have brought their divine
art to such perfection. Carry back your thoughts to –
grunt – to time when all mankind fed upon imperfectly
cooked steak. Think that all the treasures of the East
and West have been ransacked to furnish for me this
meal, and that you will never, never, never see such
a dinner again as long as you live.'

At all events, I never saw such a meal again as long
as *he* lived.

'We will now,' he said, with a backward wave of his right hand, 'consider dinner as a science.'

'Oh, sir!' I exclaimed, 'I am so hungry.'

'It's beautiful to see you hungry, but I must not let you hurry. Eat as much as you like when you begin, but gently, gently – easily and gently. Think of the future. Think of ME.'

I stared at him in wonder.

'Think of you, sir?'

'Why, what would happen to me if you really destroyed your appetite, or even yourself in swallowing a bone?'

I thought he must be mad.

'Young man,' he went on, 'you will say a grace before meat, if you remember one.'

I did not.

'Then I will say one for you. Oh! wretched trade of stage acting. He does not even know a single grace before meat.'

Then he began to help me and we went on with dinner without further interruption. He kept up a running accompaniment of comment as I devoured the meal, and his manner gradually lost all its solemnity, until before I was more than half through the dinner he was dancing about, slapping his leg with delight, and laughing till he grew almost black in the face.

Why he was so pleased I could not tell. I was soon to learn.

'These are plovers' eggs. No better thing ever discovered to begin your dinner with. Alderman Stowport says oysters are better. That is rubbish.

I do not despise oysters – Why, he has eaten the whole six! Bravo! bravo! an excellent beginning. Let me take away the plate, my dear sir. Now we have turtle soup – gently, my young friend, gently. Ah, impetuous youth! More? Stay – green fat. Humour, humour your appetite; don't drive it; calipash and calipee. It's really sinful to eat so fast. He takes all down without tasting it. No – no more; you must give yourself a fair chance, and not spoil your dinner with too much turtle.' He put the soup aside, and took the cover off another dish. 'Salmon – with cucumber. Lobster-sauce – bless me, it's like a dream of fairyland! Fillet of sole – a beautiful dream to see him. Ho! ho! he's a Julius Caesar the Conqueror. Croquet de volaille – gone like a cloud from the sky. Don't wolf the food, my friend; there is a limit to the cravings of nature imposed by the claims of art; taste it. Ris de veau – smiles of the dear little innocent, confiding calf – a little more bread with it? Mauviettes en caisse, larks in baskets – sweet, rapturous, singing larks, toothsome cockyolly larks. He eats them up, bones and all. Ha! ha! Pause, my dear sir, and drink something. Here are champagne, hock, and sauterne; never touch sherry, it's a made-up wine, even the best of it. Come, a little champagne.'

'I generally take draught-beer, sir,' I replied, modestly. 'That is the drink to which I have been accustomed and – not too much of it; but, if you please, a little fizz will be acceptable.'

I drank three glasses in rapid succession, and found them good. He meanwhile nodded and winked with an ever-increasing delight which I failed to understand.

'Now, my Nero, my Paris of Troy, my Judas Maccabaeus' – he mixed up his names, but it mattered nothing – 'here is saddle of mutton, with potatoes, cauliflower, currant-jelly. More champagne? It's worth *sums* of money to see him. Curry? More champagne? Curry of chicken? Cabob curry of chicken, young Alexander the Great? Plenty of rice? Ho, ho, ho! Plenty of rice, he said; why, he is a Goliath – a Goliath of Gath, this young man!'

He really grew so purple that I thought he would have a fit of some kind. But the flattery pleased me all the same, and I went on eating and drinking as if I was only just beginning.

'Quail or bécassine – snipe, that is? He takes both, like Pompey. More champagne? Jelly, my Heliogabalus, my modern Caracalla, apricot-jelly? Cabinet pudding? He has two helpings of the pudding. King Solomon in all his glory never – More champagne? A little hock to finish with? He takes his hock in a tumbler, this young Samson. Cheese – Brie – and celery. A glass of port with the cheese. He takes that in a tumbler too, like Og, King of Bashan.'

I was really overwhelmed with the splendour of the dinner, the classical and biblical flattery, and the extraordinary gratification which my really enormous hunger caused this remarkable old gentleman. He clapped his hands; he nodded his head; he slapped his legs: he winked and grinned; he smacked his lips; he evinced every sign of the most unbounded delight. When I had quite finished eating, which was not before we had got through the whole list of courses, he gave me a bottle of claret, and watched me while I rapidly disposed of it. Then he produced from a sideboard, where I certainly had not seen it a moment before, a small cup of strong black coffee with a tiny glass of liqueur. As for my own part, I hope I have made it clear that I dined extremely well; in fact, I had never even dreamed of such a dinner in my life. It was not only that I was half starved, but that the things were so good. Imagine the astonishment of a young strolling actor, whose highest dreams were of sufficient beefsteak, not of the primest part, at such a magnificent feed. I felt as if I had dropped unexpectedly into a fortune. I had.

'How do you feel now?' my host asked, a shade of anxiety crossing his brow.

*   *   *

There was still the strange look in my host's eyes – a sort of passionate and eager longing.

'I am very well, thank you, sir, and more grateful than I can tell you.'

'Hang the gratitude! Tell me if you feel any sense of repletion? Does the blood seem mounting to the head? Are you quite free from any giddiness? No thickness in the speech? It's wonderful, it's providential, my finding you. Such a windfall; and just when I most wanted it. Our blessings truly come when we least expect them.'

This was strange language, but the whole proceedings were so strange that I hardly noticed it. Besides, I was extremely comfortable after my dinner, and disposed to rest.

'Now,' he went on, 'while you are digesting – by the way, the digestion is, I trust, unimpaired by drink or excess? Quite so; and what I expected in so good and so gifted a young man. Like an ostrich, as you say. Ho, ho! ha! ha! like an ostrich! It is, indeed, too much. Tell me, now, something, gently and dispassionately, so as not to injure your digestion, about your history.'

I told him all. While I related my simple story he interrupted now and then with some fresh question on the growth, the endurance, the regularity of my appetite, to which I gave satisfactory answers. When I had quite finished he went to the table – I noticed then that all traces of the dinner had disappeared – and laid out a document, by which he placed a pen. Then he drew a chair, sat down in front of me, and assumed a serious air.

'Come,' he said, peremptorily, 'let us get now to business.'

I had not the smallest notion what the business was, but I bowed and waited. Perhaps he was going to offer me a clerkship. Visions of a large salary, to suit my expansive appetite, came across my brain.

'In your case,' he began, 'the possession of so great an appetite must be attended with serious inconveniences. You have no money, in a few hours you will be hungry again; you will endure great pain and suffering, greater than is felt by men less largely endowed with the greatest blessing – I mean with appetite.'

'Yes,' I said, 'it is a great trouble to me, this twist of mine, especially when I am hard up.'

He almost jumped out of his chair.

'Why, there,' he cried, 'what is the use of words? We are agreed already. Nothing could be more fortunate. Let us have no more beating about the bush. Young man, I will rid you of this nuisance; I will buy your appetite of you.'

I only stared. Was the old gentleman mad?

'It is a strange offer, I know,' he went on, 'a strange offer, and you have probably never heard a more remarkable one. But it is genuine. I will buy your appetite of you.'

'Buy my – buy my appetite?'

'Nothing easier. Read this.'

He gave me the paper which he had laid on the table, prepared in readiness, I suppose, for me. It was as follows:

'I, Luke Lucraft, being in sound mind and in good health, and of the mature age of twenty-four, do voluntarily and of my own free will and accord agree and promise to resign my appetite entirely and altogether for the use of Ebenezer Grumbelow from the day and hour of the execution of this deed. In return whereof I agree to accept a monthly allowance of £30, also to date from the moment of signature, with a sum of £50, to be placed in my hands. I promise also that I will carefully study to preserve by regular habits and exercise the gift of a generous appetite; that I will not work immoderately, sit up late, practise vicious courses, or do anything that may tend to impair the regular recurrence of a healthy and vigorous hunger.'

Then followed a place for the signature and one for the witnesses.

'You see,' he went on, 'I ask for no unpleasant condition. I give you a free life, coupled with the simple condition of ordinary care. Do you agree?'

'I hardly know; it is so sudden.'

'Come, come' – he spoke with a harshness quite new – 'come, let us have no nonsense of that sort. Do you agree?'

I read it over again.

'Give me a little time,' I said. 'Let me reflect till tomorrow morning.'

'Reflect!' His face flushed purple, and his bloodshot eyes literally glared. 'Reflect! what the devil does the boy want to reflect about? Has he got a penny, a friend, or a chance in the whole world? I will give you five minutes – come.' He rose up and stood before me. As I looked in his face a curious dimness came over my eyes; he seemed to recede before me; he disappeared altogether. When I heard him speak again his voice sounded far, far off, but thin and clear, as if it came through some long tube. 'Luke Lucraft,' it said, 'see yourself.'

Yes; I saw myself, and though *outside* of what I saw, I felt the same emotions as if I had been the actual performer in the scenes I witnessed.

I was standing where the old gentleman met me,

starving still, and suffering pangs far worse than those under which I groaned at three o'clock. The day was advanced; the diners had all gone away, and the dining-room waiters were putting up the shutters. I spoke to one of them timidly. I told him I had eaten nothing since the morning, and begged for a plate of broken victuals. He looked in my face, called a brother-servant, and they kicked me from the door. People were rougher in London fifty years ago. Then I slunk away, and wandered somewhere among the winding streets and lanes of the old city. London at night was not so empty and deserted as it is now, and the streets had people in them. Some of them were well dressed – the wealthy merchants had not, even then, all left off living in the city; some were clerks going home; some were women out for an evening's walk. The bells rang out the hours from the city clocks, and I crept along the walls wondering what would become of me, and how I should find an end of my present misery.

Then I begged. Took off my hat and held it in my hand while I asked for something – anything – the smallest coin that would get a piece of bread.

The men passed me by with pitiless and unbelieving eyes. Heavens! if they had been hungry once, only once, in all their lives, they would never again have refused the petition of a beggar, even though he was the most lying mendicant who ever disgraced the words of charity which passed his lips. But they gave me nothing.

The women edged away from me and passed on

the other side if I timidly pressed my claim. They had nothing to fear from me. At last I asked a girl. She was more unfortunate than myself, but she was not hungry, and she gave me a shilling.

Then I found a shop open, and bought a plate of meat. That spent – I saw myself slinking, ashamed and wretched, again along the cold and empty street. When I could walk no more I found myself in Covent Garden Market, and threw myself under shelter of a roof at least, among the stalks and leaves and straw which littered the place.

I awoke early, and hungry again. I rose and resumed my miserable walk.

Hope by this time was dead within me; I could think of nothing but my intolerable hunger; could feel nothing but the pain which would not leave me; could look at nothing but food in the window.

I begged again, and begged all day without success.

It was a rougher time, that, than the present. More than one man laid his stick across my back with an impatient admonition to get to work, you lazy rogue. But I was too feeble to retaliate or remonstrate. Was there no charity in the world? I passed other beggars in the streets who looked fat and comfortable. People gave *them* money, but they would give me none. The time wore on, and my craving for food became irresistible.

I passed a shop which had a tray outside of baked potatoes. The owner had his back to me. I *stole* one. Yes, I stole one. No one saw me. He did not see me as I slunk past him with guilty face, and swiftly sped round the nearest corner to eat the stolen morsel.

What is the use of a single baked potato? Presently I returned to the same place with the intention of taking another. But they were all gone. I went on, looking for another provision shop. I came to a place where hot smoking sausages were bubbling in a pan over a charcoal fire. The shop stood at a corner. There was only a girl minding it. I deliberately walked in, took a sausage from the pan, hot as it was, and stepped out again before her astonishment even prompted her to cry out.

The time seemed intolerably long. All these scenes passed before me, not as the quick and steady flight of the rapidly falling moments, but as if the agony and the shame were deliberately lengthened out.

Then came a third time when I stole, maddened by the dream of hunger. This time I was detected, pursued, and apprehended. The misery and shame of the hour when I stood before the magistrate, in that horrible vision of a possible future, I cannot even yet forget. With this a constant sense of unsatisfied and craving hunger; a feeling as if hunger was the greatest evil in the whole world; a longing to get rid of it. Last scene of all, I was lying dead, starved to death with hunger and cold, in a miserable, bare, and naked garret.

By what black art did the old man delude my senses? It was a lie, and he knew it. I should have got some honest work, if only to wheel bricks or carry loads.

'There is your future, young man' – there came up

from the distance the voice of the tempter – 'a gloomy prospect: a miserable life: a wretched ending. Now look at the other side.'

The scene changed. I saw myself, but in another guise. My hunger had vanished; I felt it no more.

This time I was happy, light-hearted, and cheerful. I remembered scenes of misery through which I had just passed, and the recollection added more sweetness to my present enjoyment. It seemed as if I should never be hungry any more, and never feel the want of food. I was like a Greek god in my exemption from the common weakness of humanity. I was rich, too, and knew that I had the command, somehow, of all that money could buy.

I was sitting in a garden, and around me were troops of girls. I heard the rustle of their dresses, caught the laughter from their lips, watched the lustre of their eyes, saw the moonlight dance among their waving locks, as they ran and played among the trees and flowers. One of them sat by me and sang to a guitar –

> Life is made for love. Ah! why
>   Should its sweetness e'er be marred?
> List! the echoes will not die,
>   Still the sweet word 'love' to guard.
>
> Nought but love. Oh! Happy youth,
>   Free from need of baser thought,
> Stay with us, and learn this truth,
>   Set with song, with music wrought.

Thine is love, an endless feast;
   Beauty – sweeter far than wine;
Joy, from lower cares released –
   Never star rose bright as thine.

I knew, somehow or other, that this was allegorical, and, as if I expressed my thought, the scene changed, and I was in real life.

Chambers in London, such as I had read of, over-looking St James's Park. I sat in them in the midst of books and pictures. I had no business to call me away from my indolent ease; I had no anxiety about the future. I got up and strolled about the streets, looking at the shops. If I fancied a thing I bought it. I went to picture galleries and saw the latest works of art; I went to the theatre and saw the performance from a comfortable box; I went riding in the park.

Then my fancy returned to my first love, and I saw myself walking in a country lane with Juliet. She was sweeter to look upon than ever, and more delightful in her frank and innocent love for me. We rambled along under the hedges while I gathered flowers for her, and talked of the happy, happy days when we should be one, soon now to arrive, and of the sweet, loving life which should be ours far away from the troubles of the world.

Dreams, idle dreams; but sweet to me, after the agony of the last, as a draught of water to a parched traveller on Sahara.

The pictures changed as fast as my fancy wandered from one thing to another. In all I was the same – free

from the downward and earthly pressure of want and
hunger, relieved from anxiety, with plenty of money,
and full of all sweet and innocent fancies.

Lies again. But by what power could this necromancer
so cheat and gull my brain?

'Very different scenes these, my dear young friend,'
he said in a winning voice, 'are they not? Now,' he
went on, and his voice was quite close to me, 'you
have had your five minutes.'

The cloud passed from my eyes. I was sitting again
in the octagonal room, the old man before me, watch
in hand, as if he was counting the seconds.

'Five minutes and a quarter,' he growled. 'Now
choose.'

'I have chosen,' I replied. 'I accept your offer.'

The influence of the things I had seen was too strong
upon me. I could neither reason nor reflect.

'I accept your offer.'

'Why, that's brave,' he said, with a gigantic sigh of
relief. 'That's what I expected of you. Boule-de-neige
– Boule-de-neige!'

He clapped his hands.

Instantly the horrible old negro appeared behind
his master's chair, as if he had sprung up from the
ground. I believe he had. He looked more like a devil
than ever, grinning from ear to ear, and his two eyes
glowing in the candlelight like two great coals. The
light fell, too, upon the seams and wrinkles of his face,
bringing them out like the hills and valleys in a raised
map. Strange as it all was to me, this ancient servitor
produced the strangest effect upon me of anything.

'Boule-de-neige is witness for us,' said the old gentleman. 'Boule-de-neige, this young gentleman, Mr Luke Lucraft, is about to sign a little deed, to which, as a matter of form, we require your signature too as witness.'

'Cluck!' said the negro. 'Dis young gegleman berry lucky – him berry lucky. What time massa take him dinner?'

'When do you think you shall be fairly hungry again?' he asked me. 'Now, no boastings – no false pretence and pride – because it will be the worse for you. Answer truthfully. It is now six.'

'I should say that at nine I should be able to take some supper, and at ten I shall certainly be hungry again. As an ordinary rule I should be ready a great deal earlier, but I have taken such an immense dinner.'

'Good.' He turned to Boule-de-neige. 'You see the young man is modest and promises fairly. I shall have supper – a plentiful supper – at ten punctually. Mr Lucraft will now sign.'

I advanced to the table and took up the pen, but there was no ink.

'Cluck!' said the infernal negro, with another grin – 'cluck! Massa wait lilly bit.'

He took my left hand in his soft and cold paw. I felt a sharp prick at my wrist.

'You will dip the pen,' said the old gentleman, 'in the blood. It is a mere form.'

'Cluck!' said Boule-de-neige.

'A mere form because we have no ink handy.'

'Cluck-cluck!'

I signed my name as desired, and, following the directions of the old gentleman, placed my finger on the red wafer at the margin, saying, 'I declare this my act and deed.'

Then I gave the pen to Boule-de-neige. He signed after me, in a firm flowing hand, 'Boule-de-neige.' As I looked, the letters seemed somehow to shape themselves into 'Beezlebub.' I looked at him with a kind of terror. The creature grinned in my face as if he divined my thought, and gave utterance to one of his hideous 'clucks'.

Then I began to feel the same faintness which I had at first experienced. It mounted upwards from my feet slowly, so that I heard the old gentleman's voice, though I saw nothing. It grew gradually fainter.

'Supper at ten, Boule-de-neige,' he was saying; 'I feel getting hungry already. What shall I do with myself till ten o'clock? I am certainly getting hungry. I think I can have it served at half-past nine. Oh, blessed day! Oh, thankful, blessed day! Boule-de-neige, it must be supper for three – for four – for five. I shall have champagne – the Perrier Jouet – the curaçoa punch afterwards. Curaçoa punch – I haven't tasted it for three months and more. Oh, what a blessed – blessed – blessed – '

I heard no more because my senses failed me altogether, and his voice died away in my ears.

When I came to myself I was leaning against the post in Bucklersbury, where I had met the old man.

A whiff of stale cooked meat from the cook-shop,

which caught me as I opened my eyes, produced a singular feeling of disgust. 'Pah,' I muttered, 'roast mutton!' and moved from the spot. My hunger was gone, that was quite certain. I felt a quietness about those regions, wherever they may be, which belong to appetite. I was almost dreamy in the repose which followed a morning so stormy. I walked quietly away homewards in a kind of daze, trying to make out something of what had happened. The first thing I found I could not remember was the name of the old gentleman. When that came back to me and under what circumstances I will tell you as we get along. Bit by bit I recalled the whole events of the afternoon, one after the other. I saw the old man, with his purple face and bloodshot eyes and white hair; I saw the wrinkled and seamed old negro; I saw the octagonal room without doors or windows; the splendid dinner; the host watching my every gesture; I remembered everything except the name of the man to whom I had sold – my appetite.

It was so strange that I laughed when I thought of it. I must have been drunk; he gave me a good dinner and I took too much wine; but, then, how was it that I remembered clearly every, even the smallest, detail?

On the bed in the one room which constituted my lodging I found a letter. It was from a firm of lawyers, dated that evening at half-past six – only half an hour after I signed the paper – stating that they were empowered by a client, whose name was not mentioned, to give me the sum of £30 monthly, to begin from that day, and to be paid to me personally.

How did they get their instructions then? And it was all true!

I was too tired with the day's adventures to think any more; and, though it was only nine o'clock, I went to bed and fell fast asleep. In an hour I awoke again, with a choking sensation, as if I was eating too much. I knew instantly what was going on, and by a kind of prophetic insight. The old man was taking his supper, and taking more than was good – *for me*. I sprang from the bed, gasping for breath. Presently, as I gathered, he began to drink too much as well. My brain went round and round. I laughed, sang, and danced; and soon after, with a heavy fall, I rolled senseless on the carpet, and remembered nothing more.

It was early in the morning when I awoke, still lying on the floor. I had a splitting headache. I had fallen against some corner of the furniture and blackened one eye. I had broken two chairs somehow or other. I was cold, ill, and shaken. I got into bed, and tried to remember what had happened. Clearly I must have made a drunken beast of myself over the dinner, and reeled home with my head full of fancies and dreams; perhaps the dinner itself was a dream and a hallucination too; if so, the pangs of hunger would soon recommence. But they did not. Then I fell asleep, and did not awake again till the clock struck twelve. How ill and wretched I felt as I dressed! My hand shook, my eyes were red, my face swollen. Surely I must have been intoxicated. I had been, up to that day at least, a temperate man, partly, no doubt, from the very wholesome reason which keeps so many of us sober – the necessity of poverty; but of course I had not arrived at four and twenty years and seen so much of the world without recognising the signs of too much drink. I had them, every one; and, as most men know too well, they are all summed up in the simple expression, 'hot coppers'. Alas! I was destined to become only too familiar with the accursed symptoms. Involuntarily, when I had dressed myself, I put my hands in my pockets, those pockets so often empty; there was money, gold – sovereigns – my pocket was full of them. I counted them in a stupor. Forty-nine, and one rolled into the corner – fifty; it was part of the sum for which I had sold my appetite; and on the table lay the letter from Messrs Crackett and Charges, inviting me to draw thirty pounds a month.

Then it was all true!

I sat down, and, with my throbbing temples and feverish pulse, tried to make it out. Everything became plain except the name of the purchaser – Mr – Mr – I remembered Boule-de-neige, the house, the room, and the dinner, but not the name of that arch-deceiver, the whole of whose villainy I was far from realising yet; and until it was told me later on I never did remember the name.

It was strange. Men are said to have sold their souls to the devil for money, bartering away an eternity of happiness for a few years of pleasure; but as for me, I had exchanged, as it seemed at first sight, nothing but the inconvenience of a healthy appetite with nothing to eat for the means of living comfortably without it.

There could be no sin in such a transaction; it was on a different level altogether from the bargain made by Faust. And there were the broad, the benevolent facts, so to speak – my pocket full of sovereigns; and the letter instructing me to call at an office for thirty pounds monthly.

Benevolent facts I thought them. You shall see. You think, as I thought, that no sin could be laid to my door for the transaction. You shall judge. You think, as I thought, that no harm could follow so simple a piece of business. You shall read. On my way out I met the landlady, who gave me notice to quit at the end of the week.

'I thought you were a quiet and a sober young man,' she said. 'Ah, never will I trust to good looks again. Me and the lodgers kept awake till two in the morning with your singing and dancing, let alone banging the floor with the chair. Not another hour after your week's up, if you was to pray on your knees, shall you stay. And next door threatening the constables; and me a quiet woman for twenty years.'

My heart sank again. But, after all, perhaps it was I myself, not the good old gentleman, my kind patron and benefactor, at all, who was the cause of this disturbance. It was undoubtedly true that I had taken a great quantity of wine with my splendid dinner. I begged her pardon humbly, and passed out.

It was now nearly one o'clock, but I felt no desire for breakfast. That was an experience quite novel to me. Still, I went to a coffee-house, according to habit, and ordered some tea and a rasher. When they came I discovered, with a horrid foreboding of worse misfortune behind, that my taste was gone. Except that one thing was solid and the other liquid, I distinguished nothing. Nor did my sense of smell assist me: as I found later, my nose was affected agreeably or disagreeably, but it lost all its discriminating and critical powers. Gunpowder, sulphuretted hydrogen gas, and tobacco offended my nose. So did certain smells belonging to cookery. On the other hand, certain flowers, tea, and claret pleased me, but I was unable to distinguish between them. Not only could I not taste them, but I had no gratification in eating them. I ate and drank mechanically, because I knew that the body must be kept going on something.

All this knowledge, however, and more, came by degrees. After making a forced breakfast I bent my steps to the lawyers', who had an office in Lincoln's Inn Fields.

The letter was received by a conceited young clerk in shiny black habiliments, a turned up nose, and a self-satisfied manner.

'Ha!' he said, 'I thought you would soon come round to us after the letter. Sign that. You haven't been long. None of them are.'

It was a receipt; and I was on the point of asking if it was to be signed in blood, when he settled the question by giving me the ink.

'There, Luke Lucraft, across the eightpenny stamp. I'm not allowed to answer any questions you may put, Mr Lucraft, nor to ask you any; so take your money, and good morning to you. I suppose, like

the rest of them, you don't know the name of
your benefactor, and would like to – yes; but you
needn't ask *me*; and I've orders not to admit you
to see either Mr Charges or Mr Crackett. They'd
trouble enough with the last but one. He broke into
their office once, drunk, and laid about him with
the ruler.'

I burst into a cold dew of terror.

'However, Mr Lucraft, I hope you will be more
fortunate than your predecessors.'

'Where are they? Who are they?'

'I do not know where they are, not for a certainty,'
he replied with a grin. 'But we may guess. Dead
and buried they are, all of them. Gone to kingdom
come; all died of the same thing, too – DT. Delicious
Trimmings killed them. Poor old gentleman! He's
too good for this world, as everybody knows, and
the more he's taken in the more he's deceived.
Anyhow, he's very unlucky in his pensioners. He
did say when the last went off that he would have
no more; he wept over it, and declared that his
bounty was always abused; but there never was such
a benevolent old chap. I only wish he'd take a fancy
to me.'

'What did you say is his name, by the way?'

The clerk looked at me with a cunning wink.

'If you don't know, I am sure I do not,' he said.
'Here is the cheque, Mr Lucraft, and I hope you will
continue to come here and draw it a good deal longer
than the other chaps. But there's a blight on all the
pensioners. Lord, what a healthy chap Tom Kirby

– he was a Monmouth man – looked when he first came for his cheques! As strong as a bull and as fresh as a lark.'

'A good appetite had he?'

'No; couldn't eat anything after a bit; said he fancied nothing. Lost his taste entirely. He pined away and died in a galloping consumption before the third month was due. Nobody ever saw him drinking, but he was drunk every night, regular, like the rest. Perhaps it's only coincidence. Better luck to *you*, Mr Lucraft.'

This conversation did not reassure me, and I determined to go over to Bucklersbury at once and see my patron. I found the post against which I was leaning when he accosted me; there was no doubt about that, for the hares and cauliflowers were still in the shop-window, only they looked disgusting to me this morning. I found the street into which he had led me, and then – then – it was the most extraordinary thing, I could not find the door by which we entered. Not only was there no door, but there seemed no place where such a door as I remembered could exist in this little narrow winding street. I went up and down twice. I looked at all the windows. I asked a policeman if he had ever seen an old gentleman about the street such as I described, or such a negro as Boule-de-neige; but he could give no information. Only as I prowled slowly along the pavement I heard distinctly – it gave me a nervous shock that I could not account for – the infernal 'Cluck-cluck!' of the negro with the cold soft hands, the wrinkled skin, and the fiery red eyes. He was chuckling at me from some hiding-place of his own, where he was safe. He had done me no harm that I knew of, but I hated him at that moment.

I was by this time not at all elated at my good fortune. I even craved to have back again what I had sold. I felt heavy at heart, and had a presentiment of fresh trouble before me. I thought of the fate of those unknown and unfortunate predecessors, all dead in consequence of drink, evil courses, and DT. Heavens! was I too to die miserably with delirium tremens, after I had sold my taste, and could only tell brandy from water, like the cask which might hold either, by the smell?

At half-past one – the luncheon time for all who have appetites – the sense of being gorged came upon me again, but this time without the giddiness. I went to a tavern in the Strand and fell sound asleep. When I awoke at six the oppression had passed away. And now I began to realise something of the consequences of my act. I say something, because worse, far worse, remained behind. I was doomed, I saw clearly, to be the victim of the old man's gluttony. He would eat and I should suffer. Already, as I guessed from the clerk's statements, he had killed four strong men before me. I was to be the fifth. I went again to Bucklersbury, and sought in every house for something that might give me a clue. I loitered in the quiet city streets in the hope of finding my tormentor, and forcing him to give me back my bond. There was no clue, and I did not meet him. But I felt him. He began dinner, as nearly as I could feel, about seven o'clock; he took his meal with deliberation, judging from the gradual nature of my sensations; but he took an amazing quantity, and by eight o'clock the weight upon me was so great that I could scarcely breathe. How I cursed my folly! How I impotently writhed under the burden I had wantonly laid upon myself! And then he began to drink. The fiend, the scoundrel! I felt the fumes mount to my head; there was no exhilaration, no forgetfulness of misery; none of the pleasant gradations of excitement, hope, and confidence, through which men are accustomed to pass before arriving at the final stage, the complete oblivion, of intoxication. I felt myself getting gradually but hopelessly drunk. I struggled against the feeling, but in vain; the houses went round and round with me: my speech, when I tried to speak, became thick; the flags of the pavement flew up and struck me violently on the forehead, and I became unconscious of what happened afterwards.

*   *   *

In the morning I found myself lying on a stone bench in a small whitewashed room. My brows were throbbing and my throat was parched, and in my brain was ringing, I do not know why, the infernal 'Cluck-cluck!' of the negro with derisive iteration. I had not long to meditate; the door opened, and a constable appeared.

'Now then,' he said, roughly, 'if you can stand upright by this time, come along.'

It was clear enough to me now what had happened:

I was in custody, in a police-cell, and I was going before the magistrate.

I dream of that ignominy still, though forty years have passed since I was placed in the dock and asked what I had to say for myself. 'Drunk and disorderly.'

I was charged by the constable – there were no police in 1823 – with being drunk and disorderly. Twenty other poor wretches were waiting their trial for the same offence; one or two for graver charges. My case came first, and had the honour of being reported in the papers. Here is the extract cut out of the *Morning Chronicle*:

A young man, who gave his name as Henry Luke, and said he was an actor by profession, was charged with being drunk and disorderly in the streets. The constable found him at ten o'clock lying on the pavement of Bucklersbury, too drunk even to speak, and quite unable therefore to give any account of himself. A cheque, signed by the well-known firm of Crackett and Charges, for £30 was found on his person. The magistrate remarked that this was a suspicious circumstance, and decided to remand the case till these gentlemen could be communicated with. One of the partners appeared at twelve, and deposed that the prisoner's real name was Luke Lucraft, that he had been an actor, and that the cheque had been given him by the firm, acting for a client who wished to be anonymous, but whose motive was pure benevolence.

The magistrate, on hearing the facts of the case, addressed the prisoner with a suitable admonition. He bade him remember that such an abuse of a good man's charity, as he had been guilty of, was the worst form of ingratitude. It appeared that on the very day of receiving a gift, which was evidently intended to advance him in life, or to find him the means of procuring suitable employment, the prisoner deliberately made himself so hopelessly drunk that he could neither speak nor stand – where, it did not appear. The magistrate could not but feel that this conduct showed the gravest want of moral principle, and he strongly advised Mr Crackett to cancel the cheque till further orders. As, however, it was a first offence, and in consideration of the prisoner's youth, the fine inflicted would be a small one of ten shillings, with costs.

That was the newspaper account of the affair. On his way out of the court, Mr Crackett stopped me.

'Young man,' he said, shaking his head, 'this is very dreadful. I warned my benevolent client against this act of generosity. You are the fifth young man whom he has assisted in this magnificent manner. The former, all four, took to drink, and died in a disgraceful manner. Take warning, and stop while it is yet time.'

I got away as fast as I could, and crept back to my lodging after the necessary miserable breakfast.

I am not ashamed to say that I sat down and cried. The tears *would* crowd into my eyes. It was too dreadful. Here I was, only twenty-four years of age, with my life before me, doomed, through my own folly, to a miserable ending and a disgraceful reputation. What good would come of having money under these dreadful conditions? Money, indeed! What had become of the fifty pounds given me only two days before? Gone. All gone but one single sovereign which served to pay my fine. Some one had robbed me. Perhaps the constables. Perhaps a street thief. It was gone. The sorry reward of my consent to the unholy bargain was clean swept away, and only the consequences of the contract remained.

In the afternoon, as I hastened home along the darkening streets, hoping to reach my lodging before the daily gorge began, a curious thing happened to me. On the other side of the street, in a dark corner, standing upright, and pointing to me with a finger of derision, I saw Boule-de-neige, the negro servant. I rushed at him, blind with rage. When I got to the spot I found nobody there. Was it a trick of a disordered brain? I had seen him, quite plainly, grinning at me with his wrinkled features. As I turned from the place I heard his familiar 'Cluck-cluck'.

Twice more on the way this strange phantom appeared to me; each time accompanied by the 'cluck' of his voice. It was a phantom with which I was to become familiar indeed, before I had finished with Boule-de-neige and his master.

It was clear that the demon to whom I had sold myself was incapable of the slightest consideration towards me. He would eat and drink as much as he felt disposed to do, careless of any consequences that might befall me. It was equally evident that he intended to make the most of his bargain, to eat enormously every day, and to drink himself drunk every night. And I was powerless. Meantime it was becoming evident that the consequences to me would be as serious as if I were myself guilty of these excesses. One drop of comfort alone remained: my appetite would fail, and my tormentor would be punished where he would feel it most. I lay down and waited till luncheon time; no sense of repletion came over me; it was certain, therefore, that he was already suffering a vicarious punishment, so to speak, for yesterday's debauch.

The next day, however, I really did meet my negro.

It was about five in the afternoon – the time when I was tolerably safe, because my owner, who took a plentiful luncheon at one, did not begin his nightly orgy much before seven. I was loitering about Bucklersbury, my favourite place of resort, in the hope of meeting the old man, when my arm was touched as I turned round. It *was* the negro. 'Massa Lucraft,' he said, 'you come along o' me. Massa him berry glad to see you.'

I declare that although the moment before I had been picturing such an encounter, although I had imagined myself with my fingers at his throat, dragging him off, and forcing him to tell me who and what he was, I felt myself unable to speak.

'Come along o' me, Massa Lucraft,' he said; 'this way – way you know berry well. Ho, ho! – Cluck.'

He stopped before the door I remembered, but had never been able to find, opened it with a little key, and led the way to the octagonal room.

There was no one in it, but the table was already laid for dinner.

'Massa come bymeby. You wait, young gegleman.'

Then he disappeared somehow.

As before, I could see no door. As before, the first

sensation which came over me was of giddiness, from which I recovered immediately. I walked round and round the room looking at the heavy furniture, the pictures, which were all of fruit and game, and the silver plate. Everything showed the presence of great wealth, and, I supposed, though I knew nothing about it, great taste. I was kept waiting for nearly two hours. That I did not mind, because every moment brought me, I thought, nearer to the hour of my deliverance. I was certain that I had only to put the case to Mr Grumbelow – I remembered his name the moment I was back in that room – to appeal to his generosity, his honour, his pity, in order to obtain my release. Mr Grumbelow – Ebenezer Grumbelow – he was the charitable client of Messrs Crackett & Charges, was he? Why, I might show him up to popular derision and hatred. I might tell the world who and what this great benefactor of young men really was.

Suddenly, as the clock struck seven, he stood upon the carpet before me, while Boule-de-neige stood at the table with a soup tureen in his hand. I declare that I did not see at any time anyone enter the room or go out of it. They appeared to be suddenly in it.

I do hope that the appearance of small details like the above, at first incredible, will not be taken as proof of want of veracity on my own part. I wish that I could tell the tale without these particulars, but I cannot. I must relate the whole or none.

'You here?' said Mr Grumbelow, looking at me with an air of contempt. He seated himself at the table and unfolded his napkin. 'Soup, Boule-de-neige.'

'Massa hungry? Dat young debbel there he look berry pale already.'

'Pretty well, Boule-de-neige, considering. You, sir, come here, and let me look at you.' I obeyed. 'Hold out your hand. It shakes. Let me look at your eyes. They are yellow. Do you know that your appetite seems to me to be failing already – already – and it is only the fourth day.'

'It is not my fault,' I said.

'Nonsense. Don't talk to me, sir, because I will have none of your insolence. I say that you do not walk enough. I order you to walk twelve miles a day – do you hear?'

'It is not in the contract,' I replied, doggedly.

'It *is* in the contract. You are to use every means in your power to keep your faculties in vigour. What means have you used?'

He banged the spoon on the table and glanced at me so fiercely that I had nothing to say.

'Massa, soup get cold,' said Boule-de-neige.

He gobbled it up, every now and then looking up at me with an angry grunt.

'Now then, you and your contract. This is pretty ingratitude, this is. Here's a fellow, Boule-de-neige, I pick up out of the gutter, starving; whom I keep expensively; whom I endow with an income; whom I deprive of the temptation to gluttony.'

'Nebber see such a debbel in all my days,' said the negro; 'nebber hear such a ting told nowhere.'

'No nor ever will. Listen to me, sir. You will walk ten, twelve, or twenty miles a day, according to the dinner I have had. And, mark you, it will be the worse for you if you do not. Remember, if I cannot eat I can drink.'

There was a fiendish glare in his blood-stained eyes as he spoke, and I trembled. My spirit was so completely gone that I had not even the pluck to appeal to his pity. Perhaps a secret consciousness of the uselessness of such an appeal deterred me.

'You will now,' he said, 'watch me making as large a dinner as your miserably languid appetite will allow.'

'I have been drunk for four nights,' I pleaded.

'Then you have no business to get drunk so easily. Your head is contemptibly weak – what did I take yesterday, Boule-de-neige.'

'Big bottle champagne, big bottle port, eight goes whisky grog.'

'I did – and that was all. Why your predecessor stood double the quantity.'

'Beg pardon, massa. Last young gegleman poor trash – last but two – him mighty strong head – head like bull – nebber get drunk.'

'Ah, we wasted him, Boule-de-neige; we fooled him away in one imprudent evening. I told you at the time that noyeau punch is a very dangerous thing.'

'Ho, ho!' the diabolical negro laughed till his teeth showed like the grinning jaws of a death's head. 'Ho, ho! him so blind drunk he tumble out of window – break him neck. Ho, ho!'

This was a pleasant conversation for me to hear.

Then Mr Grumbelow resumed his dinner.

He ate a good deal in spite of his grumbling, and then he began to drink port. I observed that the wine had a peculiar effect upon him. It made him redder in the face, but not thicker in speech. He drank two bottles, talking to me all the time. I began to get drunk, he only got the more merrily fiendish.

'This is really delightful,' he said, as I reeled and caught at a chair for support. 'I wonder I never thought of this before. It is quite a new pleasure to watch the effects of my own drink on another man's brain, I shall write a book about you. I shall call it "The Young Christian deterred, or Leaves from Luke Lucraft's Wicked Life." Ho, ha! ha, ho! I saw the account in the *Morning Post*. Heigh, heigh!' – he nearly choked as he recalled the circumstance. 'The magistrate admonishing the wicked drunkard. Ho, ho! It is like a farce. Stand up, sir, stand up. He can't stand up. Can you sing? Can you dance? He could not even dance a hornpipe. Do you feel a little thickness in your speech? Would you be able to explain to the worthy magistrate the circumstances, quite beyond your own control, which brought you into that painful position in which you stood? It is the best situation that ever was put upon any stage. There's nothing like it in fiction. Nothing. Walter Scott never invented anything half so rich. Ho, ho, ho! he is really getting drunk already. What a poor creature it is!'

He paused for a moment and then went on.

'Boule-de-neige, coffee; brandy in it – plenty of brandy, and a glass of curaçoa afterwards. A large glass, sir! I'll have a night of it. Your health, Luke

Lucraft, in this coffee; and you had better take care
of it, or I'll pack you off with noyeau punch. Pleasant
times you are having, eh? Might have been worse, you
know. You might have been starving. What? Don't fall
against the table in that way. Take care of the furniture.
It cost a great deal more money than you are worth.
So, sit down on the floor while I tell you about your
predecessors, dead and gone, poor fellows.

'Let me see. The first was William Saunders, a poor
devil of a clerk of mine. He disgraced himself in chapel
one week-day prayer-meeting, the very evening of his
signature; then he ran away, but Boule-de-neige found
him out, and brought him back. He took to praying
and crying. One day he died in St Bartholomew's
Hospital of delirium tremens. He lasted about six
months.

'The next was Hans Hansen, a Dane. He only lasted
about three weeks, because he became melancholy
directly he found he could no longer taste brandy. I
was disappointed with Hansen, and when he jumped
off London Bridge into the Thames one night, his
appetite having quite gone, I was really very sorry on
account of the temporary inconvenience it put me to;
and I determined to be very careful in his successor. I
remember I had a good deal of trouble to find one.

'However, at last I got a third man, a stout
Cumberland chap, son of a statesman. You poor,
puny little strolling actor, I suppose that you will
hardly believe that I once took four and twenty tumblers of Scotch whisky and water without affecting that
brave fellow's appetite one bit. He used to take it out in

swearing; and really he was almost too often in trouble with the magistrates. He never clearly understood that his safety lay in being home early in the evening. Once he nearly killed Mr Crackett in his own office. Poor Crackett! that eminent Christian lawyer; I should never have forgiven myself had anything happened to the worthy Crackett. Well! he went too; at least, after a good tough twelvemonth. It was my own fault, and I ought not to grumble. That noyeau punch was strong enough to kill the devil.'

'Cluck,' said Boule-de-neige.

'Then we came to Tom Kirby. None of them looked so well or promised so much; none broke down so easily. A whining fellow too; a crying, sobbing, appealing rogue, who wanted to get off his bargain. However, *de mortuis* – Your health, Luke Lucraft. Hallo! hold up.

'I tell you what I mean to do after you are worked off, Luke Lucraft. I mean to have a brace of fellows. I shall go down to the London docks, or else to the railway stations, and find a couple of trusty young porters. They are the sort of men to have. Fine, strong, well-set-up rascals. Men with muscles like rigging ropes – don't clutch at the chair, Lucraft – if you can't sit up you may lie down – I shall make them come here – give them a blow out of steak – I wasted a splendid dinner on you – and then I shall make them sign.

'The great thing, then, will be to have the appetites of two men; twice as much to eat and twice as much to drink. I never thought of that before.

'And then to bring both the rogues up here of an evening and make them wait and see me eat; watch them gradually lolling and reeling about till they tumble over each other; go secretly and hear them curse me – me, their benefactor – Ho! ho! I think I shall not be long over you, Luke Lucraft. Hallo! keep your drunken legs away from the table. Boule-de-neige, roll this intoxicated log into the street.'

* * *

When I came to my senses it was of course the next morning, and I was lying in my own bedroom, whither I had been carried by two strange men, the landlady afterwards told me, who said they were paid for the job. I had a splitting headache. I was sick and giddy; my limbs trembled beneath me when I tried to stand; my hands shook. I looked at myself in the glass. Swollen features and bloodshot eyes greeted me.

Less than a week had wrought this ruin.

The ordinary drunkard refreshes himself in the morning with tea. Nothing refreshed me, because I could taste nothing, and because my sufferings sprang from a different source, though they were the same in kind. I had to bear them as best I might.

I remembered the command which Mr – Mr – strange, I had forgotten his name again – gave me, to walk twenty miles after a 'heavy night'. I started to obey him.

Outside London, beyond Islington, where there are

now rows of houses, but were then fields, I saw a little modest cottage, standing alone in its garden. It was a cottage with four rooms only, covered over with creepers. On the board, standing at the gate, was an announcement that it was to let. A thought struck me: Here could be seclusion, at any rate. Here I could shut myself up every night, and await in comparative safety the dreadful punishment – fast becoming heavier than I could hear – which my tormenter inflicted upon me. Why should I not take the cottage, pay the rent in advance every month – for how many months should I have to pay it? – and so wait in patience and resignation the approach of my inevitable fate?

I made inquiries at once, and secured the place at a merely nominal rent. Then I moved in a little furniture, bought second hand in Islington High Street, and became the occupant, a lonely hermit, of the house. There were no houses within hearing, in case I should storm and rage in my drunken madness at night. The cottage stood removed from the road, and no callers were likely to trouble me. Within those walls I should be secure from some dangers at least. Here, night after night, I could await the attacks of surfeit and intoxication which regularly came; for my master knew no pity.

On the first evening I sat down at half-past six to prepare for what was coming. The day was drawing in, and a cold twilight – the month was March – covered the trees and shrubs in my little garden, as I opened the door and looked out.

Before me stood the negro.

My spirit was quite broken, and I could only groan.

'Do you want me to go with you again?' I asked, thinking of the last entertainment at which I provided amusement for his master.

'Massa say him berry glad you come hyar. You walk the twenty mile ebbery day, else massa know the reason why. How you feel, Massa Lucraft? Heigh! heigh! cluck. Dat most fortunate day for you when you sign dat little paper.'

He delivered his message and disappeared in the darkness. I heard his footsteps crunching the gravel in the road, and I longed, only now I had no courage or spirit left, to seize him and tear him limb from limb.

Then I shut myself in, lit one candle, and sat over the fire. I thought of the scenes by which my extravagant fancy had been excited; the garden full of lively girls – what were girls to me now? The country walks I was to have with Juliet – where was my passion for Juliet now? The ease and happiness, the lightness and innocence, of the life before me, drawn by an arch-deceiver, compared with my present, my actual misery, sitting alone, cut off from mankind, the slave and victim of a secret profligate and glutton, doomed to die slowly, unless it should please the murderer to kill me off quickly.

And then, because the first symptoms of the attack were coming on, I went to bed and stayed there.

So began my new life. A wretched life it was. There was no occupation possible for me – no amusement. I walked every day, in fair weather or foul, a measured twenty miles.

This in some degree restored vitality to my system. I never read; I took no interest in any politics. I sat by myself, and brooded.

As for my meals, I bought them ready prepared. They consisted almost wholly of bread and cold mutton. You may judge of the absolutely tasteless condition to which I was reduced, when I write calmly and truthfully that cold boiled mutton was as agreeable to me as any other form of food. I found, after repeated trials, that mutton forms the best fuel – it is better than either beef or pork – and keeps the human engine at work for the longest time. So I had mutton. As I discovered also that bulk was necessary, and that only a certain amount of animal food was wanted, I used to have cold potatoes always ready. I stoked twice a day, at eleven in the morning and about five in the afternoon. Thus fortified, I got through the miserable hours as best I could.

I look back on that period as one of unmitigated misery and despair. I was daily growing more bloated, fatter, and flabbier in the cheeks. My hands trembled in the morning. I seemed losing the power of connected thought. My very lips were thickening.

I hope I am making it clear what was the effect of my bargain on myself – I mean without reference to the sufferings inflicted on me by my tyrant. People, however, never can know, unless they happen to be like myself, which is unlikely, how great a part eating and drinking take in the conduct of life. Between the rest of the world and me there was a great gulf fixed. They could enjoy, I could not; they could celebrate every joyful event with something additional to eat; they could make a little festival of every day; they could give to happiness an outward and tangible form. Alas, not only was I debarred from this, but I was cut off even from joy itself; for, if you look at it steadily, you will find that most of human joy or suffering is connected with the senses. I had bartered away a good half of mine, and the rest seemed in mourning for the loss of their fellows. As for my pale and colourless life, it was as monotonous as the clock. If I neglected to stoke, the usual feebleness would follow. There was no gracious looking forward to a pleasant dinner; no trembling anticipations in hope and fear of what might be preparing; no cheerful contemplation of the joint while the carver sharpens his knife; no discussions of flavour and richness; no modestly hazarded conclusions as to more currants; no rolling of the wine-glass in the fingers to the light, and smacking of lips over the first sip – all these things were lost to me. Reader, if haply this memoir ever sees a posthumous light, think what would happen to yourself if eating and drinking, those perennial joys of humanity, which last from the infantine pap to the senile Revalenta Arabica, were taken away.

All things tasted alike, as I have said, and cold mutton formed my staple dish. As I could only distinguish between beer, wine, coffee, and tea by the look, I drank water. If I ventured, which was seldom, to take my dinner at a cookshop, I would choose my *pièce de résistance* by the look, by some fancied grace in the shape, but not by taste or smell. The brown of roast beef might attract me one day and repel me the next. I was pleased with the comeliness of a game-pie, or tickled by some inexplicable external charm of a beefsteak-pudding. But three quarters of my life were gone, and with them all my happiness.

If you have no appetite for eating, you can enjoy nothing in the whole world. That is an axiom. I could not taste, therefore my eye ceased to feel delight in pleasant sights, and my ear in pleasant sounds. It was not with me as in the case of a blind man, that an abnormal development of some other sense ensued; quite the contrary. In selling one, I seem to have sold them all. For, as I discovered, man is one and inseparable; you cannot split him up; and when my arch-deceiver bought my appetite, he bought me out and out. A wine merchant might as well pretend to sell the bouquet of claret and preserve the body; or a painter the colour of his picture and preserve the drawing; or a sculptor the grace of his group and keep the marble.

As regards other losses, I found I had lost the perception of beauty in form or colour. Why this was so I cannot explain. I was no longer, I suppose, in harmony with other men on any single point. Pretty women passed me unheeded; pictures had no charm for me; music was only irritating to my nerves.

Then I found that I had lost the power of sympathy. I had formerly been a soft-hearted man. I remarked now that the sight of suffering found me entirely callous.

There was a poor family living about half a mile from
me, whose acquaintance I made through buying some
of my supplies of them. They were in distress for rent;
they applied to me . . . there, I cannot bear to think of
it. I had the money and I refused them. They were sold
up, and I sat at my door and watched them on their
way to London – the mother, the two girls, the little
boy, had in hand, homeless and penniless, without
a pang and without a single prompting of the heart
to help them. God knows what became of them. May
He forgive me for the hard-hearted cruelty with which
I regarded their fate.

Had I, then, sold everything to this man?

I had been pretty religious in a way – a young man's
way. Now I had lost all religious feeling whatever. I
had once ambition and hopes, these were gone; I had
once the capacity of love, that was gone; I had once
a generous heart, that was gone; I once loved things
worth loving, I felt no emotion now for anything. I
was a machine which could feel. I was a man with the
humanity taken out of him.

This time lasted for about four months. On the first
of each month I went to receive my pay – the wages of
sin – from the clerk, who surveyed me critically, but
said nothing till the morning of the fourth month.
Then, while he handed me my money, he whispered
confidentially across the table:

'Look here, old fellow, you know; you're going it
worse than poor Tom Kirby. Why don't you stop it?
What *is* the good of a feller's drinking himself to death?
The old gentleman was here yesterday, asking me how

you looked, and if you continued steady. Pull up, old man, and knock it off.'

I took the money in my trembling hands and slunk away abashed. When I got home again, I am not ashamed to say that I cried like a child.

Delirium tremens! That would begin soon, and then the end would not be far off. It was too awful. Think of my position. I was but four-and-twenty. Not only was I deprived of the pleasure – mind you, a very real pleasure – of eating and drinking; I was the most temperate man in the world, though that was no great credit to myself, considering; and yet I bore in my face and my appearance, and felt in my very brain, all the marks and signs of confirmed drunkenness and the hopelessness of it. That hardened old voluptuary, that demon of gluttony, that secret murderer, would have no pity. He must have felt, by the falling-off of the splendid appetite which he was doing his utmost to ruin, that things were getting worse, and he was resolved – I had suspected this for some time – to kill me off by drinking me to death.

I believe I should have been dead in another week, but for a blessed respite, due, I afterwards discovered, to my demon being laid up with so violent a sore throat that he could not even swallow. What was my joy at being able to go to bed sober, to wake without a head-ache, to feel my bad symptoms slowly disappearing, to recover my nerves! For a whole fortnight I was happy – so happy that I even believed the improvement would last and that the old man was penitent. One day, after fourteen days of a veritable earthly paradise, I was walking along the Strand – for I was no longer afraid of venturing out – and met my old manager, Juliet's father. He greeted me with a warmth that was quite touching under all the circumstances. 'My dear boy, I have been longing to know your whereabouts. Come and tell me all about it. Have you dined? Let us have some dinner together.'

I excused myself, and asked after Juliet.

'Juliet is but so-so. Ah, do you know, Lucraft, sometimes I think that I did wrong to part you. And yet, you know, you had no money. Make some, my boy, and come back to us.'

This was hearty. I forgot my troubles and my state of bondage and everything, except Juliet.

'I – I – I have money,' I said. 'I have come into a little money unexpectedly.'

'Have you?' he replied, clasping me by the hand. 'Then come down and see Juliet. Or – stay; no. The day after tomorrow is Juliet's ben. We are playing at Richmond. We have one of your own parts – you shall be Sir Harry Wildair. I will alter the bills. You are sure to come?'

'Sure to come,' I said, with animation. 'Capital! I know every line in the part. Tell Juliet an old friend will act with her.'

We made a few new arrangements and parted. I bought a copy of the play at Lacy's and studied the part over again.

Next day I got over to Richmond in good time. The day was fine, I remember; my spirits were rapidly rising because it was the fifteenth day since I had

had one of my usual attacks. I was in great hopes
that the old man was really going to change his life
and behave with consideration towards me. With the
birth of hope, there revived in my heart some of my
old feelings. I had a real desire to see Juliet again, but
yet the old warmth seemed gone. It was a desire to
see one in whom I had once been interested; the desire
to awake old memories, which, I think, principally
actuated me.

I found the dear girl waiting for me with an
impatience which ought to have touched my heart,
but which, somehow, only seemed to remind me of
old times. My heart was gone – sold to my master
with everything else. Mechanically I took her hands
in mine, and kissed her on the lips as I used to do. She
threw both arms round my neck, kissed me again and
again, and burst into tears of joy.

'Oh, Luke, Luke!' she said, 'I have so longed to
see you again. The time has been weary, weary,
without you.'

We sat together for half an hour, she all the time
talking to me, and I, remembering what I used to
be with her, wondering where the old feelings were
gone, and trying to act as I used to.

'Luke, you are not growing cold to me, are you?' she
asked, as some little gesture or word of hers passed me
unnoticed.

'Cold, Juliet?' I replied. 'What should make you
think so?'

'I will not think so,' she said. 'It is too great
happiness to meet again, is it not? And you are

silent because you feel too happy to speak. Is not that so?'

Presently it became time to go and dress.

'Let me look at you, Sir Henry Wildair,' she said. 'Yes, we shall do it very well tonight. You are not looking, somehow, quite so well as you used, Luke dear. Is it that London does not agree with you? Are you working too hard? Your face is swollen and – fancy – Mrs Mould says you look as if you had been drinking.'

Mrs Mould was the dresser.

If Mrs Mould had seen me a fortnight before, she might well have said I had been drinking. A fortnight, however, of rest had done wonders for me.

I laughed, but felt a little uneasy.

We rang up at seven.

The house was quite full, because my Juliet was popular at Richmond.

I began with all my former fire and vigour, because I was acting again with her. The old life came back to me; I forgot my troubles; I was really happy, and I believe I acted well. At all events, the house applauded. Between the first and second acts a sudden terror seized me. I felt that the old man was eating again. That passed off, because he ate very little. But then he began to drink, and to drink fast.

It was no use fighting against it. I believe the villain must have been drinking raw brandy, because I was drunk in five minutes. I staggered and reeled about on the stage, I laughed wildly and sang foolishly, and then I tumbled down in a heap and could not get up again. The last thing I remember is the angry roar of poor old Kerrans, beside himself with passion, telling the carpenters to carry that drunken beast away and throw him into the road. I heard afterwards that they were obliged to drop the curtain, and that the *éclat* of poor Juliet's benefit was entirely spoiled. As for myself, the carpenters carried me out to the middle of Richmond-green, where they were going to leave me, only one of them had compassion, and wheeled me to his own house in a barrow.

In the morning I returned hastily to London, sought my cottage at Islington, and shut myself in with an agony of shame and humiliation.

I was quite crushed by this blow. For the first time I felt tempted to commit suicide and end it all. To be sure I ought to have foreseen this, and all the other dreadful things. Directly my master, my owner, got able to swallow, though he could not eat, he could drink, and ordered the most fiery liquor he could procure, with a view to kill me off and begin with another victim.

But Providence ruled otherwise.

Then began a week of cruel suffering. My master sent me word by Boule-de-neige that he intended to finish me off. My appetite, he said, had been long failing, and was now perfectly contemptible. He complained that I had neglected my part of the contract, that I must have been practising intemperance – the horrible hypocrite – to have reduced so fine an appetite to nothing in a short four months. Therefore he felt obliged to tell me that in a week or two I should probably find the agreement ended. That was his ferocious way of putting it. He meant that in a week I should be dead. His words were prophetic, but not in the sense in which he meant them.

He drank brandy now. He drank it morning, noon, and night. He drank it, not because he liked it, but in hopes of despatching me. I was no sooner partially recovered from one drunken bout than I plunged into another.

I lost all power of walking. I could not move about. I lay the whole day sick and feverish on my bed, or, if I got up at all, it was only to change it for an easy chair. I could eat nothing.

Then I began to have visions and to see spectres in my loneliness and misery.

First I saw all over again the scenes of my early life – my poor deserted mother; the tramp who took charge of me; the sleep in which I nearly perished; the strolling actors with whom I wandered; the girl with whom I fell in love. Only among them all there hovered perpetually the ugly face of Boule-de-neige, spoiling the pleasant memories, and corrupting the current of my thoughts with his 'Cluck-cluck', and his demoniac grin.

'How you do, Massa Lucraft? How you feel your stumjack this morning? Ole massa him berry fierce. Him gwine to make the noyeau punch tomorrow. Dat finish um off. Dat work um up. You wait till tomorrow, Massa Lucraft.'

I could only groan.

'You nice young gegleman,' he went on, with a grin.

'You berry grateful young gegleman. Massa him gib you thirty pounds a mouth, and you spend it all in 'temperate courses. Bad; berry bad, dam bad. What you say when you die – eh? Ho! ho!'

The creature seemed always with me during this time. If I opened my eyes I had the feeling that he was hovering about my bed. If it was dark I thought I saw his eyes glaring at me from some corner. If I was asleep he would waken me with his 'Cluck'. What he did in my cottage I never knew. The room was filled with the visions which passed through my brain, succeeding each other again and again like the acts of a play repeated incessantly. I saw the octagonal room with the old gentleman eating and drinking. I saw myself at Richmond. I saw myself before the magistrates; and I looked on as an outsider, as a spectator of a tragedy which would end in death and horror.

It was two days before the period allotted to me by my master, at eight o'clock in the evening, as I was sitting in my lonely cottage, expectant of the usual drunken bout, when I felt a curious agitation within me, an internal struggle, as if through all my veins a tempestuous wave was surging and rushing. I lay down.

'This is some new devilry of the old man,' I said to myself. 'Let him do his worst; at least, I must try to bear it with resignation.' I began to speculate on my inevitable and approaching end, and to wonder curiously, what proportion of the sin of all this drunkenness would be laid to my charge.

To my astonishment nothing more followed. The

tumult of my system gradually subsided, and I fell asleep.

In the morning I awoke late, and missed the usual headache. I had, therefore, I was surprised to find, actually not been drunk the night before. I rose with my customary depression, and was astonished to discover that my nerves were steadier and spirits higher than I had known for a long time.

I mechanically went to the cupboard and pulled out my cold mutton and potatoes. Who can picture my joy when I found that I could taste the meat again, and that it was nasty? I hardly believed my senses; in fact, I had lost them for so long that it was difficult to understand that they had come back to me. I tried the potatoes. Heavens, what a horrible thing to a well-regulated palate is a cold boiled potato!

At first, as I said, I could not believe that I had recovered my taste; then, as the truth forced itself upon me, and I found that I could not only taste, but was actually hungry, I jumped and danced, and was beside myself with joy. Think of a convict suddenly released, and declared guiltless of the charges brought against him. Think of a prisoner on the very ladder of the gallows-tree, with the rope round his neck, reprieved and pardoned. Think of one doomed to death by his physician receiving the assurance that it was all a mistake, and that he would gather up long years of life as in a sheaf. And think that such joy as these would feel, I felt – and more!

I went to the nearest coffee-shop and ordered bacon, eggs, and tea, offering up a short grace with every plate as it came. And then, because I felt sure that my old tormentor must be dead, I repaired to my lawyers', and saw the clerk.

'Ah,' he said, 'the poor old man's gone at last! Went out like the snuff of a candle. His illness was only twenty-four hours. Well, he's gone to heaven, if ever man did.'

'What did he die of – too much eating and drinking?'

'Mr Lucraft,' said the clerk, severely, 'this is not the tone for *you* to adopt towards that distinguished man, your benefactor. He died, sir – being a man of moral, temperate, and even abstemious life, though of full habit – of apoplexy.'

'Oh!' I said, careless what the clerk said, but glad to be quite sure that the diabolical old villain was really dead. I suppose that never was such joy over the repentance of any sinner as mine over the death of that murdering glutton, for whom no words of hatred were too strong.

'I think you've got to see our senior partner,' said the clerk. 'Step this way.'

He led me to a room where I found a grave and elderly gentleman sitting at a table.

'Mr Lucraft?' he said. 'I was expecting you. I saw your late patron's negro this morning. He told me that you would call.'

I stared, but said nothing.

'I have a communication to make to you, on the part of our departed friend, Mr Ebenezer Grumbelow. It is dated a few weeks since, and is to the effect that a sum of money which I hold was to be placed in your hands in case of his death. This, it appears, he anticipated, for some reason or other.'

'Ebenezer Grumbelow'. That was the name which had so long escaped my memory – 'Ebenezer Grumbelow'.

I said nothing, but stared with all my eyes.

'My poor friend,' the lawyer went on, 'after remarking that unless you change your unfortunate habits you will come to no good, gave me this money himself – here is the cheque – so that it will not appear in his last will and testament.'

I took it in silence.

'Well, sir' – he looked at me in some surprise – 'have you no observation to make, or remark to offer, on this generosity?'

'None,' I said.

'I do not know,' he continued; 'I do not know – your signature here, if you please – what reason Mr Grumbelow had in taking you up, or what claim you possessed upon his consideration; but I think, sir, I do think, that some expression, some sense of regret, is due.'

I buttoned up the cheque in my pocket.

'Mr Grumbelow was a philanthropist, I believe, sir?'

'He was. As a philanthropist, as a supporter of charities, as a public donor of great amounts, Mr Grumbelow's name stands in the front. So much we all know.'

'A religious man, too?'

'Surely, surely; one of our most deeply religious

men. A man who was not ashamed of his saintly profession.'

'Cluck-cluck!'

It was the familiar face of Boule-de-neige at the door.

'You know, I suppose,' said the lawyer, 'Mr Grumbelow's body-servant, a truly Christian negro?'

'Was there,' I asked, 'any clause in Mr Grumbelow's letter – any conditions attached to this gift?'

'None whatever. It is a free gift. Stay, there is a postscript which I ought to have read to you. You will perhaps understand it. In it Mr Grumbelow says that as to the services rendered by him to you, and by you to him, it will be best for your own sake to keep them secret.'

I bowed.

The date of the cheque corresponded with the first illness of the old man – his affection of the throat. Probably he was afraid that I should reveal his infamous story.

'I may now tell you, Mr Lucraft, without at all wishing to break any confidence that may have existed between you and the deceased, that a friend of Mr Grumbelow's – no other, indeed, than the Rev. Jabez Jumbles, a pulpit name doubtless known to you – intends to write the biography of this distinguished and religious man, as an example to the young. Any help you can afford to so desirable an end will be gratefully received. Particularly, Mr Lucraft, any communication on the subject of his continual help given to young men, who regularly disappointed him, and all, except yourself, died of drink.'

I bowed again and retired.

Did anyone ever hear of such a wicked old man?

Outside the office I was joined by the negro.

'What have you got to say to me, detestable wretch?' I cried, shaking my fist in his withered old face.

'Cluck-cluck! Massa not angry with poor old Boule-de-neige. How young massa? Young massa pretty well? How de lubly abbadide of de young gegleman? How him strong stumjack? Cluck-cluck!'

He kept at a safe distance from me. I think I should have killed him if I had ever clutched him by the throat.

'Ole massa him always ask, "How dat young debbel? Go and see, Boule-de-neige." I go to young massa's cottage daraway, and come back. "Him berry dam bad, sir," I say; "him going to be debbel berry fast, just like dem oders. De folk all say he drink too much for him berry fine constitution." Cluck-cluck! Ole massa he only say ebbery night, "Bring de brandy, Boule-de-neige; let's finish him." 'Cluck-cluck!'

Here was a Christian negro for you!

'Tell me, what did your master die of?'

'Apple perplexity, massa.'

'Ah! what else? Come, Boule-de-neige, I know a good deal; tell me more.'

'Massa's time up,' he whispered, coming close to me. 'Time quite up, and him berry much 'fraid. Massa Lucraft want servant? Boule-de-neige berry good servant. Cook lubly dinner; make massa rich, like Massa Grumbelow.'

'I'd rather hire the devil!' I exclaimed.

'Cluck-cluck-cluck!' grinned the creature; and really he looked at the moment as much like the devil as one could wish. 'Cluck! dat massa can do if massa like.'

I rushed away, too much excited by the recovery of my freedom to regard what he said.

I was free! What next?

First the restoration of my shattered nerves.

There was no permanent injury done to my constitution, because, after all, the drink had not actually gone down my throat, nor was it I who had consumed the gallons of turtle soup, the tons of fish, the shiploads of cattle with which he had punished me for that woeful signature of mine.

The contract, in some inexplicable manner, affected me with the punishment of my purchaser's excesses by a kind of sympathy. I remained a strictly temperate man for a month. I recovered gradually the tone of my system; my features lost their bloated look. I became myself again.

And then I sought the injured Kerrans.

It was no use trying to tell him a story which he never would have believed. I simply told him that I was taken suddenly and hopelessly ill on that fatal night. I asked him to remember, which is quite true, how I began the piece with a fire and animation quite impossible in a man who had been drinking; how I had certainly nothing between the scenes, during which intervals I was talking with him, and how the thing came upon me without any warning. If you try, you know, you can make yourself quite drunk with brandy in two minutes. This is just what Mr Grumbelow did to me.

Kerrans, good fellow, outraged in his best feelings, was difficult to smooth down.

He had asked me to act with Juliet in the hope of restoring to the girl her lost good spirits. I came; the misfortune happened, and she was worse than ever. But he forgave me at last, and allowed me another chance. This time it was not Juliet who threw her arms around me; it was I who implored her forgiveness, and the renewal of her love. I was cold no longer. I left off remembering, and lived again in the present. I was a lover, and my girl was trembling and blushing, with her hand in mine.

It all happened more than fifty years ago. The only record which remains of the events I have described are on the tablet to the memory of Ebenezer Grumbelow in St Rhadegunda's Church, City: and the little faded scrap from the *Morning Chronicle*, which I always carry in my pocket-book, and which tells the tale of my shame.

Juliet never believed my story, and I left off insisting on its truth.

She lies in Norwood Cemetery now, but we kept our golden wedding ere she died; and children and grandchildren live to bless her name.

The Man Who Couldn't Taste Pepper

G. B. STERN

Over the years, the huge diversity of national and regional foods has inspired hundreds of books of recipes, and led to the opening of innumerable restaurants specialising in the different cuisines. Gladys Bertha Stern (1890–1973), better known by her initials as G. B. Stern, was an enthusiast of international cooking and her work as a novelist and scriptwriter in Britain and Hollywood gave her the opportunity to patronise restaurants in many countries. Her story 'The Man Who Couldn't Taste Pepper' is set in Vienna in the year 1922 and features a small restaurant with the delightful name of 'The Little Hot Dog'. It is a story of a man with a very strange affliction and, of course, features death . . .

'So you like paprika, Niki?'

'I do. And for itself, not just because it's a national food. Though there's always a thrill about national food – like national anthems.'

Bouillabaisse at Marseilles,' mused Franz, '*Fritto del mare* at Venice. Saddle of mutton in London. Ice-cream-soda in America – or is it pie?'

'There's something exciting in paprika,' went on Veronica. 'And it's such a glorious vermilion when it's in powder; a different red from cayenne. Though

I don't think those people really appreciate it. Do you think they take our Little Hot Dog for a sort of Simpson's? I mean – one doesn't usually wallop into a nine-course dinner here, does one?'

'One can, but one doesn't. I'm glad you have a proper appreciation of paprika, Niki – though I knew a man once who couldn't taste pepper at all, black, white, cayenne or paprika.'

'Suppose one couldn't smell roses or hear Chopin! Tell me about your man, Franz. You haven't told me a story for ages. And I can't dance while those people are eating; it makes me feel like a tiger after a heavy kill, to watch them. What happened if you popped a whole lot of pepper into whatever your man was eating?'

'Well, what happened was that he killed a man and had to fly the country.'

'Ai-eee! Tell your darling-angel Niki. She likes red things – blood and paprika and soldiers' coats and lobsters.'

'It was twenty years ago – when wine was wine, and there were plenty of soldiers' coats, though not red ones. And the blood ran fast in your veins, and life was like one of Strauss's waltzes – all throb and sentiment, with a sob at the end of it. And I was a young lieutenant of dragoons, and I had an English friend – an acquaintance, rather, for I met him in a bar at midnight, and we knocked about together for a while. And La Belle Denise was dancing here at The Little Hot Dog, and he was madly infatuated with her – he and a Spaniard from Seville – I've even forgotten their names, though the Spaniard was called Juan de something, and the Englishman, I think, Charles.

'I don't believe she cared a flick of the eyelid for either of them, but they amused her, and she played off one against the other, till the two men hated each other to killing point. I've seen Juan finger his knife more than once when the Englishman was dancing with Denise. One of them would give her a bouquet that would cost a couple of million kronen nowadays, and the other would reply with a string of pearls, and next night the first would produce a ruby bracelet. And so it went on.

'She made a sort of game of keeping them exactly equal. A tour de force in equilibrium. We used to bet on it. A tilt in her favour on the Spanish or the English side, and the betting simply flickered like a compass needle.

'It got to be an absolute contest between them as to which could do the most extravagant and fantastic thing in her honour. Juan once had this place draped in black, and lit by luminous skeletons; Charles had the courtyard of the Imperial Hotel flooded and gave a Venetian fête in gondolas; Juan had a special tzigane band sent for from Hungary; Charles gave her seven brindled mastiffs, each with a spiked silver collar.

'Feeling ran very high at the "Dog". Everyone had money on it, and everyone was a fierce partisan of one or the other; and things got to such a pitch that one of Charles' men wouldn't drink with a Juanite, and vice versa.

'I tried to get Charles out of it. Things were going a

bit too far. But he wouldn't listen to me. The silly fool said he wanted to marry Denise, and take her back to England. As if one married a dancer! Especially a dancer like Denise. And as if she'd have had him – a younger son, who'd already squandered on her the little he had besides his pay. I found this out, you see, when I was trying to show him how futile it was to contemplate marriage with a bird of paradise like Denise. Why, she'd been the *chère amie* of at least two Russian Grand Dukes, and her jewels were worth a small fortune. And there were rumours about a reigning monarch. Anyway, they say the Queen of Moldavia was markedly cold to her husband after Denise left Blatzen.

'When I found that Charles couldn't be made to see reason, I approached La Belle Denise herself. "What, mademoiselle," I said, "do you hope to get by keeping these two silly moths fluttering round the flame of your incomparable beauty? Mademoiselle is charming, she is ravishing; one has but to see her to become her slave. But an Englishman chooses for his wife someone a little less exciting – more domestic. One who can cook and sew, and who will be a good mother to his children. A Spaniard, too, admires the homely virtues; and for him a marriage is arranged by the parents. *N'est ce pas?*"

'Denise flashed her yellow eyes at me. "You think, then, that I could not be a good wife? Bah! I have nothing to learn from your *Hausfrau*, or your pudding-faced English miss! You shall see, *mon ami*; me, I invite you to dinner, *chez moi* tomorrow night; you and those two poor *drôles*. The arrangement, the cuisine, everything I shall make myself."

'So the next evening found the three of us knocking at her flat. Denise opened the door herself. To my intense amusement, she was wearing an obvious fancy-dress of domesticity – blue cotton, beautifully cut, of course, a white mob cap, and an apron. As a matter of fact, she'd never looked prettier. She took us into the sitting-room, which was also rather in fancy dress: no exotic flowers, a work-box prominently displayed, a cosy fire burning brightly in the grate, and all the photographs tucked away, except two old-fashioned daguerrotypes of what might have been her father and mother, or might have been bought at the curio shop round the corner. The atmosphere was completed by a thoroughly bourgeois cat – none of your blue-blooded Persians! – asleep on the hearthrug, and a large doll propped in a baby's chair.

' "This," said Denise, taking it up and caressing it, "is my child, my own little one. Her name is Joan, a little English miss." She glanced wickedly at Juan. "You no like, *mon ami*? Then her name is Juanita."

'And all that evening she worked that doll like the very devil, till her rival adorers were simply at boiling point. It's a bad trick among women, Niki – clever women – and I'm telling you this so that you shouldn't do it, that when they know there's someone in the room who wants to embrace them, they deliberately and tantalisingly embrace something else – a dog, or a kitten, or even a sofa-cushion. It can drive a man to frenzy.'

'Yes,' mused Veronica, 'I suppose it could.' And absent-mindedly she began to kiss her own shoulder, very softly. Franz looked up. 'Fortunately,' he remarked, 'I am as leather. I've been pickled by the years . . .

'But Charles and Juan were very far from being leather that night. They were in a highly inflamed condition; and I, like a fool and a schoolboy, just to spite Denise, went and made it worse.'

'Oh, Franz, what did you do?'

'I tilted the entire contents of a pot of cayenne pepper into the omelette. The omelette, you see, was to be Denise's *chef d'oeuvre*. Her ultimate proof to me that she was thoroughly domesticated, thoroughly capable of running a home and making a man comfortable. She laid the table with her own hands. Tripping to and fro between the kitchen and sitting-room, giving a last polish to the glasses, calling us to come and admire the pile of snowy table napkins in the linen cupboard.

'Oh, it was well staged, the whole scene. I'll grant her that. And she could cook, the little devil; she knew her job. "But wait"! she cried. "Wait till you taste my omelette. There will not be a crumb left for *la p'tite* Juanita, I promise you that. But she – she prefers the rosbif." And she twinkled first at one and then at the other, and flung a glance of sheer triumph at me, and invited me to come into the kitchen and help beat the eggs.

'It was while she was carrying in the plates, that I tipped the pepper into the omelette. My object, you see, was to make her look a fool. I laughed when I pictured the grimaces of Charles and Juan. But what followed was more fantastic than funny.

'I refused omelette, on the grounds that I did not care for eggs. As for Denise, she insisted, still in the spirit of domestic masquerade, on remaining cook and waitress, and not eating, herself, till the others were done. So that the omelette was divided – with exact equality, as usual! – between Charles and Juan.

'Charles took a mouthful. "Delicious," he said, and fell to. But Juan began choking and spluttering and sneezing. He grew purple in the face. When he could speak, he glared fiercely first at Denise, then at Charles, who was halfway through his omelette. "So you try to poison me and me alone, because it is this English pig that you love? But he shall not live to love you long." And he smacked Charles twice across the face with his open hand.

'Charles sprang to his feet. A duel, of course, was inevitable. The very last thing that I had wanted.

' "I do not understand your talk of poison, Señor. I find the omelette of mademoiselle delicious. But you have called me a pig and struck me in the face. I am not a man to be insulted by a dago. When will you meet me and with what weapons?"

'I was simply amazed. Was Charles acting? If so, his nonchalance was superhuman, with all that pepper in his mouth and down his throat and up his nose. Denise, knowing nothing of the trick I had played, was merely insulted at the Spaniard's treatment of her cookery. With the sweetest of all smiles at Charles, and a cold flash of her eyes at Juan, she quitted the room. Then I burst out:

'"Charles – did you taste nothing wrong?"

'"Nothing," he replied.

'"That omelette – it was chockful of pepper – I tipped it in myself, for a joke!"

'Then I understood. Charles, by reason of some curious idiosyncrasy of palate, *could not taste pepper*. He had calmly eaten an omelette which was enough to make any ordinary man half-dead with choking and sneezing – exactly the effect it had had on Juan. Hence the quarrel – and from what I knew of Juan, one of them would have to die. He, obviously, did not believe a word of the pepper story, and Denise's parting glance of sweetness at Charles had not improved matters.

'Juan chose pistols. They were each to go and stand in opposite corners of a pitch dark room, with lighted cigarettes between their lips, and fire at the glowing end. I was sorry, for Charles was a fine swordsman but an indifferent revolver shot.

'We went in Denise's salon. I drew the blinds, placed them in position and extinguished the lights. Then the dancer and I had to wait with what patience we could while those two lunatics tried to kill each other.

'Six shots in quick succession. A seventh – a groan and a heavy fall. Like a madman I wrenched open the door, fumbled for the switch. Then I heard Charles' voice: "I believe I've killed him, Franz."

'Juan lay in a crumpled heap, the blood spreading through his shirt front in an ugly brown stain. In his hand was a still burning cigarette. Charles looked, and then turned away with a hunch of the shoulders. "So he cheated till the last!"

' "What d'you mean?"

' "Don't you see? He had his cigarette in his hand; I kept mine in my mouth all the time . . ."

'I managed to get him away. Duelling was more common then than now, but still it would have been an ugly thing for him if they'd been able to connect him with the sensational find of Juan's body in Denise's flat. As it was, we made it look like suicide. Everybody knew that he had been madly infatuated with her, and she, in her most exquisite clothes, reproached herself bitterly at the enquiry, and vowed that she would enter a convent and remain there for the rest of her life. I never heard from Charles again.'

'And did she go into a convent?' Niki asked.

Franz lit a cigarette with care, and shook his head, smiling a little to himself, as if amused at some ancient memory.

'And did you ever find out which of the two she had really loved?'

'No. She never told me. Not even during the perfectly charming six months we had together immediately after the regrettable affair.'

Final Dining

ROGER ZELAZNY

The final tale of this section in a way brings history full
circle by using the events of the Last Supper as the
theme of a murder story set firmly in the present day.
That fateful gathering of Jesus and his disciples might well
be cited as the most famous instance of a meal which
engendered a death – albeit that Christ's 'murder' was
ordered by the Roman judiciary after Judas' treacherous
act of betrayal. Fantasy writer Roger Zelazny (1937–)
has used these facts as the basis for his account of
a painter working on a picture of the 'Last Supper',
who finds himself drawn inexorably into a last meal
and a terrible act of murder. 'Final Dining' is a story
in the best historical tradition as well as being chillingly
contemporary.

I felt the cat's tongue lick of his brush, lining my
cheeks, darkening my beard.

He touched my eyes and they were opened. First
the left, then the right. Instantly.

There was no blur of sudden awakening. I stared
back into his own dark eyes, intent upon my face. He
held the brush delicately as a feather, his thumbnail a
spectrum of pigment.

He stood there, admiring me.

'Yes!' he breathed at last. 'They *are* right! Lines of guilt, shame, terror – arrowing those target eyes!

'But they face into the light, nevertheless,' he continued, ' – unflinching! – with all the insolence and pain of Lucifer. They will not drop as he dips the bread . . .

'Beard needs more red,' he added.

'Not much more,' I said.

He squinted.

'Not much more, though.'

He blew gently upon my face, then covered me.

Portrait sitting in fifteen minutes, he thought. *Have to stop.*

He was moving around. I felt him light a cigarette.

Mignon is coming at ten.

'Mignon is coming,' I said.

Yes. I will show you to her. She likes to look at paintings, and I've never done anything this good before. She doesn't think I can. I will show her . . . Of course, she doesn't know art . . .

'Yes.'

I heard a knock on the door.

He let her in. I felt his excitement.

'You're always on time,' he said.

She laughed, with the chime of an expensive clock.

'Always,' she said, 'until it's finished and I can see it. I'm eager.'

She is wearing her portrait smile already, he mused, hanging her coat on the rack. *She is sitting in the dark chair now. Dark as her hair. Green tweeds, and a silver pin. Why not diamonds? She's got them.*

'Why not diamonds?' I asked.

'Why not diamonds?'

'Huh? – Oh, my pin?' She touched it, glancing down at a youthful breast. 'You haven't painted that low yet, have you? I'm posing for a mantelpiece, not a cover story on family fortunes. So, I decided I'd rather have something simple.'

She's smiling again. Is she mocking me?

'What's that one you have covered?'

She walked to the canvas.

'Oh,' he said. Delighted. Anticipating. 'It's nothing, really.'

'Let me see it.'

'All right.'

The cloth rustled and I looked up at her.

'Goodness!' she said. 'Peter Halsey's "Last Supper"! – My, but it's fine.'

She moved farther back, intent.

'He looks as if he's about to step out of the frame and betray Him all over again.'

'I am,' I said, modestly.

'He probably is,' Peter observed. 'He's rather special.'

'Yes,' she decided. 'I've never seen those exact colours before. The depth, the texture – he's very unusual.'

'He ought to be,' he replied. 'He came from the stars.'

'The stars?' she puzzled. 'What do you mean?'

'His pigment was ground from a meteorite I found this summer. Its redness grabbed my attention right away, and it was small enough to throw in the trunk.'

She studied my brushwork.

'For something this good, you've painted it awfully fast.'

'No, it's been around for some time,' he said. 'I was waiting for the right notion of how to do him. That red stoned gave me the clue, the same week you began your sittings. Once I got started he practically painted himself.'

'He looks as if he enjoys it all,' she laughed.

'I don't mind a bit . . .'

'I doubt that he minds.'

'. . . for I am that organic changeling, left for a rock fancied as a footstool by the gods.'

'Who knows his origin?'

He covered me, with a matador's flourish.

'Shall we begin?'

'Yes.'

She returned to the chair.

After a while, he tried to read her posing eyes.

'Take her. She's willing.'

He put down the brush, stared at her, at his work, at her.

He picked up the brush again.

'Go ahead. What's to lose? And think of the gain. That silver could be diamonds on her breast. Think of her breast, think of the diamonds.'

He put the brush down.

'What's the matter?'

'I'm tired, all of a sudden. A cigarette and I'll be ready to go again.'

She rose, stretching her arms overhead.

'Want me to heat that coffee?'

He looked up, over at his cheap hot plate.

'No, that's all right. Cigarette?'

'Thanks.'

His hand shook.

She'll think it's fatigue.

'Your hand is shaking.'

'Tired, I guess.'

She sat on his studio bed. He seated himself beside her, slowly, half-reclining.

'Hot in here.'

'Yes.'

He took her hand.

'You're shaking, too.'

'Nerves. DTs. Who knows?'

He raised it to his lips.

'I love you.'

A frightened look widened her eyes, slackened her mouth.

'. . . and your teeth are lovely.'

He began to embrace her.

'Oh, please . . .!'

He kissed her, firmly.

'Don't. If you don't mean it . . .'

'I do,' he said. 'I do.'

'You're wonderful,' she sighed, 'and your art. I always felt . . . But – '

He kissed her again, then drew her down beside him. 'Mignon.'

' — '

Peter Halsey looked out from his balcony, over the landscaped garden with its Augustan walks, the picturesqueness, the eighteenth-century prettiness, and down to the guard rails, the cliffs, and the long, steep slant into the Gulf.

'It is good,' he said, and turned back toward his suite.

'Good,' I repeated.

I hung upon the side wall. He stopped before me.

'What are you smirking at, you old bastard?'

'Nothing.'

Blanche entered from the bedroom, right, patting her wide halo of sunset-pink.

'Did you say something, honey?'

'Yes. But I wasn't talking to you.'

She looked up at me, pointing with her thumb. 'Him?'

'That's right. He's the only good thing I've ever done, and we get along well.'

She shuddered.

'He looks something like you, at that — only meaner.'

He turned.

'Do you really think so?'

'Uh-huh. Especially the eyes.'

'Get out of here,' he said.

'What's wrong?'

'Nothing,' he controlled himself. 'But my wife will be back soon.'

'All right, daddy. When will I see you again?'

'I'll call you.'

'Okay.'

A swish of black skirts and she was gone.

Peter did not see her to the door. Not her sort. He studied me a little longer, then crossed the room to the mirror and stared into it.

'Hm,' he announced. 'There *is* a little resemblance – subconscious pun or something.'

'Sure,' I said.

He strolled back toward the balcony, hands in the pockets of his silk dressing gown.

Once more, he looked at the ocean.

'Mater Oceana,' he invoked, 'I am happy and unhappy. Take . . . Take away my unhappiness.'

'What is that?'

He did not answer me, but I knew.

Outside, I heard Mignon coming. The door swung open. I knew.

He stepped back into the room, looking at her.

'My, you're fresh. Why do you bother with beauty parlours?'

'To stay this way for you, dear, I'd hate to have you lose interest after two months.'

'Small chance of that.'

He embraced her.

I hate you, you rich bitch! You think you can run my life now, because you're footing the bills. You didn't make

*the loot either. It was your old man – Go ahead, ask me if
I worked today.*

She pulled away, reluctantly.

'Do any painting this afternoon, dear?'

No, I was in the bedroom with a blonde.

'No, I had a headache.'

'Oh, I'm sorry. Is it better now?'

'No, I still have it.' *You!*

'What about this evening?'

'What about it?'

'What was that French restaurant we passed yesterday?'

'Le Bois.'

'I thought you might like to try it. We've eaten in all
the others.'

'No, not tonight.'

'Where, then?'

'How about right here?'

She looked troubled.

'I'll have to call downstairs now, then.'

*I'll bet you can't even cook. I never have had a chance to
find out!*

'That'd be fine.'

'You're *sure* you don't want to go out?'

'Yes, I'm sure.'

Her face brightened.

'They'll set up a table in the garden, and send the
food out on carts – for special guests.'

'Why go to all that bother?'

'Mother said she and Dad had it that way when they
honeymooned here. I've been meaning to suggest it.'

'Why not?' he shrugged.

Mignon looked at her watch. She raised her hand, hesitated, then tapped on the bedroom door.

'Aren't you dressed yet?'

'Just about.'

Why don't you die and leave me in peace? Maybe then I could paint again. You have no real appreciation of my art – of any art! Or anything else. – Phoney aesthete! What have you ever worked for? Die! So I can collect . . . and stop bothering me!

'Why not tonight?' I asked.

'I wonder . . . ?' he mused.

'You are a happy couple – honeymooners. There would be no suspicion. Keep her there until late. Pipe her champagne by the gallon. Dance with her. When the waiters have left, when the lights are dim, when there are just you two, music, the champagne, and darkness – when she begins to laugh too much, when she stumbles as she dances,' I concluded, 'then there is the rail.'

There was another tap on the door.

'Ready?'

Peter Halsey adjusted his tie.

'Coming, dear.'

* * *

God! How much of that can she drink? I'll be under the table first!

'More champagne, darling?'

'Just a little.'

He filled it to the brim.

'Bottle is getting low. Might as well kill it.'

'You haven't been drinking much,' she accused.

'I wasn't raised on it.'

The candles were all. The trellises and islands of colour now wore impenetrable cloaks. It was deep, inky, outside the wavering halo. The Strauss waltzes whirled and circled from the hidden speaker – but dignified, dim, *sotto voce*, and excluded from the table. The aromas of invisible blossoms were dying, unmingling themselves, in the refrigerator of night.

He looked at her.

'Aren't you cold?'

'No! Let's stay here all night. This is wonderful!'

He squinted at his watch. It *was* getting late.

A drink, to brace the nerves.

He quaffed the sour fire. Like snowflakes falling upward into a yellow sky, its icy jewels jetted through his head.

'Now is the time.'

He leaned forward and blew out the candles.

'Why did you do that?'

'To be alone with you, in the dark.'

She giggled.

He found her and embraced her.

'Kiss her – that's it.'

He drew her to her feet, had a hard time unclasping her arms. But he led her, arm about the waist, to the white rail.

'How lovely the ocean, when there is no moon,' she

said, thickly. 'Didn't Van Gogh once paint the Seine at ni – '

He struck her behind the knees with his left forearm. She toppled backwards, and he tried to catch her. Her head struck a flagstone. He cursed.

'No difference. She'll be bruised anyhow, when they find her.'

She moaned, softly, as he raised her warm stillness.

He leaned forward, shoving hard, and pushed her over the rail.

He heard her hit stone, once, but the *Blue Danube* covered all other sounds of descent.

'Good night, Mignon.'

'Good night, Mignon.'

'It was terrible,' he told the detective. 'I know I'm drunk and can't talk straight – that's why I couldn't save her. We were having such a good time, dancing and all. She wanted to look at the ocean, then I went back to the table for another drink. I heard her cry out, and, and – '

He covered his face with his hands, forcing a sobbing sound.

' – she was gone!'

He shook all over.

' – and we were having such a good time!'

'Take it easy, Mister Halsey.' The man put a hand on his shoulder. 'The desk clerk says he has some pills. Take them and go to bed. Honestly, that's the best thing you can do now. Your statement wouldn't be worth much, even though I can see what happened. I'll make my report in the morning.

'The Coast Guard has a cutter out there now,' he continued. 'You'll have to go to the morgue tomorrow. But just get some sleep now.'

'We were having such a good time,' Peter Halsey repeated, as he staggered to the elevator.

Inside, he lighted a cigarette.

*   *   *

He unlocked the door and switched on the light.

The suite was transformed.

It was divided into alcoves by the hastily-constructed partitions. Of the original furnishings, only a few chairs and a small table remained.

A placard stood on the table.

Beside the placard was a leather notebook. He opened it, dropping his cigarette to the floor. He read . . .

He read the names of the critics, the gallery scouts, the museum reviewers, the buyers, the makers of opinion.

It was the invitation list.

A wisp of smoke curled up from the carpet. Unconsciously, he moved his foot to crush it. He was reading the placard.

Peter Halsey Exhibition, it said, *Arranged by Mrs Peter Halsey, on the Anniversary of the Two Most Happy Months in Her Life. 1 AM to 2 PM. Friday, Saturday, Sunday.*

*

He walked from niche to niche, repainting with his eyes all the works his hands had ever executed.

His watercolours. His stab at cubism. His portraits.

She had hunted them all down, bought or borrowed all of them.

Portrait of Mignon.

He looked at her smile, and her hair, dark as the chair; at her green tweeds; at the silver pin that could have been diamonds.

' – ' she said.

Nothing.

She was dead.

And across the way, staring into her smile, with my beard of blood and bread in hand, amidst the dove-bright faces of the holy ones, with my halo also hammered from silver, I smiled back.

'Congratulations. The cheque will be in the mail promptly.'

Where's my palette knife?

'Come now! No Dorian Gray business, eh?'

Where's something that will cut?

'Why this? You painted me as I am. You could as easily have used the pigment for someone else. – Him, for example, or him. – But I was your inspiration. I! We drew life from one another, from your despair. Are we not a masterpiece?'

'No!' he cried, covering his face once more. 'No!'

'Take those pills and go to bed.'

'No!'

'Yes.'

'She wanted me to be great. She tried to buy it for me. But she *did* want me to be great . . .'

'Of course. She loved you.'

'I didn't know. I killed her . . .'

'Don't all men? – Wilde again, you know.'

'Shut up! Stop looking at me!'

'I can't. I am you.'

'I will destroy you.'

'That would take some doing.'

'*You* have destroyed me!'

'Ha! Who did the pushing?'

'Go away! Please!'

'And miss my exhibition?'

'Please.'

'Good night, Peter Halsey.'

And I watched him, shadow amidst shadows. He did not stagger. He moved like a machine, like a sleepwalker. Sure. Precise. Certain.

* * *

Ten hours have passed, and the sun is up. Soon now I will hear their footsteps in the hall. The cognoscenti, the great ones: the Berensons, the Duveens . . .

They will pause outside the door. They will knock, gently.

And after a while they will try the door.

It will open, and they will come in.

In fact, they are coming now.

They will behold the eyes, tearless windows of a sin-drenched soul . . .

They have paused outside.

They will see the lines of guilt, shame, terror, and remorse – arrowing those target eyes . . .

A knock.

– But they face into the light, nevertheless – unflinching! They will not drop!

The doorknob is turning.

'Come in, my lords, come in! Great art awaits you! – See yourselves a writhen soul – the halo hammered from insurance claims, from pride – see the betrayer betrayed!

'Come! See my masterpiece, my masters, where it hangs against the wall.'

And our teeth forever frozen in mid-gnash.

III

JUST DESSERTS

A Selection of Detective Cases

Four-and-Twenty Blackbirds

AGATHA CHRISTIE

The 1920s and 1930s are regarded as the 'Golden Age' of crime fiction, and reading the novels from this era it is intriguing to note how many victims are dispatched by the murderer at the dinner table. As one authority has noted, the dinner plate became the 'poisoner's playground', and because it was so easy to use has remained popular ever since – although the means of concealing the poison against the probing of forensic science has had to become increasingly more ingenious. A number of the most famous fictional sleuths have not only solved cases where murder was on the menu, but revealed themselves to be know-ledgeable gourmets, too: their number ranging from Charles Dickens' pioneer Inspector Bucket by way of Hercule Poirot, Jules Maigret and Nero Wolfe to Nicolas Freeling's Van Der Valk. (Freeling, incidentally, was for a time a teacher at a cookery school.) One of these detectives is featured in the following story, Poirot in the case of 'Four-and-Twenty Blackbirds' by Agatha Christie (1890–1976).

Hercule Poirot was dining with his friend, Henry Bonnington at the Gallant Endeavour in the King's Road, Chelsea.

Mr Bonnington was fond of the Gallant Endeavour. He liked the leisurely atmosphere, he liked the food which was 'plain' and 'English' and 'not a lot of made up messes'. He liked to tell people who dined with him there just exactly where Augustus John had been wont to sit and to draw their attention to the famous artists' names in the visitors' book. Mr Bonnington was himself the least artistic of men – but he took a certain pride in the artistic activities of others.

Molly, the sympathetic waitress, greeted Mr Bonnington as an old friend. She prided herself on remembering her customers' likes and dislikes in the way of food.

'Good evening, sir,' she said, as the two men took their seats at a corner table. 'You're in luck today – turkey stuffed with chestnuts – that's your favourite, isn't it? And ever such a nice Stilton we've got! Will you have soup first or fish?'

Mr Bonnington deliberated the point. He said to Poirot warningly as the latter studied the menu:

'None of your French kickshaws now. Good well-cooked English food.'

'My friend,' Hercule Poirot waved his hand, 'I ask no better! I put myself in your hands unreservedly.'

'Ah – hruup – er – hm,' replied Mr Bonnington and gave careful attention to the matter.

These weighty matters, and the question of wine, settled, Mr Bonnington leaned back with a sigh and unfolded his napkin as Molly sped away.

'Good girl, that!' he said approvingly. 'Was quite a beauty once – artists used to paint her. She knows about food, too – and that's a great deal more important. Women are very unsound on food as a rule. There's many a woman if she goes out with a fellow she fancies – won't even notice what she eats. She'll just order the first thing she sees.'

Hercule Poirot, shook his head.

'*C'est terrible*.'

'Men aren't like that, thank God!' said Mr Bonnington complacently.

'Never?' There was a twinkle in Hercule Poirot's eye.

'Well, perhaps when they're very young,' conceded Mr Bonnington. 'Young puppies! Young fellows nowadays are all the same – no guts – no stamina. I've no use for the young – and they,' he added with strict impartiality, 'have no use for me. Perhaps they're right! But to hear some of these young fellows talk you'd think no man had a right to be *alive* after sixty! From the way they go on, you'd wonder more of them didn't help their elderly relations out of the world.'

'It is possible,' said Hercule Poirot, 'that they do.'

'Nice mind you've got, Poirot, I must say. All this police work saps your ideals.'

Hercule Poirot smiled.

'*Tout de même*,' he said. 'It would be interesting to make a table of accidental deaths over the age of sixty. I assure you it would raise some curious speculations in your mind.'

'The trouble with you is that you've started going to look for crime – instead of waiting for crime to come to you.'

'I apologise,' said Poirot. 'I talk what you call "the shop". Tell me, my friend, of your own affairs. How does the world go with you?'

'Mess!' said Mr Bonnington. 'That's what's the matter with the world nowadays. Too much mess. And too much fine language. The fine language helps to conceal the mess. Like a highly-flavoured sauce concealing the fact that the fish underneath it is none of the best! Give me an honest fillet of sole and no messy sauce over it.'

It was given him at that moment by Molly and he grunted approval.

'You know just what I like, my girl,' he said.

'Well, you come here pretty regular, don't you, sir? I ought to know what you like.'

Hercule Poirot said:

'Do people then always like the same things? Do not they like a change sometimes?'

'Not gentlemen, sir. Ladies like variety – gentlemen always like the same thing.'

'What did I tell you?' grunted Bonnington. 'Women are fundamentally unsound where food is concerned!'

He looked round the restaurant.

'The world's a funny place. See that odd-looking old fellow with a beard in the corner? Molly'll tell you he's always here Tuesdays and Thursday nights. He has come here for close on ten years now – he's a kind of landmark in the place. Yet nobody here knows his name or where he lives or what his business is. It's odd when you come to think of it.'

When the waitress brought the portions of turkey he said:

'I see you've still got Old Father Time over there?'

'That's right, sir. Tuesdays and Thursdays, his days

are. Not but what he came in here on a *Monday* last week! It quite upset me! I felt I'd got my dates wrong and that it must be Tuesday without my knowing it! But he came in the next night as well – so the Monday was just a kind of extra, so to speak.'

'An interesting deviation from habit,' murmured Poirot. 'I wonder what the reason was?'

'Well, sir, if you ask me, I think he'd had some kind of upset or worry.'

'Why did you think that? His manner?'

'No, sir – not his manner exactly. He was very quiet as he always is. Never says much except good evening when he comes and goes. No, it was his *order*.'

'His order?'

'I dare say you gentlemen will laugh at me,' Molly flushed up, 'but when a gentleman has been here for ten years, you get to know his likes and dislikes. He never could bear suet pudding or blackberries and I've never known him take thick soup – but on that Monday night he ordered thick tomato soup, beefsteak and kidney pudding and blackberry tart! Seemed as though he just didn't notice *what* he ordered!'

'Do you know,' said Hercule Poirot, 'I find that extraordinarily interesting.'

Molly looked gratified and departed.

'Well, Poirot,' said Henry Bonnington with a chuckle. 'Let's have a few deductions from you. All in your best manner.'

'I would prefer to hear yours first.'

'Want me to be Watson, eh? Well, old fellow went to a doctor and the doctor changed his diet.'

'To thick tomato soup, steak and kidney pudding and blackberry tart? I cannot imagine any doctor doing that.'

'Don't believe it, old boy. Doctors will put you on to anything.'

'That is the only solution that occurs to you?'

Henry Bonnington:

'Well, seriously, I suppose there's only one explanation possible. Our unknown friend was in the grip of some powerful mental emotion. He was so perturbed by it that he literally did not notice what he was ordering or eating.'

He paused a minute and then said:

'You'll be telling me next that you know just *what* was on his mind. You'll say perhaps that he was making up his mind to commit a murder.'

He laughed at his own suggestion.

Hercule Poirot did not laugh.

He has admitted that at that moment he was seriously worried. He claims that he ought then to have had some inkling of what was likely to occur.

His friends assure him that such an idea is quite fantastic.

It was some three weeks later that Hercule Poirot and Bonnington met again – this time their meeting was in the Tube.

They nodded to each other, swaying about, hanging on to adjacent straps. Then at Piccadilly Circus there was a general exodus and they found seats right at the forward end of the car – a peaceful spot since nobody passed in or out that way.

'That's better,' said Mr Bonnington. 'Selfish lot, the human race, they won't pass up the car however much you ask 'em to!'

Hercule Poirot shrugged his shoulders.

'What will you?' he said. 'Life is too uncertain.'

'That's it. Here today, gone tomorrow,' said Mr Bonnington with a kind of gloomy relish. 'And talking of that, d'you remember that old boy we noticed at the Gallant Endeavour? I shouldn't wonder if *he'd* hopped it to a better world. He's not been there for a whole week. Molly's quite upset about it.'

Hercule Poirot sat up. His green eyes flashed.

'Indeed?' he said. 'Indeed?'

Bonnington said:

'D'you remember I suggested he'd been to a doctor and been put on a diet? Diet's nonsense of course – but I shouldn't wonder if he had consulted a doctor about his health and what the doctor said gave him a bit of a jolt. That would account for him ordering things off the menu without noticing what he was doing. Quite likely the jolt he got hurried him out of the world sooner than he would have gone otherwise. Doctors ought to be careful what they tell a chap.'

'They usually are,' said Hercule Poirot.

'This is my station,' said Mr Bonnington. 'Bye, bye. Don't suppose we shall ever know now who the old boy was – not even his name. Funny world!'

He hurried out of the carriage.

Hercule Poirot, sitting frowning, looked as though he did not think it was such a funny world.

He went home and gave certain instructions to his faithful valet, George.

Hercule Poirot ran his finger down a list of names. It was a record of deaths within a certain area.

Poirot's finger stopped.

'Henry Gascoigne. Sixty-nine. I might try him first.'

Later in the day, Hercule Poirot was sitting in Dr MacAndrew's surgery just off the King's Road. MacAndrew was a tall red-haired Scotsman with an intelligent face.

'Gascoigne?' he said. 'Yes, that's right. Eccentric old bird. Lived alone in one of those derelict old houses that are being cleared away in order to build a block of modern flats. I hadn't attended him before, but I'd seen him about and I knew who he was. It was the dairy people got the wind up first. The milk bottles began to pile up outside. In the end the people next door sent word to the police and they broke the door in and found him. He'd pitched down the stairs and broken his neck. Had on an old dressing-gown with a ragged cord – might easily have tripped himself up with it.'

'I see,' said Hercule Poirot. 'It was quite simple – an accident.'

'That's right.'

'Had he any relations?'

'There's a nephew. Used to come along and see his uncle about once a month. Lorrimer, his name is, George Lorrimer. He's a medico himself. Lives at Wimbledon.'

'Was he upset at the old man's death?'

'I don't know that I'd say he was upset. I mean, he had an affection for the old man, but he didn't really know him very well.'

'How long had Mr Gascoigne been dead when you saw him?'

'Ah!' said Dr MacAndrew. 'This is where we get official. Not less than forty-eight hours and not more than seventy-two hours. He was found on the morning of the sixth. Actually, we got closer than that. He'd got a letter in the pocket of his dressing-gown – written on the third – posted in Wimbledon that afternoon – would have been delivered somewhere around nine-twenty p.m. That puts the time of death at after nine-twenty of the evening of the third. That agrees with the contents of the stomach and the processes of digestion. He had had a meal about two hours before death. I examined him on the morning of the sixth and his condition was quite consistent with death having occurred about sixty hours previously – round about ten p.m. on the third.'

'It all seems very consistent. Tell me, when was he last seen alive?'

'He was seen in the King's Road about seven o'clock that same evening, Thursday the third, and he dined at the Gallant Endeavour restaurant at seven-thirty. It seems he always dined there on Thursdays. He was by way of being an artist, you know. An extremely bad one.'

'He had no other relations? Only this nephew?'

'There was a twin brother. The whole story is rather curious. They hadn't seen each other for years. It seems the other brother, Anthony Gascoigne, married a very rich woman and gave up art – and the brothers quarrelled over it. Hadn't seen each other since, I believe. But oddly enough, *they died on the same day*. The elder twin passed away at three o'clock on the afternoon of the third. Once before I've known a case of twins dying on the same day – in different parts of the world! Probably just a coincidence – but there it is.'

'Is the other brother's wife alive?'

'No, she died some years ago.'

'Where did Anthony Gascoigne live?'

'He had a house on Kingston Hill. He was, I believe, from what Dr Lorrimer tells me, very much of a recluse.'

Hercule Poirot nodded thoughtfully.

The Scotsman looked at him keenly.

'What exactly have you got in your mind, M. Poirot?' he asked bluntly. 'I've answered your questions – as was my duty seeing the credentials you brought. But I'm in the dark as to what it's all about.'

Poirot said slowly:

'A simple case of accidental death, that's what you said. What I have in mind is equally simple – a simple push.'

Dr MacAndrew looked startled.

'In other words, murder! Have you any grounds for that belief?'

'No,' said Poirot. 'It is a mere supposition.'

'There must be something – ' persisted the other.

Poirot did not speak. MacAndrew said:

'If it's the nephew, Lorrimer, you suspect, I don't mind telling you here and now that you are barking up the wrong tree. Lorrimer was playing bridge in Wimbledon from eight-thirty till midnight. That came out at the inquest.'

Poirot murmured:

'And presumably it was verified. The police are careful.'

The doctor said:

'Perhaps you know something against him?'

'I didn't know that there was such a person until you mentioned him.'

'Then you suspect somebody else?'

'No, no. It is not that at all. It's a case of the routine habits of the human animal. That is very important. And the dead M. Gascoigne does not fit in. It is all wrong, you see.'

'I really don't understand.'

Hercule Poirot murmured:

'The trouble is, there is too much sauce over the bad fish.'

'My dear sir?'

Hercule Poirot smiled.

'You will be having me locked up as a lunatic soon, *Monsieur le Docteur*. But I am not really a mental case – just a man who has a liking for order and method and who is worried when he comes across a fact *that does not fit in*. I must ask you to forgive me for having given you so much trouble.'

He rose and the doctor rose also.

'You know,' said MacAndrew, 'honestly I can't see anything the least bit suspicious about the death of Henry Gascoigne. I say he fell – you say somebody pushed him. It's all – well – in the air.'

Hercule Poirot sighed.

'Yes,' he said. 'It is workmanlike. Somebody has made the good job of it!'

'You still think –?'

The little man spread out his hands.

'I'm an obstinate man – a man with a little idea – and nothing to support it! By the way, did Henry Gascoigne have false teeth?'

'No, his own teeth were in excellent preservation. Very creditable indeed at his age.'

'He looked after them well – they were white and well brushed?'

'Yes, I noticed them particularly. Teeth tend to grow a little yellow as one grows older, but they were in good condition.'

'Not discoloured in any way?'

'No. I don't think he was a smoker if that is what you mean?'

'I did not mean that precisely – it was just a long shot – which probably will not come off! Good-bye, Dr MacAndrew, and thank you for your kindness.'

He shook the doctor's hand and departed.

'And now,' he said, 'for the long shot.'

At the Gallant Endeavour, he sat down at the same table which he had shared with Bonnington. The girl who served him was not Molly. Molly, the girl told him, was away on a holiday.

It was only just seven and Hercule Poirot found no difficulty in entering into conversation with the girl on the subject of old Mr Gascoigne.

'Yes,' she said. 'He'd been here for years and years. But none of us girls ever knew his name. We saw about the inquest in the paper, and there was a picture of him. "There," I said to Molly. "If that isn't our 'Old Father Time'" as we used to call him.'

'He dined here on the evening of his death, did he not?'

'That's right. Thursday, the third. He was always here on a Thursday. Tuesdays and Thursdays – punctual as a clock.'

'You don't remember, I suppose, what he had for dinner?'

'Now let me see, it was mulligatawny soup, that's right, and beefsteak pudding or was it the mutton? – no pudding, that's right, and blackberry and apple pie and cheese. And then to think of him going home and falling down those stairs that very same evening. A frayed dressing-gown cord they said it was as caused it. Of course, his clothes were always something awful – old-fashioned and put on anyhow, and all tattered, and yet he *had* a kind of air, all the same, as though he was *somebody*! Oh, we get all sorts of interesting customers here.'

She moved off.

Hercule Poirot ate his filleted sole. His eyes showed a green light.

'It is odd,' he said to himself, 'how the cleverest people slip over details. Bonnington will be interested.'

But the time had not yet come for leisurely discussion with Bonnington.

Armed with introductions from a certain influential quarter, Hercule Poirot found no difficulty at all in dealing with the coroner for the district.

'A curious figure, the deceased man Gascoigne,' he observed. 'A lonely, eccentric old fellow. But his decease seems to arouse an unusual amount of attention?'

He looked with some curiosity at his visitor as he spoke.

Hercule Poirot chose his words carefully.

'There are circumstances connected with it, Monsieur, which make investigation desirable.'

'Well, how can I help you?'

'It is, I believe, within your province to order documents produced in your court to be destroyed, or to be impounded – as you think fit. A certain letter was found in the pocket of Henry Gascoigne's dressing-gown, was it not?'

'That is so.'

'A letter from his nephew, Dr George Lorrimer?'

'Quite correct. The letter was produced at the inquest as helping to fix the time of death.'

'Which was corroborated by the medical evidence?'

'Exactly.'

'Is that letter still available?'

Hercule Poirot waited rather anxiously for the reply.

When he heard that the letter was still available for examination he drew a sigh of relief.

When it was finally produced he studied it with some care. It was written in a slightly cramped handwriting with a stylographic pen.

It ran as follows:

> Dear Uncle Henry,
>
>   I am sorry to tell you that I have had no success as regards Uncle Anthony. He showed no enthusiasm for a visit from you and would give me no reply to your request that he would let bygones be bygones. He is, of course, extremely ill, and his mind is inclined to wander. I should fancy that the end is very near. He seemed hardly to remember who you were.
>
>   I am sorry to have failed you, but I can assure you that I did my best.
>
> > Your affectionate nephew,
> >
> > George Lorrimer

The letter itself was dated 3rd November. Poirot glanced at the envelope's postmark – 4.30 p.m. 3 Nov.

He murmured:

'It is beautifully in order, is it not?'

Kingston Hill was his next objective. After a little trouble, with the exercise of good-humoured pertinacity, he obtained an interview with Amelia Hill, cook-housekeeper to the late Anthony Gascoigne.

Mrs Hill was inclined to be stiff and suspicious at first, but the charming geniality of this strange-looking foreigner would have had its effect on a stone. Mrs Amelia Hill began to unbend.

She found herself, as had so many other women before her, pouring out her troubles to a really sympathetic listener.

For fourteen years she had had charge of Mr Gascoigne's household – *not* an easy job! No, indeed! Many a woman would have quailed under the burdens *she* had had to bear! Eccentric the poor gentleman was and no denying it. Remarkably close with his money – a kind of mania with him it was – and he as rich a gentleman as might be! But Mrs Hill had served him faithfully, and put up with his ways, and naturally she'd expected at any rate a *remembrance*. But no – nothing at all! Just an old will that left all his money to his wife and if she predeceased him then everything to his brother, Henry. A will made years ago. It didn't seem fair!

Gradually Hercule Poirot detached her from her main theme of unsatisfied cupidity. It was indeed a heartless injustice! Mrs Hill could not be blamed for feeling hurt and surprised. It was well known that Mr Gascoigne was tight-fisted about money. It had even been said that the dead man had refused his only brother assistance. Mrs Hill probably knew all about that.

'Was it that that Dr Lorrimer came to see him about?' asked Mrs Hill. 'I knew it was something about his brother, but I thought it was just that his brother wanted to be reconciled. They'd quarrelled years ago.'

'I understand,' said Poirot, 'that Mr Gascoigne refused absolutely?'

'That's right enough,' said Mrs Hill with a nod. '"*Henry?*" he says, rather weak like. "*What's this about Henry? Haven't seen him for years and don't want to. Quarrelsome fellow, Henry.*" Just that.'

The conversation then reverted to Mrs Hill's own special grievances, and the unfeeling attitude of the late Mr Gascoigne's solicitor.

With some difficulty Hercule Poirot took his leave without breaking off the conversation too abruptly.

And so, just after the dinner hour, he came to Elmcrest, Dorset Road, Wimbledon, the residence of Dr George Lorrimer.

The doctor was in. Hercule Poirot was shown into the surgery and there presently Dr George Lorrimer came to him, obviously just risen from the dinner table.

'I'm not a patient, Doctor,' said Hercule Poirot. 'And my coming here is, perhaps, somewhat of an impertinence – but I'm an old man and I believe in plain and direct dealing. I do not care for lawyers and their long-winded roundabout methods.'

He had certainly aroused Lorrimer's interest. The doctor was a clean-shaven man of middle height. His hair was brown but his eyelashes were almost white which gave his eyes a pale, boiled appearance. His manner was brisk and not without humour.

'Lawyers?' he said, raising his eyebrows. 'Hate the fellows! You rouse my curiosity, my dear sir. Pray sit down.'

Poirot did so and then produced one of his professional cards which he handed to the doctor.

George Lorrimer's white eyelashes blinked.

Poirot leaned forward confidentially. 'A good many of my clients are women,' he said.

'Naturally,' said Dr George Lorrimer, with a slight twinkle.

'As you say, naturally,' agreed Poirot. 'Women distrust the official police. They prefer private investigations. They do not want to have their troubles made public. An elderly woman came to consult me a few days ago. She was unhappy about a husband she'd quarrelled with many years before. This husband of hers was your uncle, the later Mr Gascoigne.' George Lorrimer's face went purple.

'My uncle? Nonsense! His wife died many years ago.'

'Not your uncle, Mr *Anthony* Gascoigne. Your uncle, Mr *Henry* Gascoigne.'

'Uncle Henry? But *he* wasn't married?'

'Oh yes, he was,' said Hercule Poirot, lying unblushingly. 'Not a doubt of it. The lady even brought along her marriage certificate.'

'It's a lie!' cried George Lorrimer. His face was now as purple as a plum. 'I don't believe it. You're an impudent liar.'

'It is too bad, is it not?' said Poirot. 'You have committed murder for nothing.'

'Murder?' Lorrimer's voice quavered. His pale eyes bulged with terror.

'By the way,' said Poirot, 'I see you have been eating blackberry tart again. An unwise habit. Blackberries are said to be full of vitamins, but they may be deadly in other ways. On this occasion I rather fancy they have helped to put a rope round a man's neck – your neck, Dr Lorrimer.'

'You see, *mon ami*, where you went wrong was over your fundamental assumption.' Hercule Poirot, beaming placidly across the table at his friend, waved an expository hand. 'A man under severe mental stress doesn't choose that time to do something that he's never done before. His reflexes just follow the track of least resistance. A man who is upset about something *might* conceivably come down to dinner dressed in his pyjamas – but they will be his *own* pyjamas – not somebody else's.

'A man who dislikes thick soup, suet pudding and blackberries suddenly orders all three one evening. *You* say, because he is thinking of something else. But I say *that a man who has got something on his mind will order automatically the dish he has ordered most often before*.

'*Eh bien*, then, what other explanation could there be? I simply could not think of a reasonable explanation. And I was worried! The incident was all wrong. It did not fit! I have an orderly mind and I like things to fit. Mr Gascoigne's dinner order worried me.

'Then you told me that the man had disappeared. He had missed a Tuesday and a Thursday the first time for years. I liked that even less. A queer hypothesis sprang up in my mind. If I were right about it *the man was dead*.

I made inquiries. The man *was* dead. And he was very neatly and tidily dead. In other words the bad fish was covered up with the sauce!

'He had been seen in the King's Road at seven o'clock. He had had dinner here at seven-thirty – two hours before he died. It all fitted in – the evidence of the stomach contents, the evidence of the letter. Much too much sauce! You couldn't see the fish at all!

'Devoted nephew wrote the letter, devoted nephew had beautiful alibi for time of death. Death very simple – a fall down the stairs. Simple accident? Simple murder? Everyone says the former.

'Devoted nephew only surviving relative. Devoted nephew will inherit – but is there anything *to* inherit? Uncle notoriously poor.

'But there is a brother. And brother in his time had married a rich wife. And brother lives in a big rich house on Kingston Hill, so it would seem that rich wife must have left him all her money. You see the sequence – rich wife leaves money to Anthony, Anthony leaves money to Henry, Henry's money goes to George – a complete chain.'

'All very pretty in theory,' said Bonnington. 'But what did you do?'

'Once you *know* – you can usually get hold of what you want. Henry had died two hours after a *meal* – that is all the inquest really bothered about. But supposing that meal was not dinner, but *lunch*. Put yourself in George's place. George wants money – badly. Anthony Gascoigne is dying – but his death is no good to George. His money goes to Henry, and Henry

Gascoigne may live for years. So Henry must die too – and the sooner the better – but his death must take place *after* Anthony's, and at the same time George must have an alibi. Henry's habit of dining regularly at a restaurant on two evenings of the week suggests an alibi to George. Being a cautious fellow, he tries his plan out first. *He impersonates his uncle on Monday evening at the restaurant in question.* It goes without a hitch. Everyone there accepts him as his uncle. He is satisfied. He has only to wait till Uncle Anthony shows definite signs of pegging out. The time comes. He writes a letter to his uncle on the afternoon of the second November but dates it the third. He comes up to town on the afternoon of the third, calls on his uncle, and carries his scheme into action. A sharp shove and down the stairs goes Uncle Henry. George hunts about for the letter he has written, and shoves it in the pocket of his uncle's dressing-gown. At seven-thirty he is at the Gallant Endeavour, beard, bushy eyebrows all complete. Undoubtedly Mr Henry Gascoigne is alive at seven-thirty. Then a rapid metamorphosis in a lavatory and back full speed in his car to Wimbledon and an evening of bridge. The perfect alibi.'

Mr Bonnington looked at him.

'But the postmark on the letter?'

'Oh, that was very simple. The postmark was smudgy. Why? It had been altered with lamp black from second November to third November. You would not notice it *unless you were looking for it*. And finally there were the blackbirds.'

'Blackbirds?'

'Four-and-twenty blackbirds baked in a pie! Or blackberries if you prefer to be literal! George, you comprehend, was after all not quite a good enough actor. Do you remember the fellow who blacked himself all over to play Othello? That is the kind of actor you have got to be in crime. George *looked* like his uncle and *walked* like his uncle and *spoke* like his uncle and had his uncle's beard and eyebrows, but he forgot to *eat* like his uncle. He ordered the dishes that he himself liked. Blackberries discolour the teeth – the corpse's teeth were not discoloured, and yet Henry Gascoigne ate blackberries at the Gallant Endeavour that night. But there were no blackberries in the stomach. I asked this morning. And George had been fool enough to keep the beard and the rest of the make-up. Oh! plenty of evidence once you look for it. I called on George and rattled him. That finished it! He had been eating blackberries again, by the way. A greedy fellow – cared a lot about his food. *Eh bien*, greed will hang him all right unless I am very much mistaken.'

A waitress brought them two portions of blackberry and apple tart.

'Take it away,' said Mr Bonnington. 'One can't be too careful. Bring me a small helping of sago pudding.'

The Long Dinner

H. C. BAILEY

The aristocratic sleuth Reggie Fortune, a practising physician and surgeon who acts as special adviser to Scotland Yard, has been described as 'probably the most popular detective in England between World Wars I and II'. Rather plump and younger-looking than his years, Reggie is a gourmet who enjoys virtually all fine food and drink. He is also said to be a man who loves life and feasts on its pleasures – as the reader will discover in the case of 'The Long Dinner'. Fortune was created by H. C. Bailey (1877–1961), a classical scholar and newspaper drama critic who delighted in making little jibes at English class-consciousness. In this story, however, it is snobbery over food which leads to a murder . . .

'I dislike you,' said Mr Fortune. 'Some of the dirtiest linen I've seen.' He gazed morosely at the Chief of the Criminal Investigation Department.

'Quite,' Lomas agreed. 'Dirty fellow. What about those stains?'

'Oh, my dear chap!' Mr Fortune mourned. 'Paint. All sorts of paint. Also food and drink and assorted filth. Why worry me? What did you expect? Human gore?'

'I had no expectations,' said Lomas sweetly.

A certain intensity came into Mr Fortune's blue eyes.

'Yes. I hate you,' he murmured. 'Anything else you wanted to know?'

'A lot of things,' Lomas said. 'You're not useful, Reginald. I want to know what sort of fellow he was, and what's become of him.'

'He was an artist of dark complexion. He painted both in oils and water-colours. He lived a coarse and dissolute life, and had expensive tastes. What's become of him, I haven't the slightest idea. I should say he was on the way to the devil. What's it all about? Why this interest in the debauched artist?'

'Because the fellow's vanished,' said Lomas. 'He is a painter of sorts, as you say. Name – Derry Farquhar. He had a talent and a bit of success years ago, and he's gone downhill ever since. Not altogether unknown to the police – money under false pretences and that sort of thing – but never any clear case. Ten days ago a woman turned up to give information that Mr Derry Farquhar was missing. He had some money out of her – a matter of fifty pounds – three months ago. She don't complain of that. She was used to handing him donations – that kind of woman and that kind of man. What worries her is that, since this particular fifty pounds, he's faded out. And it is a queer case. He's lived these ten years in a rat-hole of a flat in Bloomsbury. He's not been seen there for months. That's unlike him. He's never been long away before. A regular London loafer. And his own money – he's got a little income from a trust – has piled up in the bank. August and September dividends untouched. That's absolutely unlike him. Besides that: one night about a fortnight ago – we can't fix the date – somebody was heard in the flat making a good deal of noise. When Bell went to have a look at things, he found the place in a devil of a mess, and a heap of foul linen. So we sent that to you.'

'Hoping for proof of bloodshed,' Reggie murmured. 'Hopeful fellow. Shirts extremely foul, but affordin' no evidence of foul play. Blood is absent. Almost the only substance that is.'

'So you don't believe there's anything in the case?'

'My dear chap! Oh, my dear chap,' Reggie opened large, plaintive eyes. 'Belief is a serious operation. I believe you haven't found anything. That's all. I should say you didn't look.'

'Thank you,' said Lomas acidly. 'Bell raked it all over.' He spoke into the telephone, and Superintendent Bell arrived with a fat folder.

'Mr Fortune thinks you've missed something, Bell,' Lomas smiled.

'If there was anything any use, I have,' Bell said heavily. 'I'll be glad to hear what it is. Here's some photographs of the place, sir. And an inventory.'

'You might pick up a bargain, Reginald,' said Lomas, while Reggie, with a decent solemnity, perused the inventory and contemplated the photographs.

'Four oil paintings, fifteen water-colours. Unframed,'

he read, and lifted a gaze of innocent enquiry to Bell.

'I'd call 'em clever, myself,' said Bell. 'Not nice, you know, but very bright and showy. Nudes of ladies, and that sort of thing. I should have thought he could have made a tidy living out of them. But a picture dealer that's seen 'em priced 'em at half a dollar each. Slick rubbish, he called 'em. I'm no hand at art. Anyway – it don't tell us anything.'

'I wouldn't say that. No,' Reggie murmured. 'Builds up the character of Mr Farquhar for us. Person of no honour, even in his pot-boilin' art. However. Nothing else in the flat?'

'Some letters – mostly bills and duns. Nothing to show what he was up to. Nothing to work on.'

Reggie turned over the correspondence quickly. 'Yes. As you say.' He stopped at a crumpled, stained card. 'Where was this?'

'In a pocket of a dirty old sports coat,' Bell said. 'It's only a menu. I don't know why he kept it. Some faces drawn on the back. Perhaps he fancied 'em. No accounting for taste. Looks like drawing devils to me.'

'Rather diabolical, yes,' Reggie murmured. 'Conventional devil. Mephistopheles in a flick.' The faces were sketched, in pencil, with a few accomplished strokes, but had no distinction: the same face in variations of grin and scowl and leer: a face of black brows, moustache, and pointed beard. 'Clever craftsman. Only clever.' He turned the card to the menu written on the front. 'My only aunt!' he moaned, and, in a hushed voice of awe read out:

DÎNER
Artichauts à l'Huile
Pommes de Terre à l'Huile
Porc frais froid aux Cornichons
Langouste Mayonnaise
Canard aux Navets
Omelette Rognons
Filet garni
Fromage à la Crème
Fruits, Biscuits

'Good Gad! Some dinner,' Lomas chuckled.

'I don't say I get it all,' Bell frowned. 'But what's it come to? He did himself well some time.'

'Well!' Reggie groaned. 'Oh, my dear chap! Artichokes in oil, cold pork, lobster, duck and turnips – and a kidney omelette and roast beef and trimmings.'

'I've got to own it wants a stomach,' said Bell gloomily. 'What then?'

'Died of indigestion,' said Lomas. 'Or committed suicide in the pangs. Very natural. Very just. There you are, Bell. Mr Fortune has solved the case.'

'I was taking it seriously myself,' Bell glowered at them.

'Oh, my Bell!' Reggie sighed. 'So was I.' He turned on Lomas. 'Incurably flippant mind, your mind. This is the essential fact. Look for Mr Farquhar in Brittany.'

Bell breathed hard. 'How do you get to that, sir?'

'No place but a Brittany inn ever served such a dinner.'

Bell rubbed his chin. 'I see. I don't know Brittany myself, I'm glad to say. I got to own I never met a dinner like it.' He looked at Lomas. 'That means putting it back on the French.'

'Quite,' Lomas smiled. 'Brilliant thought, Reginald. Would you be surprised to hear that Paris is asking us to look for Mr Derry Farquhar in England?'

'Well, well,' Reggie surveyed him with patient contempt. 'Another relevant fact which you didn't mention. Also indicatin' an association of your Mr Farquhar with France.'

'If you like,' Lomas shrugged. 'But the point is they are sure he's here. Dubois is coming over today. I'm taking him to dine at the club. You'd better join us.'

'Oh, no. No,' Reggie said quickly. 'Dubois will dine with me. You bring him along. Your club dinner would destroy his faith in the English intelligence. If any. And I like Dubois. Pleasant to discuss the case with a serious mind. Good-bye. Half past eight.' . . .

With a superior English smile, Lomas sat back and watched Reggie and Dubois consume that fantasia on pancakes, Crêpes Joan, which Reggie invented as an expression of the way of his wife with her husband. . . .

Dubois wiped his flowing moustaches. 'My homage,' he said reverently.

By way of a devilled biscuit, they came to another claret. Dubois looked and smelt and tasted, and his eyes returned thanks. 'Try it with a medlar,' Reggie purred.

'You are right. There is no fruit better with wine.'

They engaged upon a ritual of ecstasy while Lomas gave himself a glass of port and lit a cigarette. At that, Reggie gave a reproachful stare. 'My only aunt! Forgive him, Dubois. He's mere modern English.'

'I pity profoundly,' Dubois sighed. 'A bleak life. This is a great wine, my friend. Of Pauillac, I think, eh? Of the last century?'

'Quite good, yes,' Reggie purred. 'Mouton Rothschild 1900.'

Dubois's large face beamed. 'Aha. Not so bad for poor old Dubois.'

They proceeded to a duet on claret. . . .

Lomas became restive. 'This unanimity is touching. Now you've embraced each other all over, we might come to business and see if you can keep it up.'

Dubois turned to him with a gesture of deprecation. 'Pardon, my friend. Have no fear. We agree always. But I will not delay you. The affair is, after all, very simple – '

'Quite,' Lomas smiled. 'Tell Fortune. He has his own ideas about it.'

'Aha,' Dubois's eyebrows went up. 'I shall be grateful. Well, I begin, then, with Max Weber. He is what you call a profiteer, but, after all, a good fellow. It is a year ago he married a pretty lady. She was by courtesy an actress, the beautiful Clotilde. One has nothing else against her. They live together very happily in an apartment of luxury. Two weeks ago, they find that some of her jewels, which she had in her bedroom, are gone. Not all that Weber had given her, the most valuable are at the bank, but diamonds worth five hundred thousand francs. Weber comes to the Sûreté and makes a complaint. What do we find? The servants, they have been with Weber many years, they are spoilt, they are careless; but dishonest – I think not. There is no sign of a burglary. But the day before the jewels were missed a man came to the Weber apartment who asked for Madame Weber and was told she was not at home. That was true in fact, but, also, Weber's man did not like his look. A *gouape* of the finest water – that is the description. What you call a blackguard, is it not? The man was shabby but showy; he resembled exactly a loafer in the Quartier Latin, an artist *décavé* – how do you say that.'

'On his uppers. Yes. Still more interesting. But not an identification, Dubois.'

'Be patient still. You see – here is a type which might well have known *la belle* Clotilde before she was Madame Weber. Very well. This gentleman, when he was refused at the Weber door, he did not go far away. We have a *concierge* who saw him loitering till the afternoon at least. In the afternoon the Weber servants take their ease. The man went to a café – he admits it – one woman calls on a friend here, another there. What more easy than for the blackguard artist to enter, to take the jewel case, to hop it, as you say.'

'We do. Yes.'

'Well, then, I begin from a description of Monsieur the Blackguard. It is not so bad. A man who is plump and dark, with little dark whiskers, who has front teeth which stand out, who walks like a bird running, with short steps that go pit pat. He speaks French well enough, but not like a Frenchman. He wears clothes of orange colour, cut very loose, and a soft black hat of wide brim. Then I find that a man like this got into the night train from the Gare St Lazare for Dieppe – that is, you see, to come back to England by the cheap way. Very well. We have worked in the Quartier Latin, we find that a man like this was seen a day or two in some of the cafés. They remember him well, because they knew him ten years ago when he was a student. They are like that, these old folks of the Quartier – it pays. Then his name was Farquhar, Derek Farquhar, an Englishman.' Dubois twirled his moustaches. 'So you see, my friend, I dare to trouble Mr Lomas to find me in England this Farquhar.'

'Yes. Method quite sound,' Reggie mumbled. 'As a method.'

'My poor Reginald,' Lomas laughed. 'What a mournful, reluctant confession! You've hurt him, Dubois. He was quite sure Mr Farquhar was traversing the wilds of Brittany.'

'Aha,' Dubois put up his eyebrows, and made a gesture of respect to Reggie. 'My dear friend, never I consult you but I find you see farther than I. Tell me then.'

'Oh, no. No. Don't see it all,' Reggie mumbled, and told him of the menu of the long dinner.

'Without doubt that dinner was served in Brittany,' Dubois nodded. 'I agree, it is probable he had been

there not so long ago. But what of that? He was a
painter, he had studied in France, and Brittany is
always full of painters.'

'Yes. You're neglectin' part of the evidence. Faces
on the back of the menu.' He took out his pocketbook,
and sketched the black-browed, black-bearded countenance. 'Like that.'

'The devil,' said Dubois.

'As you say. Devil of opera and fancy ball. The
ordinary Mephistopheles. Associated by your Mr
Farquhar with Brittany.'

'My dear Fortune!' Dubois's big face twisted into a
quizzical smile. 'You are very subtle. Me, I find this
is to make too much of little things. After all, drawing
devils, it is common sport – you find devils all over our
comic papers – a devil and a pretty lady – and he drew
pretty ladies often, you say, this Farquhar – and this is
a very common devil.'

'Yes, rational criticism,' Reggie murmured, looking
at him with dreamy eyes. 'You're very rational,
Dubois. However. Any association of the Webers
with Brittany?'

'Oh, my friend!' Dubois smiled indulgently. 'None
at all. And when they go out of Paris, it is to Monte
Carlo, to Aix, not to rough it in Brittany, you may be
sure. No. You shall forgive me, but I find nothing in
your menu to change my mind. I must look for my
Farquhar here.' He shook his head sadly at Reggie.
'I am desolated that you do not agree.' He turned to
Lomas. 'But this is the only way, *hein*?'

'Absolutely. There's no other line at all,' said Lomas,

with satisfaction. 'Don't let Fortune worry you. He lives to see what isn't there. Wonderful imagination.'

'My only aunt!' Reggie moaned. 'Not me, no. No imagination at all. Only simple faith in facts. You people ignore 'em when they're not rational. Unscientific and superstitious. However. Let's pretend and see what we get. Go your own way.'

'One does as one can,' Dubois shrugged.

'Quite. Fortune is never content with the possible. We must work it out here. I've put things in train for you. We have a copy of Farquhar's photograph. That's been circulated with description, and there's a general warning out for him and the jewels. We're combing out all his friends and his usual haunts.'

'"So runs my dream, but what am I?"' Reggie murmured. '"An infant cryin' in the night. An infant cryin' for the light –"' Well, well. Are we downhearted? Yes. A little Armagnac would be grateful and comfortin'.' He turned the conversation imperatively to the qualities of that liqueur, and Dubois was quick with respectful responses. Lomas relapsed upon Olympian disdain and whisky and soda.

When he took Dubois away, 'Fantastic fellow, Fortune, isn't he?' Lomas smiled. 'Mind of the first order, but never content to use it.'

'An artist, my friend,' said Dubois. 'A great artist. He feels life. We think about it.'

'Damme, you don't believe he's right about this Brittany guess?'

'What do I know?' Dubois shrugged. 'It means nothing. Therefore it is nothing for us. However, one must confess, he is disconcerting, your Mr Fortune. He makes one always doubt.'

This, when he heard of it, Reggie considered the greatest compliment which he ever had, except from his wife. He also thinks it deserved. . . .

Some days later he was engaged upon the production in his marionette theatre of the tragedy of *Don Juan*, lyrics by Lord Byron, prose and music by Mr Fortune, when the telephone called him from a poignant passage on the rejection of his hero by hell.

'Yes, Fortune speaking. "Between two worlds life hovers like a star." Perhaps you didn't know that, Lomas. "How little do we know that which we are." Discovery of the late Lord Byron. I'm settin' it to music. Departmental ditty for the Criminal Investigation Department. I – '

'Could you listen for a moment?' said Lomas sweetly. 'You might be interested.'

'Not likely, no. However. What's worryin' you?'

'Nothing, except sympathy for you, Reginald. I'm afraid you'll suffer. To break it gently, we've traced Farquhar. But not in Brittany, Reginald.'

Reggie remained calm. 'No. Of course not,' he moaned. 'You weren't trying. I don't want to hear what you've missed. Takes too long.'

A sound of mockery came over the wire. 'Are you ever wrong, Reginald? No. It's always the other fellow. But the awkward fact is, Farquhar hadn't gone to Brittany, he'd gone to Westshire. So that was the only place we could find him. We have our limitations.'

'You have. Yes. *C'est brutal, mais ça marche.* You're

clumsy, but you move – sometimes – like the early cars. What has he got to say for himself?'

'I don't know. We haven't put our hands on him yet. We – what?'

'Pardon me. It was only emotion. A sob of reverence. Oh, my Lomas. You found the only place you could find him, so you haven't found him. The perfect official. No results, but always the superior person.'

'Results quite satisfactory,' Lomas snapped. 'We had a clear identification. He's been staying at Lyncombe. He's bolted again. No doubt found we were on his track. But we shall get him. They're combing out the district. Bell's gone down with Dubois.'

'Splendid. Always shut the stable door when the horse has been removed. I'll go too. I like watching that operation. Raises my confidence in the police force.' . . .

As the moon rose over the sea, Reggie's car drove into Lyncombe. It is a holiday town of some luxury. The affronts to nature of its blocks of hotel and twisting roads of villas for the opulent retired have not yet been able to spoil all the beauty of cliff and cove.

When Reggie saw it, the banal buildings and the headlands were mingled in moonlight to make a dreamland, and the sea was a black mystery with a glittering path on it.

He went to the newest hotel, he bathed well and dined badly, and, as he sat smoking his consolatory pipe on a balcony where the soft air smelt of chrysanthemums and the sea, Dubois came to him with Bell.

'Aha.' Dubois spoke. 'You have not gone to Brittany then, my friend?'

'No. No. Followin' the higher intelligence. I have a humble mind. And where have you got to?'

'We have got to the tracks of Farquhar, there is no doubt of that. What is remarkable, he had registered in his own name at the hotel, and the people there they recognise his photograph – they are sure of it. In fact, it is a face to be sure of, a rabbit face.'

'The identification's all right,' Bell grunted. 'The devil of it is, he's gone again, Mr Fortune. He went in a hurry too. Left all his traps behind, such as they were. The hotel people think he was just bilking them. He'd been a matter of ten days and not paid anything, and his baggage is worth about nothing – a battered old suitcase and some duds fit for the dust-bin.'

'Oh, Peter!' Reggie moaned. 'No, Bell, no. I haven't got to look at his shirts again?'

'I'm not asking you, sir. There's no sort of reason to think there was anything done to him. He just went out and didn't come back. Three days ago. I don't see any light at all. What he was doing here, beats me. You can say he was hiding with the swag he got in Paris. But then, why did he register in his own name? Say he was just a silly ass – you do get that kind of amateur thief. But what has he bolted for? He couldn't have had any suspicions we were on to him. We weren't, at the time he faded out.'

'But, my friend, you go too fast,' said Dubois. 'From you, no, he could not have had any alarm. But there is the other end – Paris. It is very possible that a friend in Paris warned him the police were searching for him.'

'All right,' Bell grunted. 'I give you that. Why would he make the hotel people notice him by bolting without paying his bill? Silly again. Sheer silly. He'd got a pot of money, if he did have the jewels, like you say. Going off without paying 'em just sent them to inform the police quick.'

'That is well argued. You have an insight, a power of mind, my friend.' Dubois's voice was silky. 'But what have we then? It is quite natural that Farquhar should disappear again, it is not natural that he should disappear like this. For me, I confess I do not find myself able to form an idea of Farquhar. That he is the type to rob such a woman as Clotilde, there is evidence enough – he had the knowledge, he had the opportunity. So far, there are a thousand cases like it. But that he should then retire to such a paradise of the bourgeois, that is not like his type at all.'

'That's right,' said Bell. 'No sense in it anyway.'

'No. As you say,' Reggie murmured. 'That struck me. Happy to agree with everybody. We don't know anything about anything.'

'*Bigre!* You go a little strong,' Dubois rumbled. 'Come, there is at least a connection with Clotilde, and her jewels are gone. Be sure of that. Weber is an honest man – except in business. And what, now, is your hypothesis? You said look for him in Brittany. This at least is certain – he had not gone there. What the devil should he have to do with this so correct Lyncombe? As much as with our rough Brittany.'

'Yes. Quite obscure. I haven't the slightest idea what he's been doing. However. Are we downhearted? No. We're in touch with the fundamental problem now. Why does Mr Farquhar deal with Brittany and Clotilde and Lyncombe? First method of solution clearly indicated. Find out what he did do in Lyncombe. That ought to be an easy one, Bell. He must have been noticed. He'd be conspicuous in this correct place. Good night.'

The next day he sat upon the same balcony, spreading the first scone of his tea with clotted cream and blackberry jelly, when the two returned.

'What! Have you not moved since last night?' Dubois made a grimace at him.

'My dear chap! Just walked all along one of the bays. And back. Great big bay. Exercise demanded by impatient and fretful brain. Rest is better. Have a splitter. They're too heavy. But the cream is sound.'

Dubois shuddered. 'Brr! You are a wonderful animal. Me, I am only human. But Bell has news for you. Tell him, old fellow.'

'It's like this,' Bell explained. 'About a week ago – that's three or four days before he disappeared, we can't fix the date nearer – Farquhar went to call at one of the big houses here. There's no doubt about that. It's rather like the Paris case. He was seen loafing round before and after – as you said, he's the sort of chap to get noticed. The house he went to belongs to an old gentleman – Mr Lane Hudson. Lived here for years. Very rich, they say. Made his money in South Wales, and came here when he retired. Well, he's eighty or more; he's half paralysed – only gets about his house and grounds in a wheeled chair. I've seen him; I've had a talk with him. His mind's all right. He looks like a mummy, only a bit plumped out. Sort of yellow, leathery face that don't change or move. Sits in his chair looking at nothing, and talks soft and thick. He tells me he never heard of Farquhar: didn't so much as know Farquhar had been to his house: that's quite in order, it's his rule that the servants tell anybody not known he's not well enough to see people, and I don't blame him. I wouldn't want strangers to come and look at me if I was like he is. I gave him an idea of the sort of fellow Farquhar was, and watched him pretty close, but he didn't turn a hair. He just said again he had no knowledge of any such person, and I believe him. He wasn't interested. He told me the fellow had no doubt come begging for money; he was much exposed to that sort of thing – we ought to stop it – and good day Mr Superintendent. Anyhow, it's certain Farquhar didn't see him. The old butler and the nurse bear that out, and they never heard of Farquhar before. The butler saw him and turned him away – had a spot of bother over it, but didn't worry. Like the old man, he says they do have impudent beggars now and then. So here's another nice old dead end.'

'Yes. As you say. Rather weird isn't it? The flamboyant debauched Farquhar knockin' at the door – to get to a paralysed old rich man who never heard of him. I wonder. Curious selection of people to call on by our Mr Farquhar. A pretty lady of Paris who's married money and settled down on it; a rich old Welshman who's helpless on the edge of the grave. And neither of 'em sees Mr Farquhar – accordin' to the evidence – neither will admit to knowin' anything about him. Very odd. Yes.' Reggie turned large, melancholy eyes on Dubois. 'Takes your fancy, what? The blackguard artist knockin', knockin', and, upstairs, a mummy of a man helpless in his chair.'

'Name of a name!' Dubois rumbled. 'It is fantasy pure. One sees such things in dreams. This has no more meaning.'

'No. Not to us. But it happened. Therefore it had a cause. Mr Lane Hudson lives all alone, what – except for servants?'

'That's right, sir,' Bell nodded. 'He's been a widower this long time. Only one child – daughter – and there's a grandson, quite a kid. Daughter's been married twice – first to a chap called Tracy, now to a Mr Bernal – son by the first marriage, no other children.'

'You have taken pains, Bell,' Reggie smiled.

'Well, I got everything I could think of,' said Bell, with gloomy satisfaction. 'Not knowing what I wanted. And there's nothing I do want in what I've got. The Bernals come here fairly regular – Mr and Mrs Bernal, not the child – they've been staying with the old man just now. Usual autumn visit. They were there when Farquhar called, and after – didn't go away till last Wednesday; that's before Farquhar disappeared, you see, the day before. Farquhar didn't ask for the Bernals, and they didn't see him at all, the servants say. So there you are. The Bernals don't link up any way. That peters out, like everything else.'

'Yes. Taken a lot of pains,' Reggie murmured.

'What would you have?' Dubois shrugged. 'To amass useless knowledge, – it is our only method; one is condemned to it. Ours is a slow trade, my friend. We gather facts and facts and facts, and so, if we are lucky, eliminate ninety-nine of the hundred and use, at last, one.'

'Yes. As you say,' Reggie mumbled. 'Where do the Bernals live, Bell?'

'In France, sir,' said Bell, and Reggie opened his eyes.

'Aha!' Dubois made a grimace, and pointed a broad finger at him. 'There, my friend. The one grand fact, is it not? In France! And Brittany is in France! But alas, my dear Fortune, they do not live in Brittany! Far from it. They live in the south, near Cannes; they have lived there – what do I know? – since they were married, *hein*?' he turned to Bell.

'That's right,' Bell grunted. 'Lady set up house there with her first husband. He had to live in the south of France – gassed in the war.'

'You see?' Dubois smiled. 'It is still the useless knowledge. And your vision of Brittany, my friend, it has no substance still.'

'I wonder,' Reggie mumbled, and sank deep in his chair. . . .

He is, even without hope, conscientious. That night he examined another set of Farquhar's dirty linen, but neither in that nor the rest of the worthless luggage found any information. Prodded by him, Bell enquired of the Hudson household where the Bernals were to be found, but could obtain only the address of their Cannes villa, for they were reported to be going back by car. Dubois was persuaded to telegraph Cannes and received the reply that the Bernal villa was shut up; monsieur and madame were away motoring, and their boy at school – what school nobody knew.

'Then what?' Dubois summed up. 'Nothing to do.'

'Not tonight, no,' Reggie yawned. 'I'm going to bed.'

'To dream of Brittany, *hein*?'

'I never dream,' said Reggie, with indignation. . . .

But he was waked in the night. He rubbed his eyes and looked up to see Dubois's large face above him. 'Oh, my hat,' he moaned. 'What is it? Why won't it wait?'

'Courage, my friend. They have found him. At least, they think so. Some fishermen, going out yesterday evening, they found a body on the rocks at what they call Granny's Cove. Come. The brave Bell wants you to see.'

'Bless him,' Reggie groaned, and rolled out of bed. 'What is life that one should seek it? I ask you.' And, slipping clothes on him, swiftly he crooned, ' "Three fishers went sailin' out into the west, out into the west, as the sun went down" – and incredibly caught the incredible Farquhar.'

'You are right,' Dubois nodded. 'Nothing clear, nothing sure. The more it changes, the more it is the same, this accursed case. It has no shape; there is no reason in it.'

'Structure not yet determined. No,' Reggie mumbled, parting his hair, for he will always be neat. 'We're not bein' very clever. Ought to be able to describe the whole thing from available evidence of its existence. Same like inferrin' the age of reptiles from a fossil or two – "dragons of the prime, tearin' each other in the slime, were mellow music unto him." Yes. The struggle for life of the reptiles might be mellow music compared to the diversions of Mr Farquhar and friends. Progressive world, Dubois.'

'Name of a dog!' Dubois exclaimed. 'When you are philosophic, my stomach turns over. What is in your mind?'

'Feelin' of impotence. Very uncomfortable,' Reggie moaned, and muffled himself to the chin and made haste out.

In the mortuary Bell introduced them to a body covered by a sheet. 'Here you are, sir.' He stepped aside. 'The clothes seem to be Farquhar's clothes all right. Sort of orange tweed and green flannel trousers. But I don't know about the man.'

Reggie drew back the sheet from what was left of a face.

'*Saprelotte!*' Dubois rumbled. 'The fish have bitten.'

'Well, I leave it to you,' said Bell thickly. . . .

Under a sunlit breeze the sea was dancing bright, the mists flying inland from the valleys to the dim bank of the moor, when Reggie came out again.

He drove back to his hotel, and shaved and bathed and rang up the police station. Bell and Dubois arrived to find him in his room, eating with appetite grilled ham and buttered eggs.

'My envy; all my envy,' Dubois pulled a face. 'This is greatness. The English genius at the highest.'

'Oh, no. No,' Reggie protested. 'Natural man. Well. The corpse is that of Mr Farquhar as per invoice. Prominent teeth not impaired by activities of the lobsters. Some other contours still visible. The marmalade – thanks. Yes. Hair, colourin', size and so forth agree. Mr Farquhar's been in the sea three or four days. Correspondin' with date of disappearance. Cause of death, drowning. Severe contusions on head and body, inflicted before death. Possibly by blows, possibly by fall. Might have fallen from cliff; might have been dashed on rocks by sea. No certainty to be obtained. That's the medical evidence.'

'You are talking!' Dubois exclaimed. *'Flute!* There we are again. Whatever arrives, it will mean nothing for us. Here is murder, suicide, accident – what you please.'

'I wonder.' Reggie began to peel an apple. 'Anything in his pockets, Bell?'

'A lot of money, sir. Nothing else. The notes are all sodden, but it's a good wad, and some are fifties. Might be five or six hundred pounds. So he wasn't robbed.'

'And then?' said Dubois. 'It is not enough for all the jewels of Clotilde, but it is something in hand. Will you tell me what the devil he was doing at the door of this paralysed millionaire? It means nothing, none of it.'

'No. Still amassin' useless knowledge, as you were

sayin'.' Reggie gazed at Dubois with dreamy eyes. 'I should say that's what we came here for. Don't seem the right place, does it? However. As we are here, let's try and get a little more before departure. Usin' the local talent. Bell – your fishermen – have they got any ideas where a fellow would tumble into the sea to be washed up into Granny's Cove?'

'Ah.' Bell was pleased. 'I have been asking about that, sir. Supposing he got in from the land, they think it would be somewhere round by Shag Nose. That's a bit o' cliff west o' the town. I'm having men search round and enquire. But the scent's pretty cold by now.'

'Yes. As you say,' Reggie sighed. His eyes grew large and melancholy. 'Is it far?' he said, in a voice of fear.

'Matter of a mile or two.'

'Oh, my Bell.' Reggie groaned. He pushed back his chair. He rose stiffly. 'Come on.'

Shag Nose is a headland from which dark cliffs fall sheer. Below them stretches seaward a ridge of rocks, which stand bare some way out at low tide, and in the flood make a turmoil of eddies and broken water.

The top of the headland is a flat of springy turf, in which are many tufts of thrift and cushions of stunted gorse.

'Brr. It is bleak,' Dubois complained. 'Will you tell me why Farquhar should come here? He was not – how do you say? – a man for the great open spaces.'

'Know the answer, don't you?' Reggie mumbled.

'Perfectly. He came to meet somebody in secret

who desired to make an end of him. Very well. But
who then? Not the paralysed one. Not the son-in-law
either. It is in evidence that the son-in-law was gone
before Farquhar disappeared.'

'That's right. I verified that,' Bell grunted. 'Bernal
and his wife left the night before.'

'There we are again,' Dubois shrugged. 'Nothing
means anything. For certain, it is not a perfect alibi.
They went by car; they could come back and not be
seen. But it is an alibi that will stand unless you
have luck, which you have not yet, my dear Bell,
God knows.'

'Not an easy case. No,' Reggie murmured. 'However. Possibilities not yet examined. Lyncombe's on
the coast. Had you noticed that? I wonder if any
little boat from France came in while Farquhar was
still alive.'

Dubois laughed. Dubois clapped him on the shoulder. 'Magnificent! How you are resolute, my friend.
Always the great idea! A boat from Brittany, *hein*?
That would solve everything. The good Farquhar was
so kind as to come here and meet it and be killed by
the brave Bretons. And the paralysed millionaire, he
was merely a diversion to pass the time.'

'Yes. We are not amused,' Reggie moaned. 'You're
in such a hurry. Bell – what's the local talent say about
the tide? When was high water on the night Farquhar
disappeared?'

'Not till the early morning, sir. Tide was going out
from about three in the afternoon onwards.'

'I see. At dusk and after, that reef o' rocks would be

comin' out of the water. Assumin' he went over the cliff in the dark or twilight, he'd fall on the rocks.'

'That's right. Of course he might bounce into the sea. But I've got a man or two down there searching the shore and the cliff-side.'

'Good man.' Reggie smiled, and wandered away to the cliff edge.

'Yes. It is most correct,' Dubois shrugged. 'I should do it, I avow. But also I should expect nothing, nothing. After all, we are late. We arrive late at everything.'

Reggie turned and stared at him. 'I know. That's what I'm afraid of,' he mumbled.

He wandered to and fro about the ground near the cliff edge, and found nothing which satisfied him, and at last lay down on his stomach where a jutting of the headland gave him a view of the cliffs on either side.

Two men scrambled about over the rocks below, scanning the cliff face, prying into every crevice they could reach . . . one of them vanished under an overhanging ledge, appeared again, working round it, was lost in a cleft . . . when he came out he had something in his hand.

'Name of a pipe!' Dubois rumbled. 'Is it possible we have luck at last?'

'No.' Reggie stood up. 'Won't be luck, whatever it is. Reward of virtue. Bell's infinite capacity for takin' pains.' . . .

A breathless policeman reached the top of the cliff, and held out a sodden book. 'That's the only perishing thing there is down there, sir,' he panted. 'Not a trace of nothing else.'

Bell gave it to Reggie. It was a sketch-book of the size to slide into a man's pocket. The first leaf bore, in a flamboyant scrawl, the name Derek Farquhar.

'Ah. That fixes it, then,' said Bell. 'He did go over this cliff, and his sketch-book came out of his pocket as he bounced on the ledges.'

'Very well,' Dubois shrugged. 'We know now as much as we guessed. Which means nothing.'

Reggie sat down and began to separate the book's wet pages.

Farquhar had drawn, in pencil, notes rather than sketches at first, scraps of face and figure and scene which took his unholy fancy, a drunken girl, a nasty stage dance, variations of impropriety. Then came some parades of men and women bathing, not less unpleasant, but more studied. 'Aha! Here is something seen at least,' said Dubois.

'Yes, I think so,' Reggie murmured, and turned the page.

The next sketch showed children dancing – small boys and girls. Some touch of cruelty was in the drawing – they were made to look ungainly – but it had power; it gave them an intensity of frail life which was at once pathetic and grotesque. They danced round a giant statue – a block in which the shape of a woman was burlesqued, hideously fat and thin, with a flat, foolish face. There were no clothes on it, but rough lines which might be girdle and necklace.

'What the devil!' Dubois exclaimed. 'This is an oddity. He discovers he had a talent, the animal.'

Reggie did not answer. For a moment more he gazed at the children and the statue, and he shivered, then he turned the other pages of the book. There were some notes of faces, then several satires on the respectability of Lyncombe – the sea front, with nymphs in Bath chairs propelled by satyrs and satyrs propelled by nymphs. He turned back to the dancing children and the giant female statue, and stared at it, and his round face was pale. 'Yes. Farquhar had talent,' he said. 'Played the devil with it all his life. And yet it works on the other side. What's the quickest way to Brittany? London and then Paris by air. Come on.'

Dubois swore by a paper bag and caught him up. 'What, then? How do you find your Brittany again in this?'

'The statue,' Reggie snapped. 'Sort of statue you see in Brittany. Nowhere else. He didn't invent that out of his dirty mind. He'd seen it. It meant something to him. I should say he'd seen the children too.'

'You go beyond me,' said Dubois. 'Well, it is not the first time. A statue of Brittany, eh? You mean the old things they have among the standing stones and the menhirs and dolmens. A primitive goddess. The devil! I do not see our Farquhar interested in antiquities. But it is the more striking that he studied her. I give you that. And the children? I will swear he was not a lover of children.'

'No. He wasn't. That came out in the drawing. Not

a nice man. It pleased him to think of children dancin' round the barbarous female.'

'I believe you,' said Dubois. 'The devil was in that drawing.'

'Yes. Devilish feelin'. Yes. And yet it's going to help. Because the degenerate fellow had talent. Not wholly a bad world.'

'Optimist. Be it so. But what can you make the drawing mean, then?'

'I haven't the slightest idea,' Reggie mumbled. 'Place of child life in the career of the late Farquhar very obscure. Only trace yet discovered, the Bernals have a child. No inference justified. I'm going to Brittany. I'm goin' to look for traces round that statue. And meanwhile – Bell has to find out if a French boat has been in to Lyncombe – you'd better set your people findin' the Bernals – with child. Have the Webers got a child?'

'Ah, no.' Dubois laughed. 'The beautiful Clotilde, she is not that type.'

'Pity. However. You might let me have a look at the Webers as I go through Paris.'

'With all my heart,' said Dubois. 'You understand, my friend, you command me. I see nothing, nothing at all, but I put myself in your hand.' He made a grimace. 'In fact there is nothing else to do. It is an affair for inspiration. I never had any.'

'Nor me, no,' Reggie was indignant. 'My only aunt! Inspired! I am not! I believe in evidence. That's all. You experts are so superior.' . . .

Next morning they sat in the *salon* of the Webers.

It was overwhelming with the worst magnificence of the Second Empire – mirrors and gilding, marble and malachite and lapis lazuli. But the Webers, entering affectionately arm in arm, were only magnificent in their opulent proportions. Clotilde, a dark full-blown creature, had nothing more than powder on her face, no jewels but a string of pearls, and the exuberance of her shape was modified by a simple black dress. Weber's clumsy bulk was all in black too.

They welcomed Dubois with open arms; they talked together. What had he to tell them? They had heard that the cursed Farquhar had been discovered dead in England – it was staggering; had anything been found of the jewels?

Nothing, in effect, Dubois told them. Only, Farquhar had more money than such an animal ought to have. It was a pity.

Clotilde threw up her hands. Weber scolded.

Dubois regretted – but what to do? They must admit one had been quick, very quick, to trace Farquhar. They would certainly compliment his *confrère* from England – that produced perfunctory bows. What the English police asked – and they were right – it was could one learn anything of who had worked with Farquhar, why had he come to the apartment Weber?

The Webers were contemptuous. What use to ask such a question? One had not an acquaintance with thieves. As to why he came, why he picked out them to rob – a thief must go where there was something to steal – and they – well, one was known a little. Weber smirked at his wife, and she smiled at him.

'For sure. Everyone knows monsieur – and madame.' Dubois bowed. 'But I seek something more.'

They stormed. It was not to be supposed they should know anything of such a down-at-heel.

'Oh, no. No,' said Reggie quickly. 'But in the world of business' – he looked at Weber – 'in the world of the theatre' – he looked at Clotilde – 'the fellow might have crossed your path, what?'

That was soothing. They agreed the thing was possible. How could one tell? They chattered of the detrimentals they remembered – to no purpose.

Under plaintive looks from Reggie, Dubois broke that off with a brusque departure. When they were outside – 'Well, you have met them!' Dubois shrugged. 'And if they are anything which is not ordinary I did not see it.'

Reggie gazed at him with round reproachful eyes. 'They were in mourning,' he moaned. 'You never told me that. Were they in mourning when you saw 'em before?'

'But yes,' Dubois frowned. 'Yes, certainly. What is the matter? Did you think they had put on mourning for the animal Farquhar?'

'My dear chap! Oh, my dear chap,' Reggie sighed. 'Find out why they are in mourning. Quietly, quite quietly. Good-bye. Meet you at the station.' . . .

The night express to Nantes and Quimper drew out of Paris. They ate a grim and taciturn dinner. They went back to the sleeping car and shut themselves in

Reggie's compartment. 'Well, I have done my work,' said Dubois. 'The Webers are in mourning for their nephew. A child of ten, whom Weber would have made his heir – his sister's son.'

'A child,' Reggie murmured. 'How did he die?'

'It was not in Brittany, my friend,' Dubois grinned. 'Besides it is not mysterious. He died at Fontainebleau, in August, of diphtheria. They had the best doctors of Paris. There you are again. It means nothing.'

'I wonder,' Reggie mumbled. 'Any news of the Bernals?'

'It appears they have passed through Touraine. If it is they, there was no child with them. Have no fear, they are watched for. One does not disappear in France.'

'You think not? Well, well. Remains the Bernal child. Not yet known to be dead. Of diphtheria or otherwise! I did a job o' work too. Talked to old Huet at the Institut. You know – the prehistoric man. He says Farquhar's goddess is the Woman of Sarn. Recognised her at once. She stands on about the last western hill in France. Weird sort o' place, Huet says. And he can't imagine why Farquhar thought of children dancin' round her. The people are taught she's of the devil.'

'But you go on to see her?' Dubois made a grimace. 'The fixed idea.'

'No. Rational inference. Farquhar thought of her with children. And there's a child dead – and another child we can't find – belongin' to the people linked with Farquhar. I go on.'

'To the land's end – to the end of the world – and

beyond. For your faith in yourself. My dear Fortune, you are sublime. Well, I follow you. Poor old Dubois. Sancho Panza to your Don Quixote, *hein*?' . . .

They came out of the train to a morning of soft sunshine and mellow ocean air. The twin spires of Quimper rose bright among their minarets, its sister rivers gleamed, and the wooded hill beyond glowed bronze. Dubois bustled away from breakfast to see officials. 'Don Quixote is a law to himself, but Sancho had better be correct, my friend.'

'Yes, rather,' Reggie mumbled, from a mouth full of honey. 'Conciliate the authorities. Liable to want 'em.'

'Always the optimist, my Quixote.'

'No. No. Only careful. Don't tell 'em anything.'

'Name of a name!' Dubois exploded. 'That is necessary, that warning. I have so much to tell!'

In an hour, they were driving away from Quimper, up over high moorland of heather and gorse and down again to a golden bay and a fishing village of many boats, then on westward, with glimpses of sea on either hand. There was never a tree, only, about the stone walls which divided the waves of bare land into a draught-board of little fields, thick growth of bramble and gorse. Beyond the next village, with its deep inlet of a harbour, the fields merged into moor again, and here and there rose giant stones, in line, in circle, and solitary.

'Brrr,' Dubois rumbled. 'Tombs or temples, what you please, it was a gaunt religion which put them up here on this windy end of the earth.'

The car stopped, the driver turned in his seat and pointed, and said he could drive no nearer, but that was the Woman of Sarn. 'She is lonely,' Dubois shrugged. 'There is no village near, my lad?'

'There is Sarn.' The driver pointed towards the southern sea. 'But it is nothing.'

Reggie plodded away through the heather. 'Well, this is hopeful, is it not?' Dubois caught him up. 'When we find her, what have we found? An idol in the desert. But you will go on to the end, my Quixote. Forward, then.'

They came to the statue, and stood, for its crude head rose high above theirs, looking up at it. 'And we have found it, one must avow,' Dubois shrugged. 'This is the lady Farquhar drew, devil a doubt. But, *saperlipopette*, she is worse here than on paper. She is real; she is a brute – all that there is of the beast in woman, emerging from the shapeless earth.'

'Inhuman and horrid human, yes,' Reggie murmured. 'Cruelty of life. Yes. He knew about that, the fellow who made her, poor beggar. So did Farquhar.'

'I believe it! But do you ask me to believe little children come and dance round this horror. Ah, no!'

'Oh, no. No. That never happened. Not in our time. Point of interest is, Farquhar thought it fittin' they should. Very interestin' point.' Reggie gave another look at the statue, and walked on towards the highest point of the moor.

From that he could see the tiny village of Sarn, huddled in a cove, the line of dark cliff, a long rampart against the Atlantic. Below the cliff top he made out a white house, of some size, which seemed to stand alone.

His face had a dreamy placidity as he came back to Dubois. 'Well, well. Not altogether desert,' he murmured. 'Something quite residential over there. Let's wander.'

They struck southward towards the sea. As they approached the white house, they saw that it was of modern pattern – concrete, in simple proportions, with more window than wall. Its site was well chosen, in a little hollow beneath the highest of the cliff, sheltered, yet high enough for a far prospect, taking all the southern sun.

'Of the new ugliness, eh?' said Dubois, whose taste is for elaboration in all things. 'All the last fads. It should be a sanatorium, not a house.'

'One of the possibilities, yes.' Reggie went on fast.

They came close above the house. It stood in a large walled enclosure, within which was a trim garden, but most of the space was taken by a paved yard with a roofed platform like a bandstand in the middle. Reggie stood still and surveyed it. Not a creature was to be seen. The acreage of window blazed blank and curtainless.

'The band is not playing.' Dubois made a grimace. 'It is not the season.'

Reggie did not answer. His eyes puckered to stare at a window within which the sun glinted on something of brass. He made a little inarticulate sound, and walked on, keeping above the house. But they saw no one, no sign of life, till they were close to the cliff edge.

Then a cove opened below them in a gleaming stretch of white shell sand, and on the sand children were playing: some of them at a happy-go-lucky game of rounders, some building castles, some tumbling over each other like puppies. On a rock sat, in placid guard over them, a man who had the black pointed beard, the heavy black brows, which Farquhar had sketched on his menu. But these Mephistophelean decorations did not display the leer and sneer of Farquhar's drawing. The owner watched the children with a grave and kindly attention which seemed to be interested in everyone. He called to them cheerily, and had gay answers. He laughed jovial satisfaction at their laughter.

Reggie took Dubois's arm and walked him away. 'Ah, my poor friend!' Dubois rumbled chuckles. 'There we are at last. We arrive. We have the brute goddess, we have the children, we have even the devil of our Farquhar. And behold! he is a genial paternal soul, and all the children love him. Oh, my poor friend!'

'Yes. Funny isn't it?' Reggie snapped. 'Dam' funny. Did you say the end? Then God forgive us. Which He wouldn't. He would not!'

Dubois gave him a queer look – something of derision, something of awe, and a good deal of doubt. 'When you talk like that' – a shrug, a wave of the hands – 'it is outside reason, is it not? An inspiration of faith.'

'Faith that the world is reasonable. That's all,' Reggie snarled. 'Come on.'

'And where?'

'Down to this village.'

The huddled cottages of Sarn were already in sight. Then odours, a complex of stale fish and the filth of beast and man, could be smelt. Women clattered in sabots and laboured. Men lounged against the wall above the mess of the beach. A few small and ancient boats lay at anchor in the cove, and one of a larger size, and better condition, which had a motor engine.

They found a dirty *estaminet* and obtained from the landlord a bottle of nameless red wine. He said it was old, it was marvellous, but, being urged to share it, preferred a glass of the apple spirit, Calvados. 'Marvellous, it is the world,' Dubois grinned. 'You are altogether right. Calvados for us also, my friend. It is more humane.'

The landlord was slow of speech, and a pessimist. Even with several little glasses of Calvados inside him he would talk only of the hardness of life and the poverty of Sarn and the curse upon the modern sardine. Reggie agreed that life was dear and life was difficult, but, after all, they had still their good boats at Sarn – motor-boats indeed. The landlord denied it with gloomy vehemence: motors – not one – only in the *Badebec*, and that was no fishing-boat, that one. It was M. David's.

'Is it so?' Reggie yawned, and lit his pipe. He gazed dreamily down the village street to the hideous little church. From that – under a patched umbrella, to keep off the wind, which was high, or the sun, which was grown faint – came a fat and shabby *curé*. 'Well, better luck my friend,' Reggie murmured, left Dubois to pay the bill, and wandered away.

He met the *curé* by the church gate. Was it permitted to visit that interesting church? Certainly, it was permitted, but monsieur would find nothing of interest – it was new; it was, alas! a poor place.

The *curé* was right – it was new; it was garish, it was mean. He showed it to Reggie with an affecting simplicity of diffident pride, and Reggie was attentive. Reggie praised the care with which it was kept. 'You are kind, sir,' the *curé* beamed. 'You are just. In fact they are admirably pious, my poor people, but poor – poor.'

'You will permit the stranger – ' Reggie slipped a note into his hand.

'Ah, monsieur! You are generous. It will be rewarded, please God.'

'It is nothing,' said Reggie quickly. 'Do not think of it.' They passed out of the church. 'I suppose this is almost the last place in France?'

'Sometimes I think we are forgotten,' the *curé* agreed. 'Yes, almost the last. Certainly we are all poor folk. There is only M. David, who is sometimes good to us.'

'A visitor?' Reggie said.

'Ah, no. He lives here. The Maison des Iles, you know. No? It is a school for young children – a school of luxury. He is a good man, M. David. Sometimes he will take, for almost a nothing, children who are weakly, and in a little while he has them as strong as the best. I have seen miracles. To be sure it is the best air in the world, here at Sarn. But he is a very good man. He calls his school "of the islands" because of the islands out there' – the *curé* pointed to what looked like a reef of rocks. 'My poor people call them the islands of the blessed. It is not good religion, but they used to think the souls of the innocent went there. Yes, the Maison des Iles, his school is. But you should see it, sir. The children are charming.'

'If I had time – ' said Reggie, and said good-bye.

Dubois was at the gate. Dubois took his arm and marched him off. 'My friend, almost thou persuadest me – ' He spoke into Reggie's ear. 'Guess what I have found, will you? That motor-yacht, the yacht of M. David, she was away a week ten days ago. And M. David on board. You see? It is possible she went over to England. A guess, yes, a chance, but one must avow it fits devilish well, if one can make it fit. A connection with all your fantasy – M. David over in England when Farquhar was drowned. Is it possible we arrive at last?'

'Yes, it could be. Guess what I've heard. M. David keeps school. That wasn't a bandstand. Open-air class-room. M. David is a very good man, and he uses his beautiful school to cure the children of the poor. He does miracles. The old *curé* has seen 'em.'

'The devil!' said Dubois. 'That does not fit at all. But a priest would see miracles. It is his trade.'

'Oh, no. No. Not unless they happen,' Reggie murmured.

'My friend, you believe more than any man I ever knew,' Dubois rumbled. 'Come, I must know more of this David. The sooner we were back at Quimper the better.'

'Yes. That is indicated. Quimper and telephone.' He checked a moment, and gazed anguish at Dubois. 'Oh, my hat, how I hate telephones.'

Dubois has not that old-fashioned weakness. Dubois, it is beyond doubt, enjoyed the last hours of that afternoon, shut into privacy at the post office with its best telephone, stirring up London and Paris and half France till sweat dripped from his big face and the veins of his brow dilated into knotted cords.

When he came into Reggie's room at the hotel it was already past dinner-time. Reggie lay on his bed, languid from a bath.' My dear old thing,' he moaned sympathy. 'What a battle! You must have lost pounds.'

'So much the better,' Dubois chuckled. 'And also I have results. Listen. First. I praise the good Bell. He has it that a French boat – cutter rig with motor – was seen by fishermen in the bay off Lyncombe last week. They watched her, because they had suspicions she was poaching their lobsters and crabs, which they unaccountably believe is the habit of our honest French fishermen. She was lying in the bay the night of Tuesday – you see, the night that Farquhar disappeared. In the morning she was gone. They are not sure of the name, but they thought it was *Badboy*. That is near enough to Badebec, *hein*? In fact, myself, I do not understand the name Badebec.'

'Lady in Rabelais,' Reggie murmured. 'Rather interestin'. Shows the breadth of M. David's taste.'

'Aha. Very well. Here is a good deal for M. David to explain. Second, M. David himself. He is known: there is nothing against him. In fact he is like you, a man of science, a biologist, a doctor. He was brilliant as a student, which was about the same time that Farquhar studied art – and other things – in the Quartier Latin. David had no money. He served in hospitals for children; he set up his school here – a school for delicate children – four years ago. Its record is very good. He has medical inspection by a doctor from Quimper each month. But, third, Weber's nephew was at this school till July. He went home to Paris, they went out to Fontainebleau, and – piff!' Dubois snapped his fingers. 'He is dead like that. There is no doubt it was diphtheria. Do you say fulminating diphtheria? Yes, that is it.'

'I'd like a medical report,' Reggie murmured.

'I have asked for it. However – the doctors are above suspicion, my friend. And now, fourth – the Bernals are found. They are at Dijon. They have been asked what has become of their dear little boy, and, they reply, he is at school in Brittany. At the school of M. David, Maison des Iles, Quimper.'

'Yes. He would be. I see.'

'Name of a name! I think you have always seen everything.'

'Oh, no. No. Don't see it now,' Reggie mumbled. 'However. We're workin' it out. You've done wonderfully.'

'Not so bad.' Dubois smiled. 'My genius is for action.'

'Yes. Splendid. Yes. Mine isn't. I just went and had a look at the museum.'

'My dear friend,' Dubois condescended. 'Why not? After all, the affair is now for me.'

'Thanks, yes. Interestin' museum. Found a good man on the local legends there. Told me the Woman of Sarn used to have children sacrificed to her. That'll be what Farquhar had in his nice head. Though M. David is so good to children.'

'Aha. It explains, and it does not explain,' Dubois said. 'In spite of you, M. David remains an enigma. Let poor old Dubois try. I have all these people under observation – the Webers, the Bernals – they cannot escape me now. And there are good men gone out to watch over M. David in his Maison des Iles. Tomorrow we will go and talk to him, *hein*?'

'Pleasure,' Reggie murmured. 'You'd better go and have a bath now. You want it. And I want my dinner.' . . .

When they drove out to Sarn in the morning a second car followed them. In a blaze of hot sunshine they started, but they had not gone far before a mist of rain spread in from the sea, and by the time they reached the Maison des Iles they seemed to be in the clouds.

'An omen, *hein*?' Dubois made a grimace. 'At least it may be inconvenient – if he is alarmed; if he wishes to play tricks. We have no luck in this affair. But courage, my friend. Poor old Dubois, he is not without resource.'

Their car entered the walled enclosure of the Maison

des Iles, the second stopped outside. When Dubois
sent in his card to M. David, they were shown to a
pleasant waiting-room, and had not long to wait.

David was dressed with a careless neatness. He was
well groomed and perfectly at ease. His full red lips
smiled; his dark eyes quizzed them. 'What a misery
of a morning you have found, gentlemen. I apologise
for my ocean. M. Dubois?' he made a bow.

'Of the Sûreté.' Dubois bowed. 'And M. Fortune,
my distinguished *confrère* from England.'

David was enchanted. And what could he do
for them?

'We make some little enquiries. First, you have here
a boy – Tracy, the son of Mme Bernal. He is in good
health?'

'Of the best.' David lifted his black brows. 'You will
permit me to know why you ask.'

'Because another boy who was here is dead. The
little nephew of M. Weber. You remember him?'

'Very well. He was a charming child. I regret infi-
nitely. But you are without doubt aware that he fell ill
on the holidays. It was a tragedy for his family. But the
cause is not here. We have had no illness, no infection
at all. I recommend you to Dr Lannion, at Quimper.
He is our medical inspector.'

'Yes. So I've heard,' Reggie murmured. 'Have you
had other cases of children who went home for the
holidays and died?'

'It is an atrocious question!' David cried.

'But you are not quite sure of the answer?' said
Dubois.

'If that is an insinuation, I protest,' David frowned. 'I have nothing to conceal, sir. It is impossible, that must be clear, I should know what has become of every child who has left my school. But, I tell you frankly, I do not recall any death but that of the little nephew of Weber, poor child.'

'Very well. Then you can have no objection that my assistant should examine your records,' said Dubois. He opened the window, and whistled and lifted a hand.

'Not the least in the world. I am at your orders.' David bowed. 'Permit me, I will go and get out the books,' and he went briskly.

'Now if we had luck he would try to run away,' Dubois rumbled. 'But do not expect it.'

'I didn't,' Reggie moaned.

And David did not run away. He came back and took them to his office, and there Dubois's man was set down to work at registers. You wish to assist?' David asked.

'No, thanks. No,' Reggie murmured. 'I'd like to look at your school.'

'An inspection!' Dubois smiled. 'I shall be delighted. I dare to hope for the approval of a man of science so eminent.'

They inspected dormitories and dining-room and kitchen, classrooms and workshop and laboratory. M. David was expansive and enthusiastic, yet modest. Either he was an accomplished actor, or he had a deep interest in school hygiene, and his arrangements were beyond suspicion. In the laboratory Reggie lingered.

'It is elementary,' David apologised. 'But what would you have? Some general science, that is all they can do, my little ones: botany for the most part; as you see, a trifle of chemistry to amuse them.'

'Yes. Quite sound. Yes. I'd like to see the other laboratory.'

'What?' David stared. 'There is only this.'

'Oh, no. Another one with a big microscope,' Reggie murmured. 'North side of the house.'

'Oh, la, la,' David laughed. 'You have paid some attention to my poor house. I am flattered. You mean my own den, where I play with marine biology still. Certainly you shall see it. But a little moment. I must get the key. You will understand. One must keep one's good microscope locked up. These imps, they play everywhere.' He hurried out.

'*Bigre!* How the devil did you know there was another laboratory?' said Dubois.

'Name of a dog! Is there anything you do not see?' Dubois complained. 'Well, if we have any luck he has run away this time.'

They waited some long while, and Dubois's face was flattened against the window to peer through the rain at the man on watch. But David had not run away, he came back at last, and apologised for some delay with a fool of a master, heaven given him patience! He took them briskly to the other laboratory, his den.

It was not pretentious. There were some shelves of bottles, and a bench with a sink, and a glass cupboard which stood open and empty. On the broad table in the window was a microscope of high power, and some odds and ends.

Reggie glanced at the bottles of chemicals and came to the microscope. 'I play at what I worked at. That is middle age,' David smiled. 'Here is something a little interesting.' He slipped a slide into the microscope and invited Reggie to look.

'Oh, yes. One of the diatoms. Pretty one,' Reggie murmured, and was shown some more. 'Thanks very much.' A glance set Dubois in a hurry to go. David was affably disappointed. He had hoped they would lunch with him. The gentleman with the registers could hardly have finished his investigations. He desired an investigation the most complete.

'I will leave him here,' Dubois snapped, and they got away. 'Nothing, my friend?' Dubois muttered.

'No. That was the point,' Reggie said. ' "When they got there the cupboard was bare." '

As their car passed the gate, a man signalled to them out of the rain. They stopped just beyond sight of the house, and he joined them. 'Bouvier has held someone,' he panted. 'A man with a sack.' They got out of the car and Dubois waved him on.

Through the blinding rain-clouds they came to the back of the house, and, on the way up to the cliffs, found Bouvier with his hand on the collar of a sullen, stupefied Breton. A sack lay on the ground at their feet.

'He says it is only rubbish,' Bouvier said, 'and he was taking it to throw into the sea, where they throw their waste. But I kept him.'

'Good. Let us see.' Dubois pulled the sack open. 'The devil, it is nothing but broken glass!'

Reggie grasped the hand that was going to turn it over. 'No, you mustn't do that,' he said sharply. 'Risky.'

'Why? What then? It is broken glass and bits of jelly.'

'Yes. As you say. Broken glass and bits of jelly. However.' Over Reggie's wet face came a slow benign smile. 'Just what we wanted. Contents of cupboard which was bare. I'll have to do some work on this. I'm going to the hospital. You'd better collect David – in the other car. Good-bye.' . . .

Twenty-four hours, later, he came into a grim room of the *gendarmerie* at Quimper. There Dubois and David sat with a table between them, and neither man was a pleasant sight. David's florid colour was gone, he had become untidy, he sagged in his chair, unable to hide fatigue and pain. Dubois also was dishevelled, and his eyes had sunk and grown small, but the big face wore a look of hungry cruelty. He turned to Reggie. 'Aha. Here you are at last. And what do you tell M. David?'

'Well, we'll have a little demonstration.' Reggie set down a box on the table and took from it a microscope. 'Not such a fine instrument as yours, M. David, but it will do.' He adjusted a slide. 'You showed me some beautiful marine diatoms in your laboratory. Let me show you this. Also from your laboratory. From the sackful of stuff you tried to throw into the sea.'

David dragged himself up and looked, and stared at him, and dropped back in his chair.

'Oh, that's not all, no.' Reggie changed the slide. 'Try this one.'

Again, and more wearily, David looked. He sat down again. His full lips curled back to show his teeth in a grin. 'And then?' he said.

'What have you?' Dubois came to the microscope. 'Little chains of dots, eh?' Reggie put back the first slide. 'And rods with dots at the end.'

'Not bad for a layman, is it, M. David?' Reggie murmured. 'Streptococcus pyogenes, and the diphtheria bacillus. I've got some more – '

'Indeed?' David sneered.

'Oh, yes. But these will do. Pyogenes was found in poor little Weber: accountin' for the virulence of the diphtheria. Very efficient and scientific murder.'

'And the others?' Dubois thundered. 'The other children who went home for their holidays and died. Two, three, four, is it, David?'

David laughed. 'What does it matter? Yes, there are others who have gone to the isles of the blessed. But, also, there are many who have been made well and strong. I mock at you.'

'You have cause, Herod,' Dubois cried. 'You have grown rich on the murder of children. But it is we who laugh last. We deliver you to justice now.'

'Justice! Ah, yes, you believe that.' David laughed again. 'You are primitive, you are barbarous. Me, I am rational, I am a man of science. I sacrifice one life that a dozen may live well and happy. These who stand in the way of the rich, their deaths are paid for, and with the money I heal many. What, if life is valuable, is not this wisdom and justice? Let one die to save many – it is in all the religions, that. But no one believes his religions now. I – I believe in man. Well, I am before my time. But some day the world will be all Davids. With me it is finished.'

'Not yet, name of God!' Dubois growled.

'Oh yes, my friend. I am sick to death already. I have made sure of that.' He waved his hand at Reggie. 'You will not save me – no, not even you, my clever *confrère*. Good night! Go chase the Weber and the Bernal and the rest. David, he is gone into the infinite.' He fell back, a hand to his head.

Reggie went to him, and looked close and felt at him. 'Better take him away,' he pronounced. 'Hospital, under observation.'

Dubois gave the orders. . . . 'Play-acting, my friend,' he shrugged.

'Oh, no. No. That kind of man. Logical and drastic. He's ill all right. There was the diplococcus of meningitis in his collection. Might be that.' And it was. . . .

Ten days afterwards Dubois came to London with Reggie and gave Lomas a lecture on the case. 'I am desolated that I cannot offer you anyone to hang, my friend. But what can one do? The wretched Farquhar – I have no doubt he was murdered between David and Bernal. But there is no evidence. And, after all, David, he is dead, and we have Bernal for conspiracy to murder his stepson. That will do. It was, in fact, a case profoundly simple, like all the great crimes. To make a trade of arranging the deaths of unwanted children, that is very old. The distinction of David was to organise it scientifically, that is all. The child who was an heir to fortune, with a greedy one waiting to succeed, that was the child for him. Weber's nephew stood in the way of the beautiful Clotilde to Weber's fortune. Mrs Bernal's little boy was in the way of her second husband to the fortune of her father, the old millionaire. And the others! Well here is a beautiful modern school for delicate children, nine out of ten of them thrive marvellously. But, for the tenth, there is David's bacteriological laboratory, and a killing disease to take home with him when he goes for his holidays. Always at home, they die; always a disease of infection they could pick up anywhere. *Bigre!* It was a work of genius. And it would have gone on for ever but that this worthless Farquhar blunders into Brittany upon it, and begins to blackmail the beautiful Clotilde, the Bernal. Clotilde pays with her jewels, and has to pretend a robbery. Bernal will not pay – cannot, perhaps. Farquhar approaches the old grandfather, and Bernal calls in David, and the blackmailer is killed. The oldest story in the world. Rascals fall out, justice comes in. There is your angel of justice.' He bowed to Reggie. 'Dear master. You have shown me the way. Well, I am content to serve. Does he serve badly, poor old Dubois?'

'Oh, no. No. Brilliant,' Reggie murmured. 'Queer case, though. I believe David myself. He wanted to be a god. Make lives to his desire. And he did. Cured more than he killed. Far more. Then this fellow, who never wanted to be anything but a beast, blows in and beats him. Queer world. And David might have been a kindly, human fellow, if he hadn't had power. Dangerous stuff, science. Lots of us not fit for it.'

The Assassins' Club

NICHOLAS BLAKE

Nigel Strangeways, who finds himself eyewitness to a murder during a dinner of 'The Assassins' Club', is another of the highly regarded detectives to have emerged during the 'Golden Age' of crime fiction. An erudite man and an astute judge of character, he has something in common with his creator, Nicholas Blake (1904–1972) otherwise known as Cecil Day Lewis, the novelist and critic who became Poet Laureate in 1968. Lewis began writing his pseudonymous stories about Strangeways in 1935 to supplement his income, and the detective has been described as 'more believable than most fictional sleuths'. Lewis was a great admirer of the detective story which he once described as 'the folk myth of the twentieth century', and is at his best in the following example.

'No,' thought Nigel Strangeways, looking round the table, 'no one would ever guess.'

Ever since, a quarter of an hour ago, they had assembled in the ante-room for sherry, Nigel had been feeling more and more nervous – a nervousness greater than the prospect of having to make an after-dinner speech seemed to warrant. It was true that, as the guest of honour, something more than the usual postprandial convivialities would be expected of him. And of course the company present would, from its nature, be especially critical. But still, he had done this sort of thing often enough before; he knew he was pretty good at it. Why the acute state of jitters, then? After it was all over, Nigel was tempted to substitute 'foreboding' for 'jitters'; to wonder whether he oughtn't to have proclaimed these very curious feelings, like Cassandra, from the house-top – even at the risk of spoiling what looked like being a real peach of a dinner party. After all, the dinner party did get spoiled, anyway, and soon enough, too. But, taking all things into consideration, it probably wouldn't have made any difference.

It was in an attempt to dispel this cloud of uneasiness that Nigel began to play the old game of identity-guessing with himself. There was a curious uniformity among the faces of the majority of the twenty-odd diners. The women – there were only three of them – looked homely, humorous, dowdy-and-be-damned-to-it. The men, Nigel finally decided, resembled in the mass sanitary inspectors or very minor Civil Servants. They were most of them rather undersized, and ran to drooping moustaches, gold-rimmed spectacles and a general air of mild ineffectualness. There were exceptions, of course. That elderly man in the middle of the table, with the face of a dyspeptic and superannuated bloodhound – it was not difficult to place him; even without the top-hat or the wig with which the public normally associated him, Lord Justice Pottinger could easily be recognised – the most celebrated criminal judge of his generation.

Then that leonine, mobile face on his left; it had been as much photographed as any society beauty's; and well it might, for Sir Eldred Travers' golden tongue had – it was whispered – saved as many murderers as Justice Pottinger had hanged. There were one or two other exceptions, such as the dark-haired, poetic-looking young man sitting on Nigel's right and rolling bread-pellets.

'No,' said Nigel, aloud this time, 'no one would possibly guess.'

'Guess what?' inquired the young man.

'The bloodthirsty character of this assembly.' He took up the menu-card, at the top of which was printed in red letters:

THE ASSASSINS

Dinner, December 20th

'No,' laughed the young man, 'we don't look like murderers, I must admit – not even murderers by proxy.'

'Good lord! are you in the trade, too?'

'Yes. Ought to have introduced myself. Name of Herbert Dale.'

Nigel looked at the young man with increased interest. Dale had published only two crime-novels, but he was already accepted as one of the *élite* of detective writers; he could not otherwise have been a member of that most exclusive of clubs, the Assassins; for, apart from a representative of the Bench, the Bar, and Scotland Yard, this club was composed solely of the princes of detective fiction.

It was at this point that Nigel observed two things – that the hand which incessantly rolled bread-pellets was shaking, and that, on the glossy surface of the menu-card Dale had just laid down, there was a moist finger-mark.

'Are you making a speech, too?' Nigel said.

'Me? Good lord, no. Why?'

'I thought you looked nervous,' said Nigel, in his direct way.

The young man laughed, a little too loudly. And, as though that was some kind of signal, one of those unrehearsed total silences fell upon the company. Even in the street outside, the noises seemed to be damped, as though an enormous soft pedal had been pressed down on everything. Nigel realised that it must have been snowing since he came in. A disagreeable sensation of eeriness crept over him. Annoyed with this sensation – a detective has no right to feel psychic, he reflected angrily, not even a private detective so celebrated as Nigel Strangeways – he forced himself to look round the brilliantly lighted room, the animated yet oddly neutral-looking faces of the diners, the *maître d'hôtel* in his white gloves – bland and uncreased as his own face, the impassive waiters. Everything was perfectly normal; and yet . . . Some motive he was never after able satisfactorily to explain forced him to let drop into the yawning silence:

'What a marvellous setting this would be for a murder.'

If Nigel had been looking in the right direction at the moment, things might have happened very differently. As it was, he didn't even notice the way Dale's wine-glass suddenly tilted and spilt a few drops of sherry.

At once the whole table buzzed again with conversation. A man three places away on Nigel's right raised his head, which had been almost buried in his soup plate, and said:

'Tchah! This is the one place where a murder would never happen. My respected colleagues are men of peace. I doubt if any of them has the guts to say boo to a goose. Oh, yes, they'd *like* to be men of action, tough guys. But, I ask you, just look at them! That's why they became detective-story writers. Wish-fulfilment, the psychoanalysts call it – though I don't give much for that gang, either. But it's quite safe, spilling blood, as long as you only do it on paper.'

The man turned his thick lips and small, arrogant eyes towards Nigel. 'The trouble with you amateur investigators is that you're so romantic. That's why the police beat you to it every time.'

A thick-set, swarthy man opposite him exclaimed: 'You're wrong there, Mr Carruthers. We don't seem to have beaten Mr Strangeways to it in the past every time.'

'So our aggressive friend is *the* David Carruthers. Well, well,' whispered Nigel to Dale.

'Yes,' said Dale, not modifying his tone at all. 'A squalid fellow, isn't he? But he gets the public all right. We have sold our thousands, but David has sold his tens of thousands. Got a yellow streak though, I'll bet, in spite of his bluster. Pity somebody doesn't bump him off at this dinner, just to show him he's not the Mr Infallible he sets up to be.'

Carruthers shot a vicious glance at Dale. 'Why not try it yourself? Get you a bit of notoriety, anyway; might even sell your books. Though,' he continued, clapping on the shoulder a nondescript little man who was sitting between him and Dale, 'I think little Crippen here would be my first bet. You'd like to have my blood, Crippen, wouldn't you?'

The little man said stiffly: 'Don't make yourself ridiculous, Carruthers. You must be drunk already. And I'd thank you to remember that my name is Cripps.'

At this point the president interposed with a convulsive change of subject, and the dinner resumed its even tenor. While they were disposing of some very tolerable trout, a waiter informed Dale that he was wanted on the telephone. The young man went out. Nigel was trying at the same time to listen to a highly involved story of the president's and decipher the very curious expression on Cripps' face, when all the lights went out too. . . .

There were a few seconds of astonished silence. Then a torrent of talk broke out – the kind of forced jocularity with which man still comforts himself in the face of sudden darkness. Nigel could hear movement all around him, the pushing back of chairs, quick, muffled treads on the carpet – waiters, no doubt.

Someone at the end of the table, rather ridiculously, struck a match; it did nothing but emphasize the pitch-blackness.

'Stevens, can't someone light the candles?' exclaimed the president irritably.

'Excuse me, sir,' came the voice of the *maître d'hôtel*, 'there are no candles. Harry, run along to the fuse-box and find out what's gone wrong.'

The door banged behind the waiter. Less than a minute later the lights all blazed on again. Blinking, like swimmers come up from a deep dive, the diners looked at each other. Nigel observed that Carruthers' face was even nearer his food than usual. Curious, to go on eating all the time – But no, his head was right on top of the food – lying in the plate like John the Baptist's. And from between his shoulder-blades there stood out a big white handle; the handle – good God! it couldn't be; this was too macabre altogether – but it *was* the handle of a fish-slice.

A kind of gobbling noise came out of Justice Pottinger's mouth. All eyes turned to where his shaking hand pointed, grew wide with horror, and then turned ludicrously back to him, as though he was about to direct the jury.

'God bless my soul!' was all the Judge could say.

But someone had sized up the whole situation. The thick-set man who had been sitting opposite Carruthers was already standing with his back to the door. His voice snapped:

'Stay where you are, everyone. I'm afraid there's no doubt about this. I must take charge of this case at once. Mr Strangeways, will you go and ring up Scotland Yard – police surgeon, fingerprint men, photographers – the whole bag of tricks; you know what we want.'

Nigel sprang up. His gaze, roving around the room, had registered something different, some detail missing; but his mind couldn't identify it. Well, perhaps it would come to him later. He moved towards the door. And just then the door opened brusquely, pushing the thick-set man away from it. There was a general gasp, as though everyone expected to see something walk in with blood on its hands. It was only young Dale, a little white in the face, but grinning amiably.

'What on earth – ?' he began. Then he, too, saw . . .

An hour later, Nigel and the thickset man, Superintendent Bateman, were alone in the anteroom. The princes of detective fiction were huddled together in another room, talking in shocked whispers.

'Don't like the real thing, do they, sir?' the Superintendent had commented sardonically; 'do 'em good to be up against a flesh-and-blood problem for once. I wish 'em luck with it.'

'Well,' he was saying now. 'Doesn't seem like much of a loss to the world, this Carruthers. None of 'em got a good word for him. Too much food, too much drink, too many women. But that doesn't give us a motive. Now this Cripps. Carruthers said Cripps would like to have his blood. Why was that, d'you suppose?'

'You can search me. Cripps wasn't giving anything away when we interviewed him.'

'He had enough opportunity. All he had to do when the lights went out was to step over to the buffet, take up the first knife he laid hands on – probably thought the fish slice was a carving-knife – stab him, and sit down and twiddle his fingers.'

'Yes, he could have wrapped his handkerchief round the handle. That would account for there being no fingerprints. And there's no one to swear he moved from his seat; Dale was out of the room – and it's a bit late now to ask Carruthers, who was on his other side. But, if he *did* do it, everything happened very luckily for him.'

'Then there's young Dale himself,' said Bateman, biting the side of his thumb. 'Talked a lot of hot air about bumping Carruthers off before it happened. Might be a double bluff. You see, Mr Strangeways, there's no doubt about that waiter's evidence. The main switch was thrown over. Now, what about this? Dale arranged to be called up during dinner; answers call; then goes and turns off the main switch – in gloves, I suppose, because there's only the waiter's fingerprints on it – comes back under cover of darkness, stabs his man, and goes out again.'

'Mm,' ruminated Nigel, 'but the motive? And where are the gloves? And why, if it was premeditated, such an outlandish weapon?'

'If he's hidden the gloves, we'll find 'em soon enough. And – ' the Superintendent was interrupted by the tinkle of the telephone at his elbow. A brief dialogue ensued. Then he turned to Nigel.

'Man I sent round to interview Morton – bloke who rang Dale up at dinner. Swears he was talking to Dale for three to five minutes. That seems to let Dale out, unless it was collusion.'

That moment a plainclothes man entered, a grin of ill-concealed triumph on his face. He handed a rolled-up pair of black kid gloves to Bateman. 'Tucked away behind the pipes in the lavatories, sir.'

Bateman unrolled them. There were stains on the fingers. He glanced inside the wrists, then passed the gloves to Nigel, pointing at some initials stamped there.

'Well, well,' said Nigel. 'H. D. Let's have him in again. Looks as if that telephone call *was* collusion.'

'Yes, we've got him now.'

But when the young man entered and saw the gloves lying on the table his reactions were very different from what the Superintendent had expected. An expression of relief, instead of the spasm of guilt, passed over his face.

'Stupid of me,' he said, 'I lost my head for a few minutes, after – But I'd better start at the beginning. Carruthers was always bragging about his nerve and the tight corners he's been in and so on. A poisonous specimen. So Morton and I decided to play a practical joke on him. He was to phone me up. I was to go out and throw the main switch, then come back and pretend to strangle Carruthers from behind – just give him a thorough shaking-up – and leave a bloodcurdling message on his plate to the effect that this was just a warning, and next time the Unknown would do the thing properly. We reckoned he'd be gibbering with fright when I turned up the lights again! Well, everything went all right till I came up behind him; but then – then I happened to touch that knife, and I knew somebody had been there before me, in earnest. Afraid, I lost my nerve then, especially when I found I'd got some of his blood on my gloves. So I hid them, and burnt the spoof message. Damn silly of me. The whole idea was damn silly, I can see that now.'

'Why gloves at all?' asked Nigel.

'Well, they say it's your hands and your shirt-front that are likely to show in the dark; so I put on black gloves and pinned my coat over my shirt-front. And, I say,' he added in a deprecating way, 'I don't want to teach you fellows your business, but if I had really meant to kill him, would I have worn gloves with my initials on them?'

'That is as may be,' said Bateman coldly, 'but I must warn you that you are in – '

'Just a minute,' Nigel interrupted. 'Why should Cripps have wanted Carruthers's blood?'

'Oh, you'd better ask Cripps. If he won't tell you, I don't think I ought to – '

'Don't be a fool. You're in a damned tight place, and you can't afford to be chivalrous.'

'Very well. Little Cripps may be dim, but he's a good sort. He told me once, in confidence, that Carruthers had pirated an idea of his for a plot and made a best-seller out of it. But – dash it – no one would commit murder just because – '

'You must leave that for us to decide, Mr Dale,' said the Superintendent.

When the young man had gone out, under the close surveillance of a constable, Bateman turned wearily to Nigel.

'Well,' he said, 'it may be him; and it may be Cripps. But with all these crime authors about, it might be any of 'em.'

Nigel leapt up from his seat. 'Yes,' he exclaimed, 'and that's why we've not thought of anyone else. And' – his eyes lit up – 'by Jove! now I've remembered it – the missing detail. Quick! Are all those waiters and chaps still there?'

'Yes; we've kept 'em in the dining-room. But what the – ?'

Nigel ran into the dining-room, Bateman at his heels. He looked out of one of the windows, open at the top.

'What's down below there?' he asked the *maître d'hôtel*.

'A yard, sir; the kitchen windows look out on it.'

'And now, where was Sir Eldred Travers sitting?'

The man pointed to the place without hesitation, his imperturbable face betraying not the least surprise.

'Right; will you go and ask him to step this way for a minute. Oh, by the way,' he added, as the *maître d'hôtel* reached the door, *'where are your gloves?'*

The man's eyes flickered. 'My gloves, sir?'

'Yes; before the lights went out you were wearing

white gloves; after they went up again, I remembered it just now, you were not wearing them. Are they in the yard by any chance?'

The man shot a desperate glance around him; then the bland composure of his face broke up. He collapsed, sobbing, into a chair.

'My daughter – he ruined her – she killed herself. When the lights went out, it was too much for me – the opportunity. He deserved it. I'm not sorry.'

'Yes,' said Nigel, ten minutes later, 'it was too much for him. He picked up the first weapon at hand. Afterwards, knowing everyone would be searched, he had to throw the gloves out of the window. There would be blood on them. With luck we mightn't have looked in the yard before he could get out to remove them. And unless one was looking, one wouldn't see them against the snow. They were white.'

'What was that about Sir Eldred Travers?' asked the Superintendent.

'Oh, I wanted to put him off his guard, and to get him away from the window. He might have tried to follow his gloves.'

'Well, that fish-slice might have been a slice of bad luck for young Dale if you hadn't been here,' said the Superintendent, venturing on a witticism. 'What are you grinning away to yourself about?'

'I was just thinking, this must be the first time a Judge has been present at a murder.'

Dinner for Two

ROY VICKERS

The Department of Dead Ends at Scotland Yard does what
its name suggests – takes on the cases where all the clues and
bits of evidence about a case have ended up in 'dead ends'.
Detective Inspector Rason is the man from this obscure
branch of the police who has to go methodically through
what all his colleagues have already investigated in the hope
of finding something that everyone has overlooked. The
series of cases about this department were written by Roy
Vickers (1889–1965), a former court reporter who, with tales
like 'Dinner For Two', pioneered the 'inverted' detective
story in which the reader follows the police methods from
the discovery of a crime to its eventual solution.

Today, if you were to mention the Ennings mystery,
you would be assured that 'everyone knows' that
Dennis Yawle murdered Charles Ennings. In this
case, 'everyone' happens to be right, though for the
wrong reasons. The public of the day decided that
he was guilty because he denounced an attractive
young woman of pleasing manners and assumed
respectability. And 'everyone knows' that nice young
women don't commit murder, whatever their walk in
life, and that self-centred, solitary, aggressive little
men sometimes do.

Charles Ennings was a patent agent. He lived in a flat on the third floor at Barslade Mansions, Westminster, the kind of flats that are occupied by moderately successful professional men and junior directors. A bachelor, with a promiscuous impulse freely indulged, he nevertheless managed to avoid scandalising his neighbours.

His dead body was found in his sitting-room by the daily help at eight-thirty. Death, which had occurred upwards of ten hours previously, had been caused by a knife – thrust in the throat – an ordinary pocket knife such as could then be bought in any cutler's for a few shillings. The news, of course, did not appear before the lunchtime editions.

Dennis Yawle, the murderer, was a prematurely embittered man of thirty-two. He had taken a science degree in chemistry and had been employed by a well-known firm of soap manufacturers for the last nine years at a modest salary. His personality, rather than his science, had precluded him from promotion. The firm had given him a chance as manager of their depot in the Balkans; but he disappointed them in everything except his routine work. Incidentally, it was in the Balkans that he had learned how to use a knife for purposes other than the cutting of string.

In chemistry alone he was enterprising. He had worked out some useful little compounds, unconnected with soap, and had patented them through Ennings. His income had been substantially increased, but not to the point where he could prudently resign his job.

He believed that Ennings had tricked him over his

patents, which was true. He believed that he had lost
Aileen Daines because he had insufficient money –
which may have been true. Hysteria was added to
grievance by the further belief that Ennings himself
had enjoyed the lady's favours for a brief period before
discarding her for another, which was probably an
exaggeration. By that particular exaggeration many
a man has been flicked from hatred to murderous
intent.

Daily at lunchtime he would emerge from the
laboratory in North London with his colleague, Holldon. Holldon had his daily bet on the races, and
always bought a paper from a stand outside the
restaurant. He would prop it up during lunch, while
Yawle generally read a book. But on January 18th,
1933, he brought no book, because he had to stage a
little pantomime with Holldon's paper.

First, he must eat his lunch, which was not too easy.
When the coffee arrived he delivered his line, which
began with a yawn:

'Any news in that thing?'

'No. They've had to plug a murder to fill space.'

Holldon was doing everything right, even to pushing the paper across the table. Yawle's stage business
with the paper was easy enough.

'Good – *lord!*' He shot it out, and Holldon was
sufficiently startled to attend. 'I know this chap who's
been murdered. I say, Holldon, this is pretty ghastly
for me! I was with him last evening – I must ring the
police.'

'I'd keep out of it, if I were you. You have to turn

up at court day after day in case they want you to give evidence.'

'But they've called in Scotland Yard, which means that the local police can't produce a suspect.' Yawle kept it up until the other professed himself convinced.

Five minutes later he was speaking on the telephone to Chief Inspector Karslake, giving particulars of himself.

'I was at that flat last night between seven and half-past. I don't suppose I can tell you anything you don't know but I thought I'd better give you a ring.'

Karslake thanked him with some warmth, and said he would send a man to Mr Yawle's office.

'Well-I, I have rather a crowded afternoon in front of me. I could make Scotland Yard in about twenty minutes. If you could see me then, we could get my little bit tidied up right away.'

In his pocket was a crystal of cyanide to complete the tidying-up process if necessary.

To walk up to the tiger and stoke it was a desperate improvisation, necessitated by the blunders of an ill-designed murder. Indeed, it is doubtful whether his plans had ever emerged from the fantasy stage, until he struck the blow – if we except the solitary precaution of observing the porter's movements.

For three nights previously he had strolled past the flats on the opposite side of the road, noting that between seven and eight the porter was extremely busy – with three entrances and forty-five flats, most of whose tenants were arriving or departing by taxi or car. It would be child's play to slip in – and out again – without being seen.

In the fantasy, he eluded the porter, passed through an empty hall, ascended an empty staircase.

In actuality, he did elude the porter. But the hall was not empty. In the miniature lounge, consisting of one palm, a radiator, and three chairs, stood a girl who, as he fancied, bore some resemblance to Aileen Daines. That is, she was neither tall nor short; she was slim and dark, with regular features and liberal eyebrows. She glanced at the electric clock, sat down and began to sort her shopping parcels. Yawle looked straight into her eyes, but she took no notice of him, which, irrationally, inflamed his sense of the loss of Aileen.

The staircase, too, contributed its quota of trouble. Most people used the automatic elevator – that was why he had chosen the staircase. On the first turn, between floors, he all but crashed into an elderly lady from behind: it was such a near thing that she dropped a parcel.

He was himself startled and at a loss. The woman, small but imposing, fiftyish, glared at him with an indignation that had a quality of voraciousness – to his nerve-racked fancy, she looked as if she wanted to pounce upon him, spiderwise, and eat him.

'I'm most awfully sorry, madam! Very careless of me! I hope I didn't frighten you.'

The voracious, spiderlike quality vanished from a face which was ordinary enough and even pleasing. She accepted the parcel with a graceful, old-fashioned bow and the kind of smile that used to go with the bow.

He hurried on to the first floor – up the next flight, to the second.

'I say! Do you know you really *lose* time when you do two stairs at once?'

The thin, piping treble had come from a boy of about ten.

'Do I? Pr'aps you're right. I'll take your advice.'

This was a nightmare journey. The murder, still in part a fantasy, receded. Funny how that girl had reminded him of Aileen! Must have been like her, in a way. But that girl was sure of herself and happy. If only he could tell what had happened to Aileen!

The device of writing to her parents to inquire had not occurred to him. By the time he reached the third floor Aileen's present condition was deplorable and even unmentionable – as a result of the general behaviour of Charles Ennings.

When Ennings opened the door he was wearing a dinner jacket, which somehow made everything worse. He seemed younger than his fifty years, the heavy lips had become masterful, he had pulled himself in, probably with corsets. He looked successful, confident, insolent.

'I want to talk to you, Ennings.'

'By all means!' Ennings was unenthusiastic, if not positively damp. 'Between ourselves, I don't do business at home, but – come in, won't you?'

The hall was but a bulge in the corridor of the flat. Opposite were two doors some ten feet apart.

Ennings opened one and Yawle entered the kind of near-luscious sitting-room he had expected, littered with cabinet photographs of the current inamorata – not even attractive, in Yawle's eyes.

The telephone rang, as if to emphasise that Yawle's presence was an intrusion.

'No, it was a washout,' said Ennings into the receiver. 'I got home at the usual time after all, and I'm taking an evening off. Can't talk now. I have a client who's in a hurry.'

Ennings cut off. He pointed to an armchair, but Yawle remained standing. Ennings sat in the other armchair.

'Gronston's,' said Yawle, 'have put my Cleanser in every grocer's, and every oil shop and every hardware store in the country. And it's selling.'

'Of course it's selling! It's a damn fine fluid, old man. Who's saying it isn't!'

'Why do I get such measly royalties? Why is the contract signed by Lanberry's instead of by Gronston's?'

'So that's what's biting you!' Ennings had had this conversation, in one form or another, with a good many inventors. 'Between ourselves, Lanberry's is a holding company, if you know what that means – '

'I know that Lanberry's *holds* one desk in one room in a back street off Holborn. And I know that the Chairman is a clerk employed by you. I've been there.'

'You've been there!' snorted Ennings. 'So it only remains for the bloodsucking financier to burst into tears and disgorge the loot! My good young man, you're poking your nose into things you don't understand – and you're making an infernal fool of yourself.'

The main purpose, of course, was to talk about Aileen. Yawle had given no detailed thought to the matter of the royalties. Ennings and his dinner jacket – successful, confident, insolent – was riding him.

'I shall take it up with Gronston's! There's another thing – '

'Good! I hope you'll be fool enough to do just that. In the meantime you can take yourself and your business to the devil. Your business! Your *invention!* Between ourselves, there are a good few others who've rediscovered that old formula, or copied it out of a back number – '

So, in the end, Aileen's name hadn't even been mentioned.

The skill of the Balkan bandits with their short knives – very like our pocket knives – is based on a knowledge of how to hold the knife. If you hold it properly, as Yawle did, in the palm of the hand, you leave no fingerprints on the haft. Your index finger lies along the back of the blade, slides down it as the blade impacts with an upward sweep: so there's no detectable fingerprint there, either. If your aim is accurate, as Yawle's was, there is neither bother nor noise in the killing.

Ennings remained sitting in his armchair as he had sat in life.

If all the movements were performed correctly, there should be no stains. Yawle studied himself in the mirror. There were no stains. The brainstorm, the moment of hysteria, had passed, leaving him cool, tingling with a sense of achievement and well-being. He felt successful, confident, insolent.

He noted that Ennings's electric clock registered seven twenty-three. He had been in the flat for less than six minutes, all told.

He shut the door of the sitting-room. He was half-way to the front door when he heard footsteps on the landing. He backed away from the front door, found himself opposite the room next to that of the sitting-room. The dining-room. He opened the door.

The footsteps died away. The light from the corridor of the flat had fallen on a white tablecloth. Using his sleeve, he switched on the room light.

The table was laid for two, and the food was on the table. Cold food. Smoked salmon; chicken; trifle in fairy glasses, with a peach on top – canned peach! So Ennings had been expecting a girl! Who might turn up at any minute!

Yawle was in the act of opening the front door, was reaching forward for the latch, when he again heard footsteps approaching. This time he did not panic. He merely stood back, so that his shadow should not fall on the glass panel.

This time the footsteps stopped outside the door. The knocker was lifted and discreetly applied. Yawle kept still. In due course, people go away when there is no response to a knock.

But this caller did not go away. There came the unmistakable sound of a latchkey being inserted.

There was no time to rush back to the dining-room. He slipped into the sitting-room, locked himself in with the dead man, turning the key with his handkerchief.

He did not hear the outer door of the flat being shut. For a moment he was ready to believe that his over-taut nerves had tricked him – that there had been no footsteps and no latchkey.

Some ten seconds later there came a light knock on the door of the sitting-room. Then the handle was turned. Yawle held his breath.

'*Char*-lie! It's *me*-e!'

A full throated, middle-contralto. Aileen had a middle contralto voice, too. But that voice was not – could not be – Aileen's voice. If it were Aileen, would she hand him over to the police?

As, by hypothesis, it was not Aileen, there was a danger amounting to certainty that the owner of the voice *would* hand him over to the police.

Seconds passed without any sound to give him a clue as to what was happening.

Then the sound of the front door being shut.

Within a minute or so he had evolved a feasible theory of his predicament. The girl has been given a latchkey, so she's one of Ennings's harem. She thinks he's cut a date with her, so she's gone off in a huff. If she's waiting for him on the landing – but she won't be! She's on latchkey terms and would curl herself up in the flat. Give her a couple of minutes to get clear.

When the two minutes had passed he slipped out of the flat, pausing only to shut the outer door as silently as possible. The main thing was to avoid being seen or heard leaving the flat.

No footsteps. No one on the staircase. By the time he reached the second floor, his confidence returned.

That table spread with a meal for two was nothing less than a first-class alibi, provided the body were not discovered in the next ten minutes or so. No man, he could point out, would be such a fool as to murder another in a flat when he knew that a guest was momentarily expected.

He had merely to pretend that he had seen the table when he entered the flat, and he could add that Ennings had explained that he was expecting a girl friend. He need not even bother to dodge the porter.

When Yawle reached the ground floor, the porter was not there to be dodged or not dodged, being occupied with a tenant who had arrived with luggage at another entrance. Yawle strode on.

In the miniature lounge the girl who resembled Aileen Daines was adjusting her make-up. Unaware of his presence, she snapped her bag, gathered up her shopping parcels and went out of the building.

Might be Ennings's girl friend, he reflected – but without deep interest, for his ego was fully inflated. He had done what he had done – he had turned deadly peril to positive advantage. He would top it off by making use of the porter.

Luckily, he had a pen on him. He began to write a noncommital message for Ennings, but found to his surprise that his hand was shaking. Never mind! His resourcefulness was equal to any emergency.

He found the porter at the third entrance.

'I've just left Mr Ennings and I find that I've absent-mindedly pocketed his fountain pen.' It was a standard model, unidentifiable. He gave it to the porter, with a florin. 'If I were you, I wouldn't return it until the morning. The fact is, porter, he is entertaining – well, let's say a *friend!*'

By bedtime, Yawle's confidence had ebbed. Again and again he reviewed his movements, with increasing alarm. He had got clean away, but could he be dragged back? He ticked off the items.

The first person to see him enter the block had been the girl, but she obviously had not noticed him and could be ignored. Then the old lady who had looked at him like a spider. She might or might not remember him enough to give a description.

Then there was that wretched boy – almost certainly a Boy Scout obsessed with stairs and footsteps, who would love telling the police everything.

With that sterling alibi of the dinner table it would be safe to come forward, unsafe to hang back.

'There's the boy, the middle-aged woman, and the girl – all three saw you entering the building at about seven-ten, Mr Yawle?' Chief Inspector Karslake was making notes as he spoke. 'Can you remember what they looked like?'

'The boy I didn't notice – an ordinary boy of about ten or so. The woman, smallish, about fifty, old-fashioned, but not exactly old, round sort of face.

The girl – middle twenties, about my height, dark, good looking, well-marked eyebrows, slim, quietly dressed. But I'm sure she didn't know I was there – if you're thinking of asking these people whether they saw me.'

'It's only for checking up with others,' Karslake assured him. 'Please go on, Mr Yawle.'

'I went to the flat. Ennings opened the door. He was in a dinner jacket and told me he was expecting a friend to dinner. The way he said it, I guessed it was a girl. He showed me the dining-room – I suppose so that I shouldn't think he was stalling me – cold supper set for two. I said I would only keep him a few minutes. As soon as we got into his sitting-room the phone rang. He answered briefly and cut off.'

Yawle waited while Karslake wrote. He had not anticipated that everything he said would be noted.

'And then you both sat down and discussed your business?'

'If we are to be literal, I didn't sit down – wanted to make it clear that I wasn't going to stick around.'

The next bit was tricky. In the night he had worked out that the porter might have noticed when Ennings' guest went upstairs – that must have been while he was in the flat.

'We were about halfway through our business when his girl turned up.'

'And he got up to let her in?'

Confound the man with his passion for footling little details! Be careful to tell no unnecessary lies.

'She let herself in with a latchkey. I said I'd just write out a note and then – '

'Half a minute. Don't think I'm niggling, Mr Yawle. The fact is, we use everything an honest witness tells us to check on the people who are not public spirited and may be hiding something. How did you know some one had come in with a latchkey if you were shut up in a room talking business?'

'Ennings had one ear listening for that latchkey.' Yawle managed a realistic snigger. 'He got up, spoke to her, said he would be with her in a few minutes.'

Karslake passed him a chart of Ennings's sitting-room.

'Will you show me on that chart where you were standing when he went to speak to the girl?'

There was only one spot where one could stand to talk to a man sitting as Ennings had sat.

'Oh the hearth rug – here.'

'Could you identify the girl, Mr Yawle?'

'Oh, no – no! Certainly not!'

'But you must have seen her if you were standing there!' It was a statement rather than a question, and Yawle shrank from contradicting.

'Well – yes – but – in these circumstances, Inspector, I simply can't make a statement involving someone else unless I'm sure of what I say.'

'You couldn't put it better, Mr Yawle. All I want you to tell me now is what you saw. To begin with, you saw it was a girl and not a man. Tall or short? Fair or dark?'

'I don't think we need winkle it out that way. I can

go as far as this – she was of the same physical type as the girl I noticed in the hall when I was coming in. But I cannot state that she was the same girl.'

It would be better, he had decided, not to add that he had also seen the girl when he was leaving the building.

'From your description of the girl in the hall the thing a man would notice first would be those eyebrows,' persisted Karslake.

'Y-yes. But – '

'Was she in evening dress?'

'No.'

'Same sort of clothes as the girl in the hall, eh?' As Yawle did not deny it, 'Very natural that you won't state it's the same girl, because you aren't quite positive. Very proper attitude, if I may say so. Where did Ennings park the girl in the flat?'

'I don't know. He came back to me. I wanted to make that note. I'd forgotten my pen and he lent me his. I went on talking a minute or so and absent-mindedly pocketed his pen. When I got downstairs – which I suppose was about half-past seven – I looked for the porter and asked him to return the fountain pen – ' Yawle repeated the snigger ' – *in the morning.*'

Karslake had the air of an inspector who is not only satisfied but even grateful.

'I think that's about all, Mr Yawle. We shall round up the boy and the woman on the stairs so that you can identify each other. The local police will probably want you for the inquest. Otherwise, I don't suppose we shall trouble you – ' he pressed a bell push ' – if you'll be good enough to give us your fingerprints before you go.'

A junior entered with a frame and Yawle obliged.

'As far as I know,' he said when the process had been completed, 'I didn't leave any fingerprints in the flat. Don't think I touched anything except that fountain pen.'

'But look at it from our point of view, Mr Yawle.' Karslake was urbane and even confidential. 'Until we've taken your prints we can't prove that it wasn't you who had dinner with Ennings.'

'Dinner with Ennings?' echoed Yawle, genuinely puzzled.

'Well, supper if you like, as it was cold stuff. There were prints other than those of the deceased on the cutlery, the plates, the glasses, some of the dishes – someone who doesn't take salt or pepper but fairly shovels the sugar on a sweet.'

'D'you mean that meal was eaten?' gasped Yawle.

'You bet it was! Look here, I'm not supposed to show this, but you'll see it at the inquest tomorrow.'

Karslake displayed photographs of the dining-room and of the table, of the débris of a meal consumed by two persons. Yawle observed particularly the fairy glasses that had held the trifle. The glasses in the photograph were opaque, with nothing showing above the rims. Before consumption the trifle had topped the rim and the canned peach had topped the trifle.

Yawle left Scotland Yard, dazed to the point of being but barely aware of his surroundings. That dinner had been untouched when he left the flat. As Ennings was dead, he could not possibly have had dinner with the girl. Therefore, somebody else had dinner with the girl – which was absurd.

Alternatively, the flat had been burgled after the girl had gone. The burglars, notwithstanding the presence of a corpse in the flat, had sat down to a meal – which was even more absurd.

Which all proved that the dinner had not been eaten when, in point of fact, it had been eaten.

That it removed all danger from himself was scarcely heeded. That photograph gave him a creeping doubt of his own sanity. He had read of eye-witnesses making wholly false statements in wholly good faith. In some amazing way he must have seen an untouched meal when he was really looking at the débris of a meal.

That meal cropped up again at the inquest. One of the jurymen, unsupported by the others, challenged Yawle's evidence in a question to the Coroner.

'How do we know that this meal was eaten after Mr Yawle had left the flat? It might have been eaten before – I mean, it might have been lunch or anything. I'm not suggesting it was but as it's important evidence I think we ought to have that point cleared up.'

'I think I can help there, sir,' said Yawle. 'When the deceased took me into his dining-room I happened to notice particularly two fairy glasses containing trifle, with a canned peach on the top. If the police can confirm that statement I think it must prove that I saw the meal laid out before it was consumed.'

The police could confirm that statement. The jury returned a verdict of murder against a person unknown, with a rider indicating the young woman who had entered the flat with a latchkey at approximately seven-twenty.

The boy was found some six weeks later. He had spent a couple of nights with an uncle, one of the tenants, who suddenly remember that fact and reported it with profuse apologies. The boy had gone back to board in school at Brighton: the incident had utterly passed from his mind, and he failed to identify Yawle.

The elderly lady with the parcel was another unexpected stumbling block. When appeals through press and radio failed to solicit response, the Yard was ready to believe that she was an invention of Yawle's, prompted by a desire to tie the time of his presence at the flat at both ends. Innocent people often did that kind of thing.

The porter was interviewed again and again. His story remained sufficiently consistent. It was his busy time, dodging from one of the three entrances to another. There had never been any trouble with the police – they weren't that kind of tenant, and he was not given to observing their actions. He had not seen Mr Yawle until he made his request concerning the fountain pen – which was close to seven-thirty.

He had certainly noticed a young woman sitting in the hall-lounge round about ten past seven. That was nothing unusual. He had only noticed her because, as he passed, she was fiddling with her bag and dropped something, but picked it up before he could do it for her. He mentioned her eyebrows and her dress, which was not the expensive kind.

The dragnet went out through the West End, though from the description of the porter and of Yawle, she was not likely to be found in any of the bars or night clubs. The search became intensive, was carried to the theatres, including the dress circles and stalls, with the result that, some six weeks after the inquest, Yawle was asked to accompany a plainclothes man and wait outside a City office about lunch time.

Out of the office came Aileen Daines.

'Hullo, Dennis!' She shook hands with frank friendliness. 'I'm so glad to see you – I was going to write. You see, Leonard and I – yes, at Easter.'

When she had gone, Yawle rejoined the plainclothes man.

'You saw her speak to me. She is not the one we want. I know her very well indeed.'

The porter, at the same time on the next day, was not so positive. By a majority vote, as it were, of his muddled recollections, he decided that he did not think this young lady was that young lady.

'All the same, there's the bare possibility that this young lady *is* that young lady,' said Karslake when he was discussing the report with his staff. 'Used to be Yawle's girl, eh? There might be some tangled sex stuff there. We haven't enough to sail in with a request for her dabs. Now, if one of you boys could manage to watch her eating – when she isn't with her young man – we might get a line.'

None of them did see her eating, but one of them obtained her fingerprints without her knowledge. And that dropped her out of the case – and dropped the case itself into the Department of Dead Ends.

As weeks lengthened into months, Yawle ceased to worry about his sanity in the matter of the dinner which could not possibly have been – but had been – eaten. He still carried the crystal of cyanide in a dummy petrol lighter, but it had become a talisman rather than a menace.

Learning that Ennings's estate had been proved at £60,000 he went to see Gronston's, who gladly gave him details of the royalties paid to Lanberry's. Yawle brought an action against the estate for balance of royalties withheld by a fraudulent device.

The action was heard in the following Spring. Detective Inspector Rason was present, not because he expected to find in the public gallery the girl who had murdered Ennings, but because it was a routine duty to keep contact with the principals in an unsolved crime.

The hearing was very brief, for there was in effect no defence. Yawle obtained judgement for some four thousand pounds and his costs. The judge remarked that the deceased had behaved as an unscrupulous scoundrel and that Hendricks, his shabby little clerk who survived him, would do well to examine his own conscience.

Rason decided to do a little examining of the clerk's

conscience himself, for he had the glimmer of an idea. Over a pint of beer and a sandwich Hendricks was willing to talk.

'I knew there was going to be a rumpus when Mr Yawle turned up at my room,' said Hendricks. 'I gave the guv'nor the wire, but he only laughed at me.'

'When did Mr Yawle turn up at your room?' asked Rason.

'I dunno – not the date anyhow. Must've been about a week before the guv'nor copped out.'

That was the sort of thing Rason was hoping for. What business had Yawle transacted with Ennings when he knew that Ennings had been cheating him? No business. He had gone to demand restitution. And had he borrowed Ennings's fountain pen to make a note of it? Rats!

Barking up the wrong tree, muttered Rason. Proving that Yawle quarrelled with Ennings and killed him, when the job is to find the girl and prove she did.

Back in the office he was reluctant to admit that he had wasted his morning. He tried hard to squeeze a bit into the discovery that Yawle had known that Ennings was swindling him. No link-up.

Start with the girl, now! She comes in with a latchkey, has her dinner and then knifes him. Why? She must've expected him to get free. Can't pull the dewy innocent with that latchkey in her bag. Suppose she was an inventor, too? In the sitting-room she finds something, proving that Ennings has been buying her the stockings out of her own money?

The next morning he paddled back to Hendricks.

'Have you got on your books a girl middle twenties, height about five six, thickish eyebrows – '

'I've never seen any of 'em except Mr Yawle. And we got no girls. Only a couple o' widows, legatees of course.'

'Let's have the widows!'

Mrs Siegman lived in Hampstead, was middle-aged and had virtually no eyebrows. Mrs Deaker lived in Surbiton, which was an hour's drive out of London, allowing for traffic. With some difficulty Rason found a small house with a brick wall surrounding the garden on the outskirts of the suburb.

The door was opened by a good-looking girl in the middle twenties, height about five-six, dark, with well-defined eyebrows.

'Are you Mrs Deaker?'

'No. Mrs Deaker is in town. I'm her companion and at the moment her domestic staff too. Do you want to leave a message?'

Rason presented his official card.

'Oh!' said the girl, and Rason decided to spring it on her.

'What were you doing in Barslade Mansions, Westminster, the night Charles Ennings was killed?'

'Oh!' said the girl again. 'I'm not going to tell you anything until I have a lawyer.'

'In that case I'm afraid you'll have to come with me to Scotland Yard,' said Rason.

He was with her while she packed a suitcase and left a note for her employer, kept her within arm's reach while he telephoned the Yard. On the journey the only admission she made was that her name was Margaret Halling. On arrival at the Yard she made no objection to having her fingerprints taken.

Some three hours later Dennis Yawle turned up at Scotland Yard in response to a request by telephone. Some five minutes previously Margaret Halling's employer had arrived with a lawyer. All three, with some half a dozen others, were enduring time in a waiting-room.

Detective Inspector Rason thanked Yawle profusely, took him along a corridor behind the waiting-room.

'I want you to look through this little panel, Mr Yawle – they can't see you – and tell me if there's anybody in the room you recognise.'

Yawle looked through the panel. A smile broadened.

'Yes,' he said. 'I shall never forget that face! That is the elderly lady whose parcel I picked up on the stairs.'

'Well, I'm – ' Rason was more astonished than he had been for a long time. 'Excuse me, Mr Yawle.' In his agitation he pushed Yawle back to the panel, put his hand on the crown of Yawle's head, and gently twisted until Yawle could be presumed to have a view of the seat in the window.

This time there was no broad smile. Rason had the

impression that he saved Yawle from subsiding to the floor.

'That's the girl with the eyebrows – the girl I saw in the hall.'

'And she's the girl you saw when she let herself in with the latchkey?'

'I don't know. I said at the time I couldn't be sure the girls were the same.'

'That's all right, Mr Yawle – we never lead a witness,' said Rason unblushingly. He was now in extremely high spirits, for he had had another glimmer. 'Your statement in my file says they were of similar type. That passes the buck to us.'

They went to Chief Inspector Karslake's room. The chair at the roll-top desk was placed at Rason's disposal, with Karslake on his left, for this was Rason's case, and his own room was too much of a museum for interviews.

'Well, I suppose the first thing to do,' hinted Karslake, when he had heard the news, 'is to have the girl in for a formal identification.'

'No, it isn't, sir,' said Rason, picking up Karslake's house telephone.

'Mrs Deaker, in the waiting-room – ask her if she would like to see me. If so, bring her in.'

'Mr Yawle,' said Rason. 'This old girl has given Mr Karslake a good deal of trouble, one way and another.' Karslake's surprise changed to profound disapproval, as Rason went on: 'If she hands us anything you know to be phoney, I'd be grateful if you'd chip in and flatten her out.'

Yawle assented politely. The 'old woman' presented
no problem. She could do nothing but confirm his
statement.

Mrs Deaker chose to brave the detective without
the support of the lawyer, who was earmarked for
Margaret Halling.

'I think you have seen this gentleman before, Mrs
Deaker?' Rason indicated Yawle.

'Not to my recollection,' answered Mrs Deaker.
'Perhaps if you were to tell me his name – ?'

'At Barslade Mansions, Westminster, on the evening of January 17th 1933, this gentleman retrieved a
parcel you had dropped on the staircase.'

'Did he! Then it was very kind of him, and it is
ungracious of me to forget.'

'We advertised in the press and on the radio, asking you to come forward, Mrs Deaker,' said Rason
severely.

'I remember those advertisements, I didn't realise
you meant me!' She glared at Yawle. 'Did you describe
me as an *elderly* woman? That's what the advertise-
ment said!' Before Yawle could excuse himself, she
went on: 'I suppose I do seem elderly to a man of
your age. However, if we may consider the incident
of the parcel is closed I would like to tell the police
about Margaret Halling, my companion. She was there
solely because my taxi brought her there. I was dining
with a friend. Her train home from Waterloo was not
until eight-ten. It was a cold night and I told her to
sit in the lounge by the radiator until it was time
to leave.'

'Who was the friend with whom you were dining, Mrs Deaker?'

'The man who was murdered. Mr Ennings. But of course, you must know all about him, as you're still looking for the murderer. Now that we have mentioned the subject, you may wish me to account for my own movements, though they are of no significance, or I would have reported them.

'Mr Ennings was a friend – a very intimate friend – before I married, somewhat injudiciously, the man who invented the Deaker commutator. He handled my husband's affairs. In recent years, after his death, Mr Ennings and I – Mr Ennings and I resumed our friendship, which was cemented by the fact that my husband had made him trustee.

'Mr Ennings telephoned me in the morning that he might be detained at some special meeting or other. As I was doing a day's shopping, I was to come – he would have a cold meal prepared – and I was not to wait dinner for him after seven-thirty.

'As to the parcel incident, I never enter an elevator unless there is a responsible-looking man in charge. I selected the staircase – which took a long time – no doubt because I am *elderly*! I duly waited until seven-thirty, and then I sat down to dinner by myself. I waited in the flat until a little after nine-thirty and then caught the ten-five home.'

Rason had taken from the dossier the photographs of the débris of the meal.

'When did you see Mr Ennings?'

'Obviously, I didn't see him at all.'

'How did you obtain entry to the flat?'

'I lifted the knocker, as there was a light in the hall.' Her words were laboured as she went on: 'I thought I had sufficiently emphasised the fact of our friendship. I have a latchkey. Here it is.' She took it from her bag and gave it to Rason. 'I went to the sitting-room, but the door was locked. I knocked, then called his name. Then I looked about the flat, shut the front door and went into the dining-room to wait for him. Once, I thought I heard the front door being closed, but it was a false alarm, so I sat down and had my dinner.'

Yawle had reached forward and snatched from Rason's desk the photograph of the débris of the meal.

'I don't think so, Mrs Deaker!' cried Yawle. 'Look at this photograph. Two persons ate that dinner!'

They were glaring at each other.

'Half a minute, Mr Yawle!' interposed Rason. 'I thought Mr Karslake had told you everything! Did he forget to tell you that there was *only one set of fingerprints on those dishes*?'

'Then they must be mine!' sighed Mrs Deaker. 'I had hoped to escape this public humiliation. The degrading truth is that I can eat – and I often do – as much as two men! By nine, I concluded that Mr Ennings must have had his dinner. So I – I – I really *did* –'

Rason left Mrs Deaker floundering in a whirlpool of social shame.

'Well, Yawle, let's get back to that young girl you saw in the flat, whom you can't *quite* identify with the young girl you saw in the hall. Eyebrows an' all, too! Or would you rather ask Mrs Deaker some questions about that sitting-room door *that was locked on the inside*? At about twenty past seven, as near as makes no matter to you, Yawle!'

But Yawle possessed a talisman in a dummy petrol lighter that warded off all further assaults on his dignity.

Acknowledgements

The editor and publishers are grateful to the following authors, publishers and agents for permission to use copyright material in this collection: Macdonald Publishing for 'The Speciality of the House' by Stanley Ellin; Random Century Ltd for 'Bribery and Corruption' by Ruth Rendell; Fleetway Publications Ltd for 'Chef d'Oeuvre' by Paul Gallico; Davis Publications Inc for 'La Spécialité de M. Duclos' by Oliver La Farge; Hamish Hamilton for 'Three, or Four, for Dinner' by L. P. Hartley; Chapman & Hall Ltd for 'The Man Who Couldn't Taste Pepper' by G. B. Stern; Ziff-Davis Publishing Co Inc for 'Final Dining' by Roger Zelazny; Aitken & Stone Ltd for 'Four-and-Twenty Blackbirds' by Agatha Christie; Victor Gollancz Ltd for 'The Long Dinner' by H. C. Bailey; A. D. Peters Literary Agency for 'The Assassins' Club' by Nicholas Blake; The Estate of Roy Vickers for 'Dinner for Two'. While every care has been taken to clear permission for the use of the stories in this book, in the case of any accidental infringement, copyright holders are asked to write to the editor care of the publishers.